THE FOURTH LEVEL
CONTINGENT
BOOK SIXTEEN

I0563475

NICHOLAS HUNTLEY

First Edition, February 2021

nichhuntley.ca

WHITEWOLF PUBLISHING

Paperback ISBN 978-1-988765-42-6

Digital ISBN 978-1-988765-43-3

The text of this book is set in Times New Roman.

PART I

"In spite then of all recollections of the past or fear for the future, we have a present source of rejoicing; whatever comes, weal or woe, however stands our account as yet in the book against the Last Day, this we have and this we may glory in, the present power and grace of God in us and over us, and the means thereby given us of victory in the end."

– St. John Henry Newman

Act 1, Scene 1

Light poured in through the rose window from the face of Pentateuch Cathedral, shining down into the chancel, transept and nave, towards the many people who had their heads down and knelt in worship towards the bronze crucifix that hung from the ceiling. Above the stained-glass window was a mural painted on the half-domed ceiling of the chancel with an artist's depiction of the Father and Son dressed in white robes and caps, and Holy Spirit in the form of a dove, behind the Holy Mother dressed in blue robes with a hood over her head, being crowned to take her place as Queen of Heaven. All four persons were surrounded by a golden circle in Heaven, with onlookers to the left and right, Holy Saints by the golden halos that surrounded their faces as they looked in awe and happiness towards the Holy Trinity and Holy Mother. Beneath the four were a group of seven angels, each with trumpets. At the left and right corner were seven more angels at each side. Underneath this depiction of Heaven were a group of saints on steps. On each side, seven Saints could be seen at the top-most step with halos around their heads to depict their holiness, dressed in white robes like the Holy Father and Son. Beneath them on the steps below were more Saints with halos around their heads. All of them looked upwards to Heaven, as the laity could do the same.

Underneath the mural, around the rose window were arched stained glass windows that depicted key moments in the Gospel from Christ's baptism, the call of the Apostles, His teaching on the mountains, to His suffering, death and resurrection. The casing and walls around the chancel and ambulatory were constructed of a smooth chiseled stone that differed from light grey to white. The tabernacle laid below the rose window, within a small enclave surrounded by smooth stone pillars constructed in a Doric order style. Around the chancel, closer to the ground were eight stone statues of witnesses, notable Saints, each that looked down towards the marble altar in the middle. To the right-side was a raised seat, the cathedra, and a podium. There were other seats at the other side for the priests and deacons.

The floor between the chancel and the nave consisted of a shiny polished floor that continued down the central aisle of the nave, between the pews, and reflected the bronze crucifix and the mural above. The pews at the side stretched almost fifty in total at each side, next to the side aisles that were accessible by the stone arches with bright small chandeliers over the center of the arches and overtop stained glass windows where daylight poured in through, but no greater than the morning sunlight that poured in through the circular window ahead. Within each-side of the side aisles were some Stations of the Cross, five on each side, as well as a place where one could light candles for loved ones. Towards the left-side of the transept was a large wooden door that exited outside. To the right of this door were the confession boxes and a bench nearby. To the left of the door were the rest of the Stations of the Cross that continued at right-side of the transept where there was another large arched wooden door that exited outside and more stations to the right of this door. To the left was a cabinet dedicated to the Holy Saint of Harlech and containing a relic of His Holiness, St. Bailey.

Towards the rear of the church, sitting at a pew to the right was Diana with a veil around her head, covering her dark hair. She was dressed in an open raincoat, white long-sleeved shirt, black yoga pants, on her knees at the kneeler, hands together and head down in prayer. Diana's belly was swollen with the gift of life within her womb, readily visible by the size the child had grown in the last three months.

Diana remained in reverent silence for close to twenty minutes before she raised her head back up, opened her deep blue eyes, and then made the sign of the cross. She then sat onto the bench and carefully lifted herself up to make her way out of the pew. Diana knelt down carefully to make the sign of the cross before she left, pushing through the arched doors that went into the narthex of Pentateuch Cathedral, which was quiet as it was early morning. Diana removed her veil, revealing her dark hair tied in a ponytail, and looked over to the gift shop as it opened and made her way over where she looked into the glass cabinet and smiled to the East Asian lady behind.

"Looking for something special?" the lady questioned.

"Thinking about a gift for my little one," Diana replied, holding a hand at her belly. "I'm debating what saint to baptize him under."

"Have you chosen a name yet?"

"No," Diana remarked, "my… husband and I haven't chosen a name yet, but we've agreed on something familiar as a first name since the saint will be middle name. I'm between St. Bailey and St. Allan at the moment if it's a boy, and then St. Anne or St. Teresia if it's a girl."

"We have these beautiful St. Bailey tokens here," the lady said, showing Diana some gold amulets with the depiction of the Holy Saint.

"Yeah, we'd have to look into that. My husband has a token of his baptismal saint, St. Luke, so I want our son or daughter to have the same."

Diana looked at the tokens carefully and then said farewell to the lady. She left the narthex and stepped out into Bromley, looking about the light grey skies where nimbus clouds dominated. The trees on the sidewalk of Bailey Drive were in bloom and it was mild out with a minor wind that blew past. A few cars drove by and there were a few citizens on the street. At the sides of roads and lawns throughout Harlech was the leftover of snow here and there. The chirping of birds could be heard from afar. Diana took in the scenery and zipped up her grey coat. She then made her way onto the sidewalk and proceeded down, heading north to return to Keswick, turning onto Mackenzie Street, and then going west until she was at Bennett Street.

Diana made her way into her childhood neighborhood and came to the front of her apartment building. She checked her mail inside and then began to climb the four stories of the stairs up to her apartment. She took her keys and began to unlock the door. She then entered and walked through, placing her keys in a bowl at the nearest kitchen counter and taking off her jacket to hang it on the wall. Diana then returned and looked around the apartment.

Diana's apartment looked less bare than in the last three months. She took the time to decorate and buy some more furniture, although there was work to be done. For a start though, the TV stand now had a TV, the couch had a loveseat nearby and there was a carpet before them and a coffee table above. Diana's bookcase was moved next to the TV and at the other side was her desk where her computer had been moved to. There were various textbooks set aside on top of the desk and a laptop on the other side. The dining table near the kitchen had a vase of springtime flowers set in water, and the kitchen was tidy with all its new appliances. Diana passed through and went into the bedroom.

Atop of Diana's bed, on his side with the covers over his legs was Tristan, passed out and in a deep sleep. Diana looked at him and the dark scars over his torso with his tanned skin tone, including the one shaped like a wolf at his right shoulder. Tristan had retained the mass that he had built for himself over the last nearly four years. His green eyes were closed and there was a peacefulness to his face. His strawberry-blonde hair had grown fairly long, which for Tristan was more than three inches in length at the sides. At the top, his hair combed to the side was several inches long. Light poured in from the window, through the curtains and closed blinds. Before the window was a divan. In the left corner next to the divan was a crib and to the right was a dresser on the other side with various personal items of Diana and Tristan atop. The bedroom was amess with a mixture of Diana and Tristan's clothes scattered on the floor. The bed had been pushed closer towards the door to make room for the baby and the couple had bought an end table to replace the desk. Atop of the night table was a clock that read the time to be close to nine o'clock. Diana's wardrobe was the only piece that remained as it was, next to the door that went into the small bathroom.

Diana entered the bathroom to wash her hands and then exited to look over to Tristan. She went over to him and sat down at the edge of the wide single-person bed that they shared, hand at her womb, and another hand on the cheek of the man she loved. Tristan gave a faint moan and then slowly opened his eyes, looking over to Diana as she caressed him. Diana smiled down at him.

"Good morning, sleepyhead," Diana said. "Sorry to wake you up…"

"You're not sorry," Tristan deflected, turning onto his back and looking to her with a peaceful face. "You wanted to wake me."

"True," Diana agreed, "but you'll have plenty of time to sleep during the rest of spring break."

"Maybe," Tristan replied. "Charles phoned just after you left."

"Oh?" Diana questioned.

"He told us to return to the manor as soon as we could, because he wants to see us. He's sent us money to pay for a plane back to Allabrese."

"Did he give any reason? Is this just a general visit, or…?"

"I don't know," Tristan confessed, "but it'll be the first time we've seen him since January. As soon as he knew that we were together again, he just sort of fled and hasn't really talked to us. It's the first I've heard from him at least."

"Me too," Diana replied. "I wonder what he's been up to."

Tristan stretched his body and then sat up, moving closer to Diana. He looked down at Diana's pregnant stomach and then over to her.

"If we're going back to Allabrese to visit, we're going to have to tell him the news," Tristan stated. "It's been a bit rude that we haven't said anything to him, or anyone else for that matter."

"It's not like we know that many people," Diana replied. "Have you told Finn?"

"No," Tristan responded, "it hasn't really come up, and ever since I've started to live here instead of the dorm, we haven't really talked that much."

Diana looked at Tristan with disbelief.

"He's your best friend and you're giving him the treatment you gave me at the start of September-October?" Diana questioned.

"I don't think he has to be worried about me cheating on him," Tristan jeered. "Besides, he has lots of friends…"

"If we're going to see Charles, then we also have to tell him about us dropping out of school after April. He might not take that well… for you at least."

"It's not his choice," Tristan responded. "I don't want to be a doctor anymore. It's not in my interest nor is it my passion.

Don't get me wrong, I'm interested in the science, but physics and chemistry have proven to be my weak points that I can't compete against others with. And after what happened in December... between my dad and uncle, to be a police officer, that's in my blood."

"I hope you're not choosing this because of what happened to you with the Huntsman, and the discipline they instilled in you."

"No," Tristan denied, "I'm doing it because for once in my life, I felt alive out there, putting my entire mind and body to use, instead of just my mind. I feel like that's what I'm meant to do."

Diana smiled.

"I'm glad you've been able to make that decision before it was too late," Diana remarked. "I never expected it, but I'm welcoming to it."

"What about you? You want to become a nurse," Tristan said. "You found out what you wanted to do after you were in the hospital and it spoke to you."

"I have to be a nurse to our baby, and even then, when he's older, I doubt I'll have the time to transfer into nursing school and hope to graduate. I don't want to wander when I have my future duties as a mother to think of. I also have to think about our finances."

"Don't worry about the finances," Tristan remarked in a firm voice. "I'm going to take care of us. All three of us."

"You need to work on your future application to either the HPD, NPD, or RCMP," Diana replied. "My friend Lieutenant Macdonald would more than happily be a character reference for you down the line. He has connections and he's a senior detective with the HPD. And then I'm sure if we were to return to Allabrese, you could approach Jock or Aaron's dad to receive a reference from either of them."

"Yeah…" Tristan replied, lowering his head, "my primary concern is to put food on the table though. I need work experience more than anything. We can't live on the savings you've collected from your brief time with Paladin."

"Please don't stress about that too much," Diana cautioned. "We can always fallback on Charlemagne if we need to."

"No," Tristan denied, "I don't want to have to rely on him. Don't get me wrong, I love him for what he's done for us, but we're about to become parents and as a father I have to be responsible and provide for both you and this kid of ours, not Charles. Me."

Diana looked at him with slight disbelief. She then took in a deep breath and nodded.

"We're going to make it, Tristan," Diana said, putting a hand on his cheek and kissing him on the other. "You, me, and this child of ours are going to make it, so don't you worry."

Tristan looked ahead with concern and anxiety as Diana spoke to him about the future. He was not so certain as she was.

Act 1, Scene 2

The next day, Diana and Tristan checked into Harlech International Airport with their bags packed so they could travel to Allabrese. They stood before a self-check-in station at the entrance of the domestic flights where they signed-in and the machine then printed out their tickets and tags for their bags.

"Looks like we still have an hour and a half before the flight gets here," Diana said, looking at the tickets. "Do you want me to hold onto these, or do you want to?"

"Put them in your purse," Tristan responded. "I'll probably lose them otherwise."

Diana put both their tickets into her purse and then they walked off.

"Let's get some breakfast," Diana suggested. "I'm feeling pretty hungry."

"No surprise there," Tristan commented. "You're feeding for two."

Tristan looked around at the interior of the entrance of Harlech International Airport. From the causeway outside where the taxicab had taken them from Keswick, they came to a large and spacious modern entrance hall where there were various self-check-in stations throughout as well as a traditional check-in desk with attendants behind. Towards the left from the glass doors into the airport, one could walk into the international flights section of the airport, which was much larger. To the left, they could come to the terminal where domestic flights arrived, and behind they could come down an escalator and enter a miniature shopping center with various unique shops, some automatic-teller machines, some well-known Canadian restaurants, and a food court with some well-known Canadian fast-food restaurants. There was also an open bar in the corner with a view out towards the tarmac by some glass windows to the rear. Next to the escalator that went down into this sublevel shopping center, there was another that went up to an observation deck. Tristan walked with Diana, his hand in her hand, and the couple went down to dine at the restaurant as the fast-food restaurants were closed at this early hour.

The couple were seated in the restaurant and Tristan was served some coffee, while Diana received some hot water and tea bag. They then sat in a peaceful silence. Diana looked out towards the shopping center through a window in the restaurant, while Tristan had his hand stretched to the empty chair next to him. Diana looked over to him and saw that he appeared healthier and more cheerful than when she left him in October. However, she sensed an anxiety within him. Diana looked to the right and over to the TV. She then hid her head away as the TV played international news on mute.

"God, isn't it awful what's going on in the world right now?" Diana remarked. "What happened because of Zimmerman Corps and Mrs. Dulles really put a knife into the already fragile stability of the world."

"Yeah, it's not looking good out there," Tristan simply opined. "Certainly not a good time to be bringing a child into the world…"

Diana looked back at him.

"Meaning?" Diana questioned.

"What do you mean? I meant what I meant," Tristan replied. "I'm not discouraging our procreation. I'm simply stating the fact that this isn't a good time in human history to be having kids."

Diana put her hands together on the table and looked past Tristan. She then looked at him.

"I understand what you mean, but I'm going to disagree," Diana said back. "If anything, at times like these, good people need to have children to bring humanity out of the dredges. Did the Romans stop having kids during the time of the empire and near collapse? No. They had children who became the successors of Rome."

Tristan didn't respond and simply looked back at Diana. Diana looked away and back out towards the quiet shopping center.

"Are you worried about what Charlemagne might say about you being pregnant?" Tristan questioned. "After all, he was born out of a similar situation and has some mixed-emotions about it."

"I've wanted to tell Charles since I found out, but I didn't and kept it secret because I had to tell you first before him. Coincidentally, he disappeared after I told you, and I never felt comfortable sending him an email or phoning him to tell him something as important and jovial to me as the conception and existence of my own child."

"But what about the circumstance?" Tristan queried.

"It's a little… unorthodox, especially since we very nearly stopped ever seeing each other nor have we wedded, but I know for certain that this baby of ours was conceived out of love, at the island of paradise no less. He or she was not a mistake, or an accident, but a blessing and a welcomed grace. I don't know what I would have done if… we never came together like we did and I still found out that I was pregnant with your son or daughter. I know for sure I would have carried him to term though…"

"Please don't say anything else after that," Tristan requested. "I don't want to think about something like that."

"Sorry, I won't. My point though is that Charlemagne's relationship with his parents came out of frustration that he was 'abandoned' by them because they were too young, and maybe too immature to take responsibility for such a large responsibility as a child. We're not. He knows that. He has confidence that we've learned from him to not repeat the mistakes he's made. I'm confident too."

Tristan nodded and looked aside. Diana continued to look at him.

"I know that you're anxious about this baby," Diana said. "I am too, especially since this was sooner than I had thought we would have a kid, but we're still three months from the baby's due date. Tristan, I have every confidence that you are going to be a spectacular father to our child. God has given us this child of ours for a reason. Have faith in Him."

Tristan looked back at her with a plain face and then looked away again. He didn't respond. Their waitress soon returned to their table with their breakfast, and they ate away. Once they finished, Tristan sipped some coffee and continued to look away. He then suddenly turned to Diana and straightened up in his chair, bringing his hand away from the other chair as he rested.

"Hey, I was wondering..." Tristan timidly said. "What if, instead of looking for a full-time job to prep for my application with the police, I work part-time and stay in school for the three years I have left?"

"You want to finish your degree?" Diana queried.

"It's just... I've put the work into it this last year, and Charlemagne's always said that science degrees are worth a lot. I'm thinking about the future, and if something happens, or I can't be a police officer, or whatever, an A&P bachelor degree could give me a decent job somewhere, doing something in a research lab or whatever. And maybe even, if I somehow change my mind, prep me and help me get into medical school as a fallback. I want to keep my options open…"

"Do you think you can handle a full-time onslaught of science courses like this year, plus a part-time job?" Diana questioned.

Tristan shrugged.

"It shouldn't be impossible," Tristan reasoned. "Most courses nowadays are online."

"And don't forget the time you'll have to spend with your son or daughter."

Tristan didn't respond.

"Luckily, I don't have any intentions of working while we're financially stable. I want to devote all my time to this child while I can, so you won't have to worry too much, but it's still healthy to spend some time with him when he comes."

"He?" Tristan questioned

"She? Whatever."

Tristan rolled his eyes.

"Why don't you just get the baby tested so we don't have to hold our breaths," Tristan insisted. "I want to know if we have a son or a daughter in there."

"Maybe…" Diana replied, finishing her breakfast. "Even I'm dying to know, especially since it'll make picking a name half as easier."

"Oh, right… we don't names decided on yet…"

"We still have three months," Diana reminded him, "but going back to what we were talking about, it's up to you. Charlemagne is committed to putting us through education and board. You don't *have* to work (as much as you encourage the fact). He will make sure we don't become homeless."

"Work experience is invaluable," Tristan rationalized. "It's what I'm basing my entire future application on. These people value the life experience."

"You have life experience," Diana remarked. "By God, Tristan, at the age of sixteen they launched you into space, you've been to the arctic, across half the world, travelled with a former domestic terrorist, partook in a resistance, defied federal authorities in both Canada and the United States, and was part of one of the most elite mercenary units in the world. And that's not even all of it. You and I raided Waomoni's mansion with Charlemagne to save those poor children from those pedophiles, and you and I stopped a horrible invasion that would have resulted in the end of life on Earth. If anybody is qualified to be a cop, it is you right here and right now. Why should anyone give a damn about the two or three years you'll have under your belt as some security officer, or whatever…"

Tristan sighed.

"I wish it were that simple, but nobody is going to believe me if I say any of that to them during the application stage," Tristan reasoned. "As far as other people know, I'm just an ordinary person."

Diana sighed. She put her fork and knives together and then pushed her plate forward.

"If Jock could become a cop in two years since he left high school in Allabrese, and Aaron, who probably will be joining the NPD shortly, most likely can too, then I feel like your best luck would be to follow the same route they're taking."

"I'm between NPD and HPD," Tristan remarked. "I'm interested in the ERT with HPD more than the comfort and ease of Allabrese."

"It'll be a little more effort," Diana replied, "but I'm sure it would be worth it."

Tristan nodded. The couple finished up at the restaurant and Tristan paid for the meal. They then took their bags and went to the terminal to wait for the plane. The couple sat down and began to wait patiently when Tristan looked around and then looked to Diana.

"I'll be right back," Tristan said.

Diana looked at him and nodded.

Tristan left and went back towards the main lobby of the airport. He then went down to the shopping center and over to a high-end jewelry store. He then made his way to the ring display where he looked down. A woman in a black dress approached him from behind the counter.

"May I help you?" the woman questioned.

"Maybe," Tristan replied. "I'm looking for an engagement ring – I want to know what you have that is within six-thousand dollars. We're about to return to the town where we met and spent the last three years together, and I want to propose to her there."

"Well, that's about the average budget most men come in looking for wedding rings," the woman replied. "This is what I have to offer."

Tristan looked at the rings below, most of which had large diamonds in the center or other gems.

"Hm…" Tristan pondered, "none of those really suit Diana."

"How about these?"

Tristan looked and shook his head. He looked over to some other rings and then pointed out one with a smaller diamond at the top of a thin white gold band.

"What about that one?" Tristan questioned.

The store associate unlocked the cabinet and presented the ring to Tristan so he could look at it.

"This ring is zero-point-four carats, white gold," the store associate said. "Just under two-thousand dollars before taxes. Do you know what ring size your sweetheart is?"

"Uh, she has small hands," Tristan replied. "Smaller than mine."

Tristan looked at the ring more carefully.

"Beautiful time to get engaged and have a wedding with summer-spring coming up," the store associate remarked.

Tristan looked back at her with a smile.

"I want to get married on the day of our anniversary," Tristan said. "We, uh… have a child that's supposed to be due this June, and I know my girlfriend would want the kid to be born in wedlock. April 29th is also the earliest we could get married, because I'm in school."

Tristan looked at the ring before him.

"I don't know much about rings, and I hate to have to rush this decision, but Diana will eat me alive if I pay any more money," Tristan muttered. "This ring… it would suit her style… Hell, she'd love any kind of ring as long as it came from me; she's not materialistic."

Tristan finished up at the jewelry shop and then returned to the terminal to sit down with Diana. She read her latest book, *Faust* by Johann Wolfgang von Goethe, and they sat in a peaceful silence as they waited for their flight to Allabrese to arrive to take them home.

Act 1, Scene 3

Diana and Tristan arrived in Allabrese little more than an hour later when it was now late morning. The skies in Allabrese were as dark, grey and miserable as those in Harlech, if not a tinge worse. The small charter plane that took them over the county began to make its touchdown on Allabrese airfield. Diana looked down and saw the Nattau River and the town further ahead on its plateau. St. Allan's Field looked green and ripe, the western mountain chain was clear of snow, and the southern marsh looked to be a deep green-brown

Once the plane touched down at Allabrese, Diana and Tristan met with an armored car parked nearby with Lukas and Brandan before in their black-grey tactical uniforms.

"Welcome back to Allabrese," Lukas remarked, observing Diana without making a remark about her pregnancy. "Your guardian is waiting for you at home. I'll take you straight there."

Brandan set off to help Diana with her bags. He walked with Tristan to the rear of the armored SUV and they put their bags into the back of the car while Diana was assisted into the car by Lukas who held the door for her.

"Just one thing before we go to the manor," Diana interjected as she sat down. "Could you take us to the cemetery?"

"Certainly. We can make a stop there."

Tristan went around the other side and entered into the car. Lukas and Brandan then hopped into the front and drove off to drive down the freeway and then make a turn at the roundabout to go north towards the cemetery. By the time they arrived, it began to rain. Diana took out an umbrella from her purse and then stepped out. Tristan joined her and the two proceeded up the steps and into the depths of the cemetery.

Diana held Tristan's arm while he took control of the umbrella. They had a peaceful walk through to the center and then around to stop at a particular tombstone that read the name, 'Maximillian Magnus Bauer' at the top and at the bottom, 01-March-1981 to 01-November-2019. The two stood before the grave, paying their respects to the man that saved Allabrese from disaster. They stood there for several minutes as the rain continued to come down around them.

"He's not even down there," Tristan suddenly said. "His body, I mean. There was nothing to recover from the blast other than the necklace."

"It's still his memorial," Diana replied, sighing. "It would be nice if he could have been buried next to your mom though. I'm sure she would have appreciated that."

"Charlemagne already tried to have that arranged, but the convent wouldn't allow my mom's remains to be exhumed."

"Why?" Diana questioned. "Exhumation and reburial isn't contrary to Catholic teaching."

Tristan shrugged.

"I'm not even sure if there was anything left from the blast. We weren't even allowed to stay for her funeral," Tristan simply said in a grim voice.

Diana sighed. She held Tristan closer to her.

"I know what you want to call our baby if he's a boy," Diana said in a soft voice.

"What?" Tristan asked.

"Maximillian."

"No," Tristan replied, shaking his head, "I don't think we should call him that if he's a boy. I barely knew the man to make that commitment to him. He lived as he lived, whatever that was. We only knew him though for what he did to this town. No, if the baby is a girl, I want Sophia for sure, but not Maxim."

"Damn," Diana remarked, "I was hoping you'd agree to it. We're not naming the baby after my dad, that's for sure. I can agree with Sophia, it's a beautiful name, but we need a boy name in case he's a boy."

"I don't know what to name him."

Diana sighed. She closed her eyes and scratched her nose. She then opened them and looked to Tristan as he continued to look to his father's grave.

"I have an idea, but I've been unsure about it," Diana confessed.

"It's Damian, isn't it?" Tristan replied.

"Yes," Diana confirmed, "it was Scot's birth name and I always liked the sound of it – more than 'Scot' anyway. His recent death would connect the tribute, but…"

"It's also the name of the Mysterious Stranger."

"That's why I was hoping you'd agree to Maximilian instead."

Tristan looked uncertain.

"Damian – the bastard that killed her," Tristan replied. "The bastard that nearly killed Charlemagne and Manon. The bastard that kidnapped you and has apparently been tracking us since the beginning. Who even was that freak?"

"Iustina had high confidence in him."

"How aren't we certain that your friend Scot wasn't the same Damian that's been stalking us?"

"No," Diana denied, "I won't ever forget that the Mysterious Stranger had green eyes. Scot's eyes were between grey and light blue. This man was also taller than Scot was…"

"Do you think he's still out there?" Tristan questioned.

"I don't know. Ever since Zimmerman Corps and the Huntsmen went to hell with Zimmerman's disappearance, it's likely he got caught up in all that. Iustina said he disappeared around that time along with Zimmerman and all the others that partook in the expo to China."

"We could do some research," Tristan suggested. "We could see who owns the castle, and that might tell us who this guy was."

"Maybe," Diana simply replied. "Just maybe."

"I didn't tell you this, but when Finn was rescued, he said that the man who rescued him was named Damian as well," Tristan explained. "He said that he took him out of the forest and helped him come to America. Ever since you told me about what you found in that castle, I've felt the two have been the same – the assassin and the person who rescued Finn. I've been meaning to ask him more about this person, but… well, you know. It's made me think that this Damian guy wasn't in the forest by chance, but that he was hunting me down since the summer to get my blood – that's why he ran into Finn, and maybe, why he saved him since he knew who he was."

"It's possible," Diana replied, "but at the same time, it's over, Tristan. Zimmerman Corps is done for good, along with the Shadow Company. I'm surprised the Chosen haven't retaliated against us for what we did to Calavera, but it's possible they don't know that it was us that caused his death."

"Us? Helene was the one that technically killed him, twice for that matter. They can all back off. You're right, it is over. I just want to move on with my life, with you…"

"… and our child," Diana added.

Diana hugged Tristan's side and brushed her head against his left shoulder.

"Come on," Tristan suggested. "Charlemagne's waiting for us. We shouldn't keep him waiting."

Diana began to lead Tristan and the couple walked back the way they came to return to the Protection Squad where they waited for them. Diana looked to Tristan as they began to set off to the manor.

"It's far more certain than it is likely that both your parents are together in a better place now," Diana acknowledged. "The same is true of your aunt and uncle."

Tristan didn't respond and instead looked out the window with doubt and frustration in his eyes. The ride from the cemetery to Cabernet Manor was short. The SUV drove up the causeway and parked itself in front of the Cabernet home. Diana looked out the old manor and saw that it was much the same as she remembered it from last year. Once the car came to a halt, Diana and Tristan exited. Tristan and Brandan collected the luggage, while Diana went up the steps to wait for them. Tristan met up with her at the top of the steps and took out his keys to unlock the door as the rain continued to pour down. All four of them then entered, and Tristan and Elegast brought the luggage down before them on the carpet in the center of the foyer.

"Home sweet home," Diana chimed. "Thanks for your help, Brandan."

"I'll take our things upstairs later," Tristan said to them. "Thanks. Do you know where Charles is?"

"We can find out for you. He'll either be downstairs in his lab or his study," Lukas replied. "We'll call him for you."

Tristan picked up Diana and his suitcase and then began to walk with her up the stairs. They left the main entrance and came into the foyer of the north wing of the manor. He then went to his bedroom, but stopped.

"So, are we sleeping in separate beds, or?"

"I think we're past the point of pretending like we're celibate," Diana replied. "The choice is yours. Do you want us to sleep in your bedroom or mine?"

"I never liked my bedroom," Tristan said. "Let's just go to yours."

Diana and Tristan went forward down the corridor and to the end where Diana's bedroom was. She entered ahead of him as she opened the door. Tristan set their bags down near the dresser. Diana looked to her mementos on the shelf above. From left to right, there was the box of dried-up cigarettes, a vial of ectoplasm from 1136 Elmwood Crescent, the head of the robot from the Ural Mountains, her victory ribbon from the Nattau Derby, the small Anubis statue she bought at Giza, the piece of meteorite from her and Tristan's wishing star, the nutcracker Tristan salvaged for her from Kristoffer's workshop, the film reel that was given to her in France, Tristan's broken watch left behind at Northumbria-Berwick, a metal fragment recovered from the Cabernet Technologies wreckage, a purple candle from the Convent of Our Lady's Maidens, and behind was Diana's katana sword gifted her by the Oishi Clan. Diana unzipped her suitcase and took out three more items to add to the collection, including a brooch with the symbol of the Children of Moloch, the vial of Tristan's blood salvaged from Aegis Castle, and the apology card that Tristan had left on her doorstep. She then stepped back and looked at the objects with Tristan.

"Four years of adventures..." Diana remarked.

"It's been a hell of a four years," Tristan agreed. "At least it'll settle down now, hopefully.... Are you going to leave all this stuff here? Don't forget we got to pack up what remains of our stuff to take with us to Harlech."

"Are we set to stay in Harlech though? Are you sure about it?"

"For at least the next three years," Tristan replied, "and maybe more. Who knows after that... Eventually we'll have to move out of the apartment, maybe into a larger one with two-bedrooms. Eventually, we would have to move into a house – if we stay in Harlech. The path isn't certain."

"You've though a lot about this, haven't you?"

"Yeah…" Tristan confessed with a sigh and a frown, "of course, I have. It's almost everything I ever think about anymore."

"You should go to your room and see if there's any clothes left," Diana said. "We'll also have the space to take back some furniture if we're still going to drive back to Harlech to bring the pick-up truck with us."

"Hm… I'd prefer if we could bring back one of the beds with us," Tristan responded. "Just to give a little more room."

"Are you sure the bedroom can fit a bed?"

"Yeah, I think so," Tristan replied. "These double beds aren't that much larger. And if there's room, I want my desk too."

"Okay," Diana replied.

Tristan left and went into the washroom. He then crossed into his personal gym, looking around and sighing as he saw the untouched equipment. He then continued through and walked into his bedroom, which was a lot emptier than Diana's room. Tristan walked over and looked at the Latin Vulgate Holy Bible on his dresser, the photos of his aunt and uncle, his parents, and another of him and Diana. He then turned around to look at his bed and Finn's longbow on the wall. Tristan walked over to his desk and lifted up the cover to look inside the secret compartment. There were only a few pictures inside and an almost empty bottle of gin taken from the storage closet below. Tristan picked up the bottle and opened the cap. He then whiffed the contents and frowned. He put the bottle back and then closed the top of the desk. Tristan sat down on his bed and brought a hand to his face.

Diana moved some of her leftover clothes from her dresser and placed them into her suitcase, mostly summer clothes that were not in season. She then went to her closet and looked inside to her jackets, sweaters, and dresses.

"Oh jeez..." Diana sighed, "I'm going to need more space..." she muttered, going to her dresser and opening her jewelry box.

Diana went and opened Tristan's suitcase. Tristan barely packed with him any clothes and it was half-empty. She began to rummage through, looking for a pocket on the side. She reached her hand in and felt a hand wrap around a bottle. Diana took the bottle out and looked at it to see that it was a half-empty bottle of rum. She looked at the bottle with surprise and a slight frown. She then put the bottle back only to hear it clink with another. She dug the other out and saw that it was a full bottle of scotch. Diana's frown grew deeper. She quietly put the items back and then looked over to the bathroom door.

"Oh my God," Diana whispered, "I'm going to kill him..."

Diana heard the bathroom door open and then zipped Tristan's suitcase to stand up. She went across the room to her desk as Tristan entered.

"Well, I've had a look and other than a couple of photos, most of my stuff is still at the dorm," Tristan said.

"Okay," Diana simply replied, closing the door in her dresser.

Lukas knocked at the side of Diana's door. The couple looked over to him.

"Charles is in his study, waiting for you," Lukas announced. "He'll see you now."

"Okay," Diana said to him in a soft voice. "We'll be right down."

Act 1, Scene 4

Diana and Tristan entered into the library and walked towards the door into Charlemagne's study where Brandan opened the door for them to enter through. Diana went in first followed by Tristan who looked over to Charlemagne as he stood at the side of his desk with a fist down on top. The room was dim with only light from a fire that burned from the fireplace and there was a warm glow that produced with it. The study was organized much as it was beforehand with seats in the middle of the study, pointed towards the fireplace, a cabinet that contained the Panzerknacker Charlemagne recovered from the Arctic with an StG44 at its side. The Walther P38 pistol was also nearby. There were some of Charlemagne's paintings hung on the wall as well as various photos in the display case on the other side of the fireplace and within the bookshelf.

Charlemagne looked to Diana and Tristan with short white hair atop of his head, combed to the side. His moustache was as it always was, neat and combed down, but there was a distinct look of tiredness across Charlemagne's face and his skin was almost as white and fair as snow. He wore his traditional suit and held his head high as he looked to the couple, holding a stern face that soon turned to a smile as he extended a hand towards Diana and Tristan so that they could take a seat. Charlemagne's eyes looked to Diana's pregnant stomach, but he did not say anything as he instead walked over and sat down with them at an armchair while they sat on the loveseat. Charlemagne then placed his hands on his lap and looked to them.

"How was your flight into Allabrese?" Charlemagne politely questioned in a firm voice. "Quiet, I assume."

"Yes," Diana replied with a smile, placing her hands on her belly. "Charles, I'm sure it's obvious to you, but I didn't want to tell you over the phone, by email, or text message – I'm pregnant – almost seven months, expected to deliver in June."

Charlemagne raised his head and gave a soft smile.

"This is wonderful news," Charlemagne remarked. "In all honesty, I had no idea, I swear. I've kept my promise to give you your liberties away from the Protection Squad, so I have not heard from you since January. I'm genuinely pleased by this good news – it has made my day. It's a good thing the pair of you came together and made up, because it would have been a shame otherwise. Seven months…"

"Most likely conceived late-August," Tristan pointed out. "When we were in Isla Paraiso…"

"Yes, that sounds about right then," Charlemagne replied. "Well, I'm delighted to know that the pair of you have not only been united, but have taken the next step… When do you plan to wed?"

Diana looked to Tristan.

"Probably soon," Tristan answered. "We're both still in school, you know, but on that note… there's something else we thought we should tell you about our future plans."

"I'm going to put my studies on hold at Declan Walham," Diana said. "Obviously, I can't be a mother and a student at the same time, but if I can in the future, I do want to return because I've become interested in the possibility of a career as a nurse."

"Really?" Charlemagne questioned with intrigue.

"Yes," Diana replied. "Of all the jobs I've seen people have, none has interested me as much as the work my nurse was doing at St. Luke hospital, and I feel like, once I've finished my duties as a mother, I'd like to return to that."

"Also," Tristan said, "the last couple of months has made me realize something too. I don't think I want to be a doctor anymore."

Charlemagne looked at him with surprise as well as concern.

"I want to do something with my life where I can put all my skills to use," Tristan explained. "As a doctor, I won't be doing that... I'll be in an office, or maybe in a trauma room, clinic, or whatever, sitting down or standing, making tough, calculated decisions on something that doesn't really interest me that much. I'm not that sort of person. I also don't think I'm as smart as I thought I was. I mean, I'm certainly above-average – my marks in high school attest to that, but being at university has told me that I'm not fit for medicine, and my time on the streets chasing Diana and fighting the Syndicate told me that I'm fit for that – investigations, mystery-solving, and putting my whole body and muscles into it. I want to join the police and make my way up the ranks, hopefully ERT. I'm not sure if I want to drop out of school yet, but I want to know if I have your support either way in this new path of mine..."

Charlemagne looked at him and looked towards the fireplace. He sighed and then looked back to Charlemagne.

"Never did I expect such words from either of you on your vocations, nor this news that you were to become parents at such a young age," Charlemagne remarked. "Nonetheless, I have the upmost confidence in both of you by your maturity to make these decisions pertaining to your futures, so yes. You have my support."

"Thanks..." Tristan replied. "It means a lot to know that."

Charlemagne sighed and placed his hands on the rests of his armchair.

"Anything else you have to tell me?" Charlemagne questioned.

Diana and Tristan looked at each other. Diana then looked to Charlemagne.

"Not that we had planned to tell you, there hasn't really been anything else that's been new to us," Diana replied.

"Have you set on a name for the child? Do you know the gender?" Charlemagne inquired.

"No," Diana denied, "we're still thinking about names and we don't know if we have a he or she yet."

Charlemagne nodded. Tristan looked to him.

"What about you? How have you been?" Tristan questioned. "You look... different. I don't mean to be rude, but you don't look well."

Charlemagne looked to Tristan and then stood up. He approached the fireplace and looked down into the fire.

"I finished the project that I had been working on for so long with Barry," Charlemagne said in a quiet voice. "I had it moved to the bunker below us and have been running trials on it."

"What even was that project of yours?" Tristan queried. "You never told us."

"Yes," Charlemagne replied instead, "instead of explaining, why don't I go and show you? Come."

Charlemagne turned away from the fireplace and went towards the front door. He opened it and waved the couple to come join him. Diana and Tristan stood up and they went through to stop before the bookcase that acted as a hidden door. Charlemagne went to the book that opened it and pulled at it. The bookshelves then opened like doors and they stepped through to come to the freight elevator that took them down.

Diana and Tristan stayed together as Charlemagne stood in the center and the cart slowly came down the shaft to take them several yards beneath the mansion. Tristan looked ahead and saw the device that Charlemagne had been working on tirelessly over the last several months beneath Cabernet Industries, and possibly for many more months. The device had the appearance of a telephone box, but with no windows and instead a case made of the slick shine of alien alloy harvested from the rest of the Panzerknackers salvaged from the Arctic. The shine of the box was more focused as the lights in the lab turned on to create bright setting for them to come around the platform where the box sat on and admire it from the front.

"You, uh… you built a box?" Tristan questioned, scratching his head.

"Over the last several years, I've taken an interest in the two orbs that our lives had become so focused on, especially Zimmerman. I believe that our former foe was interested in the same sort of technology that I was, and do believe that the device the pair of you saw at Pentateuch Cathedral was the result of his own efforts to harvest the powers of these two orbs whose powers are said to consist of the control of time and ability to teleport wherever one desires. I have seen with my own eyes the power of teleportation in practice when your father and the other psionic soldiers shot around, and I've put together the four pieces of crystal from the Amulet of Ra and brought them together with the sister orb in the Scepter of Alexander the Great to combine them in what may just be, man's deadliest weapon, in the wrong hands. This device, in theory, contains the power of teleportation and time travel in one – it is in that sense, a time machine."

"You're joking, right?" Tristan remarked.

Diana looked at Tristan slightly annoyed.

"No, I am not. Although, my abilities to control the powers of the orbs by mechanical means has been difficult, and what were once schematics to construct a smaller devices has turned into this larger device, I have created a device that can activate the powers of these orbs by electrical energy – in theory, this device should take one forward into the future and to any dimensional point they so desire. Forwards, however, is the key word. The power of the time orb has never been the power to needlessly jump through time, forward and back, because that would been, as I thought, impossible, but instead to speed up time and find oneself in the future as has been hypothesized by many contemporary scientists. However, with my interest in this device has also come, since the events that occurred in Allabrese a year and a half ago, in the ability to go beyond that. The device you see before you works, but before you ask how I was able to travel forward in time and return to where I am now, I must confess that I have spent the months I had in solitary while you were in school, attempting to hone my own psionic powers believing I held the power. Zimmerman proved himself, the last moment we saw each other, to be talented in the art of psychokinesis as an awakened man, so I thought, by my own sufferings, especially in the grief over Finn, that I could. In truth, although I have not been able to activate the teleportation orb, I have felt the orb of time speak to me…. It is strange… It is as though these orbs have a mind of their own, and it's caused me minor distress to know what powers, either sinister or holy, these could be. The orb has taken me back in time from the periods I have jumped to. Firstly, this occurred when the orb and I travelled forward by a couple of hours and then were able to come back again. I didn't think such a feat was possible, but it occurred, but we only moved back to the moment in which I had left from. I have come to think of this phenomenon as elastic travel, in which, one travels forward and then comes back again like an elastic band, only going so far as the laws of nature allow. Like with the teleportation orb, as explained by your father, Tristan, it appears that the more of the orb there is, the more the power there is that can come out, but also, as I've learned from experiments with the time machine, one can opt for more energy.

I do not yet know the conversion or equivalency rate that psionic power has with electrical power, but it has taken a lot of electrical power to attain a few hours in the time machine and back again. Nonetheless, once the machine was ready, I attempted to be sure that these phenomena were not my own hallucinations or visions, but real events, by having Barry witness my later experiments, and sure enough, this has all been in reality. However, here is the problem that I cannot wrap my head around – since by natural means, one teleports or travels forward by the wishes that they set their mind own, to replicate such desire through a machine was difficult. I have yet been able to perfect that as, when I set the machine to take me forward a couple of hours, it instead took me years ahead into the future and not to the place I desired. No matter what one does, it will take you to that time and place, who knows how many years forward, into the ruins of this laboratory bunker."

Tristan took a deep breath.

"Well, that's a lot to process…" Tristan remarked.

Charlemagne went to his desk where various monitors were. He picked up a case there and then showed it to the couple.

"This is what remains of the orbs," Charlemagne said, presenting to them half of the orb from the scepter and three shards from the Amulet of Ra. "The rest is in the device. I would have liked to have retrieved the rest of the crystal from Zimmerman Corps because I have less than one-tenth of the dark orb than was in the original Amulet of Ra. Zimmerman had a shard set in a ring of his… There should be in the least thirty-five shards out there somewhere. My original intentions were to create two handheld devices, but I've been reduced to handheld orbs instead. How would the pair of you like to try the machine with me?"

"What?" Diana questioned. "Are you serious? I'm not getting into that the way I am."

"I assure you, Diana, there is no harmful effect on life by travelling through the machine, but I understand your concern nonetheless," Charlemagne replied. "It is best if you stay here…. How would you like to join me then, Tristan?"

"Uh…" Tristan hesitated, "sure," he caved with a smile, "let's see just what you've made here, because it sounds so insane that I feel like I have to experience this one to believe it."

"Tristan…" Diana said back to him with an annoyed voice.

"Diana, Charles said it was safe. What's the worst that can happen?"

"Jeez, I don't know," Diana sarcastically replied. "How about, you get separated from Charlemagne and stuck in the future?"

Charlemagne didn't respond.

"That's not going to happen…" Tristan assured her. "You heard him, the machine only goes one-way to a set time and place. We won't get separated, and we've seen these orbs work when other people grab onto them – that's how all three of us teleported with my dad from Nattau Bridge to Cabernet Laboratories. We'll be fine."

Diana crossed her arms.

"If you're going, then I want to come to," Diana remarked. "I'm not going to let you abandon me, but only forward and then back again. Okay?"

"Come, it will be a harmless adventure," Charlemagne insisted. "Step into my craft, and I will take you to experience what mankind has not been able to experience before."

Diana and Tristan followed Charlemagne who had the case with the light and dark orb in his hand by a handle. Charlemagne opened the sliding doors into the time machine, and all three of them fit into the cramped space lit by a dim blue light. He then closed the doors.

"All ready?" Charlemagne questioned.

"Yeah," Tristan responded with a playful look of disbelief. "Hit it..."

Charlemagne pressed the switch and the machine powered up, causing each of them to become dizzy. Tristan brought a hand to the side of the machine. Everything then went black.

Act 2, Scene 1

Charlemagne, Diana, and Tristan fell less than several inches beneath them as they travelled and arrived into a dark nothing. Tristan looked around and saw some light pour in from the ceiling behind them, giving some light, but it was not much. Charlemagne took a flashlight from his jacket and turned it on, giving them some better light. He then began to shine it around so that they could see they were in some sort of spacious cavern with metallic platforms installed, such as the one below their feet, around as floor. There were also thick metallic supports that went upwards high above the original ceiling of the bunker by at least double. The space allowed some second-floor platforms on the side. There were also some vault-like watertight doors against some of the cave walls that were shut and went deeper. Ahead of them was a wide desk against a cave wall with some cracked monitors and a chair overturned on its side. Behind them was a rectangular grid with a shaft that extended upwards, through the ceiling, and up to surface. However, the elevator cart was crashed on the floor, but there was still a ladder on the side of the closest pillar on the left.

"Is this...?" Tristan queried.

"It appears as if this is the bunker, but modified to have more space, and yet, completely abandoned," Charlemagne stated.

"How far into the future are we?" Tristan asked.

"I have no idea," Charlemagne replied. "My experiments were less oriented to exploration, as they were to the function of the orbs and machine. I have only gone up this ladder to the manor, and no more ahead. A part of me worries about what I might learn and its effects on the future."

Tristan looked about.

"This… this shouldn't be scientifically possible," Tristan remarked. "How is any of this real?"

"I ask myself the same, and although it seems real, I am in as much disbelief as you, because his shouldn't be realistically possible," Charlemagne said. "I have some hypotheses about how this is possible, the possibility that this is nothing more than a hypothetical glimpse of what may be, to the sheer possibility that this is physically the future. Either way, it seems as though the bunker below the manor becomes expanded, which gives me the idea to do the same as I would certainly appreciate this much space, although I imagine it to be incredibly costly to excavate through this much stone beneath the Earth."

"You said you've gone up to the mansion?" Diana repeated.

"Yes," Charlemagne replied. "The elevator is broken, but there is a ladder here we can climb up to reach the remains of what was Cabernet Manor."

Diana looked to Tristan who appeared concerned. Charlemagne went to the elevator shaft and shined his light at the ladder. Tristan went forward and helped Diana climb up. He then joined behind her, followed by Charlemagne. At the top, Diana climbed through an open hatch that entered into the small space behind the bookshelves, which had been torn out. Diana stepped forward and looked into the remains of the Cabernet library.

The bookshelves were aligned as they were in the present timeline, but they were bare of any books and some of them were torn over on their side. To the right, the door into Charlemagne's study was torn out. Diana and Tristan continued to the left to get a better view of rest of the library. The far corner where the grand piano used to be was ripped out entirely for them to look up to the dark grey skies and the wide window that looked to the front lawn was shattered. Where the couches once were was nothing but a folded carpet. Where the desks had been, there was nothing. Above them, the railing of the second-floor platform was missing a section. There was also a hole in the ceiling where light poured through.

Charlemagne walked into his study and saw that it had a different atmosphere to it. The wall that looked to the patio was blown out and none of the furniture that was presently in the study was anywhere to be seen. The fireplace contained ashes that were scattered outwards. At the windows behind where the desk should have been, there were some torn curtains that blew with the wind. Charlemagne stepped forward and looked at the scraps of paper and litter that was on the floor. He picked up a small metallic brass rectangular plate and brought it into his hands. The name plate read his brother's name, 'Salmar Clovis Cabernet.' Charlemagne frowned and brought the plate over to the mantle of the fireplace.

Diana and Tristan exited out from the library and came into the small corridor before the main foyer. The window to their right was shattered. They continued into the main foyer and looked ahead to see the chandelier collapsed on the floor. The windows on their left were shattered and the front doors ripped out and on the floor. Some of the stair railings were torn out, but the rest of the staircase was intact. A hole in the ceiling showed some crows above, who flew off upon sight of them. Diana and Tristan continued across, while Charlemagne came out of his study through the hole in the wall.

Charlemagne looked out to the patio and saw that the pool was empty with grime on the sides of the walls. The vegetation in the garden was withered at some places and overgrown in others with stems pouring over the balustrades and taking up some of the paths that used to be below. The fountain in the center of the gardens was filled with a murky water.

Charlemagne could see some crows atop of the fountain pieces. He then looked over to the patio on the left and saw the wedding arch was thrown over into an overgrown thorn shrub. The walls of the mansion were battered, holes in some, and almost every window shattered in some way. Likewise, the roof had some holes that went into the attic and even so far as into the ceiling. Charlemagne walked out of the patio and into the foyer through the torn out door on his right.

Diana and Tristan went through into the small living room where there was nothing but a hole in the wall that stepped out into the front garden. They stopped to look out and ahead towards the horizon where Allabrese was. There was nothing specific that was out of the ordinary of the view of the town, but it was also slightly foggy ahead, or perhaps smoky as there was a smell of smoke and garbage in the air. The couple continued into the dining room and saw that it was completely bare. They then went into the kitchen, which was much the same. The refrigerator door was open and there were some broken jars on the floor and litter here and there. A massive hole in the wall exposed the northside of the house, stretching down to the floorboards and up to the ceiling, looking down to the causeway where the stables and garage was. The door into the storage closet was wide open and the door into the stable attic ripped out. The elevator shaft was dark and the safety guard ripped out so that one could fall through. Tristan went into the roof of the garage and saw that some of the beams in the ceiling had fallen over. There was also a hole in the roof where light poured in through. There were none of the vehicles that Tristan knew, from Charlemagne's black sedan, the grey pick-up truck, or even the excavator, below. Some of the sides of the stables were turned over. Diana joined Tristan and looked down. Her eyes went to the stable where Zephyr had made his home, but there was nothing there, or even the renovations that once were.

Charlemagne walked up to the master bedroom and entered inside. The room was entirely different to his current bedroom, the walls were painted a dark green for example, and the base of a bed was on the other side of the room. This was not Charlemagne's bedroom. He went towards the windows and looked out to the Rocky Mountains. The fields behind the house consisted of a tall grass that stretched forward. He looked out from the balcony and then returned inside, stepping on a glass frame at his feet and then picking it up with his gloved hand. The photo in the frame was of Charlemagne and his brother, shaking hands. Charlemagne did not recognize the photo, but the pair of them were in the boardroom at Cabernet Industries headquarters in downtown Allabrese. Charlemagne looked approximately how he looked now, if not slightly younger. Salmar looked much as he looked before his mental breakdown, but his hair was shorter and he had the same stocky appearance that he inherited from their father. Both of the men were in suits, shaking hands as they looked to the camera. Charlemagne glanced at the photo suspiciously and took over to a dresser to place atop of.

Diana and Tristan returned from the garage and went upstairs to the north wing. They stopped and went to what was once Allodia's bedroom and Charlemagne's workshop. The two stepped inside and saw that instead of the pink the walls were painted once before, they were a dark beige. There was an empty frame of a bed to the right side without a mattress and the door into the bathroom, which was amess. The porcelain toilet had been smashed and the glass panels around the shower were moldy. They walked out and went to Tristan's bedroom, which was once Salmar's bedroom. They entered and saw that the walls were not painted green, but instead a brownish-red. There was some rubble on the floor as the ceiling had collapsed through and the entire roof exposed to the outside. They walked through to the next room where the gym was and looked inside. The dark room was empty. The mirrors on the wall were gone and instead there was only the grey wall and nothing more. To Diana's bedroom, and what was once Charlemagne's bedroom, the walls were the same blue they once were, but the furniture had been removed including every door, even the closet door, but not including the French window, which was instead beaten up with the glass cracked, but not shattered. Diana walked into the bathroom with Tristan to observe that it appeared differently than how it was in the present. There was no corner tub, or large mirror pane before the windows, but instead the room had been made smaller with a door that went into a closet at the other side where the toilet presumably was. At the corner of this extension there was a shower, and a smaller counter-top with the sink next to it, closer to the left wall as the door into the gym had also been removed to make space. There was a table beneath the blinded windows on the left. Diana looked into the closet where the toilet was and saw that it had been uprooted with a hole in the floor. She then exited and joined Tristan who looked around with serious eyes.

"Remind me," Tristan said, "isn't this how the bathroom pretty much looked when we moved in?"

"Hm..." Diana thought aloud. "I can't remember. All I remember is that the original bathroom was pretty much in a state like this, maybe a little better and that the door into the room next door existed. This has definitely been renovated again though."

Diana and Tristan exited from the bathroom and came back into Diana's former bedroom.

"What do you think happened to this place to make it look like this?" Diana questioned.

"Who knows," Tristan responded. "Literally anything could have befallen the manor, but from what it looks like to me, it's almost as if war happened. I mean, with all the holes around, the mess of dry wall pieces and dust on the floor, and the broken windows…"

"Who knows how far into the future we are," Diana remarked. "We could be in the near-future…"

"Or distant future," Tristan pointed out. "It's not certain."

"Let's go and find Charlemagne," Diana said. "I've had enough of this…"

Diana and Tristan left and came to the main foyer.

"Charles!" Tristan shouted. "Where are you?!"

Charlemagne's ears twitched as he heard Tristan's shout. He turned around from the balcony at his master bedroom.

"I'm over here in my bedroom!" Charlemagne yelled back.

Diana and Tristan made their way over and found him by the balcony.

"Have you had a good look around?" Charlemagne asked.

"Yeah," Tristan replied. "The manor looks like it's been through hell…"

"Find anything interesting?" Charlemagne then asked.

"Were we supposed to?" Tristan responded.

"No, it was a question of curiosity," Charlemagne responded. "I've found several effects of my brother, including a nameplate in the study and a photograph on the floor, which I've placed over there."

Tristan looked over to the photo frame on the dresser.

"Do you know what troubles me?" Charlemagne questioned them.

"Do you think this manor fell because of your brother's care?" Tristan guessed.

"No," Charlemagne denied. "The photo... there is some auspicious about it. I don't remember a photo like that being taken, especially at that age. It appears to be recent (relevant to our time period) if not taken a couple years beforehand. Perhaps, when I was fifty-six or seven."

"How far into the future are we, Charles?" Tristan asked again.

"I have no idea, really," Charlemagne replied, looking back out. "A century at the most, and a decade or two in the least."

"I saw Allabrese in the distance," Tristan said. "The town seems to be there still."

"If we were more than a century or two into the future, then I doubt this manor would be in the state like this where I can find relics of my generation left behind. It's interesting, really... in a morbid and macabre manner."

Diana and Tristan didn't respond. Charlemagne turned around and looked to them, holding the case with the orbs in his hand.

"Anyways, I appreciate the fact that you've come with me to this strange world," Charlemagne said. "I do appreciate the company, especially since in my age, I don't feel like I can journey around like I used to and it's good to be with others in case something were to happen. I'd like to look around a bit more, but we're simply not equipped for that right now, so why don't I take us back to our own time period. Hm?"

"Sure..." Tristan replied. "Do you want to return though? And explore a little bit more, maybe find out what happened here?"

"Certainly," Charlemagne responded. "From what I can estimate from my past explorations is that time continues to flow and the machine takes us here at a fixed time gap between our present and this future. In other words, several months have passed here since I made my initial trip in January and February, but what season it is right now in this world, I have no idea. It is possibly early-autumn based on this temperature, but then again, it was colder when I had started to come, and snowing."

Tristan didn't respond.

"Anyways," Charlemagne said, placing the case on the dresser. "Let's return home."

Act 2, Scene 2

Later that night, Tristan looked up to the ceiling over Diana's bedroom while she slept on her side with her back to him. His eyes wandered into the darkness, staring up as though in deep thought. He then turned onto his side and brought his chest to Diana's back and arm around to place a hand over her stomach. He maintained his eyes open and brought his head close to the back of her head, breathing gently and closing his eyes at the scent of his woman. Tristan opened his eyes briefly and then closed them as he set off to drift into sleep.

Tristan's eyes opened wide as he felt a kick come from Diana's womb. He moved his hand away and turned back onto his back, placing the hand on his forehead. He then gave a stressful moan and sat up, crossing his arms over his bare chest and then climb out of bed. He stood up and went towards his suitcase, but stopped as he looked over to Diana who looked straight forward as if she was ready to open her eyes at any moment. Tristan looked down and then over to her. He then stepped back and instead picked up his shirt on the floor and pulled it down. Tristan then left, closing the door behind him and leaving it ajar. Diana continued to sleep peacefully while Tristan wandered down the mansion halls and then came down to the kitchen. The time on the microwave stated that it was close to four o'clock in the morning. He moved into the storage closet where he turned on a light. Tristan's eyes shot around and saw that the supplies were looking bare ever since they moved out.

Tristan picked up a bottle of gin and took it into his hands. He then left and went into the trophy room, stopping at the French window as he looked out and over to see that the light was on in Charlemagne's room. He stood before the door to the patio and concentrated to see if he could spot some movement, but the room was stale. Tristan frowned and began to return to the main foyer where he left the bottle of gin on a table and then climbed up to the stairs to Charlemagne's bedroom. He entered the foyer and then went down to the wide door that went into the master bedroom, knocking on it, but hearing no response. He knocked again and then brought a hand to the doorknob to enter through. Tristan entered and saw that the lamp at the side of the bed was turned on, but the bed was made and Charlemagne could not be seen. He looked around and saw an envelope placed on top of a thin table in the corner of the room where there were some picture frames. Tristan went and picked up the envelope, quickly opening it and reading the letter, which said:

'Dear Diana and Tristan, the news that you have shared with me today has shined a ray of hope on me on the future of this world, because I have upmost confidence that the pair of you will be good parents to the son or daughter that will be born in June. What the world needs in its present state are both good parents and good children to create from the ashes what bad parents and bad children have destroyed. Unfortunately for me, I was never a good parent as I failed my only son by abandoning his mother out of a lustful desire, and thus abandoning him as well. By the grace of God, I was given a second chance when I was entrusted by Him to take care of the two of you, and I hope that in my last four years, I have been able to impart on you everything that I could possibly hope to pass on.

Before you worry, this is not a suicide note. When I wrote to you to visit, it was less of a courtesy invite, and more of a desire to have you come and assist me with a minor problem. However, never did I anticipate that you would both be parents now, even if your child has not been born, and thus I could never force onto either of you the responsibilities of my own errors and the desire to have you help me solve the problem I have created. Therefore,

I have set off, with my uniform and my rifle, back to this desolate world that we journeyed to yesterday on my own, with the crystals, so that I can take ownership for my failures. Please, do not follow me, because it will be unlikely that we can meet in this place as time continues to flow parallel to our own world even if the time period is not parallel to our own. Do not anticipate my return soon, but return I will, and if I do not, then I am sorry that I have passed on this burden of loss to you both.

Sincerely and with much love, Charlemagne'

"Not a suicide note," Tristan mocks. "It's basically a confession note for a suicidal mission," he grumbled, closing the letter.

Tristan placed the letter back on the dresser and went back downstairs. He then went into the library and opened the secret doors that went down into the shaft. Tristan called the elevator up and then went down on his own to the depths of the basement where the lights turned on. The computer ahead was quiet. Tristan looked around, but Charlemagne was gone. He sat down at the chair and brought it around. He then leaned back and brought hand to his temples, groaning.

"Diana is going to freak out..." Tristan muttered.

Tristan looked towards the time machine with a look of suspicion. He then stood up and went back upstairs. He exited out and then went into Charlemagne's study. The room was empty. He went back into the library and then into the main foyer where he grabbed the bottle of gin. He then walked into the living room and sat down, opening the bottle and drinking straight from it before tilting his head down with a hand at the side of his head by the temple. He gave a deep moan of relief as he swallowed the fiery liquor and continued to drink for several minutes until he was deeply inebriated, swaying side to side.

Tristan put the cap back on the bottle and then looked around, finally hiding it underneath the couch before standing up.

From the living room, Tristan went into the kitchen and opened the refrigerator to rummage through. He took out a plastic jar of peanut butter and then went over to take a spoon out from a drawer. He opened the jar and took out a spoonful of peanut butter, bringing it into his mouth and then chewing it around before swallowing. He then breathed into his hand, smelling the nutty smell, and then closed the jar and put it back in the fridge. Tristan returned upstairs and quietly entered the bedroom. He then went to the bathroom to relieve himself, going to the sink to wash his hands and then quickly washing his face and then taking some mouthwash from a drawer to rinse and then spit into the sink. Once he was done, he checked his breath and then quietly put the mouthwash away before returning to the bed, taking his shirt off as he was at the foot of the bed, and then climbing up and back into place next to Diana as he quickly passed out.

Diana opened her eyes and turned her neck over to Tristan who was on his side with his back to her. She began to hear him quietly snore, which caused her to sit up and lean over him. She sniffed at him and smelt the peanut butter on him. She looked at him estranged and then lay back down with an uncertain face. Her eyes looked over to Tristan's suitcase, but it was more or less in the same position as it was before she fell asleep. She lay back down on her side and snuggled her back closer to his, intertwining their feet as she fell back asleep with a peaceful sigh.

• • • •

The next morning, Diana awoke and looked around the room as it was bright with light pouring in through the cracks in the blinds. She turned onto her opposite-side and brought herself closer with Tristan who faced her as he slept, looking at him with his closed eyes as he peacefully snored away. She touched her forehead to his and closed her eyes again, opening them as she felt the baby kick in the womb. Diana brought a hand to her womb and gave a quiet yell. She took a deep breath and smelt the peanut butter on Tristan, seeing a bit of it at the corner of his mouth. Diana brought her hand to it the encrusted butter and scraped it off. She then whiffed around his mouth and looked at him uncertain. She smelt a mixture of peanut butter as well as Tristan's simple odor. Diana placed a hand on his cheek and then continued to look at him. She watched him for several minutes, observing him until the baby kicked again and her own stomach grumbled. Diana rolled her eyes and stood up, bringing the covers around so that Tristan was tucked in before she set off to go downstairs.

Diana entered the kitchen and opened the refrigerator. Charlemagne did not subsist on much and very little was inside. She took out a bag of bread and brought it over near the sink. Diana looked down and saw a dirty spoon at the bottom with some traces of peanut butter left behind. She picked it up and sniffed it. She looked at with the same uncertain face and the placed it back down, looking around and frowning. Diana went on with her business and made some toast before going into the dining room to sit down and quietly eat it with some tea at the side.

Once Diana had finished her breakfast, she entered the kitchen again and washed her plate, the spoon, and a butter knife she used to smear butter and jam on her toast. She then placed these objects on the drying rack before going upstairs and entering the bathroom. Tristan opened his eyes as he heard the shower run. He turned onto his back and then brought a hand to his forehead. Diana exited from the bathroom, dressed for the day in a long-sleeved white shirt and dark black yoga pants. She smiled to Tristan and moved her nightgown onto a hangar to place it in the closet. Diana then walked over to sit down at the side of the bed.

"Good morning," Diana said in a quiet voice as Tristan put on his watch, seeing the time to be close to ten o'clock.

"Morning," Tristan replied, rubbing his eyes. "When did you wake up?"

"Less than an hour ago," Diana answered, looking at him. "What time did you sleep?"

"Around the same time as you," Tristan responded, "but I woke up in the middle of the night as per usual."

"I saw that you had a late-night snack," Diana said to him.

"Hm? Oh right… Yeah," Tristan lied. "Same as usual."

"Come on, I'll make you some breakfast. I had some toast, but I could really go for some hardboiled eggs right now…"

"Sure," Tristan responded. "I'm going to have a shower then and meet you downstairs."

"Okay," Diana replied, standing up.

Diana left. Tristan went to shower and get dressed. Diana took some eggs from the fridge and put nine in a small pot to set them to boil. She then took out some bread and began to toast it. By the time Tristan's toast was ready, he entered into the kitchen and took it into his hand along with a cup of coffee.

"The eggs will be a moment," Diana said. "I put in enough for all three of us… Charlemagne must have gone to sleep late last night… Unless he's already gotten up."

Tristan paused before the door as he heard this. He then continued through and went to have his breakfast. Diana later joined him with a small bowl of peeled eggs, cut in half and salted.

The couple quietly ate. Diana then took the plates and Tristan helped her wash them. Diana sighed as she put the washcloth stretched out over the ridge between the sink and edge of the counter. She turned off the tap.

"It's almost eleven o'clock and Charles hasn't woken up. Do you think he's alright?" Diana asked.

"We could knock on his door," Tristan suggested. "If there's no response, he's probably downstairs."

"Good idea."

Diana and Tristan went upstairs. Tristan stood-by as Diana knocked on Charlemagne's bedroom door. No response obviously came. She knocked again and then turned to Tristan. He shrugged. Diana opened the door and pushed through. Tristan followed from behind as they entered the bedroom to see that a bedroom light was on. Diana went over to turn it off while Tristan walked over to the small desk to pick up the letter.

"Diana..." Tristan said in a depressed voice. "You should look at this..."

Diana walked over and took it from Tristan's hand. She then took out the letter that he had already read and began to skim through it.

"Oh my God..." Diana muttered. "Read this..."

Tristan took the letter into his hands and looked at it for a moment. He then embraced Diana as she buried her head into his shoulder.

"What is he thinking?" Diana questioned as she sobbed.

"Take it easy," Tristan cautioned her. "This kind of stress isn't good for the baby... God knows the baby's been through enough stress already because of us..."

Tristan sighed and said, "Charlemagne went off on his own, thinking he'd leave us be since we're the way we are now, but I would have offered to have helped him anyways. I wish he asked me. I would have helped him with whatever his 'problem' is. I'm going to help him."

"Are you nuts?" Diana questioned, moving away from him. "You have no idea where he could have gotten to since he left. He could be anywhere, and without the power to control the orbs and without the orbs at all, you won't be able to return. You might get lost!"

"It couldn't have been more than eight hours. He must be somewhere around Allabrese right now. I'll approach him, offer my proper help, and then make him return so we can re-equip. It'll be simple."

"No," Diana denied, embracing Tristan. "I don't want to see you go out there."

"Diana, you can't hold me back like this," Tristan scolded. "Is this how you're going to be when I'm out on the streets as a police officer, or even earlier as a security guard, or later with the ERT? You know we've been through much worse – I've been through much worse."

"It's not just that though," Diana warned him. "It's the fact that this is a world in which you might not be able to return from."

Tristan sighed and said, "I'll find Charles... He's a sixty-year old man with a quarter of the strength he once had. He couldn't have gotten far. He'll have to return once he sees me."

Diana shook her head and then looked back at him.

"He'll have to return if he sees me with you," Diana suggested. "Think about it..."

Tristan looked at her uncertain and then remarked, "Diana..."

"If you're going, Tristan, then I'm going too. It's a compromise..."

Tristan sighed and then replied, "Fine, but we have to go and be quick about it. We'll also have to take a bit of supplies with us."

Diana and Tristan prepared themselves for the excursion. Tristan put on his raincoat from yesterday and some hiking boots from his room. He then came downstairs to the basement with Diana, who wore her own boots and raincoat. Tristan picked up some spotlights from the emergency preparedness closet nearby and a set of binoculars. He then came into the basement where Diana waited for him. Tristan then opened the doors and the couple walked in to travel forward to save Charlemagne.

Act 2, Scene 3

Charlemagne had travelled down the highway from Cabernet Manor, crossing the Nattau River as the Nattau Bridge was intact, and went through St. Allan's Plains and uphill into the suburbs of Allabrese. There was a distinct atmosphere of abandonment across the farmland where the burnt shells of barns could be seen alongside the wreckage of military vehicles, armored cars, tanks, and helicopters across the land. The atmosphere continued into the suburbs where the houses were abandoned, the area vacated entirely, windows broken, doors ripped off, and the ruins of some houses left around with overgrowth encroaching on the sides of walls and roofs. The lawns of the suburbs were tall and there were even some abandoned cars, most of which had been siphoned for the gasoline they held, tires taken for the rubber, and engines stolen at the front. The sight was more or less apocalyptic. Charlemagne went down the road and soon entered into downtown Allabrese where he saw the Nattau Police Department HQ on his right, burnt to the ground and a pile of rubble.

Charlemagne wore his field uniform for the Protection Squad, which included the poncho that covered his torso and hood. It was approximately early morning with the sun attempting to shine through the dark clouds as it started to rain. Charlemagne carried an assault rifle on a strap around his back alongside a rucksack with various supplies, including a sleeping mat. In his hand, he held a Geiger counter, which showed there to be very little to no radiation nearby. He continued forward down the main road and came to the front of Cabernet Industries HQ, which was burned out and charred. The windows were shattered, the outsides left black. Charlemagne then looked over to the manor that was the Civil Center to see that it had been left intact, but the windows were shattered too and an overgrowth of vines could be seen on the side. Ahead, Charlemagne could see the Curtia Dawson Memorial Library and see that it was in a similar state as city hall. The park in the middle of town was overgrown and as Charlemagne made his pass down to the road, some deer scattered and ran off. Charlemagne went down and then left down the road that went towards the mountains. He stopped before the grocer and looked ahead.

The grocery store at the corner of the street had been looted long ago by the empty shelves that could be seen from outside, but Charlemagne saw some papers on the floor in the entrance, which he went towards, putting the Geiger counter away, and leaning over to pick up the paper. Charlemagne saw that the sheet was a newspaper from the local weekly tabloid. He looked at the front page and read the headline, stating an evacuation of the town. The paper was brittle and old, but in the corner the date read to be approximately September 12, 2042, based on the shape of the barely visible letters. Charlemagne attempted to read the main article on the paper, but the print was too faded to see. He dropped the newspaper and continued down the street to come around to the library. He then began to climb the stairs to enter through the front entrance.

Charlemagne looked around the main foyer of the library to see that the old architecture had survived for the most part even if the glass and walls were in ruins. He walked through to the left and went to some bookshelves. A majority of books had been taken and the shelves were bare. Charlemagne went over to where the public computers would be and saw that they had been pillaged. He then went across the other side to see that all of the books had been taken from there. Charlemagne then returned to the front of the library to exit out and came to the top of the stairs. He looked around and began to cross towards the ruins of the Cabernet Industries HQ.

Charlemagne entered through the front doors and saw that some of the plaques on the wall had survived the fire. He went towards them and began to wipe the ash off some of them, recognizing some of the older ones as business awards and such. He then stopped at a plaque towards the right, which read, 'Charlemagne de la Cabernet Memorial Scholarship' at the top. Below were a list of names with space for more, starting from the year 2038 and stopping at the year 2040, listing only three names in total, all of which he did not recognize. Charlemagne stepped away from the wall and began to return back outdoors. He looked around and then went forward towards the civic center.

Charlemagne entered through the front doors of city hall and then looked around. The wallpaper on the walls were torn and the carpet removed from the floor, leaving the archaic floorboards underneath. Charlemagne turned on a flashlight and began to look around the building, entering the hallways on the side and searching around. A lot of the furniture in the old administration building remained, including filing cabinets, desks, and chairs. Charlemagne entered into one office to open the cabinet, but saw that most of the papers had been removed and a lot of the stationery and equipment in the office taken with the contents as there were no computers or cables of any kind around.

Charlemagne continued through the civic center and went upstairs. He passed the familiar office of the social service agent that attempted to help him with Diana, Mr. Gregson, and saw that his office had been abandoned. He then went around to a central corridor that led to a set of double doors into the mayor's office. He pushed through and entered into the empty room, looking around. The mayor's office was a study, slightly larger than Charlemagne's study, shaped in a wide-T with the stem at the end and enclaves at the side. At the end of the room there were large windows that looked out to a back garden. The room was bare, however, so he could not admire what must have once been an elegant office space. The chandelier in the ceiling in the center of the room was intact, however. Charlemagne exited out and returned to the main foyer. He then went downstairs and into a corridor in the back where he went down and entered a stairwell that took him downstairs into the basement. He then came to a corridor that went downwards to a closed door that read, 'Archives' in the front. Charlemagne attempted to open the door, but saw that it was locked. The glass above had been smashed and cracked, but the door was more or less intact.

Charlemagne knelt down and began to lock-pick the door, opening the door and entering and seeing the room to be as it left behind. He walked past a front desk where there were two computer stations, one facing the door and one on the opposite-face, and down a narrow corridor into an open rectangular space where there were various filing cabinets in alphabetical order, some in association with specific sorts of documents such as building plans, property ownership, zone planning, birth records, and death records. Charlemagne went to the death records and began to search for his surname. He then went through and found the records in the 'Ca' category, stopping at his own name and withdrawing the record. Charlemagne then began to read a copy of his death certificate, which included various documents, including a coroner's report. According to the assessment made by a physician, Charlemagne de la Cabernet was pronounced dead at his home by paramedics with strangulation marks on his neck. Primary cause of death was listed as asphyxiation with no probable secondary causes. The paper was not signed by Charlemagne's personal physician, Dr. Moore, but by an unknown doctor with an illegible signature. The date in the corner read, 'October 19, 2037.' He continued to flip through and read the coroner's report, which confirmed that Charlemagne had died of asphyxiation and that several bones had been found to have been broken in the neck. Below, the paper stated that the results of the investigation had been forwarded to the Nattau County Police Department and their investigation. Charlemagne took a deep breath as he finished reading the police report. He then placed the papers back into the filing cabinet, looking down the 'Ca' out of curiosity, but saw no names that he recognized other than 'Cavanagh,' as in, Sean Cavanagh.

Charlemagne closed the filing cabinet and began to leave. He came outside, putting away his spotlight, and looked around. He then spotted a trail of smoke from the southeast. He looked at the smoke with intent and reached around for his rifle, holding it in his arms and going down the street and towards the smoke. He entered into the east suburbs that went towards Champion Plains, reaching another street where the smoke could be seen coming from a house ahead. He went down the street and raised his rifle as he got closer, taking more caution with his steps. Charlemagne rushed to the exterior walls of the abandoned home and then approached the front door, passing it and going around the other side of the house to a gate. Smoke billowed through a hole in the roof on this side, so Charlemagne passed quietly beneath some windows to reach the gate. Luckily, some overgrowth covered the windows slightly. Charlemagne pulled on the latch at the side of the gate and then began to continue down around the rear of the house into the backyard where a tall grass covered the entirety of a formerly large and diverse garden with plenty of flowers in bloom and even two apple trees with green, developing fruits.

Charlemagne approached the glass shutter at the rear of the house and looked inside. He could not see anyone. He made a cautious side-step approach to look deeper into the home, but there was nothing to see. Charlemagne then stepped up onto the concrete step and attempted to open the door, but it was locked. He continued around the side and came to another door. He brought a hand around the doorknob and gently attempted to open it, but the door was locked. Charlemagne lowered his rifle and took out his lock-pick set to attempt to quietly unlock the door. He then turned the knob and began to push through, coming into an empty garage. Charlemagne looked ahead to a door that went deeper into the house. He put his lock-pick kit away and took his rifle in hand to go to the door.

Charlemagne went up the steps to the door and then opened it, walking through and coming into the corridor of the house. The house was built with a crawlspace foundation, which caused each step he took to echo slightly beneath the floorboards. Charlemagne came around and went down the corridor and around to see a fireplace ahead, but with nobody insight. He knelt down with a foot before him and pointed the gun towards the fire. He looked to the windows and saw that the overgrowth had not been manipulated. He maintained this position and took quiet breaths as he focused forward. After several minutes had passed, Charlemagne stood up again, continuing forward and turning at a French window that looked into the living room, kitchen and dining room, which connected with the sliding door that went into the back garden. He then quickly turned back to face the other room ahead where there were some torn couches near a fireplace. The fire had been set atop of a tile floor with some wood. Charlemagne stopped ahead and searched down the room. He then continued forward, instantly turning and aiming his weapon to his right as he felt the presence of someone there.

Charlemagne's eyes widened as he looked to the person before him. He instantly lowered the gun and raised a hand up. Manon looked towards him, wearing a similar poncho to him, but holding a Walther P99 pistol with both hands, pointed forward towards him, ready to shoot. She looked as surprised as she was, but she lowered the gun and took a sigh of relief. Manon appeared much as she appeared two years ago with her short medium-brown hair, which was amess in her current dress.

"Oh, *Charles*," Manon remarked, putting her handgun into the holster on her belt, underneath her poncho, and then embracing Charlemagne. "Where have you been? I though you would never come!"

"I'm sorry," Charlemagne apologized, looking over to the fire. "I worked as fast as I could, but don't you worry. It's over…"

Charlemagne lowered his rucksack and took out a space blanket. He then patted down the fire before putting the blanket away and picking up his rucksack.

"We're not safe here," Charlemagne noted.

"*Charles*, what an 'orrible fate that has fallen onto this town," Manon said. "What are we going to do…?"

"Foremost, I'm going to get you out of here," Charlemagne replied. "Come on, we've got to return to the mansion so that I can take you back to the past. Have you been in contact with anybody else?"

"No," Manon rejected. "There has not been anyone else in these parts in the last several days…"

"I suppose that's both good and bad," Charlemagne responded. "Come now though, love. We have a minor hike ahead of us – We can talk more once we're on the road back to the manor. Come on."

Act 2, Scene 4

Charlemagne and Manon trekked down the freeway and crossed the Nattau Bridge. The two were more or less silent. Charlemagne led the way with his rifle in hand as they passed the roundabout and began to go back towards the manor as it became late morning.

Meanwhile, Diana and Tristan emerged from the shaft that went beneath the house and began to climb out of the hatch. Diana went forward and looked over to Tristan behind him. They then continued forward with the spotlights in their hand, entering into the main foyer as Charlemagne and Manon climbed up the causeway. Charlemagne rested his rifle, holding it in his hands, but not pointed forward. He walked calmly towards the steps up the front door, but then focused his head forward as his ear twitched at the sound of a footstep. Diana and Tristan stepped out of the manor and were instantly met with both Charlemagne and Manon who drew their weapons towards them.

Tristan rose his hands up as he saw them point their guns at him.

"Tristan?" Charlemagne questioned, lowering his rifle. "What in hell's blazes are you doing here?! Diana?!"

"What is going on?" Manon inquired, lowering her gun back into her holster. "*Charles?*"

"Nothing too drastic," Charlemagne responded, looking over to her.

"We read your note and thought you had finally decided to go on a suicide mission," Tristan replied. "Why didn't you ask me to help? I would have come with you – you could have needed the protection."

"I would have needed the protection…? When you clearly haven't even decided to come with a gun?" Charlemagne replied. "What kind of place do you think this is? Harlech? What were you thinking – especially you, Diana, in the state you are in, coming here?"

"We were thinking of you," Diana retaliated. "You left us a vague note that didn't really leave us confident in your goals…"

"Had you been thinking of me, you would have respected my wishes to do this alone," Charlemagne replied, climbing up the steps so they were in the main foyer of the manor.

"I thought you said they would not come, *Charles*," Manon pointed out, entering behind him. "Can't you see? They are eager…"

"Look at her," Charlemagne said, pointing to Diana with her pregnancy. "They cannot risk their lives for me – if something were to happen, I'd be damning their only child out of my own selfishness! What kind of a man would I be then, even after what's happened, hm?!"

"This doesn't justify leaving us," Tristan replied. "I could have helped…"

"Do you at least care to explain what the hell is going on? Why Manon is here?" Diana inquired.

"You haven't even told them?" Manon remarked. "Honestly, *Charles*, what have you spent the last week doing?"

"Okay," Charlemagne replied, raising his hands up to both of them. "Everybody calm down so that I can explain," he said, taking a deep breath. "My intentions with Diana and Tristan, trusting their hard-earned skills, was to have them help me with what has happened (which I will get to in a minute). However, as I said in my letter to you, I never expected them to be in a position where they would not be able to assist me. I brought them here after they arrived to see what they would think of the future, and because of their depressive reaction, I thought it too risky to even bring Tristan, especially given Diana's hefty reluctance."

Tristan looked to Diana. She glared back at him.

"The plan was to get them familiar with the world, but I had to call that short because of this unexpected news," Charlemagne said.

"But why?" Tristan interrupted, anxious. "Tell us what's going on...!"

"Let me finish!" Charlemagne shouted back at him before taking a deep breath. "The truth is, at the start of January, your roommate, Tristan, came to me that day Diana had been released from the hospital and when I had stepped out from the ICU. He approached me just as Ms. Black had finished talking to me and confessed that he was Finn Cunningham, my only begotten son, and that he had survived the wildfire in which he knew from you, Tristan, that I had known of his existence and that I had been searching for him, thinking that he had perished in the fire. At that very moment, my heart sank and was then lifted up with such raw emotion.... My boy... the boy that I had left abandoned... he was alive. In the days that I remained in Harlech, we met and kept in contact, but then inevitably his schoolwork began to hinder his opportunity to meet with me, so we settled to meet this spring break. With a date in mind, I made the cautious decision to inform Manon who accepted the opportunity after a phone call in which I had to convince her of this once in a lifetime opportunity. On Friday, Finn arrived at the manor and met with me, and at that moment, I presented Manon to him, firstly as an acquaintance of mine, but then as his mother. I gave him a tour of the manor. I showed him the laboratory in the basement, my prized possessions, and I was astonished at his knowledge and input – this was surely my son – my dearest Finn, of whom I was well pleased with.

All seemed well until we sat down in the study, just as we did when you both arrived at the manor, before the fireplace, and the subject turned as Finn asked why we had abandoned him.... So, I told him the truth... I explained to him firstly how I had met his mother, our history stretching back to our childhoods, and then I told him about what happened with me and Judith. He did not respond to my abandonment of Manon well. Manon took over for me and explained that I didn't know about her pregnancy, and neither did she until it was too late to have informed me. We had separated and didn't see each other until almost two years ago due to the fact that I happened to be in France and was researching a personal topic regarding my family. Manon explained that she carried him to term, named him Louis, and that she gave him up to be adopted by that English couple, explaining the difficulty in the task. Finn's response to her was as belligerent. He didn't say that we were bad parents, or bad people, but passed onto us the guilt we deserved. Finn told us about his life under the roof of Mr. and Mrs. Cunningham, the neglect he faced, the suffering he endured without a father that understood him, and there was only so much I could listen to until I simply couldn't listen anymore and needed to speak out.

I apologized to him. I announced my regrets, but I also argued in my defense that I had been clueless of his existence, and that Manon did not bare that fault for what I had done to her. I attempted to explain to him that this was simply the fate of the world that had been passed on, but by a blessed change to come together here on Earth, we were able to meet. Finn was not impressed. He said... he didn't believe me. He then left. I didn't chase after him... that was my regret as I heard him from past the door, opening the door to the shaft I had shown him, taking the elevator down to the lab. By the time I had caught up to him, it was too late. He had taken the time machine, setting the date to several days before January 17, 2000, but unknown to him that the machine only travelled to this place, one-way..." he said with a sigh. "Naturally, I thought to chase after him, but I wasn't sure of what he was capable of, especially if I went in armed. Manon met with me in the basement and I explained to her the situation, that he had travelled through to the future, and that he was trapped in there. She then volunteered to go in with me, but I rejected that and said that we would need more than that. Manon insisted though that one of us go in after him while the other sought for help, and she drew the short straw in that bargain. I equipped Manon with what I could and gave her instructions, telling her that I would need at least twenty-four or so hours, if not a little more to get the assistance, and after she left, I attempted to keep that promise. I contacted Mr. Heavner to put together a special team, but because of the lack of specifics, time constraint, and risk factors involved in such an operation, I told him to stand-by while I looked to you two... the heroes from Harlech.... I phoned Tristan that morning, having not slept, and instructed him to come to the manor at once. And then we met, and you know the rest..."

Diana shook her head. Tristan was silent.

"Dammit, Charles," Diana remarked. "You should have told us. He's my cousin. Tristan's best friend. Of course – dammit, of course, we would have helped!"

"What more did you want from me?! He's my biological son! I was rife with panic, and I... I choked. And now... Manon and I have no idea where he could have gotten to, because in her day and a half in this world, she's lost track of him and has not seen him."

"You shouldn't have lied to us!" Diana shouted back. "Dammit, Charles, this is serious!"

"I very well know that!" Charlemagne responded before scoffing. "And as if you two should be one to even scold me for withholding the truth when the pair of you seemingly have kept Finn's survival from me this entire time that you've started university!"

"Hey, Finn told us not to tell you, and we had to respect that wish!" Tristan replied. "He went almost a year without telling either of us about his survival!"

Diana growled and said, "I'm so sick of this – the secrecy between all of us…! Dammit, between Tristan and you, I'm sick of all of it! You though, Charles – this is beyond what I'd expect from you, although, why am I even surprised when you won't take those gloves of yours off."

Charlemagne was struck back by this jab from Diana. He went quiet. Diana and Tristan looked at him. Manon was simply confused.

"*Charles…*" Manon said. "What is she talking about?"

Charlemagne looked down. He then began to remove his gloves and present his hands to Diana and Tristan. Tristan looked forward without much surprise, while Diana was horrified.

"Oh my God…" Diana whispered. "What—what's happened to your hands?"

"Cancer, specifically a severe form of melanoma" Charlemagne confessed. "I've—I've had cancer for the past year. I was told by my GP that I had little more than a year to live, and… that was at the start of April last year… just before we left for Asia."

Diana frowned.

"You've had cancer for the past year, and you've kept that from us?" Diana questioned.

"For the past year, I've attempted endless attempts to cure this, but... I've been unsuccessful. This time machine... it was my last hope at a cure, by seeking knowledge from the future to hopefully cure what has pained so many in the present, but as you can see... the future is bleak. I've had several tumors removed across the body over the last six months, but there's one that has begun to press into my stomach that has become too large to operate on. I don't know when that cancer will worsen for certain, but as you can see... it's too late for me. My final moments could be at any point in the next months."

"Oh my God..." Diana remarked, bringing her hands to her face. "Charles, why?"

"I'm sorry," Charlemagne simply replied, "but as you can see, there is not much left for me to lose but the little time I have left on this planet. I'm sure we can all agree that this time would be better spent finding Finn though."

Charlemagne lowered his rucksack and brought it to the floor. He then removed the orb of time and the space orb from where he tucked them away. He then held them in his hands as he looked over to Diana and Tristan.

"I'm going to take the three of you back to our world and then I'm going to re-equip to return here and find Finn myself," Charlemagne said. "I don't want to hear any more about it. Understood?"

"Why?" Tristan questioned. "Charles, I fully understand why Diana should return because of the baby, but dammit, why can't I help? I've proven myself to be more competent in the field than you, and yes... I have a lot to lose if I don't return, but Finn is my best friend! I'm going to help you whether you like it or not – I've handled much worse from the Chosen to the Harlech Syndicate."

"This isn't like any of those," Charlemagne deflected. "This isn't some quest to prove yourself to Diana nor is a mission to rescue a bunch of children from that Jewish clique! This is a rescue mission in what is probably the most dangerous circumstances – a world that we do not understand."

"Wait, what?" Diana questioned. "Jewish? Why did you say that?"

Charlemagne's eyes opened as the couple faced him. His face went red.

"Sorry, it was a slip of the tongue..." Charlemagne replied. "I apologize."

Tristan looked at him suspiciously.

"I don't see what you could have possibly have originally meant by that," Diana responded. "Charles, what did you mean – dammit, stop with the lies!"

Charlemagne grumbled.

"*Charles*?" Manon asked.

"Oh, please..." Charlemagne complained, "as if it is really that oblivious... The Chosen... all of them are Jewish people, ever last one of them!" he pointed out. "How has this surpassed you? Kau Waomoni's mother was a Jewish woman that fornicated with an islander. Dr. Naser Cohen, also known as Dr. Nash Bishop, an Israeli citizen and Mossad operative. All of the Chosen I had met at Waomoni's manor were Jewish... God's alleged Chosen people – when they're nothing more than the children of Moloch as they say, of whom is their father, the Devil. Has this really passed on you? Ever since the end of the war... ever since the 1960s, they've come to wage war against Western Civilization in a plot to destroy civilization at their benefit, going after my own grandfather and having him assassinated when he attempted to reveal the truth. They are the ones that are responsible for the moral decay, and thus the societal and overall decay of Western Civilization! Certainly, perhaps not all Jewish people are Chosen, but all Chosen are Jewish people, the worst of them might I add! Don't you see?"

Tristan looked ambivalent at what Charlemagne revealed to them while Diana shook her head with tears, hands clasped before her face.

"No…" Diana denied. "I don't believe you. You're… a… an anti-Semite!"

Charlemagne rolled his eyes.

"Tell me you're lying," Diana said, shaking her head and walking towards him. "Please…"

"I'm sorry to disappoint you, Diana, but it is the truth of the matter," Charlemagne replied, lowering his hands with an orb in each hand. "I'm taking us home…"

"No…" Diana cried, grasping Charlemagne hands with the space orb. "You monster! I won't let you abandon Finn like this!" she remarked in a panic.

"Diana!" Tristan shouted, grabbing hold of her.

"Dammit, woman!" Charlemagne yelled as Diana grabbed the space orb from his hand.

"Finn has to come home with us!" Diana shouted in her distress, causing the space orb to glow. "I won't let you abandon him!"

Charlemagne flinched as the couple blinked out from where they were before him as he continued to hold the time orb in his hand. He looked at where Diana and Tristan were and began to shake.

"Oh my God…" Charlemagne muttered, falling to his knees. "No…!"

"What has happened?" Manon questioned. "*Charles*!"

Charlemagne brought his hands to the side of his head as he had a minor mental breakdown at Diana and Tristan's teleportation.

"I've... I've trapped them here..." Charlemagne noted. "Dammit, I've lost them all!" he shouted, falling over forward in tears. "Good Lord, why?!"

Manon knelt down and placed a hand on Charlemagne's back. He mourned the loss of his children as they became lost and stuck in this unknown world to them.

Act 3, Scene 1

Diana and Tristan flashed through space and fell over on their landing, rolling down a grassy hill and coming at the base where there was the rush of water by a stream. Tristan stood up on his knees and hands, looked forward towards the small creek and then up to the night sky on a new moon night. The skies above were clear, but there was a cold chill in the air. Diana looked around into the darkness and fell onto her bottom. She then brought her knees up and continued to cry. Tristan looked at her, annoyed.

"Oh my God..." Diana said, "what have I done? I'm sorry, Tristan..."

"Relax," Tristan replied in a calm voice, standing up and brushing his jeans.

Tristan walked over to where they landed and picked up three small gems from the ground. He looked at each of them as they were broken apart as well as cracked.

"No..." Diana said to him, continuing to cry, "I mean, I didn't mean to do that. I... "

Tristan hushed her and placed the orbs into his hand, covering them with the other. He then knelt down next to Diana.

"Take my arm..." Tristan said.

Diana quietly did so. Tristan then closed his eyes and began to concentrate. To no avail. He opened his eyes and closed them again. He maintained them closed and focused, but still, they remained where they were.

"You don't understand..." Diana continued to say to him, removing her hands from his arm and attempting to take the beads, "I should have known that something like that would have happened, because... it's happened before."

"What?" Tristan questioned. "What are you talking about?"

"In Egypt, when Miklos was chasing me at the Tomb of Alexander the Great, there was a ledge that I couldn't reach. The Amulet of Ra, which I didn't even know I had since Olga snuck it into my bag, sensed that I need to teleport there... it sensed my desperation, and somehow, I was there just like that. The same happened again later near the actual tomb where I was about to be entrapped by Miklos, back when he was crazy with greed, and the orb teleported me to a safer place. I had no idea at the time, but the orb sensed my need... and it delivered me to safety."

"You managed to teleport when you were only fifteen?!" Tristan remarked. "That's insane!"

"I thought it was insane at the time, and I kept it to myself because I thought I misunderstood, in the heat of it all, what happened. I double-guessed myself for a whole year and then some until we met your dad, and then I understood for sure what happened. For some reason, I had, or rather, have that gift..."

"Do it again then!" Tristan said to her. "Take us back to the manor."

Tristan poured the crystals into Diana's hands. She placed a palm over them. Tristan held on to her. She closed her eyes and shut them tight. She then focused, but nothing. Tristan looked at her until she opened her eyes and continued to cry.

"I can't do it!" Diana yelled, putting them back into Tristan's hand. "I'm sorry, but I can't... For some reason, I don't control this power... I don't even know what to think of it anymore, I'm sorry!"

Tristan growled at her and replied, "Diana, please get a grip over yourself."

Tristan poured the beads into a pocket in his inner coat, which was coincidentally where the engagement ring was in a small velvet case. He then stretched an arm over and embraced her.

"Please, calm down, Diana," Tristan whispered to her. "I need you to be calm, like me. Our son or daughter needs you to be calm so we can return to Allabrese and raise him as we planned…"

Diana breathed hard. She started to stop crying.

"Breathe easy…" Tristan quietly said to her, "you're with me," he said, taking her hand, "we're together, so look at the bright-side. Even if we were stuck here, we're together… and we're alive. Isn't that all we need?"

Diana calmed down. She instantly grabbed ahold of Tristan and hugged him tight with both arms.

"I love you so much," Diana remarked, eyes watering again. "Tristan, you have no idea of the love I have for you – to be apart from you has been proven to me to be a tremendous sorrow, and I don't want to ever experience that again."

Tristan embraced her and replied, "I do know, because every moment with you comes with an expression of that love simply by what you do for me. I know what you mean though… it won't happen. The experience of separation from you haunts me… but now isn't the time to remember that tragic moment. We can't sit around here in the middle of nowhere."

Diana and Tristan parted and stood up. Tristan helped Diana onto her feet. He picked up their spotlights and put one away into the small backpack that he had. He then lit the spotlight in his hand and began to look around. The couple had been taken to an open plains with tall grass. The air around them was chilled, but not below freezing. He shined the light down the stream and saw a shoddily crafted wooden bridge that crossed over and connected with a dirt road. Diana and Tristan made their way over to this bridge and proceeded to look left and right.

He then looked at his watch and began to determine that left went south while right went north. Tristan paused for a moment. He looked around and then began to head northwards with Diana.

The couple journeyed down the dirt road, passing through the large plains and coming into a deciduous forest before coming out again to reach another set of plains that continued onwards. They walked for close to three hours without coming into contact with another human being, or even another animal although the hoots of an owl could be heard as well as the howl of a wolf from afar. The couple rested at the base of a tree in the wide plains and there Tristan gathered some fallen branches to make a small fire for them. Diana rested against the back of the tree while Tristan took out some of the rations he had for them to eat. Once the couple had eaten, they continued to rest their heads at the back of the tree. Diana soon fell asleep, which prompted Tristan to do the same.

Tristan opened his eyes several hours later as the sun began to rise. He looked around and rubbed his eyes, looking forward to see that the fire had burned out. He then stood up and picked up his backpack, bringing it around his back and looking around as daylight began to brighten this foreign land. Tristan turned north and saw before them, in the direction they were headed, a tall mountain chain that went from east to west in the horizon. The mountains in the chain were snow-capped and appeared to be far away. Tristan brought a hand behind his neck as he looked over to the mountains.

"I have no idea where we could be..." Tristan whispered.

Diana began to awaken. Tristan went over to her so that she could see him as she awoke. Diana looked around and then grunted.

"Don't tell me we're still here," Diana groaned.

Tristan looked ahead, down the dirt road and began to see a caravan pulled by horses approach them.

"Hey, this might be our break," Tristan said to her, waving over to the caravan.

Diana looked over and stood up. She stood back as Tristan flagged the attention of the caravan driver. He was a man with fair skin and dark hair, wearing a tunic underneath a coat and a fur hat.

"Excuse me!" Tristan shouted to him. "Help us!"

The caravan stopped beside them and the driver looked down to them. He began to speak in an unrecognizable language, which was spoken in an accent similar to Russian. However, Tristan could not understand a single word of this completely different language to Russian.

"I definitely don't have a clue where we could be," Tristan replied. "*Govoritye po Russki?*" he asked in Russian.

"*Da,*" the man replied. "*What do you want?*" he asked in Russian."

"*We need help,*" Tristan responded. "*We don't know where we are and we're lost.*"

"*You don't know where you are? You are in Gruziya!*" the man said to them. "*What language do you speak? It sounds like English.*"

"*It is English. We're not from here,*" Tristan clarified, "*but I'm fluent in Russian. What mountains are those?*" he asked, pointing to the mountains.

"*The Kavkaz mountains,*" the man responded. "*One more question, young boy. I have to deliver this milk!*"

"*Where's the nearest village so that we can take refuge in?*" Tristan asked.

"If you follow the road and turn left at the fork, you will come to Venamisa, my village, but beware… the warlord in this region is an unpredictable man."

The man whipped his horses and then set off again. Tristan watched him off.

"Well?" Diana questioned.

"*Gruziya…*" Tristan said to her. "*Kavkaz* – I have no idea what either of those are, *Gruziya* sounds a little familiar."

Tristan took out his phone and turned it on. He then unlocked it and saw that he had very little battery. He selected a translator application and attempted to spell 'Gruziya,' which corrected him and provided him an English translation.

"Georgia," Tristan said to Diana. "We're in Georgia… and those are the Caucasus Mountains."

"Oh my God…" Diana responded, bringing a hand to the side of her face, "we're on the other side of the world."

"How is that even possible?" Tristan questioned. "We had three small crystals. My dad said that one was barely enough to make a journey across the county, and that every additional one strengthens the power."

Diana wiped her eye as a tear fell. She then explained, "Charlemagne said… each crystal has a minimum power input, but that the power put into the crystal can be exceeded by additional power from an external source, i.e. mechanical or psychic energy, thus increasing the output."

"So, we were transported here, almost ten-thousand kilometers away from North America because you unleashed a bunch of energy then, right then and there?"

"I was mad…" Diana simply replied.

"I'm not blaming you for this," Tristan clarified. "It's just… I'm trying to understand what the hell is going on and why we came here."

"I said… I said that I wanted to go home."

"Georgia isn't exactly home," Tristan remarked with a bitter tone.

Diana replied, "I'm sorry. I don't know why we came here either."

Tristan took a deep breath and looked down the road. He then said, "Okay, that dude said that there's a village nearby. We better head that way and see what kind of village we're talking about. Maybe these crystals have a cool down, or maybe they're broken. All I know that is that we need to make our way back to Allabrese before Charlemagne abandons us here."

"He… he won't abandon us," Diana quietly replied.

"I hope not," Tristan remarked, "but don't forget that he's due to get worse and die at any moment. If we're not quick, we might be stuck here."

Diana nodded. The couple continued to hike down the road as they ventured forward to find this village known as Venamisa. The sunlight from the sun brought a slight warmth to the land that contrasted the nighttime chill. A wind brushed against the tall grass around them. Tristan stretched an arm around Diana's waist from the back and she rested her head down at his shoulder as the two walked together towards the village. The couple reached an oak wood forest that they passed through. Sunlight filtered through the leaves and came down in rays onto the calm dirt path. The gentle rustle of leaves could be heard around them until they exited the forest and reached another large field, cultivated as farmland on the way to the village ahead at the side of some tall hills.

Tristan could see a large stone structure ahead of the village at the top of a hill covered by some trees with another forest to the left and right. The Caucasus Mountains stood behind these hills at a closer range as they loomed down on them. The structure had a plain design and appeared like either a monastery or a castle. The couple continued down the path as they passed the wheat fields on their left and right with short stone walls bordering the dirt road that went towards the village. The fields were allotted and broken up by these stone walls, each of which gave residence to a house with some additional structures. Tristan took Diana to the end of the road and they entered into the village.

Diana and Tristan looked around as locals looked to them in their strange clothes. The women wore thick dresses over their bodies that went down to their ankles, long-sleeved with veils covering their heads. The older men wore large coats that went down just below the knee. They also wore trousers and handmade boots with heels that stuck out like the women's shoes. Around their waists were belts made of either leather or rope. The young boys and teenagers close to Tristan's age wore similar clothing, but at a lighter variant than the thick coats like the men. Their tunics were lighter, made of a silk-like fabric, some made of a fabric similar to the dresses worn by the females. Of course, these were not coats, but supposed to be long-sleeved shirts. Diana and Tristan passed through and came to a city square with a well before a church-like structure.

"*Does anybody speak Russian?*" Tristan questioned to the crowd of onlookers in Russian, holding Diana near him.

"*What seems to be the problem?*" a man asked from behind in Russian.

Tristan turned and faced the man. The old man wore a black cloak over his entire body with a black cap that covered his head. He had a bushy dark-grey beard and wooden cross that hung from his neck by a long rope.

"*We're not from here,*" Tristan responded. "*We need refuge and assistance returning to our homeland.*"

"Where is that you are from?" the priest asked.

"North America," Tristan replied. *"Specifically, Canada."*

"Canada?" the priest questioned with astonishment. *"Does such a country even exist in that part of the world anymore?"*

"What do you mean?"

"What do I mean?" the priest asked. *"What do you mean, what do I mean? If you are from this land you speak of, then surely you should know of the war that tore that land, like many, apart. How is that you are from that foreign land, yet you speak Russian as if you are from up north. At the same time, how is that you are so dark-skinned, and seemingly, oblivious of what has marked us for the last several years to be from the northlands – Your appearance... you look as though you are from the West, but where? Scandinavia?"*

"Nyet," Tristan responded. *"I'm Germanic. I also speak English if that proves I'm not from here."*

"Yes, that is it..." the priest said. *"You are definitely not from here. You are strange. Even beyond this dress of yours, you do not look like one of us. Have you travelled from this land of yours?"*

"Nyet," Tristan replied. *"We... we don't know where we came from because simply appeared nearby. The last thing we remember is being in the Americas."*

"Oh, kidnapped?"

"Sure," Tristan lied. *"Tell me though, what's happened to the world? Why is everything so... medieval?"*

"What do you mean? Is that a serious question? Do you not know? Hmph," the priest grunted, *"perhaps you are too young to remember and your parents never told you."*

"I'm only eighteen," Tristan replied.

"You would have been eight-years old when it all ended then. There are many that distort the truth of what happened and

provide their own accounts. Let me explain then, at least, what happened in this land. The short answer to your question: war – war between Great Powers of the world brought our formerly united country (Gruziya) in the middle of the Great Conflict that caused the collapse of all civilizations, but that cause was itself caused by another cause and also an effect. Like all effects, there comes a cause that enables that effect to take place – cause and effect. You would not remember that 'cause' which I speak of, because it happened long before your time – the economic depression that plagued us for years, and then finally, the war. For the last ten years, we have finally known peace at the end of it all, but our country is gone like many more. Now, at least in these parts, there are only small kingdoms that rule individual lands and peoples. Because of that, it is not safe to travel alone around here – there are also many bandits. Surely, you must have known that though. Isn't it the same where you are from?"

"*Da*," Tristan replied without certainty. "*I understand now.*"

"*Good*," the priest responded. "*I'm afraid because of this, there is no feasible manner in which you could be able to travel back to the West, except perhaps by travelling to one of the larger cities in the larger kingdoms up north to broaden your prospects. However, that will come at a cost. You should speak with our king, Lord Arkady. He is the king of these parts and may be able to assist you.*"

"*Ladna*," Tristan responded as the priest pointed towards an extension of the road ahead.

"*Follow the road and you will arrive at the gates of his castle*," the priest said. "*Tell the guards that Sima sent you to see the king, and they will let you pass.*"

"*Spasiba*," Tristan responded, looking towards and then back to the priest. "*We will go and see this Lord Arkady then.*"

"*Udachi*," the priest replied.

Act 3, Scene 2

Diana and Tristan followed the uphill road that led to an archway with gates that led further to the stone structure that was Lord Arkady's castle. The couple were stopped by two guards, dressed in a similar garb as the men in the village, but with ballistic vests over their thick tunics and AK-47 rifles in their arms. The men also wore modern combat helmets and boots as well as kneepads and elbow-pads. The men shouted towards Diana and Tristan approached them.

"We are here to see Lord Arkady," Tristan said in Russian. *"We have been sent by Sima!"*

"Sima sent you? Who are you?" a soldier questioned.

"We are travelers in need of help," Tristan replied. *"We wish to journey north, but need supplies."*

The soldiers examined Diana and Tristan then looked to each other. They spoke in Georgian and then one of them left to go up the road, speaking with a guard inside at the exterior of the castle. He then returned.

"Go ahead," the soldier said. *"Our king holds court ahead. You will be taken to him."*

"Spasiba," Tristan replied.

Diana and Tristan passed through the gate and made their way down the road where they were led to the front of a large door at the front of the castle. The doors opened and they were then led down a corridor that went towards a large room where a man sat on a throne at the end. The corridor was simply decorated with a red carpet with torches on the wall. The throne was a simple, elegant chair where a large man sat and looked forward. His court was decorated with various luxurious goods, including fur pelts, golden shields, pots, and chalices, and other goods. On the opposite-wall from where they came out from, arched windows looked out towards the land beyond. There were also some overtop windows left and right as well as soldiers at the side, before columns, dressed in the ones outside.

Lord Arkady wore clothes similar to the others. He had thick eyebrows that were slanted towards his nose. He had fairish skin, slightly towards a caramel hue, but not orange like Tristan and instead darker. He also had dark hair, noticeably by his trimmed dark beard. Over his head, he wore a fur-rimmed hat. He looked fairly young, perhaps in his thirties. He wore a silk-like red tunic with gold rims that went down to his knees. He also wore the same baggy trousers as everyone else, but in a dark blue, and his hand-made boots had a fur rim and were large. The tunic he wore was short-sleeved, exposing a long tattoo across his right-arm of a dragon. He was a large, rugged man with muscular arms and legs, and he appeared like he would be much taller than Tristan by several inches. He frowned as he looked at them, slouched in his chair and arms over the rests of his throne. He lifted his arm up lazily and shouted at them in Georgian. The soldier before them spoke to the king in Georgian. Lord Arkady then looked past them as the soldier stood aside.

"*Russians?*" Lord Arkady questioned them in Russian. "*What are they doing here?*"

Tristan stepped forward.

"*We are not Russians. We are from Canada,*" Tristan said. "*By some misfortune, we were abandoned by our captors and now we want to petition for some help to return home. We have spoken with a priest here, Sima, who told us to go to you.*"

"*Canada? Canada does not exist anymore. How is that you can speak Russian, yet claim to be from Canada?*"

"*I know Russian from my time with a band of mercenaries,*" Tristan explained. "*My primary language is English.*"

"*English?* You speak?" the warlord asked in English.

"Yes," Tristan replied.

"Hmph," Arkady grunted and then continued to speak in Russian. "*A useful language to know as it is still widely known... more-so than Russian. Listen here, I do not know why that old mystic would send you to me, because I do not have the means to send you across the seas, or even across the world. You are young, however, and you appear to be strong... If you prove yourself to me as a fighter, then there may be some way I can help...*"

"*Fighter?*" Tristan questioned.

Arkady shouted to his soldiers in Georgian. One of them produced a sword from their hips and presented it to Tristan. Tristan took it into his hand.

"*The ability to fight by the sword is an archaic fighting-style that is now a game. Defeat my guards here, and I will see what I can do for you,*" Arkady explained, crossing his arms.

Tristan looked over to Diana. The soldier who gave the sword to Diana moved her out of the way.

"Stand back," Tristan warned her.

The other four soldiers in the room drew their swords.

"What's going on?" Diana questioned, looking around.

"I have to fight to prove myself to him," Tristan explained. "Hold on."

Tristan was given a wooden shield to hold. He placed his arm through and then lifted up the broadsword as he looked over to the others as they were equipped with shields.

"*Brdzola!*" Arkady shouted once they were ready.

The soldiers encroached on Tristan. He looked at all of them and then over to the warlord.

"Do you want me to kill them?" Tristan asked.

Arkady laughed and slammed a fist in his armchair rest.

"Bring them to their knees!" Arkady shouted back to him. "Do not kill them! Soldiers like these are hard to come by!"

Tristan nodded. He then looked back over to the four soldiers. He approached one of them and watched as he lifted his sword up to bring over to Tristan. Tristan quickly raised his shield, causing the blade to hit the wood. He then jabbed his sword over, but the soldier moved out of the way. Tristan quickly brought the sword over and down to his shoulder, but the swords clashed. Tristan forced the sword to the side and then brought it towards the armored chest of his opponent who moved back.

"*Garet!*" Arkady shouted.

The soldier fell to his knees and dropped his sword. Tristan then turned to the other three as one of them charged towards him. He raised his shield, feeling the vibration of the sword against the wood. The man hit twice. Tristan attempted to push back. The soldier attempted to hit again, but Tristan used his shield to pat him back, drawing his sword over to jab him in the left side.

"*Garet!*" Arkady yelled before shouting at him in Georgian.

Tristan turned to the other two. He jumped back as a soldier gave a horizontal slice. He then attempted to jab his sword forward, hitting the opponent's shield. Tristan raised his shield as his opponent went for a vertical strike. Tristan hit his sword back, hitting hard against his opponent's sword to cause it to fall to the floor. He then pointed his sword at his foe as he attempted to grab it.

Arkady growled and shouted, "*Garet!*"

Tristan then faced his final opponent who looked towards him. He charged forward, hitting Tristan with his shield against shield. Tristan kept one eye open as he felt the vibration of their forces. He then spotted his opponent's sword come towards him.

He raised his sword up to deflect. His sword then hit against his own shield as it was pushed towards him. Tristan then jumped back as the knight attempted to jab him.

The soldier looked towards him and raised his sword. Tristan raised his and they clashed again. Tristan attempted to pit his strength against his opponent's but his opponent backed off and then attempted a horizontal slice, slicing Tristan's shield. Tristan raised his sword up and attempted to hit down. He hit his opponent's shield and then quickly pulled back. He then hit down hit his opponent's sword, bringing it down before trying to raise it up and swipe towards his opponent. He moved out of the way. The two circled each other.

Tristan quickly moved forward, bringing his sword up to hit down on him. His opponent raised his shield up, prompting Tristan to move in with his shield and bash towards him. He held his ground as Tristan hit back at him, and Tristan brought his sword around and towards his exposed arm, resting just over the shoulder by the neck.

"*Garet!*" Arkady shouted.

The soldier knelt down and let go of his sword.

"*You have fought well,*" Arkady said to Tristan before shouting at the men in Georgia. He then looked over to Tristan again to ask, "*What is your name?*"

"Tristan."

"*Very well,*" Arkady replied. "*As a new subject of this land and a knight in my tournaments, I will gift to you a plot of land nearby, large enough for you to develop your own home for you and your woman. Keep in mind, as a subject of my kingdom, you must pay a monthly tribute to me, your king. If you fight well, you should have plenty to pay me and eventually, be able to leave and return to wherever it is that you come from. Tomorrow, you will be fitted for chainmail, and in six days, you will fight in the next competition."*

Arkady waved them off. He also spoke to a soldier in Georgian extensively. The sword Tristan was given was taken off him. Diana and Tristan were then led out from the castle and made to wait outside where a man on a horse came out and began to lead them downhill, back to the village, and then out to the outskirts where they stopped at a small plot of land by the forest and near a dirt track at the side.

"There's nothing here," Tristan said to the soldier in Russian. *"How are we supposed to live like this?"*

"Why do you ask me?" the soldier replied. *"You will have to figure that out yourself..."*

The soldier then left them. Diana looked at the small plot of land. The space was approximately an acre in size. Tristan sighed.

"What are you going to do?" Diana asked.

Tristan looked at her.

"Why don't you stay here?" Tristan suggested. "Rest a bit. It's almost nighttime in Allabrese. I'm going into town and seeing what can be done..."

"Okay..." Diana responded. "Be careful."

Tristan left and walked back into town. He took the engagement ring from out of his jacket and opened it. He then looked at the ring inside and sighed.

"Sorry..." Tristan remarked.

Tristan walked into town and began to meet with some peasants at a small market. He asked about the local currency and heard that they went by chips cast from silver and occasionally gold, according to weight. Tristan spoke with several peasants that spoke Russian, attempting to pawn the ring until finally, he met a blacksmith. The large man examined the ring and looked at it.

"*This is real,*" the blacksmith noted as several others, interested in the ring, looked on. "*You have pure gold here – white gold too, and this diamond... authentic.*"

"*How much can it sell for?*" Tristan asked.

"*It is very valuable,*" the blacksmith simply said, returning the ring to Tristan. "*What do you need?*"

"*I need a house built so that I can shelter me and my wife,*" Tristan replied. "*And anything else to help with that...*"

"*Hmph,*" the blacksmith replied. "*I will sell you one of my horses, a fine breed of work horses, and to help you with your fights, I will also craft you a sword like none other.*"

"*I can't live by a horse and a sword,*" Tristan remarked.

"*A house should be no problem. I will speak with Sima and we will rally some of the townspeople to help you build a home, as an expression of the charity of this town. I can also provide you with some help from my sons, some friends, and also put into consideration the costs of some finer lumber, even a bed and some furniture (my youngest son is a magnificent carpenter), and all in exchange for this ring. The sword will take some time to create, but I can take you to my family farm so that you can pick a horse out to help with the construction. Deal?*"

"*You'll help me build a home, some furniture, give me a horse, and build me a sword for the ring?*" Tristan questioned.

"*Yes,*" the blacksmith promised. "*Deal?*"

Tristan sighed and replied, "*Okay... deal then.*"

"*Ahah, thank you very much, my son,*" the blacksmith remarked, shaking his hand.

Tristan forfeited the diamond ring to the blacksmith. The other competitors in the bid for the ring groaned and left.

"*Come, let me show you to my home and you can pick a horse...*" the blacksmith said, leading Tristan out of his workshop.

The blacksmith lived in a town at the side of town where his workshop was underneath. Nearby, there was a pen with various workhorses, some older than others. Above the workshop and barn was a two-story wooden home with steps that led up to the main door.

"*Pick whatever horse that you like... except the older ones. Pick a young one...*" the blacksmith encouraged.

Tristan looked at the horses and saw that almost all of them had brown coats with white manes and hair at the hooves. Some others had beige or black hair. He picked the darker one, with a dark brown coat, and white hair. The blacksmith then led this horse out and passed the lead to Tristan. The blacksmith yelled over to one of his sons who took over the lead from Tristan.

"*My son will get the horse ready to pull some lumber form behind. Come... I will take you to Sima so that we can get started with the construction of your home...*"

• • • •

Diana watched from a tree that she had fallen asleep under as a group of local men came by with a horse and some tools. They began to clear the land. Tristan soon arrived and walked over to Diana.

"What's going on?" Diana questioned.

"I talked to the priest, and he's put together a team of locals to help construct us a house," Tristan explained.

"Really" Diana remarked. "Wow, that's very generous of them all. What's the catch?"

"None," Tristan responded. "I mean, if we're going to have to stay here, we'll have to attend church with the rest of them, but I suppose it's just community kindness."

"It's Christian kindness," Diana noted. "Finally, some good news…"

"Yeah, anyways," Tristan remarked, "I'm going to go and help build the house with the others – put at least that skill to use…"

"Okay," Diana replied, "I'll be over here then."

Diana sat down and watched from afar as the men began to work. She saw a load of lumber removed from a carriage that was drawn by the large dark brown draft horse. This wood was set aside while some men went into the forest and began to chop down some thin trees and return them where another group of men began to shave them and another chopped some nudges into the far-left and right sides. Once the land was cleared, some pieces of lumber were inserted so that a rectangular grid was created in the dirt. Afterwards, a shaven log cut in half was taken over and placed on top of the frame. A man passed a hammer to Tristan, who had removed his jacket and rolled up his sleeves. He hit down the first nail, and then the others continued as they went on with the construction. The logs were placed atop of each other, stacked neatly until they began to form a low wall. This continued with each corner being nailed down into each other until the wall was approximately seven feet tall. Inside the box, lumber had been brought in to act as a vertical beam that kept the wood in place. Diana then watched as they took a saw to the house and began to cut out a doorway, some windows, and then went inside to continue stacking the wood as they stood atop of steps.

At midday, the men took a break as the women from the village brought over some lunch. Once the men had refueled, they continued on. The plywood lumber was placed on top of the logs as they began to construct the ceiling. At the front and back of the cabin, lumber was stacked in a triangle, logs placed before it, and the ends of the logs cut off so that they all created a slope down. A firepit had been lit near the house where men began to burn the backs of the rest of the lumber, charring it. This lumber was then placed atop of the cabin to form the roof. Meanwhile, some men went into the house with a wheelbarrow of concrete and began to insulate the foundation before some wood was placed down. Tristan helped finish the roof as a third team took what logs remained and began to create a pen at the side, laying down the logs to create a four-foot tall fence. At the side of the house, a small shelter was propped up within the pen. The grass was cleared from this space afterwards.

By the time the sun began to set, the men finished up and Tristan thanked them by shaking their hand with a smile on his face. Diana stood up, having dozed off, and went over to stand by Tristan. The work horse had been moved into the pen where a metal trough had been placed with some hay and water. Once the last workman had left, Diana went into the cabin and looked inside. The room was spacious and in the corner was a mat.

"Wow," Diana remarked, "they worked fast…"

"What do you think?" Tristan questioned. "Is it enough?"

Diana sighed and looked back at him, saying, "It's more than enough. At least we won't have to sleep outside again…"

"And look," Tristan said, walking over to lift the mat where a hatch had been constructed, "we'll hide the money I earn here to pay the warlord at the end of the month. It's perfect. We also have the horse, which is nice, and the town blacksmith said that he'd bring over some furniture made by his son so we won't have to sleep or eat on the floor. He also invited us over to his house for dinner, but we'll have to think of dinner for ourselves going forward..."

"That's okay," Diana responded.

"I'm going to pawn one of the flashlights... and if I have to, my watch and phone. We're going to need money to pay for some more stuff, such as food..."

"I wish I could offer something to pawn, but... I don't have anything... My earrings aren't even real silver..."

"Don't you worry, Diana," Tristan assured her. "I've got this handled. Next Friday, I'm going to win and then we'll have lots of money to not have to worry about anything. Trust me."

"Isn't there anything else you can do for the town other than pitting your body against others?" Diana questioned. "It's barbaric..."

"I'm not going to lose," Tristan assured her. "I have too much riding on this competition to lose. We're going to raise the funds, and with that money... We might just be able to return to Allabrese. You'll see..."

Diana sighed. Tristan walked over to her and took her hand.

"Come on, let's go and have dinner," Tristan said to her.

Act 3, Scene 3

Charlemagne held the orb of time in his hands, knelt down at the floor as he attempted to activate its powers as he stared down towards it. Manon held a hand at his shoulder.

"I don't understand," Charlemagne said, breaking his concentration and clenching the orb in his hand. "Why isn't it letting me return to our time?"

"Perhaps you need the other one," Manon replied.

"No," Charlemagne denied. "I shouldn't need it, because this is a matter of time travel, and I never had any power in controlling that other crystal. For whatever reason, the orb won't let me leave…"

"So, we are stuck here?" Manon concluded.

"We should look for Finn," Charlemagne instead responded. "We'd be safer if we travelled with him, especially if something were to happen to me… I don't want to leave you alone if my cancer suddenly decides to worsen."

Charlemagne put the half-orb into his coat and stood up. He left the briefcase behind and picked up his rifle.

"You stepped into the time machine less than half an hour after him," Charlemagne said. "He could not have gone far from the cavern below…"

"You sent me into a dark cave," Manon replied. "How long did you expect me to take before I could have found the ladder and climbed out – not to mention that it was already dark when I had escaped from underground."

"Either Finn left before you did, or he was right behind you… He would have been avoiding you…"

"When I came to the mansion, I looked for him, called for him, but he did not reply," Manon explained. "I looked for him, but did not see him. I then stayed the night here until the morning, which was when I left and went to the town."

"Surely he must understand that this is not the time period he thought he was going to," Charlemagne reckoned. "He also could not have gone too far and must have heard your cries. He's avoiding us… He's probably still mad at us, but he's looking for something in the meantime… as I was…"

"What do you mean?" Manon asked.

"I think he understands that this is not the past, but the future, and so he's taking advantage of that fact to learn about this land before he has to face us. He must have seen or heard you, which told him that there would be a way out eventually (otherwise, why would we bother going after him), so I don't think he'll have gone too far. If he goes too far, he won't be able to leave."

"Are you certain?" Manon questioned.

"The alternative is that he's come to this desolate place, seen the destruction, and taken joy to that fact, so he'll remain here to see what he can make of himself. However, from what I have come to learn from him, he does not wholly resent the modern world. He is optimistic of the present and what he can make of it, at least from what I know. What I do know for certain is that he's obviously upset at us, so perhaps we should wait and see."

"You want to wait?" Manon repeated.

"What more can we do? We don't understand this world, and neither does he. Finn is a survivalist, however. He spent an entire month in a forest on his own, and I'm sure he'll be able to survive out here just the same. When he decides that he's had enough, he'll want to return and with that, the rationalization to confront us. How mad at us could he really be?"

"What do you want to do then?" Manon finally asked.

"I want to organize and make sure that when he does return to us, there will be a way out. I need to examine this crystal and see what has gone wrong. In the meantime, I want to establish a beacon for Finn so that he knows where we are when he decides to return. In the daytime, a column of smoke will suffice, but in the nighttime, I want this house to be lit by lights so that it can be seen from across the river. And then we wait…"

Manon brought a hand to her cheek and turned away.

"Don't you worry, Manon," Charlemagne assured her. "This will be no different than our time in Azerbaijan. I'll need to find some tools though and go to the hydropower generator quite a way from here though. This house is independent from the mainstream power grid and harnesses electricity from a stream slightly northwest from here that comes from the mountains. Once we have that activated, I'll be able to hopefully open some of the doors downstairs as I've seen that they're electronically locked. If there are supplies within them, they will be most useful. I'm going to collect some wood to build us a fire in the foyer."

Charlemagne put his rifle down and walked over to the chandelier. He pushed the chandelier back against the wall, clearing the central space. He then set off to scavenge for supplies and collect firewood. Manon sat down at the bottom of the stairs in the meantime, emotional over the situation, lighting a cigarette as she watched Charlemagne put together the kindling and then used Manon's lighter to ignite a flame. He then put some wooden planks taken from around the house into the fire, enlarging it until they had a modest bonfire. Charlemagne stood up before the fire and then turned to Manon.

"I've found some tools scattered in the maintenance closet," Charlemagne said to her. "I'm going to take them and go out across the field to fix the generator. The battery here appears to be in one-piece, so I believe the problem may be at the dam. Stay put and if trouble comes, hide."

Manon didn't respond as Charlemagne picked up his rucksack, rifle and then set off to walk across the field behind the manor. She stayed behind as he went across the tall grass, looking back to see smoke rise from the mansion, signifying their location. Charlemagne journeyed over the grass, which came up to hips. He walked with careful steps, looking down as he walked, holding a saddened face. The grey skies began to let loose a drizzle of rain.

Charlemagne continued to cross the grassland, stopping less than halfway as he nearly fell into a large crater, approximately ten feet in diameter. He looked down and recognized the location, especially the hole in the middle where the meteorite vessel had fallen years ago. Charlemagne walked around the hole, took out his compass, and then continued northwest.

From Cabernet Manor to Scruton Creek, the hike took approximately an hour and then several more minutes to go upstream and reach the small hydropower dam where water poured through gates at a point where the creek was artificially made to narrow, letting loose a cascade that poured downwards over a fall of five feet, and flowed southward where the creek went several miles before stretching around a mountain further south to empty into the Nattau River. At the sides of the dam were concrete barriers that concentrated and controlled the flow to avoid splashback. To the sides of these barriers was a bank of artificially placed rocks. On the westside there was nothing more than grass and trees as the forest continued uphill towards the mountain, while on the eastside there was a small concrete slab with a green shed, a small fenced paddock with a transformer inside, and a gravel road to the east that went northeast into a forest beyond. A worn-out signpost at the northeast corner of the concrete slab stated that the premises were monitored by CCTV with cameras above pointed east to the end of the road and then south to the shed. The shed contained a metal door protected by a rusted padlock and chains. Charlemagne walked over to the dam and climbed up the metal steps at the side that gave rise to a bridge to cross to the other end. He looked north to the calm, bountiful river that stretched northwards and then over to the mighty rapids that went southbound. Approximately a couple meters down the stream there were two metal barriers at the side of the river with markings to measure the gauge of the river. There was also a concrete pipe that stuck out from the side. The rapids were almost halfway up the postmark.

"Hm…" Charlemagne thought aloud, "the water has been let loose."

Charlemagne went to the green shed and hit the padlock with the butt of his rifle until it broke off. He then unraveled the chains and opened the door to look at the hole in the ground with the ladder that went down into the depths of the manor's power. Charlemagne brought his rifle around and squatted down to sit down with feet into the hole so he could climb down the ladder. The shaft went down a couple feet. Charlemagne took out a spotlight and found himself in a narrow tunnel that went around and south with a large pipe at the side where water would normally pour though from the north river. He checked the valves at the side and saw that they had been closed off so no water poured. At the end of the tunnel, Charlemagne came to a metal platform that looked down into a cuboidal room where the turbine generator was connected to the same wall where the tunnel exit was. Beside the turbine were some switchboards with a computer station to the side and a workshop bench. On the opposite-wall from the turbine was the water filtration basin. The metal platform that came from the tunnel was short and went down by a set of metal steps. Underneath the stairs there were some shelves with some boxes. The pipe in the tunnel ended shortly before the exit, going through and wrapping around to connect with the turbine. Charlemagne shined his light around the room.

Foremost, Charlemagne went towards the switchboard to see that the switches were all off and dials set to off. He then shined his light at the generator before going back up the steps to the three individual valves that controlled the flow of the water into the station. Charlemagne released the valves and then returned back into the power station where he went to the switchboard and began to crank a lever. He then pressed a switch and watched as the box roared to life. Charlemagne then went over to some dials to set them up, but within a short burst, the machine died down.

"Dammit..." Charlemagne responded.

Charlemagne turned the dials down again and then returned to the startup circuit-breaker where he crouched down to open a cabinet below where there were some fuses. He removed one of the fuse cartridges, a fairly large-sized cylindrical rod and took it over to the workbench. He removed his rucksack and placed it at the side of the workbench. He then took out some wrenches so he could open the fuse cartridge and remove the burnt-out fuse itself. Charlemagne took this fuse and went over to the shelves beneath the stairs to fetch a new fuse. He then returned to the workbench and proceeded to replace the fuse, tightening it within the cartridge afterwards, and then going over to the circuit-breaker to replace the fuse. He then closed the doors and proceeded to start the process again at the startup panel.

Charlemagne cranked the lever to prime the machine. He then pressed a switch and then another, causing the machine to start. He then moved over to the switchboard and began to turn on switches and crank dials. The motor began to hum as the turbine began to spin. Within a few more seconds, the entire facility came to life again. Charlemagne looked over to the computer as it began to turn on. He picked up his spotlight from where he left it at the workbench and then went over to the top of the stairs to switch on the lights. The power station was lit up. He walked down the tunnel and came up to the transformer. The transformer hummed. Charlemagne then returned downstairs to run some diagnostics on the computer, seeing everything to be alright before he packed up to return to the manor.

Manon sat by the fire as Charlemagne entered through the front doors. She looked over to him.

"Did you do it?" Manon asked.

"One moment," Charlemagne quietly responded, removing his rucksack and placing it down by the stairs.

Charlemagne walked over to the maintenance room behind his study and walked over to the switchboard. He began to switch on the power and then went over to turn on the lights in the room. They turned on without a problem. Manon entered the room.

"You did it," Manon said with some relief.

"We should now have power throughout the house, wherever lightbulbs haven't burnt out or been broken..." Charlemagne said. "I'm going to go downstairs to open those locked doors."

Charlemagne left the room and entered into the library through the hole in the study. He then climbed downstairs where the lights switched on their own as he entered. Charlemagne looked at the entire basement and then went to one of the locked doors. He approached the pin pad and began to test some sequence of numbers, 0-8-1-0, 0-7-2-2, 0-9-0-2, 0-1-1-7, 0-8-1-6, 1-1-0-1, and finally, 0-9-1-1.

The lock let up and Charlemagne could pull the heavy door open, exposing the room on the other side. There was a small kitchen and dining area within. He went down to the next door and opened it with the same pin combination. He then opened the door and saw that the room had various beds inside. He fiddled with the emergency release on the other side before going to the other side of the cave where two more doors went into two more rooms, one was an emergency power substation, and another was another room with beds.

Once Charlemagne looked at these rooms, he went to the north side of the cave where there were some shutters. He inserted the pin and then raised the shutters, revealing the trove of non-perishable foods, equipment, and weapons that were inside and stretched down an entire corridor to the other side. Charlemagne also saw jerry cans with gasoline as well as containers and bottles of water stacked on a palette. He looked around and then went to the elevator shaft, climbing up the ladder to return to the surface.

Charlemagne looked to the chandelier that still hung from the ceiling in the library. He then went to the light switch to turn it on. The chandelier still lit up. He turned off and then returned to the fire, which was starting to dwindle. Manon continued to sit by the fire. She looked to Charlemagne as he approached her.

"We have about a two-year supply of food below, ammunition, weapons, and other equipment including beds downstairs," Charlemagne said. "I'm going to take an axe and fetch some more firewood and then I'll have a fix at the doors to the shaft so that we can hide the entrance again. Otherwise, we're set to make our stay here until Finn returns to us."

Act 3, Scene 4

Tristan was outfitted in a set of chainmail that weighed down upon him, covering his entire torso down to his pelvis. The chainmail was short-sleeved and was placed upon a wool undershirt that poked out around the top of his neck like a short turtleneck and covered his arms up to his wrists. Atop of the chainmail was a *feldgrau* tunic, hand-made and short-sleeved, shorter and smaller than the chainmail. At the four rims of the shirt were patterned designs in white. Likewise, over his tunic, he wore a long sleeveless white jersey to designate him from the others. Tristan's forearms were covered by leather gauntlets attached to fingerless gloves underneath. At his legs, he wore beige trousers and tall hand-made leather boots that went just up to his knees. Around his waist, he wore a simple leather belt and across his chest and back he wore a leather strap that held the scabbard behind with his hand-made broadsword crafted for him by the town blacksmith. Around Tristan's head was more chainmail that covered the sides and the back, leaving his face exposed. Atop, he was given a small iron helmet. Tristan stood in a tent where he was made to wait as the first of the competition fought against each other.

Tristan's position was sixteenth in the bracket with fifteen other fighters from across the land, which meant three fights ahead if he survived the initial two. At the sound of the trumpet, Tristan was guided out from his tent and towards the arena where a crowd of onlookers from across the land had gathered to cheer. Diana watched with the blacksmith family from the sidelines. The arena was a wooden structure within Venamisa with stands around that surrounded a rectangular plot of dirt where the fighters were brought to. Tristan looked forward to face his competition, a man that wore significantly different armor to him as he wore a full-suit of metal armor with a similar jersey across the front, but in a bright yellow with an insignia across the torso.

Tristan stood before his opponent and brought a hand to his sword to draw it. The sword that the blacksmith had constructed was sharp and fine, approximately twenty-eight inches in length with the grip rapped in in leather straps. The crossguard was thick and spread out in cylindrical shape, thicker in the middle. The pommel, the piece at the end, was shaped like an axe-blade. Tristan pulled his sword out his sword and raised his wooden shield.

The competitor across from him had an iron shield that he banged like a madman before drawing his sword from its holster. Tristan looked over and saw that he was not a tall man, but short. Nonetheless, he took cautious steps as they met each other at the center of the arena. His foe brought his longsword down and into the dirt. Tristan raised his broadsword to strike at his arm, but his foe protected himself with his shield. He then hit back with his own shield while the man raised his longsword up and then attempted to swipe at Tristan.

Tristan took advantage of his flexibility and rolled out of the way, standing up and striking with his sword, hitting the shield and causing his sword to kick back as sparks flew. Diana watched from the stands with an unimpressed and worried expression. Tristan swung his sword again and hit the longsword. He then stepped back and took a hit on the shield, fielding the impact of the larger sword against his flimsy shield issued by Arkady. Tristan jumped back again and gave himself some space from his foe.

The foe brought his longsword back down towards Tristan, who dodged out of the way and then brought his broadsword up and over, hitting his wooden shield with the metal one before jumping back. Tristan then hit his foe in the side of his right thigh. The crowd gasped. The competition continued. His foe growled at him and then brought his sword down towards Tristan.

Tristan rolled out of the way and attempted to swipe low, but his foe kicked back, causing Tristan's sword to fly off. He quickly jumped for it and then turned to cover himself as the longsword came down again. Tristan exhausted himself into not only holding the sword back, but also causing it to fling back, using his shield then to brush back as well while he crawled backwards and stood up. Tristan adjusted himself and waved his sword in the air before holding it steady as he concentrated and looked down at his foe.

The foe swiped at Tristan with his longsword. Tristan deflected with his sword. His foe then took another swipe at him, but Tristan bounced back with his broadsword. And then unexpectedly, his foe hit at Tristan's side with his shield, causing him to knock down to the ground. The crowd was astonished by such a move. Diana flinched and looked uneasy. The foe moved in with his sword.

Tristan got onto a knee and covered himself as the blow came. A second blow came shortly afterwards. Tristan hit back with a strike at the lower leg. He then stood up and protected himself with his wooden shield as another hit came, causing the shield to crack. He quickly stepped back and away from his foe as he came towards him with the sword, swinging it towards him. Tristan ducked down and rolled to the side, hitting back at the other leg and then rushing forward to strike from the back.

The blow caused his foe to step forward and hunch over. Tristan swung his sword and hit him in the helmet as he was about to turn. The impact caused the man to fall to the side and drop his sword. Tristan then lunged forward and brought his sword to the mercy of his foe.

"*Dasruleba!*" a referee shouted.

Tristan's foe shook his head and stood up. Tristan stepped back and was guided to the center where his arm was raised so that the crowd could applaud him.

"Oh, thank God," Diana muttered.

Tristan swiped his sword in the air and then put it away back into the scabbard. He was promptly guided out and returned to his tent. There, he was permitted to rest and eat while an intermission was held before the quarter and then semi-finals.

At noon, the competition continued with the eight fighters that remained. Coincidentally, Tristan was now the only that represented Venamisa. The quarterfinals went by uneventful for Tristan, who triumphed over another man with a set of knight armor. In the late afternoon, he was prepped to take on his foe for the semi-finals.

Tristan was brought out from his tent and taken to the arena. He then met with his foe across from where he was brought through. Tristan's foe wore a suit of armor with a tunic overtop that went down to the ankles. His foe was a large man. He had no shield, but only a large claymore, or great sword, which was a kind of sword longer and thicker than a broadsword and longsword. Where the broadsword Tristan had was twenty-eight inches, the longsword of his initial foe approximately thirty-six inches, the claymore was a rife forty-five inches in length and required two-hands to wield. Tristan stood before his opponent and drew his sword.

Tristan's opponent raised his claymore and began to approach him. Tristan walked forward and the two began to encircle each other. They then clashed swords with Tristan retrieving his sword and attempting to jab his foe in the torso.

His foe retaliated by kicking him back. Tristan jumped back and hit at his foe's foot. He then jumped back again as the claymore came down and smashed into the dirt, causing a cloud of dust to rise. Tristan then attempted to move around the side, but his foe swiped his claymore, knocking Tristan back with a brutal blow. Diana cringed. His foe approached him as he was on the ground.

Luckily, Tristan's sword was still in hand and his foe moved with slow steps. He struggled to stand, crawling away with the same hand he had his sword before standing up. His foe swiped his claymore left and right towards Tristan. Tristan jumped back. He then slashed down his sword as he had done previously. Tristan didn't chance another blow and instead simply dodged to the side and hit his on the arm, aiming for the points that the armor met to expose a weak spot. He quickly moved back as his foe swiped with his claymore. He gave himself a bit of room and looked forward to his foe as he moved towards him. Tristan looked at him with anticipation. He kept his feet moving side to side by an inch, slightly raised from the ground by his toes, knees bent and ready to strike or dodge at any moment.

Tristan's foe moved in with his sword. Tristan moved to the side as he swiped towards him. He was the near the edge of the arena and moved so that he could be behind his foe. They then stared each other down as his foe was now backed against the wall. His foe moved towards him. He brought his sword down towards Tristan. Tristan clashed with his sword and then swiped at the claymore with his shield, taking his sword to whip it across his foe's helmet, hitting back. His foe tilted his head back. Tristan moved in again and brought his sword down onto right-side of the collar bone. Tristan's foe grabbed him by the arm, entrapping him as he raised the claymore with the other hand.

Tristan blocked the half-forced blow of the claymore with his shield, attempting to break free as he continued to hold on to his sword. He raised his legs up as his foe held on to him, kicking his foe in the head with both feet and then bringing them back towards him for another as she was let go, instead using the momentum to flip back and land on his feet. The crowd gasped. Diana watched with intent. Tristan brought his sword down and hit his foe in the wrist that held on to the claymore, kicking it down at the blade. He then whipped his sword to the helmet of his foe, coming around his left as he attempted to punch him and then kicking him down by the calf. Tristan then jumped up and whipped at him at the side of the helmet, knocking him at the side with his shield so that he fell to the floor. He kicked the claymore away and then lurched forward to point his sword towards the bottom of his foe's helmet. Tristan panted as he had his competitor at his mercy.

"*Dasruleba!*" a referee shouted.

Tristan's foe had his hands raised as he looked back at him. Tristan lowered his sword and cut through the air. He then returned it to the scabbard as the referee came to bring him to the center of the arena. Diana gave a sigh of relief and then watched as Tristan was dragged off back to his tent. The intermission before the competition was less than an hour, which was an hour extra of rest than Tristan would receive before his fight in the final fight.

By evening, Tristan was brought out from his tent and brought to the arena where he confronted the other finalist. Tristan's foe for this round was a man at least ten-years older than him, approximately the same height and wearing a set of rusted chainmail armor that came down to his thighs. He also wore baggy pants and leather boots. He did not wear a tunic like Tristan. Over his head, he wore a helmet that came down half-way before continuing as chainmail that even extend over his mouth. He did not wield a broadsword however, but a one-handed battle axe with a round wooden shield. Tristan brought his hand around to the grip of his sword and then pulled it out.

The two foes moved in to face each other. Tristan kept his feet hot as he shuffled in anticipation. The two began to encircle each other. Tristan's foe immediately moved in to deliver a blow with his axe. Tristan raised his shield and brought his sword down, hitting his foe's shield. The axe split apart Tristan's shield, hitting his gauntlet on the other side with a sharp pain. Tristan jumped back and looked at his shield as the two pieces fell over and into the dirt. He then looked over to his opponent as he came for him with his axe, swinging it towards him. Tristan jumped back and out of the way as he was defenseless without the shield.

Tristan's foe moved him backwards towards the edge of the arena where Tristan finally deflected with his broadsword, moving to the side so that he could get around. His opponent was aggressive in attempting to ensure he had Tristan cornered, forcing him to move to the other side as he attempted to get away. His foe bashed him with his shield, hitting him back and into the wall that surrounded the arena. Tristan quickly brought his sword up, grabbing the end of the blade with his hand to deflect the incoming swing with both arms. The sword then caught onto the underside hook of the axe. His foe attempted to pull down. Tristan kicked back and managed to free himself before he could be disarmed. He then quickly side-stepped so that he was no longer pressed against the wall.

Tristan brought his sword down to attempt to hit his foe, but his foe deflected with his shield and then brought his axe over to slice at Tristan with a horizontal slice. Tristan narrowly dodged the blow as he tossed his waist back and then moved away. His foe moved in with his shield raised. Tristan attempted to move to the side to keep him at the side. His foe came down with the axe, scraping the side of Tristan's chainmail at his left shoulder and brushing by. Tristan moved back with alarm at the near miss. His foe then closed in home, charging at him with his shield forward. Tristan pointed his sword forward and hit at the shield, blocking him back momentarily before he slapped his sword away with the shield and then came down with the axe.

Tristan's sword flew aside. Tristan instantly moved in to grab him by the wrist and then grab the handle of the axe in a quick move that ripped the weapon from his arms. He then jabbed at his foe in the head with the end of the handle. Tristan dropped the axe and then grabbed the shield, tearing it from his opponent and then slapping him across the head with it, causing it to fly off. He then dodged down as his foe attempted to punch him, grabbing hold of him at the waist and securing both arms as he lifted him up and then brought his foe down with a mighty throw. The crowd was blown back by the sudden move. Tristan elbowed his foe in the head while his foe threw a punch from the ground and hit Tristan in the cheek just below the eye.

Tristan's foe pushed him back. Tristan quickly went to grab the shield and then went to his sword. His foe took his axe and then threw it towards Tristan as he was armless. He blocked with the shield and then quickly tossed it back at him like a frisbee, hitting him in the head. Tristan swiped his sword from the ground and charged at his opponent, jumping forward and striking him at the shoulder. The impact on the chainmail caused his foe to fall onto his knee.

Tristan brought his sword back down where he had hit, but did so gently as he had his competitor at his mercy. However, they did not see eye-to-eye on that. His foe grabbed the sword and pulled it off him. Tristan deflected with his gauntlet as he attempted to swipe at him with his own sword. He then grabbed hold of his foe's arm by the wrist, bringing his other arm to hit his foe in the eyes with the side of his hand and then bringing his arm up and around to lock the elbow joint. Tristan then quickly and swiftly brought his foe down onto the ground, holding his foe's arm as he knelt down atop of his foe and took the sword from the ground and raised it up to point at his foe's face.

"*Dasruleba!*" the referee shouted.

Tristan's foe smashed a fist into the dirt. Tristan let go of his foe's arm and quickly backed off. He then brought his sword into his scabbard and turned as the referee went towards him. His foe cursed at him as he was helped onto his feet by some attendants. The crowd clapped and cheered for Tristan as he had won the competition. Tristan looked across to them with a smile as he panted. Arkady looked down and gave slow claps for the new champion. Diana simply looked over to Tristan with relief. Tristan smiled to her and saw her relief as well as a little smile that crept through. Tristan's foe was walked off.

The referee lowered Tristan's arm while he continued to bask in his victory. Tristan removed his helmet to reveal his medium-length dark strawberry-blonde hair that was drenched in his sweat. Finally, Tristan was led out from the arena where he was taken back to his tent.

Tristan placed his helmet on the table inside and then went to drink some water. He brought his head down into the basin of water and then looked over as the tent flaps opened. Arkady walked in with some guards. Tristan looked over to him.

"*You have done well, Krasniyi,*" Arkady said in Russian to him.

An attendant walked in with a small canvas bag. He handed it to the warlord.

"*Here, your reward for your fighting,*" Arkady remarked. "*You are a formidable warrior, and if you continue to bring this sort of honor to my kingdom, then we will be good friends.*"

Tristan walked over and took the heavy, but small bag.

"The next competition is a week away," Arkady remarked. *"Report to the castle at sunrise next Monday for training. Until then, rest and spend some time with that wife of yours."*

"Spasiba..." Tristan replied.

Arkady left with his guards. Tristan brought the bag over to the table and placed it down. He then looked inside at the silver coins that were within. He gave a sigh of relief and closed the bag. He then sat down and leaned over the table to rest after a steady day's work.

Act 4, Scene 1

Diana sat at the hand-crafted table within the couple's cabin where she had the fragments of the space orb before her in her hands. She looked towards the shards and then closed her eyes so that it were as if she could see them through her eyelids. The dark gems were motionless almost as if they were nothing more than ordinary rocks.

Diana and Tristan's cabin was better decorated than when it had been built. For a start, they had a hand-carved double bed where the hay-filled mattress laid on top of and there were some woven blankets and hand-made pillows. In the opposite-corner of the far wall from the door there was a stove in the corner with iron pipes that came out of the roof as a chimney. Towards the corner to the right of the entrance into the house was a table with two chairs. The windows had been mended with glass panes and opaque curtains installed atop that could slide open and closed. With the windows covered, the cabin was dark and lit by the stove, which gave them warmth as it was a cloudy and cold day. Diana wore a hand-made gown that went down to her ankles. She also wore hand-made shoes that Tristan had bought for her with some of the winnings he had earned.

Once several minutes had passed and nothing had happened, Diana opened her eyes. She spilt the shards onto the table and then wiped her eyes as tears fell from them.

Tristan opened the front door and looked over to Diana as she cried. He held a look of awkwardness and discomfort as he walked in on her in emotion. Tristan wore a peasant shirt, or *kosovorotka*, which was a loose, skewed and long collared shirt that came down over his lap. He also wore a pair of beige trousers, belt and hand-made boots. Over his torso was the leather strap with the scabbard and his sword behind him. His hair had also grown, extending out from the back and sides. Across his face, he had a bruise from his first competition on his cheek and he was unshaven. Tristan quietly closed the door behind him. Diana jerked her head over to him. She held her head up by her hands and elbows on the table.

"Oh, Tristan," Diana cried out, "it's useless. We're stuck here. The crystals… they don't work anymore… I've broken them.

Diana scooped up the crystals into her hand and the squeezed her hand around them. She continued to cry.

"All I want to do is to return home, to Allabrese…" Diana said.

Tristan looked on as nothing happened. She opened her hand and poured them out.

"I thought…" Diana remarked with a hic, "I thought that if I waited a bit, they'd recharge. I thought… if I got emotional, they'd work, but nothing seems to work. It's been two weeks, and it feels like we'll never return to Allabrese, never return to our time period – nothing."

Tristan looked at her and sighed. He then went over and placed a hand on her back.

"Hey, don't cry…" Tristan attempted to discourage, "you know… you know that thing that you sometimes say to me… about how sometimes, things happen for a reason, and such?"

"Yeah?" Diana questioned.

"Maybe, just maybe, this is one of those instances, you know? Maybe, we're meant to come out here, at this time period, and maybe our meeting with Charlemagne, him being in our life… maybe that was to come to this moment so that we could leave and come to this town. You know? I mean, what's so bad about this place anyways? The people are nice. I have a steady job. We're homeowners. And in a couple weeks more, you're going to give birth and we'll be parents. Is this really a bad place to raise a kid?"

"Dammit, Tristan, what about our friends and family? Charles... Finn..." Diana complained.

"I thought you hated Charles," Tristan responded. "Last time we were with him, you called him a 'monster' and an 'anti-Semite' because of his correlation of the Chosen-Shapeshifters with Jews. Besides, it's not like Finn is any different... He practically believes the same... he thinks Jews control the media and such... They're all crazy."

Diana looked back at him in offense.

"Tristan, they're still our friends and family," Diana objected. "I don't know if you've realized, but being pregnant has made me very emotional..."

Tristan avoided responding.

"I didn't mean to burst out at him like that – I was worried about Finn and also you... For God's sake, Charles has cancer! He could die and leave Manon alone in this world, and Finn... who knows what could have happened to him. He could have been killed my now, or kidnapped!"

"It's been two weeks," Tristan replied. "If something bad has happened to any of them, I'm sure it would have already happened..."

Diana looked back at Tristan with another annoyed glance. She stood up and looked over to Tristan with distaste.

"Why are you so calm about this?" Diana questioned. "Finn is your best friend. Charlemagne is our guardian. Manon is a family friend and the mother of your best friend! You should be as worried about me as I am for them!"

Diana moved in towards Tristan. He took a step back. She moved her head forward and towards his face. She sniffed at him.

"You've been drinking…" Diana muttered.

Tristan didn't respond.

"Oh my God!" Diana shouted. "Of course, you've been drinking!" she yelled, raising her arms up as she went to the other side of the room. "Why am I not surprised that even in this hellhole, you've managed to find a source of liquor to satisfy your quench and addiction?!"

"I'm not addicted," Tristan deflected. "Hey, I have a right to a little privacy, and to a bit of relaxant every once in a while. Don't I? I work my ass of in these competitions…!"

"Hmph!" Diana grunted at him. "As if it were about relaxation! You're an escapist, Tristan. Liquor to you isn't the same as sitting down in a hot spring or a hot bath. It's about burying all that raw emotion within, the anxieties, the facts about life, and all of the other crap you worry about. It's probably why you loved to surf so much in Isla Paraiso… I can't believe you!"

"Where are you getting all this from?!" Tristan questioned. "You've caught me at one drink, and suddenly I'm an alcoholic?! Chill out."

Diana laughed at him and replied, "Oh, this isn't one drink, Tristan. Do you honestly believe that I wouldn't catch you even before this? You stowed two bottles of rum into your suitcase when we came to Allabrese. Who does that? And I checked online, and apparently, peanut butter is one of those foods that masks the smell of alcohol. So, all those late-night snacks I thought you were getting at four in the morning – yeah, they were only the discrete trips you made to leave the bathroom and get a secret swig of the bottle while I'm asleep. And that's only what I've observed so far – who knows how much longer it's been. You've probably been at it ever since Charles let you have that bit of champagne on our graduation date."

"Charlemagne has nothing to do with this, Diana!" Tristan shouted back. "I swear…!"

"Okay, so when? When did you suddenly want to pretend like you're some sort of champ having a bit of alcohol?" Diana asked.

Tristan was quiet. He took a deep breath.

"Okay, I swear," Tristan confessed, "I only had a taste of it starting in January last year. I was anxious, okay? It soothed me. It made me feel ecstatic – like all the problems atop of me were lifted. That's it. It was a stressful moment…"

Diana put her hands on her face and turned away from him.

"So, after your mother died, is that it?"

"For God's sake, Diana!" Tristan shouted.

"Admit it!" Diana yelled, turning to him.

"Admit what?" Tristan yelled back. "I didn't do anything. All I did was have a few drinks, so what? I thought that other kids my age were probably doing it all the time, and if I were still friends with Peter and Aaron, I would have been doing it for sure? It isn't unethical. It's liquor! So, I had a few drinks around that time, it isn't like I was doing it every day! You saw me for almost every hour of every day when we were at Isla Paraiso. I didn't have a single drink throughout that whole trip! Even into September, I didn't have a drink except once when Finn and I went to a frat party."

"And what about when we broke up. Huh? How many did you have then?" Diana questioned.

Tristan was silent. He shrugged.

"Answer the question!" Diana shouted at him.

"A few. What? I don't keep track of how much I drink!" Tristan yelled.

"How many, you bastard!" Diana yelled, throwing a shoe at him.

Tristan deflected. "Piss off!" he yelled. "If you're so smart and think you know me so well, then why don't you do the math? You left me and it felt like everybody hated me for what I did to you. Even Finn wouldn't stop bothering me and making me feel guilty."

Diana shook her head.

"How...?" Diana questioned. "How did you even manage to get booze in Harlech?"

Tristan sighed.

"Finn got me ahold of a fake ID," Tristan replied, "but I swear, I'm not an alcoholic! Whatever you think about me, Diana, it's a lie. How can you even blame me though? I'm not a normal kid – I mean for God's sake, look at me? I'm fighting in these bizarre swordfight competitions where the only reason I've made it this far is because of the Sambo I learned from a bunch of Russian mercenaries, through a computer simulation that violated my mind! And sure, maybe I have been drinking a little more than usual recently, but if there's any reason to that, it's not because I'm a messed-up person with a messed-up head. It's because we're trapped in the middle of Georgia, in God-knows-what-year, plus only two months ago, I learned that I was going to a father to a child that I don't even want right now. So yeah, maybe I'm a little stressed, and maybe, just maybe, that's why I'm drinking."

Diana's jaw had dropped at Tristan's remark. He looked back at her with a frown.

"What did you just say about our child?" Diana questioned with anger.

Tristan's face dropped as he too realized what he said. He raised his hands up before him as Diana approached him.

"Diana..." Tristan reasoned. "I..."

"Get out."

"You can't tell me to get out," Tristan replied. "This is my house!"

"Get out! Get out! Get out!" Diana shouted, hitting him with closed fists. "Get out, you miserable bastard! You absolute fiend! Get out…! Get out of my life and leave me! I don't want to see you anymore, you adulterous pig!"

"Hey, Diana!" Tristan complained as she hit him, attempting to stop her. "Stop it!"

Diana pushed him back towards the door. Tristan became angry and grabbed her by the wrists and then pushed her back. Diana went further back than he intended, and a result, she hit the side of the table, nudging the table slightly.

"Oh crap…" Tristan muttered.

Diana looked back at him with tearful eyes, her head down. He took a step back and turned to open the door. Tristan left without another word. Diana looked towards the door as it closed and then hunched over, losing strength in her legs and steadying herself by an arm on the table. She took the other hand brought to her face as she cried. She soon regained the strength of her legs to stand and brought the other hand to her cheek. Diana wiped her tears and looked to the floor.

"Oh my God," Diana remarked in sad realization. "I've become my mother – in love with a pathetic drunk…"

Tristan heard these words as she placed the saddle on his horse, Tempest. He then climbed atop of her and then whipped her forward, jumping over the fence and made his way off as there was still daylight.

Act 4, Scene 2

Tristan rode off, but did not go into town. He rode Tempest towards the main road that led out of town, the same road that he and Diana had walked along to reach Venamisa. Tempest rode with speed and vigor down the road. Tristan looked steadily down the road as they came into the forest and then continued through. He whipped Tempest to ride faster, speeding along through the forest and reaching the great plains behind. He continued through and passed the tree that he and Diana had slept under during the night that they first came to Georgia. He went into the dark forest that he and Diana had walked through at night and then came into the hilled plains with the stream ahead. Tristan continued down the road until he reached the bridge.

Tempest reared at the end as Tristan brought her to a halt. He then hopped off and went over to the spot that he and Diana had landed at when he arrived. He then began to look around the grass and dirt, searching around carefully before slamming a fist down into the ground.

"Where is it?" Tristan shouted.

Tristan came to the riverbank and began to look down into the water. The stream ran at a gentle pace and the water was absolutely clear. He could see the fish that swam around as well as the rocks at the bottom of the river. His eyes scanned the riverbed, but there was nothing odd down there. Tristan continued to look until his eyes defocused and instead came to focus on the surface of the water. He looked at himself and his reflection.

Tristan's unshaven facial hair was not enough to give him a beard as it was too short and the hairs were too spread out. His hair had become unkempt though and at this length, the darkness of his hair was noticeable. A tear fell from Tristan's eye and into the river. Tristan yelled out and brought a fist down at his reflection, distorting his shape and standing up. He returned to Tempest and climbed atop of her. He then turned her around and rode back into town.

Tristan rode through town and stopped by the well. He hopped off Tempest and then began to lead her by her lead as he went towards some of the market stalls. Tristan stopped before a food stall and picked up some raw food. He also went and bought some flint, paying for the goods with silver coins stashed in the pouches at the side of Tempest's saddle. Finally, Tristan went down to a stall and paid for two bottles of Venamisa's very own wine.

"Again?" the vendor said as Tristan picked up the bottles and laid down the coins.

Tristan glared at him. He took the bottles and brought them down into a pouch in Tempest's saddle and then began to lead her out and towards the city square before the church. The sun had begun to set as it was now evening. He looked into the water in the well and listened to the clucks of chickens from nearby.

"Shouldn't you be returning to that wife of yours?" Sima asked, approaching the well from nearby.

"She... she kicked me out of the house," Tristan responded. "I have nowhere to sleep tonight. I don't think she'd want me to return."

"For a woman that pretty, you have done well," Sima remarked. "However, I could not help but notice that neither of you wear a wedding ring. I have said that she is your wife only because that is what you have told of what is true. Is it true?"

"No," Tristan clarified. "We- we were together though and she is pregnant with our child. Diana has only ever been with me. We gave ourselves to each other years ago when we met. I wanted to propose to her and I bought a ring, but when we arrived here, I had to sell the ring so that I could pay for the horse, the house, and this sword. I wanted to get married this month…"

"The burdens that fall upon you then are not of random chance, but burdens of your sins," Sima remarked. "There are two types of sufferings, those that we deserve and those that we do not. Your premarital relations are the former, and the fact that you have gone three years until only recently your woman has given you a child tells me that you have also engaged in the use of contraceptives. Do you know why contraceptives is considered immoral?"

"No," Tristan replied.

"Christ taught us that when a man comes together with his wife, the two will become one flesh. What it means to be one flesh, means that a man and a woman are united, two parts to become one whole. This unity that a man and a woman create mimics the unity that is God, and it is from here that life is created as God, the Almighty Creator, created all life on Earth. This unity is only achieved when one comes together with their wife in the manner that all men and women are called to do so with their respective spouses – through the Sacred Mystery of marriage. A marriage is a unity and that is why the act of sexual intercourse is limited to those that have married, because of the serious act that it is and consequences that it evokes. A marriage comes together by four conditions, and that is that the husband and wife are free to come together, intend to come together fully (that is, give their full-self to each other), are and will be faithful together, and finally, will be fruitful together. Likewise, the whole act of unity that is sexual intercourse is to be done in this same way. When one uses contraceptives, they inhibit the condition of fullness and fruitfulness. Thus, a contraceptive distorts the act of sexual intercourse to make it into something other than its purpose was – to procreate. For this reason, too, masturbation is a sin, because what is intended by God for this act is spoiled and turned into an object of pleasure."

Tristan sighed.

"Diana has had that – we've been free with each other, full with each other, faithful (at least back then), and fruitful. For most of our recent years together, I've questioned the speed of our relationship. I've felt like there's never been any pace to it... it's all felt... distorted. Don't get me wrong, I love Diana very much, but the circumstances of our meeting have always felt forceful, like we've been glued together, and because of that we've been smushed together to be what we are. And I've always felt like she's been ahead of me... I- I don't want to get married yet, but I have to for the sake of this kid. I want to get married with Diana eventually, but..."

"If you were not ready to confront these circumstances, then you should not have come together with this woman, and it is for this reason why premarital sex is as dangerous as it is. The act of seeing her off would have been less painful for the two of you had you not become as emotionally invested as you have, no less through intercourse. However, by your sinful actions, you have entwisted yourself in a trap in which you believe you cannot escape from – the Devil laughs at that. The Devil entraps one and it is this entrapment that becomes like damnation – a torment."

"I- I wouldn't leave Diana for anything..."

"Even for her own good?" Sima questioned.

"I mean, that's different..."

"Different?" Sima asked with a laugh. "We are speaking of her eternal wellbeing – her opportunity to receive eternal life by rejecting sin and accepting the will of Christ. Do you not believe that you have led her astray from good?"

"I- I wouldn't leave her, I just…"

"You want what you want, but what you want cannot be done. We live in an imperfect, Fallen world in which sometimes the two paths before one are equally horrible. However, that is not the reality of the situation as God sees it. What have you done? You've led a woman into falsehood – to believe that she would be with you, and it would be perfect, when it has not been. Women are easily subdued. And, you've taken that which she can never have again (her virginity) and you have run off with it, leaving her with the taint of another man should she wish to marry someone else – a burden. You are not concerned with her wellbeing, because had you been, you would have stepped aside and placed your foot down. You would have said to her, 'My darling, I love you, but I do not wish to burden you as I am not ready to advance to this moment that can only be achieved through Holy Matrimony,' and should she accept this from you, then you carry on until you are ready, if not, you find someone who is your pace. Instead, you have consistently conceded to her, and perhaps even coaxed her to give to you with false expectations to her. And now that the consequences of these steps face you, the burden falls atop of both of you and the Devil laughs in glee."

Tristan sighed and simply asked in return, "What do I do then?"

"Confess your sins and admit your faults," the priest responded, "… and then… well, the situation has become much more complicated now that the fate of a child is involved. You do not seem like you are ready to marry, but the life of that child of yours is to be considered now. You must do what is right for that child, which coincidentally may be what your wife wishes from you. In that sense, you must confront your own inner demon so that you can give to this child what is needed from you, a father who does not cower, and to your woman, a man that is ready to come together with her in Holy Matrimony."

Tristan didn't respond.

"The purpose of marriage is unity, and in that unity, we not only procreate as is our ancestral and communitarian duty to continue the cycle of life, the raising of that child, but also take hand-in-hand with our partner so that we can hope to achieve what is asked from us individually, and that is to achieve Eternal Life in Heaven, helping each other to reach that point."

Tristan sighed again. He then hopped atop of Tempest and then looked towards Sima.

"Thanks for your advice," Tristan replied. "I- I have to have a think about all this…. Do you know what I could do, or where I could go since I've been kicked out of the house?"

Sima looked back at him.

"There is a cave northwest from here," Sima simply replied. "If you are lucky, it is uninhabited and you could spend the night there."

Tristan nodded to him. He then turned Tempest around and began to gallop out of town. He then sped up and began to go on the road back to the cabin before he stopped to look over. He gave a saddened look over and then continued northwest as he ventured down a road that went into the forest and away from town.

"Stupid priest…" Tristan muttered, frowning as he continued forward. "What does he know about anything…?"

Once the road began to turn west, Tristan branched off and continued through the woods at a slower pace. He came towards some cliffs at the base of the mountain and followed them until he reached the entrance of a small cave. He hopped off Tempest and took her lead to tie her to a tree nearby. He then went forward into the cave to see that it only went so far in, but gave him suitable shelter. Tristan left to retrieve some wood.

. . . .

Later that night, Tristan sat with his back against the cave wall, looking towards the fire and the shadows that were made on the wall. He tilted his head back as he drank from the bottle of wine and then sat it down next to the other empty bottle beside him. He turned his head to the bottles and began to cry as tears fell down his face.

Suddenly, Tristan picked up the bottle and threw it against the wall of the cave, causing it to shatter into many small pieces. He then threw the other and then leaned over as he cried into his hands. He then looked over to the fire and moved over to crawl on his hands. He came closer to the fire and then lay down on his side. He gradually and slowly shut his eyes before he passed out and fell asleep on the cold floor of a cavern far away from Diana.

Act 4, Scene 3

Charlemagne looked at the bonfire that he had constructed out of various logs of trees taken from the nearby forest that surrounded the manor. The smoke from the fire was tall and wide and lifted upwards into the sky. He walked around the fire and came to the steps that went up to his master bedroom, removing his rucksack and placing it down before sitting down on the steps. He took his assault rifle and brought it to his lap. He then proceeded to polish his gun. Not much had changed in the manor in the two weeks that had passed for both Charlemagne and Manon. The two continued to live in the ruins of the Cabernet home where nothing could be done about all the destruction that had swept the manor, even with the power restored. Charlemagne took the opportunity though to board some windows and doorways throughout the house, and cleaning the library so that it was more secure. He also fixed the bookcase door that went into the shaft to the basement so that wanderers or even wild animals would not come across it. Lastly, the foyer had been fortified slightly with the back windows looking to the patio covered in wooden panels as well as the windows above that faced east and west. Towards the north side of the room, Charlemagne took advantage of the railings on the second floor to lay down some rope where he hung some hunted deer. There was also some cooking equipment near the side of the stairs going to the north wing. The doors into the ground floor of the north wing were blocked off though. The foyer bathroom was the only bathroom that was useable, so it remained accessible, and since there was no obstruction in keeping the second floor south and north wing accessible, they were left open too. Charlemagne continued to polish his gun as he sat at the steps of the staircase, looking up the smoke as it rose up to the grey skies that never seemed to disappear.

Manon appeared from out of the library. Like Charlemagne, who still wore his tactical *feldgrau* field uniform, Manon wore the poncho he had given her overtop her clothes. She walked over to Charlemagne, around the fire, and sat down next to him. She looked as depressive as he was.

"*Charles*," Manon said, bringing a fist to the side of her face as she supported it by an elbow at her knee, "it has been two weeks. I do not think our son plans to return…"

"He'll come," Charlemagne argued, continuing to clean his rifle. "Eventually…"

"How can you be so certain?" Manon inquired,

"Because, in this world, I do not disappear in the year 2021, but am killed in the year 2037 by an unknown assailant. If this world were truly the future, then we will eventually return to the present, and with Finn I may add. My cancer… will heal, and I'll live another sixteen years – that's sixteen years with Finn where I can see him grow up to be the man that takes the reins of Cabernet Industries."

"How can you be so certain that you return with him?" Manon asked.

"Because I won't leave this world until we have our son."

"Did you not tell me that you found items that suggest your brother, Salmar, comes to live here and control Cabernet Industries? And look at this world, it is an 'orrible world, *Charles*. What makes you think that anybody could be alive anymore, no less Cabernet as a family?"

Charlemagne shook his head and said, "Salmar has a life sentence for attempting to kill me, Diana, and Tristan. He was also charged with child endangerment. There's no way in hell that he'll see the daylight of Allabrese ever again. Even then…"

124

"And for some reason he was the owner of this manor and he was most likely the owner of Cabernet Industries in its final moments, instead of our son. Do you not see? We do not return with *Louis*... Finn..." Manon said. "He is lost in this world. The same with Diana and Tristan."

"Do not talk like that," Charlemagne protested, standing up. "I will not abandon any of my children! If I have another sixteen years, then damn-well, they will be another sixteen years in this hellscape. I would certainly love to return you to our time, but I simply do not have that power anymore ever since the other crystal was taken from me. We will see Diana and Tristan again, believe me," he assured her. "And with the crystals, we'll be able to return to our time and re-organize a proper rescue mission as Heavner intended."

"Why, *Charles*?" Manon questioned. "Why did you have to do this to us?"

"Pardon?"

"Why did you have to look for him?" Manon clarified. "I had lived almost twenty years in peace that our boy had been fine. Why did you have to take that from me?"

"You're going to get worked up about why I took the initiative to find my own son? And then, when I did find him, why I invited you to meet the boy that we could have raised ourselves?"

"*Mon Dieu, Charles*!" Manon cried out. "This boy... he is not the same boy that I gave birth to. He is not the boy that I held in my arms, *mon petit Louis*... because this boy that you have brought to me, he is a monster! A terrorist with who knows how much blood on his hand. I was scared right there when the two of you argued that he might have killed you; killed me for what we did to him. Who knows what he is capable of...? Perhaps, it is better that we let him loose in a world like this, like the animal that he has become. It is too late, *Charles*, to save him. We failed him."

Manon shook her head. "No, this boy is not ours," Manon decreed.

Charlemagne frowned at her. "I'm sorry to upset you," Charlemagne said with a stern face, "but this boy is positively our very own son. Heavner assured me that when he began his investigation, looking into all adopted children throughout Western Europe, he would narrow the search until he was certain that he had found the boy. When I looked at Finn's profile, I knew that this was my son. Even when I met him as Tristan's roommate, I thought there was something suspicious, but believing that he had died, I did not want to make a scene of it. And even then, I looked at that boy as though he were my son – going so far as to offer him a scholarship and apprenticeship. Of course, he was my son. He has my eyes, but your cheekbones. His hair is darker than mine, but lighter than yours – dark blonde as mixed by our pigmentation. He has my stature, but your charisma. He has our intelligence. He is not a monster. We did not create a monster."

"He has your insanity," Manon responded. "If there is anyone to blame for the capacity by which he could become this way, it is your fault. What with these anti-Semitic ideas of these 'Chosen...' I should have known that you too had become a Nazi..."

"Did you not read my grandfather's unpublished work while it was in your hands?" Charlemagne interrupted. "Certainly, my conclusions on the Jews are my own even if it was my grandfather, whose fate came to an end in the sixties because of these people, wrote the prophecy about the future of Western Civilization that he had made, and his own conclusions about Zionists and the Children of Moloch. However, my own experiences in the forty-sum years that I have lived as an adult has all confirmed these lingering suspicions. Obviously, these people took such a threat to my grandfather, a world-renowned man who in his final years, became labeled by the media as a racist and Holocaust denier because he dared to challenge a narrative that only recently then was birthed out of the war propaganda from twenty-years ago. They had seen that he intended to go public with the truth, presenting irrefutable evidence of Jewish subversion from the 1600s to the 1960s; an extensive narrative of their blood sacrifice traditions since 500 AD, the history on that cult that is the Children of Moloch, and a conclusion on the fact that these people are not Israelites or Judahites, but whose identity they had grafted as their own from those that rejected Christ, the Pharisees; followed by a prediction on the fate of Western Civilization should their subversion continue (which it has). My grandfather's last work would have been a monumental piece of history, and that is exactly why they had to kill him – why they came after us in France – and why they wanted to collect these files when they knew that your father and then you had them. The only reason why I have not gone public with them is for the sake of my own life, the children's life, and the fact that it would be too late. The revolutionary time that my grandfather lived in would have been ripe to expose the treasonous plot that had befallen Western Civilization, and even if they had not listened, the prophecy he predicted in terms of the fate of Western Civilization and the deliberate ethnic cleansing of its peoples, would have been seen to be true. Now... it would be shot down as a conspiracy theory... So, do not tell me that you did not peak at my grandfather's work... You idolized him as much as I had. This shoddy attempt to denounce him is an insult to his memory."

Manon was silent. Charlemagne sat back down next to her.

"Up to now, you have not said a word about any of this, because you already knew, even if you may or may not believe it. You respected my grandfather. You also know me. Nobody has come to know me better than you have, and the same has gone for me to you. We've known each other since we were schoolchildren. You had never loved me for my ideas, but my heart, and because of that you could never in good conscience believe that I am someone other than who I am. I have to say that the same is with our son. You do not know him, but he has a good heart even if he is far more radical than me. He simply is young and inexperienced – what I would have given to have allowed him to experience life as my grandfather had with me."

Charlemagne and Manon turned to the front doors of the manor as they heard a brake screech followed by the shut of car doors.

"What was that?" Charlemagne questioned.

"*Spara per uccidere questo piccolo bastardo*," a voice remarked from outside.

Charlemagne stood up and raised his rifle as he looked to the door. He turned to Manon.

"Take the stairs up to the library and then go down to the basement," Charlemagne quietly said to her.

"What are you going to do?" Manon questioned.

"I'm going to defend my home," Charlemagne simply replied.

Charlemagne continued to point his rifle towards the door while Manon ran up the steps and disappeared into the south wing. He took side-steps up the staircase, keeping his rifle pointed towards the door as he saw men come up the steps. He took point at the top of the stairs, behind the railings and opened fire at the men as they appeared.

"Who are you!" Charlemagne shouted. "Get away from my home!"

"*Apri il fuoco! Apri il fuoco!*" the bandits shouted.

Charlemagne was briefly able to see what kind of men these people were. They appeared to be fairly well-built men, but they were not dressed like professional mercenaries, but they simply wore cargo pants and everyday coats with holster vests atop that held magazines. These men opened fire back at Charlemagne with their own rifles. He managed to shoot at two of them as they were about to come up the stairs, while the rest spread out and returned fire indiscriminately. Charlemagne retreated back into some full cover in the small south wing foyer corridor. He continued to lay down some fire back at the intruders.

"*Dov'è lui?*" the bandits shouted from behind the door.

Charlemagne laid down some suppressing fire towards them.

"*Non riesco a vedere,*" another bandit replied.

"*Al piano di sopra a sinistra!*" a third bandit remarked.

The bandits began to fire back towards where Charlemagne was. He retreated back and made his way into the library. He then came down the circular stairs and took cover behind a bookcase as he looked over to the library where they poured in. Charlemagne shot back at them as he saw them come.

"*Merda!*" a bandit remarked as he was hit.

Charlemagne moved forward and continued to fire back. He then disappeared into his study and moved forward to take point by the doorway that looked into the foyer.

"*Dov'è lui?!*" a bandit shouted, annoyed.

"*Biblioteca!*"

Charlemagne moved in and took cover behind the stairs. He opened fire at some bandits as they attempted to come through.

"*Foyer!*" a bandit remarked.

Charlemagne retreated back out of the patio and went over to the ruins of the French window into the trophy room. He went inside and then into the kitchen, entering the garage, and then going down to exit out and make his way around. He looked ahead and saw that the bandits had come in two pickup trucks. Charlemagne opened fire at the two bandits at the stood guard and took them down. He then went ahead to the doorway so that he could shoot at the others as to take advantage of their disorganization.

"*Fianco!*" the bandits remarked.

"*Esci da casa mia!*" Charlemagne shouted at the bandits in Italian.

Charlemagne dodged back and went towards the library window. He peaked up and then climbed through, shooting at the two bandits that had taken cover in the small corridor to the foyer. He then came up to them as one of them fell over dead. Charlemagne pointed his rifle at the one that was alive.

"*Chi siete persone?*" Charlemagne questioned. "*Casa dei Medici?*"

"*Si,*" the bandit replied, raising a hand towards Charlemagne. "*Per favore, perdonaci!*"

"*Allora, Medici vive?*" Charlemagne asked. "*Chi ti ha mandato?*"

"*Dino,*" the bandit responded. "*Dino Medici! Si, Medici y il Duce vive. Controlliamo questa regione e ti abbiamo preso come una minaccia!*"

"*Dov'è lui? Piana Calabrese?*"

"*Si,*" the bandit remarked. "Please, we will leave. Just have mercy…"

Charlemagne frowned at him. The man soon bled out and fell backwards. He was dead. Charlemagne looked at the mess around and then over to Manon who was behind him.

"So, there are others alive," Charlemagne stated. "Across the county, the Medici family survives and they believe they control this entire area like warlords. If Finn has run into them, they may have either killed or captured him sometime over the last two weeks. I need to go there and find out."

Act 4, Scene 4

Tristan sat in his cave, looking forward to the wall across from him as he sat with his back against the other wall. His feet were spread out and he simply looked forward, across the fire and towards the shadows that flame created. He sat with an arm over his abdomen, fist tightened. Tristan's face was wet with his own perspiration. His hand shook and he breathed sharply. Tristan looked over to the empty wine bottle by the entrance of the cave. He began to crawl towards it. Tristan grabbed the bottle and sat down with it in his hands. He then sniffed within the neck of the bottle before letting the bottle down and placing his hands on the rock of the cave floor. His hands trembled, but not because they struggled to hold his weight. Tristan breathed out as if he had been holding his breath. He then raised his head up and looked forward.

A cloaked figure could be seen ahead, looking at him from within the forest ahead. Tristan squinted towards the mysterious figure that looked at him. The person that looked to him was tall and wore a dark black robe that covered his entire body.

"Sima?" Tristan questioned, carefully standing up and placing a hand on the cave wall.

The face of the figure could not be seen as the darkness covered his face. Tristan took a step forward and began to walk towards the figure. He walked careful steps, limping with every step that he took as he made his way towards the mysterious man. The cloaked figure took a step back and then turned away from Tristan as he went down the forest.

Tristan followed the figure as both of them walked in a calm pace. The figure turned around to look at Tristan as they were further within the forest. Tristan could see that the figure before him was at least six feet and six inches tall. He continued to approach him as he could begin to see glimpses of his fair skinned, shaven face by the mouth. Tristan hurried up as he went deeper into the forest and away from the cave. He followed the figure until they reached a cliffside that came out of the woods. Tristan approached the figure as he looked towards him from the edge of the cliff.

The cloaked figure looked at him and Tristan saw as he finally confronted this mysterious man who loomed over him that he was a beautiful, young man with fair-skin and eyes with red irises. He had fine dark eyebrows. His nose was medium-sized, sharp and refined. His cheeks were round and jaw fine. His light and fair skin was smooth and flawless. There was no imperfection that could be seen across his face, except for thick vein that crept over the right-side of his face, stretching up from his neck and over onto the top of his perfectly bald head. The beautiful man looked down at Tristan with a smug look on his face.

"Who are you?" Tristan questioned.

The man raised a hand from his cloak and brought it towards Tristan's face. Tristan took a step back, but then looked around as his surroundings began to darken while he and the man stood in place.

"What are you doing?" Tristan remarked.

Tristan attempted to leave, but as he stepped forward, he stepped back as his foot touched down and hit onto concrete. He looked down and saw that it was a dirty sidewalk. He then looked around and saw that it was raining and he was no longer in some forest, but in the middle of a slum. Tristan looked around him and the beautiful man had disappeared. He continued to look at the environment that he had been transported to and realized that he was in Keswick at night-time in the past or present.

The lights of some shops were lit and there were people walking up and down the sidewalk. Specifically, Tristan had been taken to Mackenzie Street near Diana's apartment. The sky above was a dark grey, lit by the pollution of light that gave it a brownish appearance. Tristan was dressed in his peasant clothes, but they did not become wet as he stood in the rain and he could not feel the rain touch upon him. Instead, he continued to feel the coldness of the forest around him. A man walking along the streets passed through him from behind.

Tristan's eager expression that he had returned to Harlech soon turned to disappointment. He then looked over as he heard a ruckus from nearby. Tristan looked over to a liquor store as a security guard pushed a man out from the store and onto the streets. He walked across the street to get a closer look at the man, who appeared familiar. Tristan squinted.

"You can't kick me out!" the man shouted. "Do you know what the sign says?! It says B.C. Liquor Store! That means it's owned by the government and is public property. My taxes pay for this place!"

The man growled at the security guards as they re-entered, keeping a distance from the drunken man. Tristan continued to step forward towards the man as he picked himself up from the floor. He was dressed in a dirty, ripped canvas coat and jeans. He also wore thick Sherpa-lined boots. Over his head, he had dark brown hair. He patted his jeans and then began to walk down the street.

Tristan came onto the sidewalk and began to look over to the man as he walked away, continuing down Mackenzie Street towards the west.

"What the hell is this?" Tristan questioned. "Some sort of nightmare to prove the salient point that Diana thinks I'm like her father?"

Tristan jumped from surprise as a man moved through him. He looked over to the man and saw that he wore a coat with one of the sleeves pinned in as if the man had an amputated arm. He had balding brown hair and a short stature. Tristan squinted at him and began to follow, especially as the man followed Diana's father down the street.

Tristan walked with careful steps. He stepped down onto the road and looked ahead to where Diana's father had begun to harass some people on the sidewalk. Tristan frowned at him, but then looked over to the man with the amputated arm as he continued to follow him. Diana's father soon continued down the street, turning into an alleyway and disappearing. Tristan stopped and continued to look over to see if the man would follow around the corner. He then sped up as he did exactly that. Tristan rushed over and stood in the middle of the alleyway entrance as the armless man took his only arm out from his jacket where he held a short-barreled revolver. He walked with faster steps and then raised the gun up, shooting three shots indiscriminately, which caused Diana's father to fall forward and land on the dirty alleyway floor. Tristan watched as the armless man took a step back and then began to rush out from the crime scene.

The armless man walked towards Tristan as he fled. Tristan saw his face. He had an unshaven face and a sort of rat, or mouse-like look to his face. It was a sort of malnutritious face, although the man had a stocky body with a short stature. Tristan turned and saw the way that the man went, but then looked over to Diana's father. He walked over to him.

Tristan came up to the body and saw a pool of blood around. Nobody had seen the body yet. He looked ahead as some people crossed the alleyway from the street ahead, Trutch Street, but paid no attention to the body. The gunman had shot Willis in the back, near the heart in three clean shots. Tristan crept around the side of the face and looked at the unshaven face of the man who shared facial characteristics with Diana. His eyes were wide open, but they did not move. Tristan breathed fiercely and then looked over to some pedestrians who had stopped to look over at the body.

"What are you looking at?" Tristan questioned them. "Don't just stand there, call an ambulance!"

Tristan looked at them with disillusion. He then looked back at the body and over to the other side of the alleyway as he saw the cloaked figure stand nearby.

"What the hell is this supposed to be? A warning? How exactly is this supposed to encourage me to stop drinking, huh? I'm not anywhere close to the fiend that this scumbag was – I don't know if you've noticed, but I'm actually trying to quit, so these bizarre hallucinations are not really arguing in favor of me continuing to try to quit."

Tristan looked around him as his surrounding began to darken. He took a step back and looked around with a panic. He stayed where he was and then soon his surroundings brightened as he came to a new location. Tristan looked around and saw that he was at Diana's apartment, but not in the present-time, or future, but past. The apartment was decorated differently than how Diana and he had come to make the place home. There was very little furniture, although the furniture there was had been positioned similarly to how Diana and Tristan had the apartment. Where the white table was, there was a white round table, and where the couch was there was a plain brown one that looked over to a thick-reared TV. The kitchen looked entirely different as it was in its original form with laminate countertops and original white appliances, alongside a gas stove. Tristan looked over to the woman that sat at the table.

The woman had light brown hair and a slim figure. She also had fair skin. The woman was hunched over the table as she sat with a mug around her hand. She cried and cried. Tristan looked over to the bedroom door to see that it was shut. He then stepped aside and went around to get a better look at the young woman that was at the table. Diana's mother shared certain facial characteristics with her daughter, especially the cheek bones. However, a majority of Diana's appearance had come from her father, especially the hair. The woman continued to cry in a manner in which she tried to stay quiet.

Tristan looked behind him as he heard a knock on the door. Diana's mother looked over and stood up. Tristan looked at her straight on to see that she was approximately the same height as Diana. She passed through Tristan and went around into the corridor to the front door. Tristan followed, but stayed at the end of the corridor while the woman answered the door. She removed a chain atop and then unlocked the door, opening it and looking towards the man at the other side. Tristan squinted and recognized the man as the same armless man from earlier.

"Felix," Diana's mother said, "what are you doing here?"

"I heard about Willis, Scarlett," the man named Felix said. "I came to offer you some company in what must be a hard moment for you."

"Oh God…" Diana's mother remarked. "The police were not here too long ago… I didn't say much about Will's work, so I'm glad you came."

Diana allowed the man to enter. She then closed the door behind him. The two walked back into the kitchen.

"What happened? Did this happen while he was out collecting money?" Diana's mother asked.

"No," Felix replied. "Willis had the day-off today. We weren't due to collect until tomorrow."

"Then how has this happened? Will could be really awful sometimes, but he never had any enemies," Diana's mother said, going over to sit down. "Who could so a thing like this to us? I- I can't believe it."

"Sometimes," Felix said, "these things simply happen for no reason, and there's nothing you can do. I'm sorry for your loss," he remarked, placing a hand over Diana's mother's hand.

Tristan frowned towards him.

"What the heck is going on here," Tristan remarked. "What is this supposed to be?"

Diana's mother flicked the man's hand away. She crossed her arms and turned away from him. Tears continued to roll down the sides of her face.

"Will and I have known each other since we were fourteen years old," Diana's mother said. "We met in high school and we had never been apart since. I don't know how I can go on living – having to support Diana. I…"

"You'll have to do what's best for her," Felix responded.

"I- I can't do anything for her. Will was a terrible father, but at least he brought in money from time to time, which gave us food."

"Take it easy…" Felix replied, coming around behind Diana's mother to place his hands on her shoulder. "It'll be alright."

Tristan looked at Felix suspiciously. He slurred his words and walked with a sort of dazed motion. Diana's mother flicked him back.

"Will you back off?" Diana's mother remarked, standing up and walking away from him. "You're coming on too strong – I've just lost my husband."

"Oh God," Felix replied, falling to his knees and grabbing Scarlett's hand. "I'm sorry... I- I've always loved you. I- I'm sorry. I feel terrible about what I've done."

Diana's mother looked down at him with disgust.

"You need to leave," Scarlett said. "Now. You're going to wake up Diana."

"Please, give me a chance. I can be a better father than Willis ever was," Felix pled. "I- I can bring in money..."

Felix stood up and moved in on Scarlett. She attempted to push him back. He brought his hand onto her arm.

"Come on," Felix remarked, bringing himself too close to Diana's mother. "Give me a chance."

"Hey! Get off me!" Diana's mother quietly yelled.

Felix became more aggressive as he forced himself onto Diana's mother. Scarlett did not stand for this and finally elbowed Felix across the face, causing his nose to bleed. Felix retrieved the pistol from his pocket and hit Diana's mother across the face with it, but accidentally caused it to fire and shoot her through the head. Felix's eyes widened as she fell to the floor.

"Oh my God!" Felix shouted. "What have I done?!"

Felix fell to the floor again and crawled over to Diana's mother's corpse. He then brought his hands over to her, touching her breast in one hand while he grabbed her waist. The man cried at her body before looking up as there was a knock on the door.

"Scarlett, is everything alright in there?" a woman questioned.

Felix's eyes shot over. He stood up and began to look around. He looked at the gun in his hand and then the door knocked again. Felix took the gun and shot himself through the head, falling over. Tristan simply looked over and then down to the horrifying sight that was Diana's mother on the floor with a gunshot wound through her head.

Tristan looked away and could hear panicked mumbling from the other side of the door. He shook his head and placed a hand on the edge of the apartment corridor wall as he kept his eyes away from the body.

"Get me the hell out of here..." Tristan muttered. "Please... this doesn't even make any sense. This isn't even how Diana's mom died."

Tristan looked back over, but not towards the body, but instead to creak of a door. He looked over and saw a young girl come out from the bedroom. She had a short stature, but curled and short dark brown hair and a round face. The little girl wore a blue night gown as she crept out from the bedroom and looked ahead of her. Tristan's eyes began to water as he looked at Diana stand before her mother and the creep that was Felix.

"Mama..." Diana said, her own eyes watering.

Tristan wiped the tears from his face and turned his back on the poor girl. He then sniffled.

"Please," Tristan pled, "get me out of here... I don't want to see this anymore – this is sick..."

Tristan closed his eyes and then turned back, expecting to see little Diana again, but instead, he looked towards the cave wall and realized that he had returned to reality. Tristan looked at his hands and then placed his palm against the cave wall to feel the coldness of the stone. He then looked over to the fire as it continued to burn. He walked over to the fire and sat down before it, bringing his hands into his face as tears continued to stroll down. His hands continued to tremble, but his face was pale.

"What the hell was that...?" Tristan muttered, hugging his knees and shaking his head.

Act 5, Scene 1

Charlemagne drove down the road towards Medici Manor late in the same evening on the same day that he was attacked by the Italian family. He had his hands around the steering wheel of one of the white pickup trucks that had driven up the manor driveway. The front hood of the pickup truck was strapped with plastic explosives taken from the cache of weaponry in the Cabernet Manor basement. In contrast to Cabernet Manor, Medici Manor was a fortress with the outer walls modified so they contained barbed wire. There were also floodlights around the perimeter and a spotlight that shined down from the tower. Lights from within the manor were turned on to evoke further brightness around the only structure other than Cabernet Manor that had lights turned on. Charlemagne drove as fast as he could down the road before taking his rifle at his side and opening the door. He jumped out from the pickup truck and left the car to drive forward the rest of the road while he landed in the field at the side, rolling his landing before looking over to the vehicle.

The pickup truck drove towards the wooden gate at the end of the road where the guards at the front dodged out of the way as the car made its impact against the wooden door and exploded. Charlemagne stood up from the field and began to open fire from where he was, shooting at the guards at the front of the manor before he ducked down and began to make his way across the cropped field so that he could get around the side. He made his way over to the outer wall, taking his pistol out to shoot at the CCTV cameras at the corner, and then went down the side to reach a smaller wooden gate.

Charlemagne placed some plastic explosives on the wooden gate and then continued down to reach the rear of the manor where there were some guards around the rear open field of the manor cordoned off by some wooden fence and connected to the barn further down. Charlemagne shot towards them as they were disorganized and out of cover. He then moved forward to take cover behind some hedges at the sides of the gravel path that went from the rear gates. He came down into the prone and began to crawl down behind the hedges before sticking his rifle through an opening to continue firing at the mobsters-turned-bandits.

Once the area was clear, Charlemagne stood up and went to prepare explosives around the wooden gates. He then shot at the CCTV cameras nearby before continuing down to the west-side where it was clear. He shot at the cameras and then prepared some more plastic explosives at the wooden gate, near the section of the wall that he had once climbed in order to get access to the crime scene of the murder of Giovanni and Bianca Medici. Charlemagne went down and shot at the last of the cameras before he took a detonator and pressed it. He looked over as the gates flew off and listened as the same was done at the other gates. Charlemagne looked around the corner to the front gates where the pickup truck wreckage lay and then went towards it.

Charlemagne could hear panicked shouting in Italian from the other side of the wall. He went towards the front gate and stopped to look inside. He could see bandits on the roof of the manor behind some balustrades as well as from some balcony windows. Charlemagne opened fire at those from the roof, surprising them as they anticipated his attack from elsewhere. He then moved to the other side and took a moment to reload. Charlemagne took some smoke grenades and began to throw two into the front of the manor so that he could push through. He waited a moment before he pressed in, keeping his head down as he went to take cover behind the fountain in the center, and then went over to the front gates of the manor where he placed some plastic explosives. He then moved away and continued around the side of the manor, stopping to look around the corner and then continuing down. Charlemagne dropped onto a knee and brought his other leg forward as he saw some bandits come from around the corner. He used the cover of the steps up to a side door and the balustrade railings as cover as he shot at these bandits.

There was not much cover around the front and sides of the manor. Charlemagne moved up so that he was directly behind the steps and then shot back towards the only bandit behind cover. He then moved up and began to prepare some more explosives to place at the side door before going back around. Charlemagne took a fragmentation grenade from his vest, cooked it, and then threw it over to the bandits ahead, spooking them while he rushed forward to get closer. Charlemagne reached the rear of the manor and the elaborate gardens behind where the bandits had spread out.

Despite all the destruction across Allabrese, Medici Manor retained its structure and the beauty of its garden as if the world had not come to an end. Charlemagne shot at the bandits within the garden, hitting the sides of the marble statues that they took cover behind. He shot at the ones that were closer to flanking him before concentrating at the others. Up ahead, around the rear perimeter of the manor, were a set of stairs that went up to the patio behind the mansion, which contained the pool. A large hedge wall rose up from behind the balustrades that looked out to the garden.

Charlemagne shot towards the bandits over there, pushing them back before he took some smoke and cleared the way for him to rush forward and come up the patio. Charlemagne shot towards the bandits on the roof as he emerged from out of the smoke. He then pulled back as they shot at him, barely missing him. He looked over and decided to go through the garden instead. Charlemagne went over and took cover behind a balustrade at the edge of the garden and looked over as he saw a few bandits in cover. He shot towards them and then reloaded.

The bandits shot back towards him. Charlemagne took another fragmentation grenade and threw it over, causing them to run out of cover for Charlemagne to shoot them before the grenade detonated and caused fragments of the statue to spill around. He continued to push against the bandits as he made his way into the gardens, keeping close to the hedge that blocked the line of sight from those on the roof. The garden had become lit by spotlights on the south balcony of the tower. Charlemagne was halfway through the gardens. The bandits continued to return fire, but eventually they were forced to retreat.

Charlemagne made his way through the other side of the garden and threw some smoke by the stairs on the other side of the patio before he continued down the path towards another side-door. He made his approach up the steps and carefully placed some of the last of his plastic explosives before he moved back and detonated all three packages. The side-door ripped off. Charlemagne made his way inside the manor, taking cover behind the casing of an open archway as he entered into the regal halls of the house. He went down and came into another corridor where it was quiet. Charlemagne could hear the shouts of the bandits in Italian from within the manor, so he moved forward.

There were several bandits within the foyer of the manor. Charlemagne turned to face them and opened fire at them. He then continued down the hallway and disappeared into a parlor. He took the moment to reload as she came around to the dining room where he stopped as bandits appeared from the other side. They opened fire at each other. Charlemagne took a fragmentation grenade and rolled it down towards them. He then stood up as they panicked out of the room, shooting at them as it detonated and shredded the other side of the table.

"*Dov'è mio figlio, bastardi!*" Charlemagne shouted at the bandits.

"*Nella sala da pranzo!*" the bandits instead remarked to each other.

Charlemagne hunched over as he felt some shots come from behind him. He quickly took cover behind the doorway into the dining room and closed one side of the double doors. He placed down some plastic explosives on the door and then quickly moved over to the other side to shut the door and then continue to the other side. Charlemagne took the detonator into his hand as he paused at the other side.

The bandits kicked the door down. Charlemagne blew the C4, causing bits of the door to fly off into the parlor and leave behind some flames on the wooden floor and dry wall. Charlemagne then looked into the corridor behind him to see that it was clear. He moved in and went towards an archway on the right that went into another corridor. He then went and moved a wooden table to cover the door across from the dining room before continuing through. Bandits from the end of the corridor began to shoot at him.

Charlemagne retaliated fire while bandits from the other side of the room he had barricaded began to bash against the door. He shot his rifle through the door, which forced them to stop. He then continued to fire down the corridor until he dodged back to reload. Charlemagne took one of the last fragmentation grenades he had and threw it down.

"*Granata!*" the bandits shouted.

The grenade detonated, and shredded the floor and the sides of the open archway.

"*È vicino alla cucina!*" a bandit yelled.

Charlemagne took a smoke grenade and threw it over. He then knocked the table over and took another smoke grenade, his last one, and threw it into the kitchen. Charlemagne stood back as he heard shouts from the other side. He then carefully walked into the room to see that it had been cleared as the smoke went off. Charlemagne walked carefully around. A large set of three arched windows looked out to the garden ahead. Charlemagne went to a set of doors that continued into a corridor ahead. He peaked around the corner and saw the smoke from the other grenade, which had filled the hall. From the other side of the corridor, there was a door that exited out onto the patio. Charlemagne opened this door and quietly left, coming down to the other door, which he opened and carried on through.

The voice of the Italian bandits could be heard throughout, slightly incoherently as Charlemagne walked through with his rifle raised. He stopped at the end of the corridor and took cover at a horizontal corridor that connected with the other side of the manor, going into the ballroom via a vestibule. There were shreds of smoke ahead. The bandits took cover around the corner and Charlemagne had them in his flank.

"*Dov'è lui?*" one of them quietly said.

"*Lui non e qui,*" another replied.

Charlemagne opened fire at them and caught them off-guard. He then continued forward down a vertical corridor as he disappeared.

"*Dov'è lui!*" a bandit shouted.

Charlemagne ran down to the end of the corridor and took cover behind an archway that went into the foyer. The remains of the front door stood before the entrance. Charlemagne looked up the stairs and saw some bandits take point at the top. He heard a voice speak over their radio.

One of the bandits replied, "*Nessuna vista di lui.*"

The voice over the radio spoke in a brash tone at them.

"*Si, mio Duce.*"

Charlemagne reloaded and then opened fire at these two above.

"*E nell'atrio!*" a bandit shouted.

Charlemagne shot the two bandits down and then began to move forward so he could climb the stairs. Another two bandits appeared from the end of a corridor ahead. He opened fire at them and took them down. He then rushed to a column at the corner of the railings and looked over as he saw more bandits arrived from below. Charlemagne opened fire at them.

"*L'intruso e sopra!*" a bandit remarked from below.

Charlemagne turned his attention across the foyer as a door opened from the second floor and bandits shot at him from the other side. He held his ground and fired back. The firepower became too overwhelming for him. He retreated and fled into a corridor, taking the moment to reload before he went further back towards some bedrooms, but away from the master bedroom and study. He went down and knocked on a door into an unoccupied bedroom and took cover behind the casing. He then sat down and pointed his rifle forward as he waited for bandits to appear. Charlemagne opened fire as they took cover around the casing of the open archway ahead.

The bandits that appeared fled backwards. Charlemagne stopped firing and waited for more to appear. He then opened fire again before stopping, and then going again. Charlemagne quickly reloaded, switching out his magazine and then continuing to fire down the corridor. The bandits held back.

"*Chi e questo ragazzo?!*" a bandit questioned from the other side.

"*Ad essere onesti, assomiglia al signor Cabernet.*"

"*Lo spirit del signor Cabernet? Non c'è da stupirsi che non morira!*"

Charlemagne continued to fire in bursts as they appeared, conserving his ammo.

"*Dove sono gli altri per prenderlo da dietro?*" a bandit asked.

Charlemagne lowered his rifle as he heard this. He then continued to open fire, standing up as he went behind, emptying his magazine to hide at a door at the end. Charlemagne opened the door and entered into a staircase that only went up to the roof. He quickly reloaded as he heard steps come from above. Charlemagne pointed his rifle and shot at the bandits as they came down before going back around the corner to see if anymore were coming towards him. He gave some shots back with his pistol before reloading and then continuing up the stairs and to the roof. Charlemagne barged through and pointed his rifle forward.

The roof, including the third floor and fourth-floor tower were clear. He moved ahead and past a bandit that had bled out, moving around so that he could come down the stairwell towards the front of the house. He then quickly went down with his rifle pointed, coming around and quietly opening the door. He looked ahead and saw that the bandits had moved ahead.

Charlemagne moved down and went towards the door to flank them. He opened fire at them as they went down the corridor with caution. Charlemagne opened fire, and they went down without a hitch. Charlemagne reloaded and then looked around. He looked towards the window and saw a bolt of lightning flash through the windows as it began to rain. Charlemagne went towards the foyer and looked down. He then went over to the corpse of a bandit as heard some static from the radio.

"*C'è qualcuno la fuori?*" a voice questioned from the other end.

Charlemagne looked down and then raised his rifle up as he continued forward, ready to confront the Duce.

Act 5, Scene 2

The next day since Tristan's bizarre vision, he continued to sit in his cave, but with his back against the furthest wall from the end of the cave so that was looking out towards the exit. His eyes were baggy and tired, and his hair was amess. He was still unshaven and three days had passed since Diana had kicked him out. Tristan's face was covered with sweat and he had made incisions on his arm with his sword dropped nearby. Tristan squeezed his arm with a hand as he sat with his legs spread out forward. He breathed heavily as if he were in pain and feverish.

Tristan closed his eyes for a moment and then opened them again to drop a worried expression as he looked ahead to see the cloaked figure once more. The figure stopped before the entrance into the cave. Tristan released his grip on his wrist and moved his hand over to take his sword. He then stood up and pointed the sword towards him. However, as the man looked over to him with his red eyes, Tristan noticed that the cave began to darken and his sword disappeared.

"No, no, no…" Tristan exclaimed dropping to his knees and shutting his eyes. "Please, not again…"

Tristan shuddered and then relaxed as he heard the smack of a gavel. He stood up and looked around. He was in a brightly lit room where light poured in through overtop windows at either side. The walls were a yellowish custard color and the bottom panels were a clear white. Above and below there were crown moldings and baseboards in the same white. The floor consisted of diagonal polished beige panels and above him were chandeliers. He stood in the middle of an aisle with white wooden benches at either side. Ahead were several figures behind a bar, with none in the audience section aside from Tristan. He was in a courtroom. Tristan looked head to the judge in black robes and then over to the bailiff that stood nearby. At the prosecution desk stood a man with silver hair next to a man with medium-length blonde hair. At the defense desk stood a man with dark hair with a man with even darker hair. A court clerk could be seen in the corner of the room. Tristan looked back over to the two men in the prosecution desk.

The man with grey hair had a slimmer stature than the man with blonde hair who was stocky. Tristan stepped aside and recognized the sides of the faces of the men to be Charlemagne with his health and color, while the other was his brother, Salmar. At the other side of the table, Tristan did not recognize either of the men. One of them had a stocky figure like Salmar, the man with the combed dark hair and shaven face, while the other had a moustache and gelled hair so that it looked even darker than the other. All four men had fair skin. The judge sat down, which prompted the others to sit down.

"I have reviewed the case carefully, and after careful consideration, I have come to a verdict," the judge said. "I have decided to place the care of Ms. Diana Anne Cambridge, age ten, into the home of Mr. Charlemagne Phillipe Cabernet over Mr. Damian Jerrick Lachlan Sutherland. Court dismissed."

The judge hit his gavel and then stood up. The others in the room stood so that he could leave. Afterwards, the others turned to face their respective lawyers. Charlemagne and Salmar shook hands, while the man known as Damian, or Scot, shook his head and then brought his fists to the table and hunched over in disbelief. Scot's lawyer attempted to leave with him, but he flicked him off of him. The lawyer then left without him.

Charlemagne and Salmar attempted to leave afterwards, but was stopped as they confronted Scot. He faced them.

"Mr. Cabernet, a peaceful word before you leave?" Scot petitioned.

Salmar looked at Charlemagne. He nodded to his brother who then left. Charlemagne and Scot looked at each other.

"Please, take good care of Diana," Scot requested. "She is a special little girl and didn't deserve the father that she had, so be sure to make up for that for her…"

"Of course," Charlemagne replied. "Diana will be in good care under my home. I promise you that – not that she would not have been in good care with you, but Crown has determined this to be the best path for her, and indeed she will be safe in the countryside where she can recover from the traumas she's experienced."

Scot nodded to him.

"Since I won't get to see her before you leave, please let her know that… if there's ever a time in which she needs me, I'll be there for her."

"I'll be sure to let her know that," Charlemagne replied.

"Goodbye then, Mr. Cabernet."

The two gentlemen shook hands. Charlemagne then left while Scot stayed behind to sulk in his loss. Tristan squinted at him and then over to the door where Charlemagne had left.

"What?" Tristan questioned. "This doesn't make any sense…"

Tristan turned around again and looked over where the mysterious figure stood at the gates of the bar. Scot had disappeared as had the court clerk and bailiff. The room began to darken. Tristan stayed put and then looked around as he found himself in the foyer of Cabernet Manor.

The foyer was bright and light shined through the large arched windows from the rear. The chirping of birds could be heard from outside. Tristan stood in the center of the foyer and turned around as he heard the front door open. Charlemagne, dressed in the same suit he wore in court, stepped through and guided young Diana inside.

The Diana that Tristan saw before him was the same youngster that he saw in the apartment in the earlier scene from her mother's death, with the curled dark hair and round face. She wore a green t-shirt and denim overalls. She also wore a light green backpack behind her as she walked into the manor with a timid face.

"Welcome to Cabernet Manor," Charlemagne said to Diana with a soothing voice. "This home is your home now. Mrs. Quinn will be here to cook and clean, and I'm sure she'll also appreciate if you want to have a chat. She's quite friendly…"

Tristan looked behind him as he saw Mavis in her black dress and apron. She looked younger than Tristan remembered her. She looked to Diana with a kind face.

"Hello, Ms. Cambridge," Mrs. Quinn remarked in her posh English accent. "How'd you do?"

Diana did not reply and instead simply looked back at her with a depressive face. Tristan looked at her with pity.

"Come now, let me take you to your bedroom," Charlemagne said. "Afterwards, we can have lunch. I'm sure you're very hungry from the flight over…"

Charlemagne walked with Diana up the steps to the north wing as he carried her suitcase for her. Diana walked slow steps and kept her head down. Tristan watched and then turned around to see the mysterious figure looking down at him from the other side. He turned back to look over to Diana, but they had disappeared and the room darkened.

Tristan found himself at Lord Phoenix Secondary School next. He was in the main office, but it was quiet and only the voices of a woman could be heard from the principal's office. Tristan walked over to the door left ajar and looked in. Mrs.

Phillips sat at the desk in a black dress, speaking with Charlemagne who was in front of her. Tristan looked in and listened.

"Diana's performance so far has been excellent," Mrs. Phillips remarked. "She's a very smart and intelligent girl, and she's excelling in all her subjects, but…"

"There is always a 'but' isn't there…" Charlemagne replied.

"The other eighth graders have become a bit estranged to her, and it's caused me to worry. She's very quiet and rarely talks to the other kids…"

"How many are there in her class?" Charlemagne questioned.

"Six," Mrs. Phillips replied. "Only six, and to be fair, all of these kids have known each other since kindergarten, but I understand that Diana came from Prince Albert with them…"

"Yes," Charlemagne replied. "I've had the same concerns addressed to me by her sixth and seventh grade teachers then… What can we do though, Sabrina? I honestly feel for the poor lass, but the trauma of her mother's death has not eased as I had hoped."

"What we could try is to bring some of that energy into some sort of craft or hobby," Mrs. Phillips suggested. "Is there anything that she likes to do?"

"Well," Charlemagne remarked, "she does like to read, and she's quite fond of playing the piano. However, these are all solitary joys of hers. What she needs is to engage in a sport of some kind. Perhaps field hockey, or soccer… I'll have a word with her and attempt to motivate her into some sort of hobby."

"Thank you, Charles…" Mrs. Phillips replied.

The room darkened again. Tristan simply looked on as he found himself outside in the sun. He looked over and saw the bright smile of a young girl in a white dress with flowers styled around the rim. Diana stood at the side of the wedding arch at the side of the south wing, holding a basket with flowers inside, and with a young boy with short blonde hair in dress pants, white-shirt, and crossed red-black tie. In turn, they stood behind an older man with a scar over his eye and grey hair – Tristan recognized him as Bogdan Alexandrov. The boy in turn was Kodiak at the age of around fifteen or sixteen. Tristan looked back at Diana and saw that she appeared much as she appeared around the time the two had begun to date, but her hair was cut slightly short up to her shoulders and straightened back.

The man and woman stood under the arch, in front of a civil servant. The man under the arch was a tall, handsome man with short blonde hair. Tristan recognized him as Yuri Saburov, also known as Sergei Bykov, while the woman in the large white dress was Allodia Cabernet. Tristan stood at the end of the aisle and looked at them with a confused glance. He looked aside and then over to the chairs at the front where Charlemagne was seated with his brother, father and mother alongside some family friends such as the Huxleys, Peter and Vivian included, the Phillips, their children, and Judith Lambert.

Diana looked to Allodia with a wide smile. Tristan looked back at her with a confused glance. He continued to look around, finally observing that he was not present.

"What the heck is going on here?" Tristan questioned, annoyed. "Is this supposed to be Diana's life without me? Supposed to make me feel self-depreciative as if I somehow ruined her life? Everybody's life?"

The people around blurred out and Tristan found himself further ahead after the wedding ceremony. He was in the ballroom where the guests were enjoying the reception. Charlemagne spoke with his parents and Salmar, while Allodia and Yuri spoke with Richard and Jacqueline Huxley alongside

Bogdan. Diana was nearby and playing with Kodiak. Both of them had a smile on their faces as they ran after each other around the room.

"Diana!" Charlemagne complained as the pair came close to the bride and groom. "Be careful, or you might break something! If you're going to play, play outside!"

Diana lowered her smile briefly.

"*Kodiak, behave yourself in this home and show some decorum as a man, not some little boy,*" Bogdan shouted to his son in Russian.

"*Sorry, father,*" Kodiak replied, dropping his smile as he looked back at his father with fright.

"*Can't you see that the two of them are having a bit of fun,*" Yuri remarked to Bogdan in Russian. "*Let them be.*"

Diana approached Allodia's side while Kodiak returned to his father's side.

"You know, one day we may just be at their wedding," Allodia said, looking down and over to Diana.

"Allodia!" Diana complained, blushing.

Kodiak blushed too. Tristan looked at them with jealousy. He crossed his arms.

"What?" Allodia questioned. "You'll find love someday too, Diana. Just you wait…"

Tristan's eyes looked behind them as he saw the mysterious figure appear. The room darkened and people froze. He found himself outside next, but not in Allabrese. He looked around and recognized the street he was on by what was across – it was the various fields at the University of Harlech and he was in front of the frat houses. He looked ahead as he saw Diana step down the sidewalk. Tristan's eyes ran over her to see that she was older than in the previous vision and wore a denim jacket with dark black jeans.

Tristan turned as Diana passed him and entered into the frat village as a party went on. He followed her and watched as she went to one of the houses. He then went after her, rushing to keep up. Diana looked around the dark house while some boys looked towards her. He was in the same house where Tristan had met Helene and fought those frat boys.

Diana walked into one of the rooms and then bumped into someone. Tristan squinted at the person through the darkness to see that they had short hair. He then opened his eyes as he recognized the person as himself, wearing a collared shirt and sweater with jeans. This Tristan had a red cup in his hand and a slightly slimmer, less muscular appearance as well as a thinner face. He smiled at Diana as the two met.

"What's your name?!" the other Tristan shouted to Diana. "My name's Tristan!"

"Diana!"

"Can I get you a drink?!" the other Tristan asked.

Diana nodded and then followed this Tristan deeper into the house. Tristan looked on with anxiety. He soon followed where he quickly lost track of them. Tristan looked about and realized there had been a time shift. The music had changed and the party had settled down. He stepped through the door and found himself not in a kitchen, but on a back patio where Diana and himself were on a couch, laughing and smiling together as both were clearly drunk. Diana fixed her hair as the other Tristan whispered something into her ear. She stood up with him and the two began to leave.

Tristan stepped after them and found himself in a room similar in size to the dorm rooms at Residence A and B, but with only a single bed instead of a bunk bed. He looked over to the bed and loosened his unimpressed expression to draw one of awkwardness as he heard the grunts and moans come from the bed. Tristan looked over as he saw himself over Diana, underneath the covers as the two engaged in intercourse. He crossed his arms as he awkwardly watched.

"Alright, you've got me," Tristan muttered as he watched himself. "I'm totally lost…"

The room disappeared in front of him and he found himself in another dorm room. The room was neater and had a single bed ahead. Tristan looked around and then turned behind him as he heard a toilet flush. The bathroom door was open. He stepped aside and looked in to see Diana with a pregnancy test in her hand as she stood before the toilet with a t-shirt on and in her underwear. Diana brought a hand to her face and looked shocked.

Tristan looked with surprise. His surroundings then disappeared and he found himself outside, near Residence A as it rained down. He looked ahead near the entrance into the commonplace and saw a figure in a raincoat rush towards the door where Tristan saw his other-self stand, opening the door. He was with two other boys.

"Tristan!" Diana shouted, reaching him as he was about to go in.

Diana caught up with this Tristan who looked at her unimpressed. He walked towards her while he turned around to the others. They went ahead inside. The other Tristan looked at Diana with minor annoyance.

"What are you doing here?" the other Tristan questioned.

"I've been looking for you," Diana said with a smile. "I have to talk to you…"

"Yeah, I know you've been looking for me," the other Tristan responded.

"Why haven't you responded to my texts?" Diana asked.

The other Tristan didn't respond. She took his hands.

"I have to tell something wonderful," Diana remarked. "I'm pregnant."

"What?" the other Tristan questioned. "Are you serious?"

"Yes!" Diana said with glee. "Isn't this great?"

"No," the other Tristan denied, "it's not. What the hell!"

"What?" Diana questioned, lowering her smile in shock at his reaction.

The other Tristan grabbed Diana by the arm and brought her away from the main path to the hidden side of the commonplace where there were tall shrubs and hedges.

"Listen to me," the other Tristan said to Diana. "You need to chill out and leave me the hell alone, okay? This kind of behavior is not okay, and this kid of yours, is not mine. Even if he were mine, you need to do us both a favor and get rid of it because I am not going to pay for that kid. Got it?"

The other Tristan stepped around Diana and looked back at her.

"Just leave me alone," the other Tristan said before walking off. "For your own good... because next time I see you around me, I'm calling the police."

Diana turned and watched him off. She was left in shock. Tristan watched on. Diana turned her head away and began to cry. Tristan looked back at her with pity as his own eyes began to water. He looked back over to his other-self with a vengeful eye as he left. Tristan shook his head as he looked back to Diana. He tightened a fist at his sides.

"No..." Tristan muttered. "No, that was not me. This isn't me. I would never act like such a tool – I... I wouldn't abandon Diana. She was the most beautiful woman I had ever met, and right from the start when I met her four years ago, I never wanted to be with anyone other than her."

Tristan then looked to the side as he saw Helene walk down the path. He looked at her with surprise, especially as she walked through him. Tristan flinched. He opened his eyes again and saw that he was back in his cave. He looked around and then over to the fire. Tristan stepped back and then went over to sit down, backing up against the cave of the wall and placing his palms on the stone. He then slid down and brought his knees to his chest, hands at the side of his head and tilted down as he cried in a distressful manner.

Act 5, Scene 3

Charlemagne walked into the corridor in the Medici Manor that went to the master bedroom at the end. He pointed his rifle forward and moved up to take cover at a set of double doors beforehand. He took his final package of plastic explosives and prepared them at the hinge of the door, near the doorknob. He quietly placed the package and then moved slightly away, keeping his back against the wall as he took out a detonator and blew the package. The door ripped to shreds and invited a volley of rapid gunfire from the other end that swept into the corridor. Charlemagne remained where he was as the gunfire continued.

"Vieni da me figlio di puttana!" the Duce shouted from the other end.

Charlemagne took his pistol and inched closer to the opening he had created. The gunfire settled. He shot into the room without turning his head. The shatter of glass could be heard. The gunfire continued from within. Charlemagne moved out of the way as shots shred through the wooden walls. He then heard the clack of the submachine gun as bullets ran out. Charlemagne took his rifle and crossed the opening, firing towards the Duce within the room and hitting him in the arm.

"Ah!" the Duce yelled.

Charlemagne stopped at the other side and then walked into the dark room that was the office of the head of the household. He walked forward with his rifle pointed and came around the desk, kicking the Thompson machine gun aside. The Duce sat on the floor, hand extended towards Charlemagne while the other was over the bloodied gash of a bullet. Charlemagne looked at him with a frown.

The Duce was an older man, approximately in his sixties with greyish-white hair and a thick beard. He wore a dress shirt tucked into black pants. He also wore black shoes and suspenders. His hair was cut short and combed to the side in a slight Caesar haircut. Charlemagne squinted at him as the Duce looked at him with a shocked face, moving away from him.

"Dino," Charlemagne said, looking towards him. "You are the leader of the Medici family?"

"Please, do not hurt me…" Dino remarked, hitting the back of a bookcase against the wall. "Take whatever you want, but please, have mercy."

"Dino," Charlemagne replied, "do you recognize me?"

"Yes," Dino responded. "I- I thought you were dead, unless… unless you're a ghost. Are you? I thought that miserable boy had killed you!"

"What boy?" Charlemagne questioned. "I don't understand…" he said before he could answer, shaking his head. "How did you become the head of the household? I thought you were regent until Arturo could become of age. Even then, if he stepped down, Bruno or Mercutio…"

"Do you not remember?" Dino replied, panting. "They're all dead, because of you…"

"Me?" Charlemagne questioned. "What are you talking about?"

"Almost thirty-five years ago, when Allabrese had the problem with the ghosts," Dino explained. "Arturo became obsessed with the memory of his grandfather, Nero, and because of that, he killed his parents, my uncle, Giovanni, and his wife, Bianca. We could not find him until the morning, and when we did, he had killed himself in the basement. A gunshot to the head… guilty, no doubt, about what he had done."

"No…" Charlemagne replied, pausing for a moment. "No, that's not what happened. I remember that night, because I came here to investigate the deaths of Giovanni and Bianca. Giovanni was hiding from the NPD, but he was lured out by his wife when Arturo confronted them. After I looked at the bodies, when I made my escape, I confronted Arturo in the basement and we spoke for a moment... He then took me to you and you let me leave."

"You bastard," Dino remarked. "I have no idea what you're talking about. Arturo died that night too. And then, on Halloween night, the ghost of Nero killed Bruno and Mercutio too... You were there because you went to stop him, but you told us that you were too late to save them."

"No!" Charlemagne barked. "I wasn't too late. I saved all three of them! Arturo nearly died, yes, but he didn't. I saved him..."

"With Giovanni's sons dead, my father in prison, I became the head of the family, but all I could do was mourn the loss in the family... and resent you for not being there to stop Nero earlier..."

"I don't understand," Charlemagne confessed.

Dino stood up and looked over to him.

"What year is it?" Charlemagne asked.

"What year is it?" Dino repeated in question format. "It is 2052."

"And what's happened to our town?" Charlemagne then asked.

"The war happened," Dino responded, picking up a cigar on the table. "The civil war that tore through our town and which nobody won from. Almost two-hundred years of fighting between the Italians and English in this town, and now there is nothing left..."

"And what's happened to Cabernet Industries? My family. Do you know?"

"No," Dino responded. "If the company or your family lives, then they are in Harlech. Only that cosmopolitan city-center and those alike across North America survive. You may also find a village or two, but there is very little behind in this New World, or anywhere else in the world. I do not quite know much about the world beyond, except that it is very decentralized... We've made a return to the Dark Ages..."

Dino hunched over his desk. Tristan eyed the pistol on the table.

"What has happened to my men?" Dino questioned. "Are they dead?"

"I'm afraid so," Charlemagne responded. "I've come looking for my son. Have any of your men captured a young boy with mixed-blonde hair?"

Dino grunted. "So, that boy was yours," he replied. "The little bastard stole from us. He made off with a truck and a bunch of our supplies. We saw the smoke from across Calabrese Plains and I sent my men after them."

"Except they didn't find him, but me," Charlemagne responded. "I need to know where my son is."

"You – you're supposed to be dead," Dino stated. "It was the most fatal news to come to this town since Giovanni, Bianca, and the children died. Everybody talked about it... They all thought that the boy had killed you – police looked for him but could not find him."

Charlemagne didn't respond.

"I've wanted to avenge the children for so long... I know you killed them. I know that when you tried to banish the spirit of Nero, they died in the crossfire."

"I assure you, that was not the case," Charlemagne simply responded, looking as Dino grabbed ahold of the revolver. "Put the gun down."

"You bastard!" Dino shouted, pointing the gun towards Charlemagne.

Charlemagne shot back at him and caused him to fall backwards dead. He looked back at him with frustration and then lowered his rifle to bring his hands to his face. He then stepped away from the desk and stood in the middle of the room, pacing around. Charlemagne took deep breaths and then knelt down, holding his rifle like a cane as he held the barrel of his rifle.

"Forgive me, Father, for the lives I have taken here," Charlemagne muttered, making the sign of the cross, "but help me find my son. Please."

Charlemagne heard a crack of lightning from outside as it continued to rain. He stood up and proceeded to leave the quiet manor where the bodies of Italian men could be seen throughout. He walked down the stairs and exited outside, looking around as another bolt of lightning struck down. He looked to the left and across to see a large buildup of smoke come from across the county. Charlemagne squinted as he could barely see the smoke, so he went forward to step out and look over the smooth farmland. Sure enough, the plumage of dark smoke could be seen extending upwards.

"What the hell...?" Charlemagne muttered. "I told her not to light a fire, besides it's nighttime, she... Oh, Good Lord..."

Charlemagne rushed back into the manor and went into the garage at the left where he knocked down the door and then went to one of the only vehicles parked around. He fetched the keys and then stepped into the black sports car, launching off so as to return to Cabernet Manor where Manon was in trouble.

Act 5, Scene 4

The next day, on the same day that Charlemagne fought with the Medici family, Tristan sat in his cave, lying on the floor on his side as he looked to the fire ahead. He held his arms around his stomach and looked forward with painful eyes. His face was sweaty, eyes bloodshot, and hair amess. His tired eyes looked as if they had not slept. He carried with him a depressive expression of defeat.

Tristan looked over to the cave entrance as he felt a shadow loom over him. He saw the mysterious figure again and then brought his head back down onto the stone floor as he continued to look to the fire.

"Go away," Tristan remarked. "I don't want to see anymore... I have no idea what any of this is supposed do to me except make me hate myself..."

The figure extended a hand towards Tristan. His surroundings began to disappear. He closed his eyes and came into the fetal position, bringing his arms around his face. He then heard the sound of a heart monitor, the desperate cries of a woman, and the sound of a baby crying.

Tristan removed his arms from himself and opened his eyes. He looked ahead and saw that he was in a room at a hospital where there were various people in scrubs with face masks and head covers over their hands, rushing around. He pushed himself off the floor as he saw the medical staff carry a naked child in their arms. Tristan looked at the baby and saw that he was ruddy with dark hair. He looked at the baby with a depressed face, but also one of compassion. His eyes went over to the woman on the hospital bed who gasped for breath.

Diana's hair was wet and her knees raised and spread apart. She looked over and extended a hand towards the child as the medical staff injected the child with various needles. Tristan looked at the child for another moment before he was brought over to Diana and given to her.

"Congratulations," a nurse said. "You've given birth to a beautiful baby boy."

"You should breastfeed him to help your uterus contract," another nurse suggested.

"Okay..." Diana replied, still gasping for breath, "I'll try..."

Diana took the baby into her arms. She looked at him with loving eyes, bringing a hand to his cheek as she lowered her gown to expose a breast and feed him. Diana nursed the child who calmed down as he suckled.

"Oh..." Diana quietly said, looking down at him, "he's... he's beautiful."

"Have you decided on a name?" a nurse asked.

"Yes," Diana replied. "Damian. He's little Damian. My beautiful little boy."

Tristan crossed his arms. He looked ahead suspiciously and stroked his facial hair. His surroundings soon disappeared, and he found himself out of the hospital and back at Diana's apartment, but with the furniture different and moved around. The apartment was clean, except from the toys in a corner that were spread apart. Tristan looked over to the dining table where Diana, significantly older than Tristan could ever have imagined and slightly wider at the hips. She appeared to be in her late twenties. Tristan saw that she was sat at the table with a sunken expression, not crying, but in a similar position as her mother had been less than two decades ago.

Diana was accompanied by a woman with greyish-blonde hair. Her face and hands were wrinkled and she was comforting Diana by holding her hand. Tristan recognized her as Allodia.

"There, there," Allodia expressed. "It's going to be alright. You're going to get through this…"

"I can't even imagine why this has to happen to me…" Diana remarked, wiping her eyes with a tissue. "There must have been a mistake in the tests. How could I have been diagnosed with Hepatitis C?"

"Is the doctor sure?"

"Yes," Diana replied. "He said that he would never offer such a serious diagnosis without certainty. He told me to come into the hospital tomorrow for a biopsy… If this gets worse, I fear what could happen to Damian. Could you do me the favor and look after him tomorrow while I go to St. Luke's?"

"Of course," Allodia responded. "I'd be happy to."

"I have to also get into contact with a lawyer to set up a will in case something happens to me now. I have to make sure the Ministry doesn't take Damian."

"If you want to leave him with me, Yuri and I would be more than happy to take him in," Allodia offered. "It's the least I can do to make up for how Charlemagne has been in the last couple of years…"

Diana sighed. "It's not his fault…" she responded. "He's had it tough, but he'll get through his adversity as I will hopefully get through mine. What I have to hope for is to get better… which reminds me that I'll have to probably stepdown from Paladin because of my condition. I don't know what I'll do for money then…"

"Hey, I told you not to worry," Allodia said. "We'll look after both you and Damian. Shame on his father for not pitching in… He's a doctor, isn't he? You should have claimed child support from him."

"No," Diana quietly rejected. "He told me to leave him alone, so that's what I'm going to do. He doesn't want anything to do with this kid, and from what I've heard, he's married now. I don't want to upset the wife he has to know about the kid he left behind."

Allodia looked back at her without assurance.

"Okay," Allodia admitted, tapping Diana's hand. "You do what you have to do, but we're going to look after you. You're a part of the family, even if Charles has fallen from his sanity, both myself, Yuri, and I'm sure even Salmar are here for you."

"Thank you, Allodia," Diana quietly said, standing up. "Thank you for coming over – I won't keep you any longer. I'm going to check on Damian and then go to bed."

Tristan looked over to the bedroom door as he heard it quietly shut. He walked over and passed through the door to enter into the bedroom, which had been altered alongside the rest of the house. There were two beds in the room, one on either side of the far wall with a window between them and a dresser. The boy rushed back to his bed and quickly got into the covers. Tristan squinted at him, but he could barely see the boy he had seen not too long ago as a baby, now an older child at least eight-years old. He stood where he was until the door opened behind him and light poured in.

Diana walked over to their son and turned on a lamp on the dresser. She then sat down at the side of the boy's bed, stroking the top of his dark brown wavy hair. Tristan walked in closer to get a better look of the boy, but could only see the back of his head.

The room darkened and Tristan was taken to another room, a hospital room again. He turned to his left as he looked over to a stretcher where Diana was sat in the bed, older than the last vision, but still young. She wore a hospital gown and was slightly raised. Her finger was clipped to an oximeter and her skin held an unnatural slight jaundice-shade of yellow.

Tristan saw a binder at the end of the bed and tried to pick it up, but he couldn't because of his lack of physical properties in this vision. He then looked back over to Diana and came around the side of the bed. Tristan looked at her with sadness.

"What's happened to you, Diana?" Tristan whispered, trying to touch her cheek.

Tristan turned to the other side of the room as he heard a rip of paper. There, in a chair, using a coffee table as a desk was little Damian, slightly older – a teenager now, with the same unkempt dark hair. The boy wore a sweater with a collared shirt as well as jeans. Behind him on the chair was a canvas jacket. Tristan saw that the boy was attempting to do some homework. He walked over to him and crouched down at the other end of the coffee table.

Damian looked like his mother, which in turn gave him an appearance slightly like Willis, but at the same time, nothing like him. His facial features were an amalgamation of his ancestors from both sides of the family, but at heart, he was like Diana except in the eyes. The eyes were jade-colored and his father's. Tristan looked up towards him as Damian's focused eyes looked to the paper before him. Tristan's own eyes began to water as he saw the boy before him. Damian grunted as he tore out another piece of paper and threw it into a garbage bin across the room, missing and hitting the side.

"What is it?" Diana questioned.

"I don't get it…" Damian responded in a deep voice similar to his father's. "I hate this…"

"Don't be like that," Diana scolded him. "You're smarter than that to be full of such low self-esteem. You can do it…"

Tristan walked around and crouched down next to the boy as he looked at what he was doing. He was doing some simple algebra. Tristan sighed and appeared resentful.

"This is stupid…!" Damian shouted.

"Damian, keep your voice down!" Diana warned. "Otherwise, the nurses will kick you out. Do you want that?"

"I don't know why I should even be studying anymore. We're broke and now that Cabernet Industries went broke too, there's no way Allodia will continue to support us."

"Don't talk about your aunt like that," Diana warned him. "They have never abandoned us, and I see no reason for them to throw us under the bus. We're a family and we'll pull through…"

"I want to get a job or something – do anything to help out. I feel helpless…!" Damian complained, looking to his mother.

"No," Diana rejected. "You have to focus on your studies. You're not going to get into medical school if you don't put the effort into keeping your marks up. You're a smart kid, you can do this…"

Damian crossed his arms and held a frustrated expression.

"Who else is going to cure me?" Diana questioned with a smile.

Damian dropped his frustration.

"Sorry…" Damian muttered.

"Now come and give me a hug…" Diana said to him.

Damian stood up and went to hug his mother. He wrapped his arms around her and hugged her tightly. Tristan watched from the other side of the room, the mother-son bond that Damian and Diana had. Tristan's eyes watered. Damian held a warm smile, which soon turned to anguish. Diana moved away from him and looked back at him.

"What is it?" Diana asked.

"Are you going to die?" Damian questioned.

"No," Diana replied. "No, of course not. If Uncle Charles could beat cancer, then certainly I can too. You just have to have a little faith, Damian. I'm not going to leave my little star all alone, and the thought of that empowers me every day to fight back… at least until my little boy can help his mama out."

Damian wiped his tears. His body shook. He hugged his mother again. Diana looked back across the room where Tristan saw that she had a look of uncertainty in her own face. Tristan took a deep breath, especially as the room darkened and he found himself outside.

Tristan looked around and saw that he was back in Keswick. He looked around and saw that the skies were a deep brownish-grey and the streets were as filthy as before. He was at Mackenzie Street again, which naturally led him to look over to as an alarm sounded and a figure rushed out from the liquor store with a sack in his hand and pistol in the other. Tristan watched the robber run off and down the street. He looked over suspiciously and then began to run after him, keeping up from a distance and going around the block.

Finally, the robber came to an alleyway at Bennett Street, next to Diana's apartment. He climbed up onto a dumpster and then up the fire escape to come to the top. Tristan looked up and then found himself transported into the bedroom, which was about the same as it was earlier. He looked over to the boy and saw him spill the money out from the bag before removing the balaclava around his face.

Damian's hair had grown longer, but dropped its wavy expression. The boy was older than the last vision by at least two years. He was about as slim as Tristan in this world and as tall as Tristan now. His clothes were torn and rundown. He counted the money before him before hiding some in a loose floorboard where he also hid the gun and balaclava. He then removed his clothes, the denim jacket and jeans mostly, hiding them in a laundry basket as sirens could be heard outside and then walking out in his underpants and undershirt. Tristan looked out the window to see the HPD cruiser pass the front of the apartment and drive off. Damian looked out the window from the living room and then returned to the bedroom to sit down, bringing his hands to his face in a distressed manner.

Tristan looked back and recognized this distress. He stepped towards the boy and saw that he had begun to cry. He stretched a hand over to the boy's shoulder in an effort to comfort him, but his hand ran right through him. His environment also began to disappear. Tristan found himself outside again, but on a brighter, grey day.

Tristan looked across from where he was and recognized the iron archway at the end of a cul-de-sac ahead. He then looked around him and saw the tombstones. Tristan's hands shook, especially as he saw the procession where various people were gathered around a coffin as it was taken through St. Allan's Cemetery.

"No..." Tristan muttered, rushing over.

Damian stood at the back of the procession, dressed in a black suit with dark hair cut short. He was as tall and skinny as Tristan saw him in the bedroom, but a bit of time had passed for him to get a haircut. The boy looked ahead and then turned around, wiping his eyes as tears fell down them, and then holding his hands in fists. Damian appeared before Tristan differently than he had seen him before. His face was thinner and cheeks more round and defined. He was a handsome boy with fine eyebrows. Damian walked off from the cemetery.

Tristan watched him off before looking back over to the procession. He attempted to follow it, but his surroundings vanished again and he found himself in a dark basement – it was the basement at Cabernet Manor, just like Tristan had seen it when he first came to this future, except there were more items around and it was not rundown. Tristan looked around and over to a man hunched over the desk at the end of the room from the elevator shaft.

The man at the table wore a cloak with a hood over his face. His arms were stretched out at the sides, but one of his arms had a robotic appearance. Tristan stepped forward and saw that this arm was an advanced prosthetic. He looked back at the hooded man suspiciously. He then turned around and looked over to see Damian as he arrived, dressed in his suit as though he had just come from the cemetery, looking over to the hooded man with a deep frown.

"You missed the funeral," Damian said to the man in an annoyed tone.

"What would have been the point?" the man quietly questioned in his English accent. "She's already dead."

"No thanks to you," Damian scowled.

The man turned to face the boy. Tristan saw that the man was of course, Charlemagne, significantly older than he currently was with a wrinkled face and white hair.

"If you want to blame me for Diana's development of hepatitis C because of her dependence on opioids, and then her regression into liver cancer, then go ahead if that'll make you feel better. The truth is, I had nothing to do with her fate. Ever since Diana left my care, she has been independent to do what she wanted with her life, because that is the sort of independent woman she was. My responsibility with her stretched from when I adopted her twenty-five years ago to when she turned of age."

"You should have done more for her..." Damian replied. "You should have been there for her when my jackass of a father left her with me, pregnant. You should have been there for her when I was born so that she didn't turn to drugs! Instead, you had to sulk about your own dead son... You're pitiful. You're no different than my own father... I hate you!"

"I'm sorry this is what you think," Charlemagne simply said with resignation.

Damian clenched two fists into his hand.

"How can you be so indifferent about everything else, while be so emotional about something that happened years ago?!" Damian shouted. "My life has sucked, but you don't see me mope about it! I've had to fend for my life out on the streets so that the city doesn't close in on our apartment! I've had to go my entire life without a father and surviving only on the support of my mom and Allodia! And worse of all, I'm a useless faggot with nothing to live for anymore... I have nothing anymore!"

Charlemagne didn't respond.

"Say something!" Damian yelled, walking over to him. "For God's sake, say something! Do something! You mute, immoveable bastard!"

Damian pushed Charlemagne forward and against his desk. Charlemagne attempted to stand up and turn to Damian, but Damian pushed him again. He then brought his hands over to Charlemagne and proceeded to strangle him. Tristan looked on with horror.

"Stop!" Tristan shouted. "Damian, stop! Please, stop!"

Damian continued as Charlemagne attempted to fight back. Tristan heard the snap of a bone and then Charlemagne's body become lifeless as his arms fell to the side. Damian unclenched his hands from Charlemagne's neck, panting and shaking. He looked at his hands. Tristan looked back at him in horror. Charlemagne's body fell to the floor, eyes wide open. Damian stepped back with his fingers scrunched up and arms frozen.

"Oh my God..." Damian remarked in a distressed tone. "What have I done...?"

Tristan looked at Damian and then saw that his surroundings began to disappear.

"No!" Tristan protested, rushing forward as he was held back. "No, let me see him! Let me help him! Please, I want to help him!"

Tristan attempted to fight the void, but instead of a new scene, he found himself in this exact void with nothing around him. He looked about and then saw the cloaked figure ahead.

"Who are you?!" Tristan questioned. "What was all of this?! Tell me! Please, this wasn't the past or future – what was this?! Was this supposed to scare me to be a good father? Was this supposed to warn me about what could happen to my son if I don't smarten up?! Please, tell me! I won't abandon him! I want to have this kid and be a good father for him – I always have, so please, tell me what this was about!"

Tristan stood before the tall man. He lowered his hood and then stretched a hand out towards Tristan's forehead. Tristan simply watched as the mysterious man placed his cold hand on Tristan's forehead. Tristan's vision began to fade as his eyes rolled back and his body lost control of his muscles. Tristan also heard a sudden, angelic sound of a sort of high-pitched whistle followed by a demonic screech similar to the sound made when his father defeated a psionic soldier, but less exacerbated.

Tristan's vision returned as he looked forward to see the cloaked figure disappear like a shadowy wind. A bright, clear bluish light stood between Tristan and the cloaked figure as he disappeared. Tristan looked back and felt a gentle wind cross over him. He closed his eyes and then opened them to see that he was back in his cave as if nothing had happened.

Act 5, Scene 5

Charlemagne drove from Medici Manor back to the freeway where he drove as fast as he could to return to Cabernet Manor. He passed through Champion Plains, went through downtown Allabrese, and then went through St. Allan's Plains to reach the Nattau River. The rain had worsened as he drove through, hindering his visibility slightly. The smoke that came from Cabernet Manor was more definitive as he went down the hill from the plateau. The lights were also on from the library and north wing. Charlemagne drove across the bridge and then went around the roundabout to come down to the cliffside and then up through the broken gates of the manor to stop where another pickup truck had parked. Charlemagne exited the vehicle and took his assault rifle up the steps to reach the foyer.

Manon sat in a chair near the fire, mouth tied by rope, legs and torso wrapped together with her arms behind her.

"Manon!" Charlemagne remarked, rushing towards her and removing the rope from her mouth. "Manon, are you okay?"

"Run, *Charles*! Run, he's going to kill you! Run!"

"What?" Charlemagne questioned.

Charlemagne ducked down as he heard gunshots fly over him. He quickly scrambled away and took cover in the corridor that went to the library. Charlemagne peaked from around the corner as he looked over to see Finn at the second floor with a rifle pointed forward.

"Finn! What are you doing, lad?!" Charlemagne questioned. "Have you gone absolutely mental?"

"I knew that my plan was contingent on you turning up, but here we are. Show yourself, you coward!" Finn shouted back. "Quit hiding from me like you've done for so long!"

"I never hid from you!" Charlemagne remarked. "The instance I knew of your existence, I did nothing more than to look for you! If I could change back time… I certainly would have to be with you!"

"I'll kill you, you pig!" Finn yelled in return.

Finn shot towards Charlemagne. Charlemagne stayed in cover.

"This is your last warning, Finn!" Charlemagne shouted. "You're playing a dangerous game, but to put our lives in danger is not acceptable!"

"Fight me!" Finn challenged, continuing to fire at him. "Spill my blood! Do what you should have done years ago! I demand it!"

Charlemagne poked his head out of cover as Finn's gun clicked. He shot back towards him, avoiding the torso and head in hopes of disarming him. Finn ducked out and went into the north wing.

"*Charles*, please, be careful," Manon cried. "He's insane!"

"Don't worry," Charlemagne remarked. "I'll take care of it…"

Charlemagne moved out of cover as Finn disappeared from his line of sight. He went past Manon and went around the fire to reach the stairs that went up to the north wing.

"Finn, stand down your weapon," Charlemagne requested. "You don't have to do this, my dear boy. Your mother and father have always loved you…"

"Liars!" Finn shouted, turning the corner and opening fire.

Charlemagne ducked and shot back towards him as he hid by the steps. Finn retreated. Charlemagne moved in and took cover against the wall. He shot towards Finn inside.

"I'll admit it again, I should have never have left your mother, but you must understand that I had no idea of your existence and neither did she. What would you have rather have had been? Raised in a single-parent household or given the chance to be with two-loving parents?"

"The Cunninghams hated me!" Finn yelled back.

Charlemagne moved in and took cover by the corner to the corridor that went to Diana's bedroom.

"As fate had it, you were placed in a miserable family – that was simply the luck of the draw, but it would have been no better than if you were raised alone by her. She did what she thought was best for you… Sometimes, there isn't an easy choice in any of these matters. What matters is, by the Grace of God, we've been able to come together again."

Finn shot towards Charlemagne from the end of the corridor. He stayed in cover and reloaded his own rifle. He then breathed carefully.

"Please, come out, my dear boy," Charlemagne petitioned. "I don't want to fight you like this – Please, give us a second chance…"

"None of this matters!" Finn cried out. "I'm done pretending like there is a point anymore! If I can't change the past, then I'll change the future!"

Charlemagne sighed. He came out from around the corner and shot towards Finn, making his way to the bedroom door that went into Tristan's bedroom. He took cover behind the doorway and waited as Finn emptied his magazine. Finn slowed down and stopped firing as Charlemagne disappeared. Charlemagne peaked around the corner and then quickly hid as Finn continued to fire

"Finn, you don't want to run heads up with me!" Charlemagne warned. "I'm not as worn out as you think I may be. I've been through worse, fought worse!"

"If you think you can bring me down, then try it, old man!"

Charlemagne sighed. He heard the click of Finn's rifle. He then came out from around the corner and moved in closer, taking cover in the caved in room. Charlemagne looked in and noticed that there was small crawlspace through the rubble. He moved out of the way as Finn shot towards him and knelt down. He looked ahead, but then remembered that the other door into the bathroom had been built over. Charlemagne quickly turned around as Finn attempted to come behind him.

Finn held his ground as Charlemagne attempted to get his hands off the rifle. He pushed his son towards the glass window and the two fell out and came onto the patio below. Finn quickly stood up and went to grab his rifle. Charlemagne took a pistol out from his vest and shot towards Finn, but he disappeared into the trophy room. He stood up and went after him. Finn escaped into the ballroom where chandeliers littered the floor and tables had been turned over.

Charlemagne shot towards Finn from the door. Finn took cover. A bit of blood dripped from Charlemagne's face as he had cut himself when they smashed through the glass. He wiped the blood off before he turned to shoot back towards Finn. Finn was pinned down. Charlemagne stopped firing and began to move in. Finn stood up and shot at his father, hitting him in the arm as he quickly rushed to take cover by a table nearby. He stood up and shot back at his son who made his escape out and into the kitchen. Charlemagne stayed where he was for a moment to look at the gash on his arm. He then stood up and went after Finn.

Finn took cover in the corridor towards the dinette. Charlemagne stayed in cover as Finn shot towards him.

"You can't outsmart me, my boy," Charlemagne warned. "This is my home. I know every secret to it and I know the rooms and walls better than you do."

"I'll outmaneuver and outspeed you," Finn remarked. "Let's see how much you can move for a sixty-year old bastard!"

Charlemagne came out from around the corner and shot towards Finn. Finn inched out of the way as the shots blew over him. He then fled and disappeared. Charlemagne watched and then ducked around to return to the trophy room. He then went down the corridor as Finn was about to come around to flank him. Charlemagne shot towards him. Finn quickly jumped out of the way and into the sitting room. He then shot back to him as Charlemagne took cover. Charlemagne reloaded and then took deep breaths.

"I told you, you can't outsmart me! This could have been your home too, you know. If you hadn't decided to play these stupid games with me! You can blame Aidan Cunningham all you want, but you will not take this rage against myself and your mother!"

"How valiant!" Finn mocked. "Where was this nobility when you abandoned her for that other woman?!"

"That other woman is dead, Finn! Even then, my heart has always been for your mother. If only you knew...!" Charlemagne yelled, "... just how much she meant to me!"

"Shut up!" Finn shouted. "Stop lying to me! You cannot make any of this any better!"

Charlemagne took his pistol and shot back blind shots towards Finn. Finn stopped firing. He spent an entire magazine and then ducked through to return to the patio. Charlemagne went to the door that went into the ground floor bathroom and then went through to come up towards Finn from behind.

Finn turned around just as he was behind him. Charlemagne picked up the barrel of the rifle as it shot into the ceiling. The two struggled with the rifle until Finn let go with one hand and punched his father across the face. Finn regained control of the rifle and aimed down at Charlemagne. He pressed the trigger, but the gun clicked. Charlemagne then stood up, but Finn hit him across the face with the butt of the gun before making his escape. Finn exited through the trophy room and went back to the patio.

Charlemagne followed him and looked over as he went to the study. Finn shot towards him from across the patio. Charlemagne took cover and checked his weapon and ammo before he moved over to a window to shoot back through it. Finn ducked down. He then crawled into prone and shot towards Charlemagne. Charlemagne backed off and reloaded his rifle. He then moved back over to the French window to wait for Finn to be out. Charlemagne quickly rushed to the other side of the French window and went down the corridor to return to the foyer, rushing down past Manon to come to the library.

Finn shot at Charlemagne from atop of the second floor of the library.

"You see this? You stuttered, and now I've got the high-ground!" Finn remarked.

"Finn, enough!" Charlemagne warned. "This isn't a game!"

"I thought it was!" Finn replied, continuing to fire at him.

Charlemagne snuck out of the way as his son continued to fire. He then came around and went upstairs, entering the corridor and stopping as a door was slammed shut towards the master bedroom. Charlemagne took cover beside the door and stopped as bullets flew through the wood. Once the gunshots stopped, Charlemagne kicked down the door and looked over as Finn stood at the direct end from the door, out of cover. He quickly stood up and rushed into cover. Charlemagne shot towards him and hit him in the knee. Finn staggered down, allowing Charlemagne to come in. Charlemagne aimed his rifle at him.

"Stand down!" Charlemagne warned.

Finn tackled him and hit him onto the wall. The two struggled against each other. Charlemagne pushed him back onto the other wall in the short corridor to the rest of the room. Finn hit his father in the face with the butt of his rifle again. He then fled out while Charlemagne raised his rifle and went after him. Finn quickly hit him in the head again as they came to main foyer.

Charlemagne fell down, but then quickly stood up as he grabbed Finn's rifle, pushing himself against it. The two pivoted and changed spots. Finn pushed his father back, overpowering him as they went down the platform. Charlemagne exerted a burst of energy and managed to pivot each other again. Finn then pushed back and then the two fell over the railing and onto the floor below. The rifle fell before Manon. Charlemagne struggled to stand while Finn quickly recovered and began to crawl for the rifle.

Finn swooped the rifle up. Manon attempted to kick at him, but she missed. He then turned around and looked over to his father as he got his sidearm out and pivoted over so that he was on his side with the gun pointed towards him. Finn shot Charlemagne in the shoulder, causing him to drop the gun. Charlemagne clenched the wound on his shoulder. Finn then went in and put a foot down atop of Charlemagne as he aimed down towards him.

"I told you," Finn grunted. "I told you that I could beat you! Now, you get what you deserve!"

"Finn, please!" Charlemagne pled. "Please, just listen for a moment – Diana and Tristan…"

"What?" Finn questioned.

"Diana and Tristan, they're here… in this world too, looking for you… If you don't listen, then all of you will be stuck here and you need to... you need to rescue them because they're separated."

Finn looked at him, confused.

"It... It doesn't matter if you want to kill me or not," Charlemagne remarked, "but please, don't punish them. They're... they're my children too, don't you understand? I've loved them with the love I wish I could have loved you – not that I would not stop loving them if I had to love you too."

"Tell me about them! Where are they?!" Finn questioned.

"I... I have no idea, but... I'm going to die, Finn. I- I have stage four stomach and skin cancer – a malignant spread melanoma in the hands," Charlemagne said, removing his gloves to show them to Finn, "which has spread to the rest of the body, but metastasized in my stomach. I won't live to the end of the year..."

"Shut up and tell me about Diana and Tristan!" Finn remarked.

"They came looking for you after I told them to stay back," Charlemagne explained, "but then... Diana became upset with me and she took... she took one of the orbs, the crystals that I apparently need to go back home. The dark one – the space crystals responsible for teleportation. She took them and somehow... she activated it and I don't where they could have gone, but... her words when the orb activated were that she wanted to go 'home,' and home to her is in Harlech. You have to go and rescue them in Harlech to retrieve the space orb and..."

Charlemagne reached into his jacket to take out the time orb. Finn took it off him.

"And use this to reach home. Diana... she seems more than capable. She will be able to return you to your time, but please... rescue them. I- I've been looking for you for the past two weeks to pass this on to you, because... I feared I wouldn't live to be able to do it myself – not that this was my only reason to find you, Finn. I'm sorry."

Finn looked down at him.

"I'm sorry not only to you, but to your mother, for abandoning the two of you. I was a naïve fool whose lust had taken the better of him, and… this is the punishment that I deserve for my wickedness. In the least, I was able to redeem myself through Diana and Tristan – they've both grown up and are to become parents soon."

Finn looked surprised.

"My work is done…"

Finn dropped some tears as he heard these words.

"You…" Finn said, stuttering as he chocked, "you love them, don't you… You really do love them."

Charlemagne didn't respond.

"My one regret is that I wasn't able to love you in the same way," Charlemagne expressed, "together, all of us, Manon – your mother, included."

Finn sniffled and wiped his eyes with the back of his fist.

"One big and happy family, eh?" Finn questioned, looking up. "All I ever wanted was that…"

Charlemagne didn't reply. Instead, he continued to lay down pressure on his shoulder as he looked up to the ceiling. Charlemagne's ability to lay down pressure soon waned and he was forced to let go. His arm fell over and he began to bleed out. Finn lowered his rifle and knelt down to apply pressure on the wound. Charlemagne looked at him as tears continued to stroll down Finn's eyes.

"I don't want you to die…" Finn acknowledged. "I'm sorry…"

"You're going to need to get this tourniquet on my arm," Charlemagne said, removing a tourniquet from his belt and bringing it onto his chest. "You'll want to wrap it around my upper arm and tighten it to stop the bleeding. Then, get your mother out from that chair and take us down to the basement so that I can patch myself up."

Finn took the tourniquet and applied as if he knew how to use one already. He then helped Charlemagne up before going over to loosen his mother from her ties. Afterwards, Finn stood Charlemagne onto his feet and took him over to the library so they could get out of the rain and Charlemagne could bandage himself before he bled out.

Act 6, Scene 1

Tristan fell backwards as he returned from the most recent vision in which Damian had killed Charlemagne. He crawled backwards and hit against the wall of the cave. Tristan's eyes were wide open, face covered in sweat and breathing rapidly. He gritted his teeth and brought his hands onto the side of his face as he growled in distress. He then brought his hands through his hair as he began to cry. Tristan finally slowly stood up and rushed out of the cave, past the horse, and into the darkness of the forest where there was a minor fog on the floor and it was raining.

From the cave, Tristan rushed through the forest and came out on the other side, on approach towards the cabin where the lights had been turned off. He quickly ran towards the cabin, but slipped in some mud and fell over, landing on his back. Tristan slammed a fist in the mud and then sat up, attempting to stand, but instead falling over again. Tristan slammed another two fists in the mud before he began to continue crying.

"Why me?" Tristan questioned, falling over in defeat. "After all that's happened to me, and now this? I thought – I thought that I'd finally be happy when Diana and I came together again, but I'm going to screw it up...? I'm going to screw the life of that kid up? I'm going to screw up the life of Diana? All because I can't get my act together? What kind of person am I? I'm... I'm pure evil."

"An evil person doesn't attempt to redeem himself," a feminine voice said from behind in a North German accent.

Tristan sat up and looked over into the forest. There, he saw Helene approach him from the forest. She was dressed in a white dress and had a white glow around her. She was translucent. Tristan crawled away from her as she approached.

"If you truly were evil, you wouldn't be so determined to make things right," Helene said. "You have the heart of a proud man though. You don't know when to stop and admit that you are one man, and that you cannot do all of this on your own."

"What are you doing here? Am I now going to hallucinate the dead?" Tristan questioned.

"Is it so farfetched to believe that the dead can rise again?" Helene asked. "When Christ returns to Earth, you can guarantee that I will be there…"

"Don't bother me with that nonsense," Tristan replied. "You know I'm an atheist. You know I don't give a damn about that mystic crap."

Helene frowned. "And that is your problem," she remarked. "You place all of the burdens of the world on your shoulders, but you are not a god. Man can never be like god because man is incapable of even being remotely like Him. There has only ever been one man to walk on this Earth and be a perfect being, and that was Christ. You doubt me even though I am in the afterlife? In Heaven?"

"You're not real," Tristan denied. "You're not real!"

"You continue to make errors," Helene said. "You made an error when you lusted over me. You make an error when you deny His existence. You will keep making errors until you vow to change your ways and be better. Look at you, in that mud, thinking you'd run to Diana and she'd change her mind about you, but you think because you had some visions of an alternate reality that you're suddenly different? No."

Tristan didn't respond.

"When we spoke on that field behind the dorms, I asked you if you thought you were a good person, and I can now say from what I have seen from you, that you are not a good person. You are simply a person. Everybody sins. However, what separated the 'bad' from the 'good' are those that are humble enough to admit that they are a sinner and attempt to change their ways. When Christ died, he blessed upon us, all of humanity, the gift of redemption and in doing so conquered evil. Him, the almighty all-loving and all-understanding God knew that humanity would be doomed to continue to sin and sin, but he gave us the means by which we can attempt to change and do better, knowing we'd fail, but willing to take on our hearts and give us the chance anyways. Before Christ, this absolution of sin did not exist. In my short life, I had never met a person that was as loving than Iustina to share knowledge of this gift with me and teach me for better. Humans are a proud species, and it was their proud society that led to their collapse in this world, and they thought themselves as gods when they could not even bestow to each other such a simple concept known as forgiveness."

Helene shook her head.

"Until you change, you cannot and should not return to Diana. She does not need a boy in her life. In a couple weeks, she will give birth to a boy – your son, but she does not need two boys in her life at this time. She needs a man. It takes a great man to be able to bend his knee down to something that is mightier than him and admit his wrongs, but also to pledge that he will do better. Diana's patience has been tried with you. You will not win her over until you become this man that she needs – a hero striving to become a saint. You placed yourself before her as a hero once when you made the sacrifice of your life. I'm afraid, this is all that there is towards it. Manhood takes a great strength of silent sacrifice for those that you love – it is this that makes you a hero, and this attitude that makes sainthood inevitable."

"A saint?"

"All those in Heaven are known as saints. If you intend to marry with Diana, you make a commitment of unity not only to raise this child and have more, but to walk with her towards sainthood together. Diana has been tolerant of your godlessness, or perhaps she does not know as I knew…"

Tristan did not respond.

"At any rate, like Christ who gave up his own life so that we could receive forgiveness and enter into Heaven as saints, you too must make the sacrifices that are necessary. You have shown effort, especially in the past days as you attempt to stab this demon of yours, your addiction, in the heart, but it is time to continue with those efforts and continue to act."

"What more can I do?" Tristan pled.

"Foremost, you must reject yourself as a deity and accept Christ as your Savior. Then, you must confess your sins to Him, admit your faults, and accept your punishment. When you have been able to save yourself, your soul, then you will be able to save others… When you have learned what it takes to be a man, then Diana may just accept you again and you will not doom this child…"

Helene then disappeared. Tristan raised a hand towards her.

"Wait!" Tristan shouted.

Tristan looked over to where Helene had stood and then lowered his hand into the mud. He looked down and stayed seated where he was. Finally, he placed a hand in the mud and laid down, crossing his arms as he continued to cry and refused to stand.

Act 6, Scene 2

The next morning, Tristan awoke in the pile of mud that he had fallen asleep. He slowly picked himself up and saw that his clothes were completely dirty. He then looked over to the cabin as he saw a bit of steam or smoke rise from the chimney. Tristan picked himself up to look over to the cabin before he slowly took some steps back and then retreated into the forest. He went down the road and came to a river near the cave where he bathed and attempted to clean the grime off his clothes, letting it dry nearby.

Tristan's stomach grumbled as he returned from the cold water of the river in the late noon. The clouds above were grey, but it was not raining although humid. His clothes had not dried, so he put on his underpants and then walked back into the forest with the wet clothes. Tempest remained where Tristan had left her, grazing the nearby grass. By the time Tristan had returned, a rain had begun to set in. The crackle of thunder could be heard from afar. He entered into the cave and walked over to a chest, opening it and taking out a bag with the silver coins that Tristan had amassed. Of Tristan's belongings, he only had this wooden chest, the sword, and a newly crafted metal shield that laid against the cave wall nearby. The shield was heralded by a depiction of a rampant lion with its paws raised. Tristan picked up a shirt from underneath at the bottom of the chest – the long-sleeved wool undershirt that he wore underneath the chainmail padding. He set the clothes aside for a moment. His pants and boots were still stained, but he didn't have a change of pants with him as this was all the clothing he had. Tristan put the bag of coins back into the small rectangular chest and then sat atop of it as he picked up his sword on the floor and placed a piece of flint near the firepit. Tristan's stomach grumbled again.

Tristan attempted to strike some sparks to ignite himself a fire, but as he brought his sword down onto the flint, he kept missing and hitting the stone floor. A tear dropped from Tristan's eyes as he continued to fail until finally he threw his sword against the cave wall and kicked the ashes of the fire pit, scattering them around. Tristan then went over and picked up his shield, tossing it over and hitting the cave wall as well. He then went to the chest, kicking it hard until it tipped over, contents opening and the silver coins spilling out. Tristan then picked up the chest and threw it against the wall as well before he fell down to his knees to cry.

"I- I can't do this anymore," Tristan muttered. "I can't do it. I can't do it. I can't do it," he repeated, bringing his palms onto the stone floor. "All the life that has been given to me, for what? I'm defective. I can't do anything right. I've failed Diana and our son."

Tristan picked up his sword from the ground and came up onto his knees, bringing the blade to his stomach as he stretched back. He breathed slowly with both hands at the grip. The tip of the sword touched against the skin of his abdomen. Tristan then closed his eyes as he charged his strength and pulled the sword back as though to stab himself through the abdomen.

"Is this your solution to your problems?" a deep voice spoke to him in a South German accent.

Tristan opened his eyes and looked over to the entrance of the cave. A flash of lightning hid his sights on the person that stood there. Tristan squinted and then his eyes opened as he realized that it was his father.

Maxim stood at the entrance of the cave, similar in appearance to how Tristan had seen and known him a year and a half ago, except he wore a white tunic, grey pants, and boots. His light strawberry-blonde hair was cut short and he was clean-shaven. Maxim stepped into the cave with his hands behind his back, head held up, and with a serious face.

"What are you doing here?" Tristan questioned.

"Is that anyway to say 'Hello' to your father?" Maxim replied, slightly offended.

"You didn't have the balls to tell me that you were my dad when you were alive," Tristan responded. "I have every shred of faith that you, like Helene before, are not real, but a symptom of me going mad without alcohol. Go away."

"I didn't know that I was your father then," Maxim said. "How could I when your mother thought I was dead?"

Tristan didn't respond. He kept his eyes pointed forward with the spirit of Maxim in the corner of his eye. His hands were on the floor before him, hunched over with one of the hands over his sword.

"I'm sorry I was never there for you, Tristan," Maxim apologized. "I know that this was the same regret that your mother held, but I believe, and in my post-mortem, support, the decision that she made to place you in the home of your aunt and uncle. What you do not realize, in your lust for the ideal, is that you would have ultimately suffered more had you been with your mother, alone, raised in that convent. The reality is that you cannot always have what you want sometimes, and sometimes what you want is nothing more than an unrealistic ideal. Look at the childhood that you were able to have because she made the sacrifice to part with you. You were able to live a normal childhood, make friends and go to school – do you know what other children would give for that? Although it was tragic what had happened to your aunt and uncle, Charlemagne did his best to provide to you what he could hope to offer."

"Ever since I walked into that house of his, I've… I've done nothing but suffer…" Tristan said with a broken voice.

"Your suffering was an inevitability – not Charlemagne's fault. Do you not understand that yet, Tristan? Your mother created you by artificial means with the best genetics from both of our ancestral lines. Your mind, your body – you were given the best, and with that, you were given a superior consciousness that has made the confrontation of reality a dreadful burden. You suffer this fate of yours because you have a good heart that wishes good for others, but is struck back by the evil that you see. You understand that this modern world is a dreadful place…" Maxim explained walking over to stand before Tristan, "and with that, with your mind and body, comes the ability to change the world, but you cannot do that on your own."

"I don't want to change the world – I just want to be normal," Tristan complained.

"Do not be so grandiose or complex," Maxim replied, squatting down. "A change in the world does not merely mean a revolution. We can all make a change, little and large, and as men, especially as a man like you, you have the resolve to be what this world lacks most of all: a hero that fights evil. A hero in the home as a father, or a hero in the fields as a soldier. Do you still not understand? You understand that there is evil in this world, yes? So, now it is time to confront that evil rather than wallow in self-pity as the Devil wants you to. What did you see in those visions, but the product of malice? Only by the heroic virtue of Charlemagne to adopt Diana, to the sacrifices of Allodia to later support Diana and her son was there any good. Imagine if there were others to intervene, such as a boy like you."

"I've already tried to do good in this world once," Tristan stated. "I tried to save those kids from those pedophiles, but it did nothing."

"You still saved those children, and also helped in the reconstruction of their village. Even then, a hero does not give up in his quest simply because an obstacle presents itself," Maxim replied. "A feat like the dismantling of the greater evil that lurks in the shadow of the entire world would take more than a raid on an island mansion. You must continue to stand up every time you are thrown to the floor with the same determination in your heart," he said, bringing a fist to his chest, "and the same resolve – this is what terrifies the Devil the most: determination. And as a son of God," he continued to explain, standing up and walking aside with his hand behind his back, "you are called to confront this evil, but not alone. God has not abandoned you, Tristan, even if you have failed to recognize His presence in your life. In order to make these changes though, you must confront the evil within you and make the effort to change your life before you can help others. A hero is a man of virtue, and that includes the virtue of humility. Man is flawed, and even the best of us require submission to something that is ultimately greater than us – God, from whom we draw our strength and fortitude. With God at your side, listening to His words, you will be able to be the man that you deep down desire to be. The man that I was not able to be. Do not condemn your son to this same fate that has stricken you and others."

"I feel like I'm being pressured into this," Tristan finally responded. "I- I'm not ready for this fate. I don't even know if I want it."

"A hero does not decide when it is his time," Maxim answered. "No less, does he decide when it is his time to fall from his horse. However, to answer the call of duty is a choice that only you can make when confronted with it. And it is a serious one at that. The time to answer that call is nigh for you."

"But you will not succeed until you choose to act, rather than contemplate," Helene said, joining from the other side of the cave. "And you must act on yourself foremost and then on your family. For those that are able to save themselves, can save others, and those that are able to save and lead their families will be able to do greater goods for the rest of the world. From there, you may just yet find peace in your heart as you so seek, instead of this frustration that torments you."

Tristan looked over to her with uncertainty. He stood up and backed up against the wall as Helene stood before him, his father at his side.

"And we will be there with you," Maxim stated, "just as God will never abandon you, ever, even if you may abandon God. So long as you seek to pervade evil in yourself, your family, and the world…"

"… and continually seek these goods that will bring truth, beauty, and love," Helene added, "you will have done what God has entrusted in you and achieve your sainthood that will inspire millions more than your sons or daughters."

"But God does not entrust in you what He does not believe you cannot do," a third, familiar, slightly monotone, but deep voice spoke. "By your essence, you are capable of so much more."

Tristan turned to the cave entrance as the room began to darken. He stood up, looked ahead and saw not the cloaked figure, but instead a figure of pure light in a lightish-blue color similar to the one that expelled the hooded man yesterday. The figure of light that stood before Tristan had an ethereal, but anthropoid shape to it with long, thin legs, two long arms, and a round head with no face. The figure was translucent and within it there was a vein-like wisp that connected around the head to a roundish bulb. Around the pure spirit were thin tentacle-like attachments like a jellyfish with brightly colored bulbs at the end, spread out like wings. Tristan looked at the figure and stepped back as the two of them stood in a void that resembled outer space with stars around them.

"Mika..." Tristan said, looking at the pure spirit.

The spirits of Maxim and Helene faded.

"What is going on?" Tristan asked. "What are you doing here?"

"Exactly what appears to be happening," Mika replied. "And secondly, I have always been here with you, protecting you."

"Why do you look like that though? Did you die too?"

"No. What you see is my true form. The Almighty One created us long ago to be the wisest and most beautiful of His creations, and in our time, we came to elevate ourselves from our Earthly appearance to join with Him in this wise and beautiful form, but there were those that did not succeed and those that did succeed, but later sought to rebel. Led by the one that the Almighty One had created to be our ruler, this being led the rebellion that took one-third of our kind, both physical and true, astray. His pride led him to believe that he could be as mighty as Him, but his ultimate failure proved contrary. A war ensued, and those of us that remained created the earthly avatar that you know me for, an ultimate, but ugly physical form that allowed us to be between the realms. In his defeat, the rebel and his followers were banished to your world where they would continue to seek the destruction and spite of the Almighty One through His most cherished creations, the Great Ones. Those of us who did not elevate themselves and who remained loyal to the rebel leader, in their failure to attempt to alter their physical forms, instead created themselves into a terrible earthly beast that you know of, while those that elevated from their earthly forms also took hold of avatars of our own creation and would seek to infiltrate and subvert, both our world and yours. The earthly ones would be doomed to never ascend; those fallen beings, would be doomed to never be able to leave their form and instead cursed as those that were left behind for their pride and treachery, to wallow in the dirt."

"Who was this rebel? What's his name?" Tristan asked.

"He has adopted many names in the cultures of this world, with the oldest name being Heyl," Mike explained. "He is the one that has led you out at night and through these many visions of the past. He is also the one that has consistently attempted to lead the Great Ones astray. He had elevated with us, but then took a corrupted avatar form that he cannot escape from and has merged with his being."

"And these earthly beasts, they're the Chosen, right?" Tristan guessed. "The shapeshifters?"

"I believe that is one of the many names they have taken," Mika responded. "The oldest name that I am familiar with is *Nefilim*. Like their master, they were thrown down to this world and left exiled at the most southern, inhospitable reaches of this planet. However, their ingenuity knew no bounds, and they escaped and integrated into a rogue people in the south, spreading their domain as they worked north, and then across the ices to reach around and make their way west to subvert the Great Ones. The Almighty attempted to uproot them after some years then and the world had been corrupted in their presence. In that time, the Almighty One entrusted *Noach* and raised a calamity that rid many but not all of them. From that calamity, the Great Ones, the sons of *Noach*, sprouted from this land that you walk on and spread out before those beasts could eliminate them. It is not by coincidence that you and Diana have come to this land. When she cried out to return to home, her request was an ancestral cry to return to the homeland of the Great Ones."

"The Caucasus?" Tristan questioned.

"Correct. Many years ago, Noach had three sons who left from this land after the calamity to establish the three realms, only two of which remains in existence – the realm of Sem and Yepet, in which Yepet's sons remained in this nearby region while some travelled north past these mountains and then went west, while some went east. Likewise, few of the sons and descendants of Sem remained slightly south, while others travelled west and then north to establish the great civilizations of these lands. Ham was the one-third of the three that turned from the Almighty. The curse of Ham led to the destruction of not only his individual spirit, but his collective spirit as his descendants would never know themselves. Heyl and his beasts would rest upon these descendants, taking more with them, especially descendants from Sem, such as Y'ishma and Esa. The *Nefilim* lost their strength after the calamity, and after generations, would slowly lose themselves too. They would continue to subvert and prey on the Great Ones, going so far as to even enter into the many kingdoms on Earth and wreak havoc, and then into the ranks of the Beloved Ones, a truly chosen and holy people, until the day came in which His Son exposed their malice and fulfilled His plan. However, even with the fulfillment of His promise, the war continues."

"You... you're an angel," Tristan concluded. "Just as Charlemagne named your species... *Angelus*. He knew! All this time – he knew!"

"Truth can be burdensome to those that are not prepared for it. When Heyl brought truth to the Great Ones in his effort to be like the Almighty One, he was severely punished to be accursed the way he is now, to wallow in the dirt like the *Nefilim*. Likewise is the same fate of all those people that attempt the same – punishment for their wickedness and pride to go against

Him. The Son acted out on the Almighty One's permission to deliver His truth to the Beloved Ones, who are no more, and from them all the Great Ones who together have created a new sort of Beloved Ones of all peoples fit for His kingdom, but as a result, the *Nefilim* and those they had subverted, punished the Son."

"That's ironic."

"Nonetheless, the day will come in which He will awaken and return to deliver his final blow against Heyl, Heyl's followers, and the *Nefilim*. A plot had ensued earlier in which we worked together against these conspirators. When we met, the rebels had ejected the vessel that held the preserved body of the Son, and the *Nefilim* attempted to have this body destroyed through their subjects in this world. This body was dormant, but His spirit continued to reign across the universe with the Father and Holy Spirit. When the day comes that He is ready, He will assume His physical form again and return to deliver His final judgement, but even I do not know when that is… All I know is what He asks from me…"

Tristan didn't respond.

"And then there comes what He asks of you…"

Tristan looked back at him.

Act 6, Scene 3

Diana lay down on the bed in the cabin as he looked ahead. She held a sad and worried look on her face. She placed a hand on her womb and then her ears twitched. Diana heard the stamp of some hooves come from outside of the cabin. She sat up and looked over to the door with anticipation.

"Tristan!" Diana remarked, standing up.

Diana heard a neigh from a horse outside and then heavy knock on the door. She stood up and went over to the door, opening it and looked out the other side as not Tristan, but Arkady stood before her. Diana stepped back as he looked at her.

"Oh jeez…" Diana muttered.

Arkady spoke to Diana in Russian. She simply nodded to him and stepped out of the way as he entered into their home. The warlord entered, removed his fur cloak and sat down at the table. He continued to speak in Russian as Diana looked to him.

"I'm sorry," Diana confessed in English, "but I don't speak Russian or Georgian."

Arkady spoke in a disgruntled manner to her. He continued to speak to her in a manner as though he was asking questions.

"Okay, you're probably here for the money if not Tristan," Diana remarked, holding her hands out to him. "Let me get it…"

Diana moved over to the bed and began to push it aside so she could access the trapdoor underneath. She opened the door and saw not the bag of coins that she and Tristan had hid, but a bunch of empty wine bottles.

"Oh no…" Diana muttered, standing up.

The warlord looked over to her. She looked back over to him.

"Listen, you need to speak with my husband," Diana asserted, enunciating her words. "My husband – the man you called, 'Red?' You need to talk to him if you want your tribute, because I don't have it."

The warlord spoke back to her in Russian. He continued to speak in a manner in which it sounded like he was asking questions. He then slammed a fist on the table, spooking Diana as she jumped and flinched. The warlord stood up and became angry with her, extending a hand out the door.

Diana simply shook her head at him and replied, "Please, I don't know where he has gone. You must have seen him. He does not live here at the moment. You need to go find him if you want your money."

The warlord growled at her. He drew his sword and pointed it towards her. Diana's eyes widened as she saw the sword. He shouted at her and then walked around the table to approach her. Diana walked forward and then around the bed, moving over to the stove where a kettle was atop. She held a hand on her stomach.

"Please, I don't want trouble," Diana stated in a terrified voice. "I'm pregnant – I can't help you. You have to find Tristan."

The warlord spoke back to her in Russian. He took Diana by the wrist and began to drag her forward.

"Hey!" Diana shouted, grabbing the kettle and slamming it into his arm.

"Agh!" Arkady cried out, letting go of Diana and grabbing his arm as Diana singed him.

Diana quickly exited out from the cabin and went outside. She then proceeded to run into the woods as Arkady stepped out and looked over to her as she escaped.

• • • •

"You have a duty to protect this woman of yours, your Diana, just as it was entrusted in me to protect the Son, our Queen, the Archon, and many more. Like our Queen, your Diana will give birth to a boy who will be entrusted a greater part than has been entrusted onto you, and it is your union together that will see this boy carry out the will of the Almighty One as he plans to stop the spread of malice as it rises in this world."

"Is this the end then? The end of humanity? The end of civilization? Does it all end soon?" Tristan asked.

"I cannot answer, as I told you, I do not know when the Son will return, or if it even is soon, but I do know that He does not wish for the Great Ones to live in a state of anticipation for these end of times. He does not want the probability to consume them and distract them, but to simply continue to live. What He wants is for his Will to triumph over this world, and he intends to do so by good men, such as your son, who are willing to fight on his behalf. He will be inspired by his father who will have sacrificed his life for this boy and his mother, and by his mother who will have sacrificed her own life in the way that all mothers are called to. The inspiration of his parents, and his own sufferings, will see to it that he becomes one of the greatest of the Great Ones since the Son had walked on this Earth. For it is the image of the Son that the Great Ones are called to mirror, knowing that he cannot reach the same perfection, but continuing to strive to, nonetheless. From those that achieved, his new Beloved Ones, he will reign as their King in a new world."

"How can I do this though? Diana and I are stuck here – How do we return? Where even are we?"

"You will need to return the very same way that you came. The stones that brought you here can only be activated by a man with a greater power than is within you or Diana. It was the objective of Heyl to reach this man, and now I am, with hesitance but knowing well that it is the only option to return you to your time and universe, entrusting you with the same objective. The world that you are in is not the future of your own world, but the present of an old world that was abandoned. When you came to this world, a pause was placed on the time of your former world so that you could be here, and that was fated. You travelled not forward in time, but to an entirely different universe. And the visions that Heyl showed you were of the alternate past that occurred in this world."

"So, it was all real then…" Tristan responded.

"Yes," Mika confirmed. "What you saw was the product by which a son born from a man like you and Diana was left abandoned, without a father to guide him properly, and instead only himself and all his power to turn against the Great Ones in a selfish and mistaken path. The world you are in is the direct consequence of his actions, which saw the complete destruction of civilization entirely. He continues to lurk in this world though, captured and imprisoned in a town south that has become the nest of the *Nefilim*, the ancient city of Jerusalem. You will need to travel south and find him, but be careful because the powers that this man has are stronger than any of these Awakened Ones than you have met, and like Heyl, he is both a trickster and a thief. I will travel with you, although we will not be able to speak to each other like this – I have already tread far enough to intervene, but I have been left no choice and needed to do so. When the time comes, I will be with you in the final fight against this man, who will inevitably attempt to come with you back to your world as he fights for his own survival, and continuation of malicious, hateful, and selfish deeds."

Tristan nodded.

"Since we had last met, a lot has happened to you and you have suffered and learned, and become wiser," Mika concluded. "You may never continue suffer to the extent that you have, should you choose to accept what the Almighty has tasked to you and listen to the words of your father, but you will continue to learn and become wiser. However, the time to accept this quest is now or never. Go. Your woman is in danger and she needs you."

"Thank you," Tristan responded.

The void around Tristan disappeared and he found himself in the cave. He looked around and then outside as the rain continued to fall down and thunder crackle. Tristan looked at his hands and then took a deep breath, clenching his fists and looking to his clothes. He put on his undershirt, tunic, and then his boots but not his pants as they were still wet. He then swiped up his sword and picked up the scabbard and leather strap. He brought his sword before him and held them. He then took a deep breath and brought the sword into the scabbard, placing it around him, grabbing his shield, and then exiting the cave to come to Tempest.

Tristan picked up the leather saddle at the exit of the cave and placed it onto his horse who panicked at the crackle of thunder and flash of lightning. He attempted to soothe her before he fixed the saddle and then climbed atop of her. He then pulled the lead off from the tree and set off with her to return to the cabin. Tempest galloped through the woods and came out to the road. Tristan then guided her along so that they could come to the town, and then over to the cabin, stomping through the mud that stopped him before.

Tempest reared in front of the cabin as Tristan stopped her. He quickly hopped off and went to the cabin door, seeing that it was left ajar. He pushed through and looked inside, seeing the bed pushed over, trapdoor open, and Diana nowhere to be seen. Tristan breathed sharply and saw that the kettle was on the floor. He stepped back outside and shouted out, "Diana!" Tristan then stepped forward and saw some tracks in the mud going into the woods. He then went back to and hopped onto his horse. Tempest reared again as Tristan turned her and they went into the woods.

• • • •

Diana rushed through the woods, pushing through the thick shrubs as she escaped for her life. The galloping of Arkady's horse could be heard behind her. Diana continued to push through as she made her escape into nowhere. She then tripped on a root and fell over, ducking down as the warlord's horse reared and then came down as Arkady attempted to swipe at her. Diana rushed forward, sliding down and slowing down as she reached a dead-end at a cliff wall in a clearing within the forest.

Arkady rode his horse over the shrubs and then came down over the hill behind, cornering her against the cliffside wall. He jumped off his horse and shouted to Diana. Diana panted and encroached the wall with her back, holding a hand at her womb. Arkady hopped off his horse and stepped towards Diana.

Tristan hopped off Tempest, seeing Arkady ahead. Arkady raised his sword and gave a sinister laugh. Tristan drew his sword and quickly sprinted forward, jumping off the side of the cliff and raising his sword as a hatred overtook him so that he could defend what he loved.

"Get away from my family!" Tristan shouted as he jumped, swiping down and clashing with Arkady.

Diana watched as Tristan intervened. Arkady had quickly turned and swiped his sword at Tristan. Their swords clashed.

Tristan's aggression empowered him to bring Arkady's sword down, bashing him with his shield and swiping at him, cutting him at the shoulder. Arkady growled at him and kicked back. Tristan held his ground as Arkady kicked his shield. He then raised his sword up and the two clashed again. Diana made her escape and moved up the hill where Tempest was.

Tristan held back as Arkady attempted to overpower him. Tristan growled and then withdrew his sword, allowing Arkady's sword to hit againt his shield. He then took a step back before shuffling at the side to try and get around the warlord. Arkady kept his distance as he only had his sword in hand and the plate of armor around his chest. Tristan had no armor other than his shield. Tristan attempted to jab at the warlord.

Arkady blocked his attempts and then began to swipe back with his sword, scratching Tristan's shield as Tristan covered himself. Tristan then went in for another jab closer to the warlord's chest, but Arkady blocked and then parried, cutting Tristan along the top of his own chest near the shoulder. Diana cringed as she saw. Tristan quickly refocused and took a step back. The two foes circled each other before Tristan raised his sword up and attempted to take a vertical swipe at Arkady. Arkady deflected and attempted to parry again, but Tristan blocked the blowback with his shield.

Tristan and Arkady circled each other for another moment until he went in with a jab straight to Tristan's throat. He raised his shield up and blocked it. He was then knocked back as Arkady kicked at him. Arkady brought his sword down towards Tristan. Tristan quickly swiped back, drawing his sword back and cutting Arkady at the cheek. Tristan then bashed his sword back before he stood up and attempted to bring his sword down at him again.

Arkady clashed back and side-stepped out of the way, raising his sword and cutting Tristan at the upper left arm. Tristan hit back and hit him on the cheek again before he pivoted and absorbed a blowback by his shield. He then jumped back and looked over to Arkady. The two foes breathed sharply as they stared each other down. Arkady maintained his sword pointed forward. He went in for another jab. Tristan deflected and clashed back at him, attempting to parry, but the warlord used his other arm to hit against his and then grab Tristan by the throat. Arkady then threw Tristan aside, causing him to land on the floor.

Tristan looked over on his side as the warlord came for him. He quickly stood up and absorbed the strike, cutting at the warlord's thigh and then knocking him back with a bash from his shield. Tristan then hit him on the other thigh, slicing a deep cut. He then raised his shield as Arkady brought his sword down against him with two hands. The sword bounced back and Tristan went in for a jab in the right shoulder as a crack of thunder could be heard. Tristan then pulled back.

Arkady grabbed his shoulder with one hand and with the other looked over to Tristan with a deep anger. He went for a diagonal strike. Tristan blocked with his shield and gave an underhanded swipe at the warlord, cutting his forearm. Arkady then swung a backhanded fist at Tristan and slapped him back. He grabbed his sword with both hands and then made his way over to Tristan to bring it down on him.

Tristan raised his shield up to cover his head. He also saw that the warlord attempted to kick him at the same time. He swiped with his sword back at the leg while he took the blow from the sword with his shield. Arkady fell over. He charged his arm with a hand on the sword and threw it towards Tristan like a javelin. The sword missed. Tristan went in to place a foot down in his armor, pointing his sword towards his fallen foe. Tristan had Arkady at his mercy, but the warlord did not seek mercy.

Arkady grabbed Tristan's leg and threw him over. He then went for his sword and quickly brought it over to Tristan as he recovered from his fall and stood up on one knee. In an instant, Tristan jabbed his sword at the warlord, stabbing him underneath his armor in the lower intestines and then drawing his sword back. Tristan looked at the warlord as he gasped for air in shock of the hit. Arkady stepped back and then fell over.

Tristan looked to him and went over with his sword pointed as the warlord fell backwards in a weakened state. A wrath built into the warlord as he saw Tristan over him. He raised his sword back up and attempted to throw it towards him like a javelin again with the last reserves of his strength. Tristan raised his shield as it launched towards him. The impact caused the shield to fly off. The warlord grabbed the bottom of his leg at the same time. Tristan saw his shield off and then saw Arkady pull out a dagger from his leg. Arkady attempted to stab at Tristan's thigh, but dropped the knife at the last moment. Tristan had brought his sword down with both hands and stabbed through the jugular notch, instantly killing the warlord.

Arkady's head fell back as he died. Tristan pulled his bloodied sword out and then stood before his fallen foe, panting. Another burst of thunder could be heard in the background. Tristan looked down and over to his sword, whipping it in the air to get some of the blood off before he took a limped step back and put his sword away.

Tristan looked over to Diana who had witnessed the whole ordeal. He looked at her sympathetically. Diana held a fist at her heart as her eyes began to water. Tristan walked towards her and then collapsed onto the ground in exhaustion. Diana quickly went over to him and helped him up.

"Diana…" Tristan remarked.

"Shh…." Diana hushed. "Save your strength… I'm going to get you back home."

Act 6, Scene 4

Diana brought Tristan back to the cabin with Tempest. Tristan was able to stand on his feet as walked in with her. She took him to the bed and sat him down. She took off his tunic and undershirt, and looked at the deep cut near his right shoulder, above his chest and the deep cut on the side of his left arm. Diana helped Tristan lie down on the bed.

"Stay put," Diana said. "I'm going to clean and dress the wound."

Diana went over and picked up a tub on a table near the stove. She also picked up the kettle and poured the water leftover inside into the indoor tub before going outside to take some rainwater from the outdoor tub for the kettle. She sat the kettle down onto the stove. She then took the tub with the little water and went to a dresser to take out one of her dresses. Diana ripped the fabric up. She took one of the sheets and doused it in water before she began to dab at Tristan's wounds.

Tristan grunted as she touched his torn skin over his chest. The blood continued to seep through.

"You're going to have to lay down some pressure while I get the other cut patched," Diana said, applying pressure.

Tristan took control of the cloth. Diana then took another piece and began to clean Tristan's arm.

"Here I thought that I'd never get to use my first aid knowledge on you," Diana said, dabbing at the cut with her cloth. "Ever since what happened in Russia, I've tried to be sure that I had the skills to help you if something ever fatal happened to you again."

Tristan didn't respond.

"I suppose, wanting to be a nurse has been a natural progression of that desire to be prepared..." Diana confessed. "I suppose I should thank you for scaring me into wanting to be like this…"

"You don't have to thank me for anything," Tristan quietly said with a raspy voice.

"I have to thank you for helping me discern what I want to do with my life and for giving me this child…"

Tristan shook his head and replied, "Don't. I don't deserve thanks for those. He's my kid too. You would have been a mother without me anyways."

Diana didn't respond.

"You know, I've had quite an interesting week," Tristan said, grunting, "since I left…"

"Save your strength, Tristan. We can talk later…"

"I had a chat with our old friend, Mika," Tristan stated. "He came to me and he told me what we need to do to return home."

Diana looked back at him with surprise.

"This world we're in… it's not even the same world we came from. It's an alternate universe… parallel to our own and slightly ahead in time. We never travelled forward in time; we travelled to another world in another universe."

"Why don't the crystals work then?"

"Because we don't have the skill," Tristan replied, grabbing Diana by the arm. "We have to travel south to Jerusalem. There, we'll find someone who has the skill to take us back to Charlemagne, and hopefully then we'll be able to return home."

"Are you sure?"

"I'm positive," Tristan assured her, letting go of her arm. "He was the one that warned me about you being in danger – that's how I was able to come find you and intervene. That alone tells me that all of it was true…"

Diana looked at him and nodded. She took another piece of cloth and began to dry the cut before setting another piece over the blood and applying pressure. She then began to wrap the dress and tie it together.

"I'm sorry, Diana," Tristan confessed as Diana began to take over the wound on the shoulder. "I'm sorry I've let you down far too many times... while I was gone... I saw so many horrible things. Bad things that have happened in this world, and..."

"Hey, calm down," Diana cautioned.

"...I'm sorry for everything I've done to you. You shouldn't have had to cope with all the crap I did to you. What kind of a man was I to do that to you? What kind of a man would I be to abandon you and our son?"

"Son?" Diana questioned as she dried his wound.

Tristan explained the series of visions that he had over the last couple days as he detoxed from alcohol. He didn't mention Helene or his father, but explained into detail what Mika had told him. Meanwhile, Diana finished to dress and bandage Tristan's other wound.

"The man that Mika wants us to meet in Jerusalem... He's our son in this universe, a product of my negligence..."

"Sounds like more than just your negligence," Diana responded, sitting at his side and holding his hand. "How could I have become a heroin addict given my mother?"

"Because your mother didn't die of heroin. She probably never even did the drug since you told me that she got into that after your dad died. She died shortly after him in this universe when that pig attempted to rape her."

"In our universe, Felix died before he could shoot my dad. The Syndicate sent him to do the deed, but someone shot him before he could, so that never happened..."

"I thought... when I saw that we had met in university... I thought that it was a kind of fate that even in an alternate timeline, we still met each other and had a son together... but then I saw what I did to you. How I told you to abort the kid and pretend like nothing ever happened to you. It makes me grateful for the circumstances we had actually met, even if those circumstances involved my parent's death, Salmar adopting me and going insane, and all that. It's all starting to make a lot more sense, Diana."

"I can't believe Charlemagne adopted me at ten-years old. It meant that he never had his midlife crisis…"

"… but it meant that Finn's death was harder on him. For some reason, Finn dies in this world and Charlemagne was aware of it. I'm not too sure what that's all about, but if I had to guess, Finn does something in relation to Aidan Cunningham where I never intervened."

"That would suggest that you saved Finn when you two met," Diana replied.

Tristan didn't respond. He instead inched up the bed and placed a hand on Diana's hand.

"Diana, what I saw was messed up, but seeing you and our son… seeing Damian without a father. It broke my heart. Diana, I want to have this son of ours that's in your womb. I want to be there for him. I want to be there when he needs help with homework, or when he's struggling to know what to do with himself. I want to be there for him when no one else can be there."

Diana smiled at him.

"Tristan, I never had any doubts, even before this, that you would be the best father to possibly raise a child with. And whatever guilt you may have about this other Tristan, please don't share them. This Tristan was not you. The Tristan that I know is you. It is the Tristan that keeps trying to win me back instead of leaving me behind."

"I'd never leave you behind, Diana. I'll never leave you or our son behind."

"Do you really think I have a son in here?" Diana questioned.

"I know it," Tristan confirmed. "I guarantee you that you're going to give birth to a son, and although he might not be exactly like the boy I saw, he'll nonetheless be our boy."

Diana didn't respond. Instead, she brought a hand over Tristan's hand.

"Diana..." Tristan said, "I'm also sorry about mocking you..."

"Mocking me?" Diana questioned.

"Your faith in God," Tristan replied. "I've... I've never believed in God until Mika told me everything that he told me. I'm... I'm not a religious person like you, but I want you to know at least what I believed and that was that I didn't believe anything. I had no faith in God. I thought the world was an empty, meaningless place, but now I understand that we live in an evil world because there are too few good men. I was one of the wicked types. I never thought of myself as evil until I cheated on you, and even then, I tried to justify my actions instead of confronting the guilt that I had wronged you. I believed that if I made a heroic effort to sacrifice my life that this would make it all better, but it didn't. I had still wronged you. I thought that this one heroic action alone would redeem myself for a whole year of wrongdoing, but I continued to lie to you. I lied to you about my alcoholism. I lied to myself about it too. I don't want to be that kind of person with you... When you met me, you met a boy and you fell in love with that boy. Now that you're a woman though, what use do you have in this boy? When you've loved me most in these recent years, it's not been when I've been immature, but when I've made sacrifices... When I volunteered to build those houses, or when we saved those kids and took that bullet for you. In those instances, I was a man… even if it was for a brief moment. Ever since I heard about you being pregnant, I've pretended to be a man around you, but I've hid my face and been drinking behind your back to make up for what I wanted – the carefree life I had as a boy, but no more… I want you to marry a man… not a boy. I want this kid to have a man as a father, not a boy."

"Oh, Tristan…" Diana remarked. "What I really want is just you as you are. I don't want you to make any extra effort…"

"It's not an effort. It's a maturity. It's a progression. It's who I want to be, especially since it's who I have to be."

Diana brought her hand to Tristan's cheek.

"If I hadn't sold the engagement ring I had bought to pay for this house, I'd propose to you right now," Tristan said.

"You did what?" Diana questioned.

"It was the only way I was able to get the horse, the sword, and this roof over our head. I wasn't going to let you sleep outdoors again."

"Tristan…" Diana said, tearing up and hugging him.

"I want to marry you, Diana," Tristan remarked. "I want to be one with you. I want to commit to you. I want to raise this kid with you. I want to go to Heaven with you."

"Tristan, you will…" Diana replied, parting from him and placing the back of her hand on his cheek. Her eyes were tearful, but not with sadness but rather joy. She continued to say, "and although I'm overjoyed by these words, how about you save the proposal when we're back in our world? I'll give you a hint though… my answer will definitely be yes."

"I love you, Diana."

"I know you do," Diana replied, kissing him on the cheek.

"I'm going to take what coins we have left and trade it in for some supplies, some new clothes, my armor, and then when we can, we're going to set off for Jerusalem," Tristan stated. "I'm going to get us back home – to Allabrese, in our own timeline, and then we're going to get married and have that child."

PART II

PART II

"To be brave in misfortune is to be worthy of manhood; to be wise in misfortune is to conquer fate."

– Agnes Repplier

Act 7, Scene 1

The clear night sky was painted with the bright glowing dots of the stars that were lightyears away and scattered across the entire galaxy around. The seemingly infinite void behind them was an extremely dark blue. The Great Rift was marked across the million dots and marked the skies like a scar or tear on the celestial fabric that covered the natural ceiling.

All around, there was nothing more than a gritty, rough dark tanned sand with bits of stones littered around. The landscape consisted of tall dunes to short hills with patches of a short grass on occasion on the shorter hills. There were also larger dry shrubs that could sometimes be seen. In the background there were steep dark tanned cliffs to the east and dunes to the west. In the midst of the desert there lay a curved dirt road between a canyon of tall hills, running through this land, which was the Judean Desert.

Tempest galloped forward along the desert road laid down before her as she hurried forward as it cooled down from the humid and intense heat that overwhelmed her and her masters. Tristan sat atop of Tempest with the reins in hand as he steered her along the road. Diana sat behind him, holding on as the horse raced forward as they made their way to Jerusalem.

Both Diana and Tristan appeared differently than they had presented themselves in Venamisa. Tristan's unshaven facial hair had grown longer to become a short beard and his hair had also grown longer as it stretched out from the back of his head and began to cover his ears. He wore a set of handmade leather boots at his feet that stretched up his legs to cover his shins, beige trousers, and the long-sleeved undershirt with his leather gauntlets and gloves that covered his forearms and hands. Atop of his undershirt, he wore the chainmail for protection like a slash vest, and over the chainmail he wore the greyish-green *feldgrau* tunic. Around his waist, he wore a leather belt with a quail attached with some arrows. Across his chest he wore the leather strap that held his scabbard with his sword, a longbow, and his iron shield that covered his entire back.

Diana's dark hair had been cut short at the back and tied in a ponytail, seen through the white veil she wore to cover her head that stretched back just over shoulders. The headcover hung below her chin and came down her chest, showing only her face and the top of her front neck. She also wore a loose-fitted long-sleeved white garment that covered her arms and her swollen abdomen that had grown larger and became even more pronounced than before. At her feet, she wore sandals. Her legs were joined together and fell to the left-side of the horse as she sat with her torso turned so that she could hold on to Tristan.

Tristan continued to lead Tempest through the desert as they soon reached a rundown concrete road with various potholes, craters, and cracks against the formerly smooth surface. At the side, there were some power line pylons that were fallen over at certain segments, while others were raised and led onwards. Tristan rode Tempest at the side of the road as they hurried along and soon began to see glimpses of civilization in the distance. The desert had smoothed out, but continued to have a rugged appearance with a sand mixed with various rocks of all different sizes that composed the landscape in addition to large tufts of moss. Tristan looked towards Jerusalem as they rode in from the north.

Jerusalem appeared from the horizon to be a wide city with various rectangular structures that were warmly lit not by electrical lights, but by torchlight and candlelight. Various structures in the ancient holy city were in ruins, decayed, and these were noticeably the ones that were unlit. Tristan rode down a road where to his left, there was a mixture of moss and a very short and dry grass. In this sort of field, there were destroyed tanks protruding through the dirt. A structure on a hill ahead was blown out from the side and left in ruins. Towards the outskirts of the town, there was a graveyard of various vehicles and some tents and shacks where some people lived. Finally, Tristan entered into the outer edge of the town itself where he saw that it was quiet and abandoned with wrecks of vehicles parked around, graffiti sprayed atop of signs with Modern Hebrew letters and concrete walls.

Tristan rode around a roundabout and began to go deeper into the city where there were destroyed structures, businesses, mounds of litter, destroyed cars stacked atop of each other, and finally some apartment complexes that had been blown out at the side, were abandoned, and some in mounds of pure rubble. The sight was worse than what could be found in Keswick. Tristan then went along and came to another roundabout that turned towards a tall concrete wall with watch towers along and a border checkpoint ahead between a modern concrete wall where the road drove through. The wall stretched and wrapped around the town. Tristan could see the rest of the city ahead, which appeared to be war torn as well, but at least inhabited.

Tempest rode up to the border checkpoint where the stalls were unmanned and gates torn out. Tristan rode through and continued onto the other side as he finally entered into the city. From the checkpoint, Tristan passed some inhabited homes lit by candlelight and torches. The road soon split into an avenue with shrubs on the side and various trees around in the gardens of some homes. He was in a residential area where there was not much in the way of structures other than some homes and various craters left behind by the war that tore through this land. Tristan rode along and soon found himself by a blown-out overpass and major road. He looked around. Tempest stopped as Tristan held her back at an intersection.

"This doesn't look like Jerusalem," Tristan said. "It's... quiet and small."

Tristan continued to ride through and followed a road that went south and out of the town. He came to another arid region with some blown up overpass highways around and followed along, coming up a road that was built along the side of a hill and looked out to the district that he had just come from. The road went uphill and followed a continuation of the border wall from earlier. To the left, the road was blocked off by a barrier made of stacked and crushed cars. The only route was right where they followed along until they came to a wide freeway that went south. The area was quiet along the highway with only some structures lit, some torn, and some simply dark. There were a lot more ruins in this part of the town. After another moment continuing down this road, he finally saw another traveler on horseback, going north with a caravan behind. Tristan went along where this traveler came from and began to enter a lit section of the town where there was a lot more life centered around a roundabout.

Within this part of Jerusalem, there were a lot of palm trees and torches lit by candlelight that created a glow for Tristan to be able to see around. The structure around looked older than most, but below there were various canopies with shops that were closed for the day. Across from the market there was an ancient wall made of brick with struts atop. Behind this wall there were older structures that were lit and inhabited. Tristan continued around the road that wrapped around the wall of the old city and saw that life in Jerusalem centered around this older portion with life continuing within. After a few moments, Tristan began to see armed personnel at the gates of the wall.

The road ended towards the eastern part where it had been blown out by a crater and the rest of the town ahead in complete ruins. Tristan turned around and began to travel west and then around south. The structures here were taller and slightly cleaner than the shabbier structures up north. There was also more of a presence of armed personnel at the street corners.

Tristan saw that there was much more traffic in these parts with people on horseback, donkeys, and not an automobile in sight. He continued south down the main road, but stopped as the road became a tunnel that was caved in. He then continued atop of a walkway on the surface, travelling south before stopping as the road ended shortly afterwards up ahead. He looked down from atop where he could see nothing but a steep drop into a massive crater to the south of the city that stretched at least three or four kilometers in radius. Tristan stopped Tempest and looked ahead.

"Well, I guess that's it then," Tristan remarked. "Welcome to Jerusalem."

"Hm..." Diana responded, "take us back into the town and let's find an inn to stay in for the night. I'm tired."

Tristan rode back into town and returned to the west gate into the old town where there were some guards at the side of the wall. They both ignored Tristan as he rode in with his horse. The streets ahead were narrow and quiet. A lot of the homes had shutters that were closed. He walked forward and soon met with a larger road that he rode Tempest down. Tristan looked around and saw that people looked towards them as they rode through.

"Maybe I'll have better luck finding an inn outside of the town," Tristan said, turning Tempest around and exiting the way they came.

Tristan rode a short distance and found a stable and inn where he could take Tempest in for the night. He jumped off the horse and took out a bag of coins from one of the saddle pockets, walking into the inn while Diana stayed behind. Tristan walked up to the desk of the rundown inn and looked over to the innkeeper, a large-nosed man with greyish-brown skin and dark grey hair.

"Hello," Tristan greeted, "do you speak English? Russki?"

"English," the man answered.

"How much for a night?" Tristan questioned. "I have silver and gold coins."

Tristan took out some coins and placed it on the desk. The man eyed the gold coins and picked one up, weighing it in his hands.

"One night, two gold coins," the innkeeper stated. "For you, wife, and horse."

"Two gold coins?!" Tristan grumbled.

Tristan picked out five more gold coins from the loot he had collected from Arkady's corpse before they left and placed them on the desk. He then took back the silver coins, tightening the strings on the bag before looking back to the innkeeper.

"I'll stay for three nights. Where can I take my horse?"

"I show you," the innkeeper responded, coming out from behind the counter.

Tristan walked out and led Tempest around to the stable where he took her to a pen. He then began to remove the saddle as well as the saddlebag with the rolled-up blanket atop. He left the saddle in the pen and removed the reins too. Diana took the bag of coins while Tristan handled all of their camping gear. He then walked out and followed the innkeeper upstairs to their bedroom, which was a small suite with a double bed, fireplace, and table. The window looked out towards the ancient wall of the old city. Tristan was given a key to the bedroom and then left alone with Diana. He placed the saddlebag on the table and took the coins from Diana so that he could return them to the pouch. Tristan then looked back to her.

"We only have enough coins to stay three days here," Tristan said, "so I'll have to work fast to find this prison where Damian is being held in. Tomorrow I'll ask around about what kind of place this is – I saw some signs in English, so maybe English is a lot more common. Meanwhile, you rest – we've had a long journey from Georgia; almost two weeks non-stop riding through nothing but desert."

"Is there anything I can do to help?"

"I wouldn't risk your aid," Tristan replied. "I don't want this baby to be born preterm either while we're still stuck here, and you're halfway through your third trimester now."

"I'll do some shopping tomorrow and see what kind of food we can eat while we're here. Can I at least do that?" Diana questioned.

"I don't know what kind of culture is in this town," Tristan answered. "I don't know if the Muslims have taken over, the Jews, or Christians. From what Sima told me about Jerusalem before we left, it was one of the only places left in Palestine where people come together of all faiths to make pilgrimages. If I have to guess, it's an autonomous state like Venamisa, but larger, probably with a king, or worse, a council. If the Children of Moloch have survived, they may be in control of this town and stationed here, or maybe they're just hiding here. Even then, I don't know what attitude they'd have towards women, or if they're anything like those Muslims we met on our way over here, so please just wear your veil when you go out. Okay?"

"I'll keep my veil on – I'm not totally out of commission though, you know," Diana remarked. "I can still hold my own in a fight… even if I've got our son in me."

"Just be careful," Tristan responded, removing his scabbard, shield and bow. "And keep your dagger on you too. We don't know really understand what kind of a world this is still. All we know is that it's hostile and dark."

"Okay," Diana replied, removing the strap at her leg that carried a dagger in it. "I'll be careful."

Diana placed her weapon with Tristan's and then looked at him as they met at the foot of the bed. She placed her arms around him, feeling the chainmail underneath his tunic.

"You be careful too. Okay?" Diana reminded him.

"Of course," Tristan smiled, placing his hands on Diana's pregnant abdomen as he leaned in for a kiss. "The fact that I have not only you, but our son to return home to empowers me to fight."

Act 7, Scene 2

Charlemagne looked forward as he drove along the remains of the Trans-Canada Highway within the Pacific Northwest where evergreen trees were at either side of the road barriers. The skies above were a medium-grey. The road was in a poor state with various potholes, cracks, and sometimes the occasional collapsed portion, but all of the bridges from Allabrese, through the Rocky Mountains, and to the coast had remained intact for their travel. Charlemagne appeared much the same as when he had come to this universe, but he had removed his poncho and grown a minor beard around his moustache.

Next to Charlemagne, Manon sat in the same clothes that she had come with, including the poncho with the handgun. In the rear of the truck, Finn was sat down with all of the supplies they brought with them, including a mounted machine gun that pointed backwards. There were also crates of gasoline, ammunition, rifles, and food for them as well as rolled-up mats, tents, and some cooking utensils. Within the cabin of the truck, between Manon and Charlemagne, was Charlemagne's rucksack. Both Charlemagne and Finn had mildly bruised faces with healing scratches around from the fight they had.

Charlemagne drove non-stop for close to eight hours, driving as fast as he could manage while Finn rested in the back with his feet stretched out, and Manon slept with her head against the window. Charlemagne looked forward with focused eyes and determination to reach their destination as fast as they could. As he drove, Charlemagne saw that it soon became evening with the skies turning orange. He then took a hand off the steering wheel and grabbed his side, cringing and holding in the sharp pain that came across him. Charlemagne quickly brought his hand back to the steering wheel.

Manon looked over to Charlemagne from out her window as she heard the minor grunt that Charlemagne let out, although he attempted to hold back.

"What is it?" Manon asked. "Are you alright?"

Charlemagne didn't respond and instead he started to slow down so that he could pull over. He turned off the engine and brought a hand into his jacket.

"Are you okay, *Charles*," Manon asked again.

"Sorry, I need to check my wounds to see if my sutures in my side have come out. Stay here…" Charlemagne said, stepping out of the car and going around to the rear.

Finn watched Charlemagne through the rear-view window and then around as Charlemagne came to the back of the truck. He stood up and went over to him.

"What is it?" Finn asked. "Your stitches come out?"

Charlemagne unbuttoned his shirt and then raised his undershirt to see that the stitches on the side of his abdomen were intact. He then lurched forward and grasped his side, just under his right ribcage.

"No…" Charlemagne responded after a pause. "No, my wounds are fine. It's been two weeks for Pete's sake…"

"Is it the cancer?" Finn then asked.

"I believe so," Charlemagne replied, cringing as he hit the side of the pickup truck. "Agh…"

Charlemagne returned to the front of the car and took out his rucksack. He opened one of the pockets and took out a small prescription container and then took his backpack with him to the back of the car. He brought it over. Finn stood up and looked over to him.

"I'm going to have to take a moment to rest," Charlemagne said. "This pain is too strong and will distract me, and I'm going to take a painkiller that will make me drowsy. Please, take the wheel and go as much as you can. We should almost be there – we've driven non-stop for almost two days. This motorway goes straight to New Harlech…"

"I'll do as much as I can," Finn responded, hopping over the car while Charlemagne climbed into the back.

"Thank you, my dear boy," Charlemagne said with relief, going over to lie down where Finn had been.

Finn opened the car door and entered. He looked over to Manon who had a look of concern on her face.

"What is *Charles* doing?" Manon questioned. "Is he okay?"

"He's not feeling too well," Finn simply said. "He's going to have a rest and told me to takeover."

Finn sat the front of the pickup truck, turned the keys, and then began to drive back onto the highway as he continued to drive down while the sun set. Manon looked at Finn with uncertainty, but remained where she was as the car went forward. Charlemagne took some painkillers and laid down before he drifted off. Finn drove forward while his father snoozed and his mother looked ahead with attention. He looked to his right from the corner of his eye as he noticed the perkiness that Manon had suddenly come under. Finn frowned in his own worry.

"I'm not going to do anything to get us killed," Finn said. "I'm sorry if I've scared you in the past three or so weeks… but Charlemagne – I mean, my dad, trusts me with this, so…"

"Your father has always seen and led to believe in the good of others," Manon interrupted, looking down as she fixed her poncho over her lap. "He was raised in the sort of environment where he could trust anyone he was presented with, except his own father. Him and his own father had never had the best relationship, so I've heard."

"How come?" Finn questioned.

"A difference of character most of all, but also a troubled upbringing. Has Charlemagne not spoken to you about his childhood?" Manon said and asked in return.

"He told me that he was raised by his grandfather – my great-grandfather, I suppose, until he died in which he was then raised by his parents in Allabrese. He never said any more than that."

"Well, I will not say much because it is not my place to gossip, but your father had resented his own father, your grandfather. Despite that, Charlemagne always had the valor and conviction of your great-grandfather within him. I must imagine that he's spoken to you in length about your great-grandfather. No?"

"Not really," Finn replied. "He only mentioned him once to me. He hasn't really told me much about the Cabernet – I mean, my family."

"Well, for a start, you were born '*Louis*' not '*Finn*,' why?" Manon said to him. "Because I named you, despite all of our separation from each other, so that you would continue to be a Cabernet even if you were unaware. You are the seventh generation of a family that came to this New World from the region of Alsace, once *Elsass*, in the German Empire – under the name of *Witzendorff*. Before the Franco-Prussian War, Elsass was French territory and it was from here that your great-ancestor had served as an officer in the La Grande Armée that was the army of Napoleon Bonaparte. After Franco-Prussian War, the family was divided with half that remained and became part of German nobility, while others came to the New World as peasants. One of these persons was your forefather, Sennett, and all of these people came to Canada with the family name, Cabernet, to honor their loyalty to France over Germany, coming also from their desire to grow Cabernet Sauvignon in this New World. Sennett Cabernet became the father of Lycidas

Cabernet, who became the father of Pepin Cabernet, who fathered Derby Cabernet, who fathered Everest Cabernet, who then fathered *Charlemagne*, and between us, you were born. Your ancestor, Lycidas, who saw the rise of fortune that was Cabernet Industries, saw that he had created an empire, so he named his son Pepin after Pepin II who fathered *Charles Martel*, who fathered Pepin the Short, who then fathered *Charlemagne*, or *Charles* the Great, who was then the father of *Louis* the Pious. By naming you '*Louis*,' I wanted to continue and respect the tradition of your ancestors, one of whom I had respected immensely, Derby Cabernet, who was your father's personal hero."

"Why?" Finn questioned.

"Because from Derby, *Charles* learned everything that he could and ever have needed to learn from a man. He learned the spirit of courage, of wisdom, and of power. He was taught the importance of truth and in keeping truth, pursuing truth, and delivering truth. *Charles* grew up seeking to be just like this man, and he did become like him while at the same time being his own person. Of course, there was always more that Derby could have passed on to *Charles*, but his life tragically came to an end when *Charles* was still a young boy. Everything else that *Charles* has learned about or from his grandfather has been in his memory, and that included his late realization in the importance of children."

"But who taught Derby to be the way that he was?" Finn then questioned. "Did Pepin teach Derby to be the way that he was, or was Derby so exceptional that he was just the way that he was?"

Manon did not answer.

"I know why you're telling me all this," Finn instead replied. "It's not to share with me that history of this family. You want me to look at Charles and be inspired by him, to be like him, because you don't like the way that I've turned out. You want me to question my identity with doubt and take from my father what you assume I have not been able to establish on my own. It's too late for that. I'm my own person. Sometimes, men are so foregone from the influence of their fathers that they have no choice but to make a name for themselves. And sure, sometimes they become exceptional people like Derby, but more often, they become total failures. Ever since I was younger, I've wanted to be an exceptional person, but I've always felt held back by the fact that I had nobody there to guide me. I've become the person I am because of me alone. I take pride in that fact. And if one day, I have a son to carry on this legacy that is the Cabernet family, I would never force him to endure what I've endured expecting him to come out on top as I have. I would be there with him, ready to guide him along as a father should, because that is what I have learned from not having a father."

Manon did not reply. Instead, Finn continued to drive down the highway as the two sat in silence. Eventually, they came out from the forest as the highway came along the coast of a wide river, the Harlech River. The road then inched away from the water as they came across acres of smooth land where crops were planted in neat fields. Manon and Finn saw that there was a small town in a distance.

A worn-out green sign at the right-side of the highway stated that they were approaching the Town of Douglas and that the City of Harlech was still almost one-hundred and fifty kilometers away. Finn drove towards the town and then began to pass by some suburbs on the right-side of the highway and farmland to the left. Afterwards, there was an exit ramp to come out to some abandoned commercial areas and roads that went out to the heart of the town, and then there were more suburbs.

Both Manon and Finn noticed that the houses in this town were lit with power although the municipality was quiet and small. Once past the suburbs, they began to pass through some farmland before turning out right so that they drove through the forest again. Another green sign before they left stated the distance of Harlech and then Lennox on the current path they were on. It was also tagged in graffiti with the words, 'Stay out' around Harlech and Lennox. Finn continued to drive for another stretch until they started to run low on gasoline, so he pulled over at a rest area.

"Charles told me to go straight to Harlech, but I don't think we should go in at night," Finn said to Manon. "It could be dangerous. I'd rather wait until morning when he's awake in case there's trouble."

Finn took out the keys from the ignition.

"I'll help you pitch your tent," Finn said, opening the door. "We'll have to wake Charles."

Manon nodded to her son. She opened the door and exited with him. The three of them then camped at the rest area for the night with less of a two-hour drive between them and Harlech.

Act 7, Scene 3

Two days later, Tristan climbed onto the top of a rooftop in Jerusalem via a drainpipe, dressed in his chainmail armor and tunic, and equipped with all his gear. He looked over to the large complex ahead. The prison was a circular fortress existing in the midst of the ancient city and surrounded by various apartments and structures around. It was a large complex with walls as high as the outer city walls, at least twenty-feet tall, round watchtowers spread apart the walls of the fortress. At the right, facing to the east, there was a superstructure that extended out from the center and attached to the perimeter walls. This superstructure had even larger watch towers that flew a blue-white flag with the six-pointed star. Tristan could see various guards similar to the ones seen patrolling around the city, stationed along the perimeter of the fortress and at the watch towers. He could also look into the center of the fortress where there was a mess of chain-link fences with barbed wire atop, organized in zones, composing several sections where there were various items within, including horses, trucks, and crates.

Like the rest of Jerusalem, the fortress was only lit by the torchlight. Tristan moved around the dark rooftops of the compact city center and came around to the rear of the superstructure where he spotted some powerlines that connected over the road and went upwards to the top of the superstructure, attaching to a thick rod or antennae. Tristan came over to this line and raised his arms up. He stretched out his arms to pull down on the dead line, exerting the force of his two-hundred pounds of weight and more some. The line was tight and sturdy, so Tristan raised himself up and began to climb across the alleyway and over to the wall where he then grabbed the edge of the structure and then raised himself over.

Tristan crouched down as he saw a guard ahead. He slowly made his approach and then brought his arms around his neck to silently take him down, knocking him out unconscious and then disarming his rifle before he looked down and over to the rest of the prison. There was no immediate entrance into the center of the fortress from outside, but instead a series of individual zones with a helicopter pad in the center, no helicopter, a zone where there were the horses, another where there were parked trucks and various large cargo crates. Tristan looked to the side where a small portion of the center, at a corner, had been blocked off from the rest by a concrete wall similar to the one around the entire former city. The wall ran from the left corner tip of the superstructure and against the outer perimeter wall, and below were two-story structures built out from the wall with cell doors on the outside and a large archway with iron-bar gates in the midst of them, facing into the outer wall. In the midst of the concrete barrier was a rectangular doorway kept open with a yellow-black border around symbolizing caution, and a metal blast door at the side with handles on the front. Tristan took out from a pouch on his belt the set of binoculars that he kept with him and began to look down towards the archway. He saw that there were a set of stairs down past the iron-bar gates

Tristan lowered his binoculars and returned them to their pouch before he went to a trapdoor on one of the four tower heads from the superstructure and began to climb down to enter a stairwell. He then proceeded down the set of circular stairs to the very bottom, which came out to a platform at the side of a ramp that went down towards a set of wooden doors and portcullis at the entrance into the fortress from the city streets. To the right, the ramp went up to the center of the fortress. Tristan made his way out, but stopped before he stopped into the open, coming down onto one knee to look up towards the top of the wall where the guards were. He then looked down and over to the chain-link fences, eyeing the individual gates that went to the other sections. Across from him at the other side of the archway he stood under, there was a gate that went into a corridor that went the direction that Tristan needed to go. He crossed the archway and came to the other side, looking over to the gate and then through the corridor to the other side. Tristan carefully moved over to face the gate, bringing his hands to the release handle and clenching it with his hands before moving the gate back and slipping through.

From this corridor, Tristan walked down and to the other side where he walked through and then made his approach towards the concrete wall where he stopped at the corner to look in. He looked towards the cells that faced outside and saw that there was nobody kept in these holding cells. On the second floor of these structures, there was a warm light from the top with the movement of shadows behind curtains. Tristan made his way across and towards the archway that went into the wall, reaching the iron-bar gates to see that it was locked.

Ahead of the gate there were stairs that went down and then turned left at the landing below, going into the sublevel of the prison. He moved away from the gate and then brushed up against the side of the archway, closer to the side-structures to look around before he moved at the side of the holding cells and then made his way up a set of stairs to the second-floor. He stopped in front of an iron door and took cover at the corner. He then listened to the inaudible speech that came from the other side, and then took a fist and banged against the door. The speech stopped. He heard footsteps approach. The door opened and Tristan pushed his way in, grabbing the guard by the hips and raising him up to toss him onto the floor. The man at the other side of the office space within stood up from his chair, alarmed. Tristan punched out the guard he was atop of and then looked over to the panicking guard as he went for his rifle against the wall. Tristan ran forward and tackled him against the wall, taking his rifle from him and hitting him with the butt of the gun before punching him down onto the floor.

With both guards taken care of, Tristan began to pat them down and search their bodies for a set of keys. He eventually found a key ring on one of them and took it with him. Tristan took apart their weapons, including sidearms, and then proceeded out so that he could reach the gate, quietly testing each of the keys until he was able to unlock the gate and open through. Tristan took the key ring and placed it in one of his pouches before he continued down the steps, stopping at the corner to look down the left side and then continuing downwards as he reached a landing that turned left again. He looked down the steps and went down as he came into the heart of the prison, which was a circular four-story chamber the same size as the prison above, but below ground with prison cells all around followed by protective corridors with iron-bar walls at the outer edge, vestibules spread out between the cell blocks, and a center where there was a watch tower that looked out to every one of the cells from top to bottom.

From the stairs, Tristan came into the outer corridor at a junction where there were gates to his left and right that went into the cell blocks on his left and right, while ahead there was an iron gate that went into a bridge that connected to the modern water tower in the center of the sublevel chamber. The watch tower in the center was modern and contained barred windows that looked down on either side. The bridge that connected to the tower was a narrow cage-like bridge with iron bars at the side and a metal grated floor. At the sides of the bridge and the sides of the tower there was barbed wire.

Tristan made his approach towards the iron bars that looked down to the bottom of the panopticon. The very bottom did not have any cells, but instead was a ruined mess with rubble and water pouring from above. The tower in the middle stood on struts with individual levels below and protected stairs that connected out from the tower to each floor with gates on the other side. There were four-stories of prison cells, labeled from one to four at the side, and at the very bottom of the pit there were arched corridors that went out. The bottom was accessible via ladders at the side of the struts from the bottommost platform. Tristan looked behind him towards the prison cells around, seeing that the corridor was dark, but there was enough candlelight from the center of the tower for him to see the basic structure of the cells, which was a wide arched like slot with metal bars and two beds in each cell. Many of the cells were occupied with people inside, in bed and asleep. Tristan looked back towards the watch tower in the center to see people inside, sitting at a table in the center.

Tristan approached the door into the right block and began to fiddle with keys so that he could enter through. Once he had the right key, he quietly opened the door with a creak and then crouched down so that he could come up to the half-wall below the bars that looked towards the watch tower. He made his way around and then to the next door at a vestibule. Tristan looked ahead through the bars and saw that there was a stairwell that went down. He peaked over the wall and over to the watch tower to see that guards still at the table, playing cards. He went to the next gate and used the same key to open his way in and then make his way over to the gate into the stairwell. He unlocked the gate and then came into the stairwell to go down to the second floor and then make his approach over to a gate that led to a set of stairs up to the watch tower. Tristan unlocked the gate and then began to climb the stairs up to the watch tower where he took out his bow and an arrow at the nearest guard, hitting him in the thigh, and then the other as he went for a sidearm, hitting him in the upper arm.

Both of the guards reached for their wounds. Tristan shot a second arrow at the guard with an arrow in his thigh as he went for his sidearm. He then quickly opened the gate and went over to the one that had been hit with two arrows, slamming his head into the side of the table to knock him out before going to the other from behind to choke him out of consciousness. Tristan retrieved his arrows from each of them and then looked out from the watch tower around to the prisoners. He looked at the desk and began to search for a catalog or manifest with prisoner names, but there were no such documents. Tristan set himself to tie up and dress the guards before he went further. Finally, Tristan took a flashlight from a pouch and left the watch tower to go and check each cell individually.

Many of the prisoners were older men, some Arabic in appearance, some Turkish, and some European, but none that were white with dark hair in his early thirties. By the time Tristan was halfway through the prisoners, he heard a noise from above. He went over to the perimeter of the third level and looked out. He could hear some murmurs in Hebrew, so he went down to the second level to complete his search with haste, but there was nobody of the description that Tristan had expected. Tristan opened the gates to a bridge that connected to a concrete platform at the bottom of the pit and went towards it. He then looked up and saw that there were guards searching the blocks for him.

Tristan lowered himself into the bottom of the chamber and then made his way towards the arched corridor that exited out. The corridor was dark. He shined his light forward, shining it above to see that one of the stairwells came down, but the metal staircase had eroded and broken off to reach the bottom floor. He continued into the left and began to follow a corridor that went briefly around and then down into a curved and wide corridor with cells at either side. These cells were smaller than the ones above, but closer together with thicker doors that could not be seen inside except through a small hatch. There were six in total. Tristan went towards one of these doors and opened the hatch, shining his light in to see a half-naked old man inside, growling in the corner. He shined his light out of the way, shook his head in minor horror, and went over to the other side, going to each one, but not seeing the prisoner he was looking for. Tristan walked to the end of the corridor once he was done and reached a wooden door.

Tristan unlocked the door and entered into a damp corridor with arched cells at the side where there were wide raised platforms with railings at the side. The corridor was lit by sconces against the wall. Each of the cells were covered with only metal doors with hatches. The whole corridor was the length of the diameter of the fortress and ran underneath the bottom of the chamber.

Immediately, as Tristan entered, he faced two guards at the end of the corridor. He took out his bow and shot two arrows towards them at the arms that held their rifle grips. He then ran down and charged towards the closest, picking him up and knocking him onto the floor. He then punched him out and looked to the other. Tristan shot another arrow at him and then hopped over the railing, jumping up onto the other side and taking the guard over before knocking him out with a headbutt and then a punch across the face. He then stood up, retrieved his arrows and looked around. Tristan checked the prisoners, but none of them had the appearance of an older Damian.

Tristan went to a wooden door at the end of the corridor and attempted to open it. However, it was locked. He took out his keyset and attempted to open the door with each key, but none opened. He put the keys he had away and rustled through the guard he knocked out in search of a key ring, but there was none on either of them. Tristan grunted and went down the corridor to a door at the other end, quietly opening it and came into a curved corridor where there were no cells, but doors that went into showers and toilets. At the end of the corridor there was a locked door. Tristan opened the door with the key set that he had and came through.

Across from Tristan, he was met with several guards that were sat around a table. The guards stood up from the table as they saw Tristan. Tristan immediately reached for his bow and shot at one as he reached for his sidearm. He then jumped out of the way as one attempted to punch him. Tristan put his bow away and quickly went in to wrap an arm around the man's torso and arm, picking him up by the leg and throwing him over to one of the other guards. Tristan then raised his fists to the other, but saw that he decided to go in for his sidearm. He took his shield out in retaliation and threw it at him like a frisbee, hitting him hard in the head. Tristan then went into the others on the floor, taking them off each other and raising a fist up.

"Do any of you speak English?" Tristan questioned. "I'm looking for Damian!"

"No!" the one before him replied.

Tristan punched him across the face and dropped him. He then went to the other two.

"How about you chumps?" Tristan asked. "The name Damian ring a bell?"

The men shouted back in Hebrew. Tristan punched one of them out before going to pick up his shield and hitting the one that had been hit by the shield once more to knock him out.

"I guess I'll keep looking then..." Tristan muttered, searching them for keys.

Tristan found a set of keys different to the one that he had on one of the guards. He picked it up and then exited out the way he came, going towards the door that he struggled to get by. He opened through, exited into a wider and taller corridor at the other side that was warmly lit, and looked around. At the sides there were more arched cells, but these had iron bars and some of them did not have gates. Tristan observed that there were no prisoners in this area and some of the cells were occupied with beds in the center that had straps. He looked around and then continued to the end where there was a set of wooden double doors. Tristan opened the door and stepped into the next room as he continued to search for Damian.

Act 7, Scene 4

Tristan came into a longer corridor than the one that he had been at, but less wide with doors at the left-side. He checked on one of these doors and saw that it led into a dark room that was a sort of laboratory with wooden tables that contained lab equipment atop in a similar mess that Charlemagne makeshift lab formerly had. Against one of the walls there was a chalkboard, some desks, and bookcases. Tristan exited out from this room and attempted to enter into others, but some of the doors were locked, while others led into similar laboratories. He used his keys to unlock the locked doors and came into private offices and even a storage closet. At the end of the corridor, Tristan came into another wide corridor, perpendicular to the last one, with arched slots out the left-side with iron bars and doors. All of these cells were unoccupied.

In the middle of the corridor, Tristan saw a large set of double doors on the opposite-wall between the cell, where there were two guards in front of the doors. He took out his bow as they saw each other and shot towards them before they could open fire at him. He then ran towards them, lifting up one of the guards and tossing him back onto the floor to punch him out. Tristan then stood up and took the rifle on the floor, hitting back at the guard on his knee and then striking him down. Tristan looked over to the end of the corridor and saw a wooden door at the opposite-end from where he came. The set of doors that he was at were locked.

Tristan retrieved his arrows and searched the guards for any keys. They were empty-handed. He went to the end of the corridor and exited out into the corridor that was perpendicular and narrow like the other where the laboratories and offices were. This corridor contained arched slots in the left wall, but without iron bars or doors, and instead crates of supplies. Tristan walked to the end and was met with two doors, one that went back into the corridor that connected to the rest of the prison and another that came into a round stairwell with steps that went up. He came upstairs and entered into a corridor significantly different to the dungeon that he was in.

The walls in these corridors were made of the same sandstone bricks, but decorated with rugs on the floor, tapestries, portraits, and paintings on the walls with the occasional lit sconce. Tristan walked down and began to open locked doors that led into more private offices. He searched the offices as he went by, but did not find any keys. He went back down towards the stairwell, and went into a corridor on the right that only had a set of double doors at the end. These doors led into a large library. Tristan continued down and came into the next corridor. He then searched these offices until finally, he found a set of two keys different to ones he already possessed. Tristan took these keys and went around the corridor above where he wanted to be, which was a simple corridor that wrapped around to the first corridor he had come to and led into the stairwell that continued either up or down.

Tristan went down and returned to the set of double doors. He inserted the keys in and unlocked the door, pushing against it to enter into a dark arched corridor that went straight forward and to another set of arched wooden double doors. Tristan took out his flashlight and went to these doors, pushing against them to enter into the dark circular room on the other side.

The chamber that Tristan entered into was circular, wide and two-stories tall. The room was dark, requiring Tristan to shine his light around. He saw stairs at either side of him that went up to a rim that ran around the side of the room and looked over to the center. The room contained various empty and small arched cells around. He shined his light left and right and then stopped in the center where there was a human being with his arms hoisted upwards by the shackles around his wrists and chains that connected to a stone pillar in the center of the room where the man's back was up against.

Tristan looked at the man with the unkempt dark hair and thick beard. His head was tilted down and he was half-naked in only a cloth around his groins. Tristan saw that this man had fair, but dirty and injured skin with wound marks across his body, including lash marks that were most visible around the abdomen, which looked as though a bird had been gnawing at his innards. The man also had a scar shaped like a thick four-pointed star on his shoulder. He was a muscular man and appeared to be within the age range that Tristan anticipated. Tristan quickly made his way over to him, seeing closer and realizing that they were about the same height and size, although the man appeared to be slightly thinner and less lean than Tristan. The man was unconscious. He looked at the shackles around the man's ankles that were connected to the pillar to see that they required a key. He lowered his flashlight onto the floor so that he could attempt to unlock the shackles. Tristan took the keys he had taken from the office, but then turned around as he heard a set of doors open from behind him.

The set of doors immediately before him opened. Tristan took his bow and pointed it towards the man that had entered into the room. He was unlike the other guards, although he was dressed similarly. The man was dressed in a dark rubber-like or ballistic armor with tall boots at his feet, gauntlets at his arm. Around his hips he had a belt, around his thighs holsters, and around his torso a tactical vest. The armor portrayed a muscular physique with imprints on the abdomen. Around his head, he wore a shiny black helmet that covered his entire face except for his lower chin and mouth.

Tristan looked back at the figure and pointed an arrow towards him. The figure raised an arm towards Tristan. Tristan grunted and closed his eyes, bringing a hand to his head as he started to yell out in pain. He dropped his bow and fell to his knees as he continued to shout. The figure then shouted out in pain in return while Tristan was relieved. Tristan looked over as the man faced his palm towards the prisoner rather than Tristan, causing the prisoner to yell out in pain. He quickly picked up his bow and shot an arrow at the psionic soldier, hitting him in the shoulder of the arm that was extended out. The soldier was then knocked back and against the wall by the prisoner. Tristan drew his sword and went towards the soldier, jabbing him and hitting against the tough armor. He then hit at his helmet, but was telekinetically tossed back and onto the floor.

The psionic soldier stood up and extended his arm out towards the prisoner, causing him to shout in pain, tilting his head back. Tristan recovered from the fall that he had and noticed that something had fallen out from one of his pouches – the pouch with his flashlight, which also kept the dark crystals. He quickly picked them up into his hands and saw that they were glowing. He placed them back into the pouch and put away his sword. He took his bow out and shot at the psionic soldier again. The psionic soldier grunted and took his hand out to face towards Tristan, but Tristan had vanished.

Tristan reappeared atop of the steps as he blinked and took his arrow back out to shoot at the psionic soldier before he blinked out again to the other side of the room. He then shot another arrow at him, hitting him in the side. The soldier fell to a knee as he grabbed the arrow to remove it. Tristan blinked and appeared before him. He took out his sword and hit at him in the corner of the neck and then at the helmet. The psionic soldier simply absorbed the brutal shock that came with the sword coming down onto him as he slowly stood up. Tristan quickly teleported out of the way and came behind the pillar.

The psionic soldier drew a sidearm and connected it with another piece to put together a heavy caliber rifle. He then proceeded to shoot towards Tristan, requiring him to back out of cover and hiding in the darkness. The soldier shouted out and Tristan saw that light appeared in the room as he set fire to the torches in the room. Tristan ducked out from the other side of the pillar and shot an arrow towards the soldier. The psionic soldier took the shot and began to move around the side as he shot towards Tristan with his rifle.

Tristan prepared another arrow and then teleported out of the way. He reappeared towards the right-side of the room from the exit, shot his arrow, and then teleported out of the way, to the left-side of the room where he shot another arrow at the thigh of the soldier, causing him to come down onto his knee again. Tristan quickly put his bow away and took out his sword. He teleported before his foe and jabbed his sword into his torso before swinging it down onto the clavicle and into the helmet. The helmet cracked. Tristan teleported out of the way as the soldier recovered. He appeared within one of the cells and took cover against the wall as the soldier began to move up the stairs to the upper level. Tristan shot an arrow towards him and then vanished as the bullets came.

The psionic soldier began to open fire towards the left-side of the room in anticipation of Tristan's arrival. He appeared on the lower level of the left-side and shot another arrow towards the soldier, hitting him in the shoulder. He then vanished and appeared behind the pillar, looking over to the prisoner to see that he had been knocked out. Tristan stayed where he was as he heard the gunshots fire. He then heard the magazine run out, so he came out from around the pillar and shot another arrow before putting his bow away and teleporting before the soldier as he took out his sword and shield. The psionic soldier attempted to punch at Tristan, hitting his shield as Tristan raised it.

Tristan slashed at the soldier with sword, piercing through the armor as he jabbed into the shoulder. Tristan then wacked him in the helmet as he shouted out, causing a part of the helmet to break and reveal the face inside. He looked in and saw an extremely, sickly pale face and bloodshot yellow eyes. The skin of the man was as white as the men in black. The man had no hair protruding through the helmet or even any eyebrow hair. Tristan looked back in astonishment, which followed with a strike towards him that knocked him back. He quickly teleported out of the way and into a cell underneath where he took a moment to recover.

The psionic soldier reloaded, but didn't immediately begin to fire. He put his sword and shield away, and listened. Tristan then jumped as the soldier appeared before him on the other side of the bars, hopping down from above. He immediately teleported as the maniac began to open fire into the cell, appearing behind him as he took the opportunity to grab him by the waist and thigh to lift him up. The psionic soldier retaliated by hitting Tristan in the head with his elbow, causing the massive weight of the man to come on top of him.

Tristan brought an arm around the soldier as attempted to choke him out. He also took hold of an arrow, pulling it out from the ballistic armor and then stabbing into the shoulder to cause the soldier some pain. The soldier squirmed and began to hit an elbow back into Tristan's chainmail. He shouted out in pain and Tristan was soon required to let go as he began to close his eyes and cringe. He let go of the arrow too and took his hands to the side of his head. The soldier got off from Tristan and attempted to grab him. Tristan vanished before he could and appeared in another cell, above, where he took another moment to recover.

The psionic soldier picked up his rifle and began to move towards the right-side of the room. Tristan prepared his bow and shot at the back of the soldier. He then vanished and came to the middle of the room, in front of some cells to shoot another arrow towards the man. The soldier shouted out and cast the palm of his hand towards Tristan as he vanished and came back to the left-side in the lower levels. The psionic soldier unleashed a wave of energy that hit at the center of the room like a shockwave from a blast, causing some of the stone to be blown back and for the barred doors to fling open.

Tristan shot another arrow back at the soldier, hitting him in the back of the calf. He fell over. Tristan teleported behind him, put his bow away and then took out his sword. He ran towards him and brought the sword down with a jump, hitting the clavicle and then the back of the neck. He then struck onto the top of the head, exposing him. Tristan then raised his sword up with both hands with intent to strike down.

The psionic soldier shouted out and unleashed a wave of energy that sent Tristan backwards and onto the floor. Tristan quickly vanished as the soldier stood up and opened fire at him. He appeared behind him and stood up, putting his sword away and looking over to the man as he was now without his helmet. The man had a complete white face with red lips, no hair. Tristan took out his bow and shot at him. He then teleported out of the way. The psionic soldier released a wave of energy at Tristan.

Tristan appeared from the middle of the room and shot another arrow at the soldier, hitting him in the shoulder. The soldier fell onto his knee again and Tristan put his bow away and drew his sword. He then teleported behind him. Tristan raised his sword. The psionic soldier pivoted around and lunged at Tristan, grabbing him by the neck and taking him down to the ground. Tristan dropped his sword.

The psionic soldier began to choke Tristan. Tristan struggled as he attempted to reach for his sword, but it was too far away. He then closed his eyes and teleported away, but he couldn't vanish without the soldier still around his neck. Tristan closed his eyes again and the pair appeared above in the air. The weight of the man against Tristan sent them towards the floor. Tristan took the moment to flip them over as he grabbed the psionic soldier, thrusting the force into him as they landed down. The psionic soldier smacked into the stone with Tristan atop of him.

Tristan grabbed his sword and then stabbed down into the jugular notch of the soldier, causing a hissing noise to come out of the soldier as he shouted in pain. Tristan then drew his sword out and backed away from the body as a storm of a dark purple energy followed around the corpse and emitted out like an aura as if it were melting like a block of ice. A terrible, demonic screech began to emit and the corpse of the soldier vanished with an expulsion of an energy that hit at him like a shockwave. Tristan held his ground and covered his face as the energy hit him. He then looked back to see that the there was nothing left of the psionic soldier except the torn remains of his clothes and some of his equipment, including the rifle and all the arrows that stuck out. Tristan put his sword away and then walked over to the prisoner so that he could release him.

The prisoner's feet were freed from the chains. Tristan then picked up his flashlight on the floor before looking up and into the face of the prisoner, which was clearer with the torchlight in the room. Tristan squinted at the face and then looked back in horror and shock. The prisoner that was in chains above him eerily like the man that he knew as Audric Zimmerman.

"No…" Tristan muttered, looking at the man carefully.

Tristan breathed sharply as he stepped back from the prisoner. He then turned around to hear the doors open again followed by the march of quick footsteps. The doors burst open and a group of guards entered into the room with their rifle pointed towards him and the prisoner. Tristan backed up and looked over to them. They shouted at him in Hebrew. Tristan grabbed Damian by the ankle and closed his eyes, but before they could vanish together, he felt Damian come alive.

The guards before them began to shout out in pain as they dropped their arms and fell over with their hands to their head as Tristan had with the psionic soldier. However, these guards had more of a panic in them. Tristan took the moment to come around the other side of the pillar and climbed the ladder so that he could break Damian out from the shackles at his wrist. He then fell over and onto the floor. Tristan came down and then helped him onto his feet. The guards were in disarray, which allowed them to go straight through.

Tristan opened his pouch as they entered into the corridor and brought the crystals out to see if they continued to glow, but they didn't. He put the crystals away and then reaffirmed his grip around the man before they continued to leave. Tristan came out the way that he had come, entering into the panopticon and going across to enter into an arched corridor that led to the stairwell upwards. He then came up to the top, exiting into the corridor that went to the surface, and then going through the enclosed corner to step out into the midst of the prison fortress. Tristan stopped as he heard a shout in Hebrew, so he looked above and saw the rest of the guards with their rifles pointed down at them.

Within a few seconds, the guards like those below began to fall into a fit of delusion as they lowered their rifles and took to their heads. Tristan quickly took Damian over to a pen where there were horses and laid him down against the wall. He picked out a horse at random, choosing one with dark hair and a black coat. He picked up a saddle and readied the horse. He then picked up Damian and brought him onto the back of the horse, laying him on his stomach and then going over to the gate that connected to the helipad and aimed down into the ramp that exited out of the fortress. He pushed the gate open and then returned to the horse. Tristan climbed up and then rode the horse around so that he could make his escape.

Tristan stopped at the portcullis and hopped down so that he could crank the gate open, locking it into place, and then going over to release the lock on the wooden doors, pushing the doors open before he returned to the horse and then rode out into the streets of Jerusalem with Damian behind him. Tristan rode out without a chase behind him, going straight to the inn where Diana waited for him.

Act 8, Scene 1

Diana sat at the table at their inn suite. Tristan quickly opened the door with Damian's arm around his neck as he dragged him in. Diana stood up and went over to help him, but stopped as she saw the face of the man that had caused them so much trouble over the years. She brought her hands together and before her face.

"Yeah, I know," Tristan responded to her lack of words. "Help me get him onto the bed."

Diana walked forward and helped Tristan. The pair sat Damian down and then picked up his feet so that he could lay down. Tristan panted as he looked over to the man. Diana looked back at him.

"Mika was right," Tristan stated to her. "I never doubted him for a moment."

"Tristan, this…"

"Is our son, in this world at least – not technically our own son…"

"It's Zimmerman," Diana said.

"Mika didn't lie to us though," Tristan replied. "He told us to seek out our son who was being held in a prison in Jerusalem, and that's who we found. Zimmerman is Damian. Damian is Zimmerman, and on retrospect, I think it's safe to conclude that Zimmerman-Damian is the Mysterious Stranger."

Diana looked down at Damian as he slept on their bed. She looked over to his shoulder and saw the star-shaped scar. Diana moved away from the bed and went towards the table to sit down.

"I can't believe this…" Diana remarked, picking up the metal cup to drink some water.

"The last time we saw him was in China... Charlemagne told us that something strange had happened at the shrine when Zimmerman touched the time orb. He disappeared right there..."

"But we're not in the future," Diana pointed out. "You said that we're technically in the present, but in a different universe."

Tristan didn't immediately respond.

"Charlemagne said that these orbs seem to be sentient in some mannerism," Tristan remarked. "Maybe it's the work of God, and/or, maybe there's something more elaborate to it, but when I was in that chamber, the crystals began to glow when I was faced with danger."

Tristan took out the crystals.

"It was like they sensed that I was in danger, so they decided to activate after weeks of being inactive," Tristan explained. "And then when I was out of the danger, they stopped working again."

Diana crossed her arms.

"When they worked for me in Egypt, I was in danger..." Diana pointed out, "but that doesn't explain how Zimmerman came here."

Tristan looked back to Damian.

"We'll have to wait for him to wake up and explain to us what the hell is going on," Tristan said. "For all we know, this could be someone else..."

"No," Diana rejected. "If this is Zimmerman, or not, I'm not sure, but I do know for sure that this is in the least the Mysterious Stranger. Look at the scar on his shoulder – I gave him that when we were in Montana. This is him."

Tristan looked back to Damian with a frown.

"He's definitely Damian in the least," Tristan remarked. "I'm going downstairs to see if we can extend our stay or get another room so that you can sleep. I'll keep watch of him overnight…"

Tristan walked over to a table where they had placed the horse's saddle. He then picked up the bag of coins and left.

• • • •

Tristan took off his armor and watched Damian into the night, seeing him awaken before the sunrise. He then looked back towards him. The man grumbled and came to his side, going back asleep. Tristan closed his own eyes and drifted off. He later woke up with the sound of a knock on the door. Tristan stood up and went over to the door.

Diana walked in and looked over to Damian who was fast asleep. She then walked past and went over to the table to sit down.

"He's still asleep?" Diana questioned.

"I wouldn't put it past the Chosen to have sedated him," Tristan remarked, rubbing his eyes. "He's seriously out of it, but we don't have to leave until noon, so… we can give him until then.

Tristan took the money bag and placed it on the table.

"Do you want to go into town and find him a set of clothes so he doesn't have to leave here like that," Tristan said. "Preferably something that can help him conceal his identity. They'll be looking for him."

"What happened in the prison?" Diana asked. "Tell me."

Tristan proceeded to tell Diana about his infiltration and then fight with the psionic soldier. He included the details about Damian helping him until he was knocked out, the crystals awakening, and then their subsequent escape where Damian caused the guards to undergo a mentally-induced panic attack.

Tristan finished off by saying that he stole a horse from the prison and that it's downstairs in the same stall as Tempest.

"I'm going to see about some breakfast then," Diana said, standing up. "Stay here and rest. I'll be right back, and maybe I'll find some clothes too. I saw a place out there that sells some garbs."

Diana looked back over to Damian.

"I never realized it before, but he's about your height," Diana stated.

"You should have an easy time finding him something in my size then," Tristan replied.

Diana left. Tristan continued to sit at the table until she returned with some clothes and food. The couple ate together and then sat quietly as they looked over to Damian sleep. By the time that it was almost noon, Tristan looked at his watch and stood up. Diana watched as he went over to nudge the man.

"Wake up!" Tristan shouted at him.

Damian grunted and came onto his back. He slowly opened his eyes and looked to the ceiling. Tristan looked at his green eyes like his. He stepped back. Diana stood up and looked over to him. Damian inched up the bed to sit up and look over to them.

"What's going on?" Damian asked.

"Yeah, we'd like to know that too," Tristan replied. "What the hell are you doing here?"

Damian grunted and lay back down. He brought a hand to his head.

"Where am I?" Damian questioned.

"You're in Jerusalem – in your own timeline," Tristan explained. "In the year 2052."

"And that begs the question of what the two of you are doing here," Damian replied

Tristan looked over to Diana as he crossed his arms

"We're trapped here," Tristan responded. "We were sent to free you because we know that you're awakened and have psionic powers. We need your help to return to our own universe. So, what were you doing in a prison owned by the Children of Moloch?"

Damian sat up again and looked over to him.

"So, you know about them?" Damian remarked.

Tristan sighed and said, "We know about the Children, the Chosen, the Global Defense Project, The Order of St. Athanasius... all those secret societies, oh... and the fact that your name isn't Audric Zimmerman, but that your true identity is Damian. We also know that you're the assassin who's sought us out, killed my mother, also probably killed my aunt and uncle too, and let's be honest, are the reason why my dad is dead."

"Tristan..." Diana remarked to him.

Tristan looked back at her and then continued to say, "And we know that you've been spying on us over the years. Diana saw your quarters at Aegis Castle. She was taken there by Iustina, her friend. I suppose this also means that you're Helene's adoptive-father, and all those other kids" he said with a sigh. "I also know about your upbringing, the fact that you born from Diana in this universe, conceived between her and the Tristan that exists, or existed (I don't know), in this universe. And with that, I also know that you killed Charlemagne when you were seventeen. I've seen it all."

"Seems like you know what's going on then," Damian barked, lying back down.

"We now about your robots too," Diana said. "Your 'legacy' and the Wells Project; the Shadow Company. All of the other superhumans in your castle. We know about your membership with the Children of Moloch..."

"Aren't you the pair of detectives…" Damian replied. "All of that is old news."

"We'd appreciate to be brought up to speed on current events then," Tristan responded. "Preferably, anything that we don't know, such as the *why* to all this."

Damian looked back at him and over to Diana. He sighed.

"Where do I begin?" Damian questioned, pivoting himself out from the bed to sit.

"China," Tristan replied. "When we last saw each other."

"Very well…" Damian said, pausing for a moment. "As you seemingly have found out, I am not from the world that you're from. I'm from this world. When I took hold of the scepter with the time orb, the orb sensed that I was not from this world, but had made my stay for almost ten years in a world that wasn't mine. I heard the whispers in my ear…"

"What whispers?" Tristan asked.

"Voices," Damian remarked. "They banished me back to the world I came from, and I appeared in the Dragon's Den in that world. As soon as I made my arrival, the Children (or what remained of them) knew, so they closed in one me as fast as they could and I was easily captured – I couldn't escape from that damn tomb, or even teleport out."

"So, that's how you were imprisoned then," Tristan said, "but why?"

"Tell us from the very beginning," Diana said. "Tell us what happened after you killed Charlemagne, when you were still a boy."

"I was hardly a boy," Damian barked back. "I was seventeen and made more of a life for myself than either of you…"

Damian stopped as he looked at Diana's pregnant belly. He sighed.

"Fine," Damian remarked. "You seem to somehow know that I killed Charlemagne, so let me explain what happened afterwards. Charlemagne in this world was less like the Charlemagne you know and surely love. The Charlemagne I knew for all of my life was much like the Charlemagne that you had known when you had met him at first. He was cold. He was emotionless. He was depressive. However, he had lived a lot more before this spell came unto him, particularly as he was in the care of Diana since she was ten instead of fourteen. In those years, he came to find both the Amulet of Ra and the Scepter of Alexander the Great on his own. As I'm sure you know, it was never about those artefacts."

"The crystals…"

"I took them after I killed him. I was drawn to them. For the next year, I lived as an outlaw while authorities of all kind searched for me. I was eventually captured by an organization you know of – the Global Defense Project. They didn't care that I had killed a man. All they wanted was the crystals they knew Charlemagne had. By then, I had uncovered the power of the crystals, but it wasn't enough for me to defend myself. They took me in. They tortured me. As I'm sure you know, the Global Defense Project is led by a committee that is in the hands of the Children of Moloch. In these times, there was no more middleman. I became a test subject for their psionic program, accelerating their research and becoming one of the first awakened soldiers, trained to use the powers that I had within me, while also being trained as a commando. They broke me. I was brainwashed. They told me I was their messiah. I believed it. They used me to wage war, their wars, but I was not all lost. I'm not sure what you know about this world…" Damian said, standing up and going to the window, "but this world is gone. This was more than a collapse of civilization… it was goaded conflict. All of it started with the civil war in the United States, which took the world into chaos as people took advantage of the fact that the superpower was distracted with its own conflict. The Children of Moloch took the chance to secure their position in the Middle East by creating Greater Israel. However, it didn't go as they thought it would, and that led to the Great Calamity. Millions upon millions; billions of lives were lost in that moment – two-thirds, or maybe it was three-quarters of the world's population, instantly vanished from the face of the Earth, and that was the end of it all."

Damian paused for a moment and then continued to explain, "After the Children of Moloch regrouped, I went to them with an idea. I proposed a second chance at success. They were distraught at the outcome of the war and listened to me. I convinced them that I had unlocked a new power, which I had, in which I could rip through reality and travel back in time. So, they entrusted me, a twenty-one year old boy, with this mission to use my powers and travel into the past to a point where I could ensure the conditions that would guarantee their success in a war against their enemies. However, I never intended to help them. They gave me the orbs and I unleashed the power that I had learned, travelling back in time... or so I thought."

"You didn't travel back in time. You created a new, younger universe," Tristan explained.

"Thanks, I figured that one out myself," Damian replied, groggy. "I had my mind set on the year 2010 – giving me enough time to make a name for myself while also changing some events in the past. The Children prepared me with the information I would need, and once I was set, I found myself thirty years in the past, in the presence of the Children of Moloch. The intensity of what I had done had ripped the orbs to shred, but I was there. In that fortress you found me in, where I presented myself to them as a god, using the Yiddish name that I was given by the Children, Audric Zimmerman, and stating that I was their messiah. They believed me, but with suspicion. After I had established myself with them, I went off to accumulate my wealth. I played the stock market and became an investor. I then made my own company, began to assimilate other companies, one-by-one, until I had the empire you know of. The crown jewel was Fitch Corporation, which with the help of Oswald Montgomery's daughter and husband, I was able to stage a hostile takeover against as we leaked his tax evasion to the IRS and FBI. With this company, I formed the Wells Project which had the sole purpose of accumulating the orbs that I once had. I also established the Shadow Company, and began to put together my plan – not the Children's plan, my own plan. I was not in their world, I was in mine. I set off to change the past and that began with my mother's life so that I could change her fate for the better. I killed that scumbag that killed her mother. I then killed her father to release them from that man. I didn't realize though that the burden of loss would cause Diana's mother to develop an addiction to opioids, just like my own mother. I kept a close watch, but also kept my distance. I never expected that she would overdose. To learn that despite my efforts, Diana suffered the loss of her mother, struck me. I had to retaliate, and that's what I did when I hunted down the people that, at first, I thought were Tristan's parents. I wanted to make him suffer, so that he could understand the pain that affected both me and Diana. When a man demonstrated interest in adopting Tristan after the death of his aunt and uncle, I kept watch and learned that this man was the man that I needed to get closer to Charlemagne – Salmar. I influenced his mind and made my acquaintance as a board member of Cabernet Industries. When I later learned that Diana had been taken into foster care, I worked to have her brought into the care of Charlemagne, but by then, he had deteriorated mentally. I needed Charlemagne alive so that I could use him to lead me to the orbs. So, I used my connections with the Chosen and used Salmar to have her brought into his care."

"How come Salmar doesn't remember this?" Diana asked.

"Because he was under mind control," Damian replied. "It was the only way I could get him to do anything, including trying to get Charlemagne to not sell his company, but the effects were too much for him and he lost his mind. To have him go after Charlemagne with bloodlust was never my intent. I lost control of him and as a result, I lost control of Tristan only to later learn that Charlemagne adopted the both of you. I was more or less indifferent to this result – if anything, it made it easier to track all of you together. I carried on with my plans and began to influence another helpless soul, Dr. Judith Lambert, and through her I set off to construct my own fusion reactor, using the Medici organization as a connection. When that failed, I made contact with another helpless soul, Yuri Saburov, who introduced me to the Huntsman Legionnaires. Through them, I set off to retrieve both personal files belonging to Charlemagne as well as the prototype robots that I would base my army on, lost in the Russian wilderness. With that, I had a steppingstone for my plans. And at this time, I began to learn of something that surprised me: the two of you had fallen in love. I didn't dare to come between you two. My intentions with Diana have always been to ensure that she was happy, and if that meant that he was happy too, then what of it?"

"Is that why you kidnapped me in France? Almost killed me in the US?" Diana questioned.

"I've never attempted to murder you," Damian deflected. "I've never attempted to subject you to any type of bodily harm.

I only kidnapped you in France as a way to get to Charlemagne and then in the United States to get to Tristan. Did you not sense that – the benevolence your captor had for you? Did it not strike you as odd?"

"Anyways…!" Tristan interjected in an annoyed voice. "Go on."

Damian sighed and continued to explain, "With both the robots and Charlemagne's personal files in my possession, I set into motion the events that would have him come to Egypt to search for the Amulet of Ra and Scepter of Alexander the Great. To start, I killed his old friend, the Russian, and found his journal so that I could push Charlemagne into the direction he would need to go in. The Huntsman kept an eye on the situation, intervening in Luxor when you were under threat of those Jihadists, and keeping everybody in the loop of what you were doing so that they could be a step ahead and ready to swoop in to collect the prize for me. Once it was all over, my agent, Dr. Southern, who I recommended to Charlemagne when he announced his intentions to find the Spear of Destiny, collected the prize and set off with it in Alexandria, which was when we met and I was forced to abandon my position as Charlemagne's friend and become his enemy. With half of the orbs, I had enough to continue my own psionics program and human experimentation to have my own supersoldiers. However, when the Children of Moloch caught wind of what Charlemagne had done in France, I was summoned on a mission to interrupt your *Bon Vacances*. I had to assure my connections with the Chosen, working with Mossad operatives and their intelligence network. I later took the problem into my own hands, seeing this as a personal problem, and concealed my identity to retrieve important documents in Charlemagne's possession. However, Charlemagne had formed his personal army and made the problem more difficult than I expected. I didn't want to kill Charlemagne; I needed him still to find the Scepter of Alexander the Great, so I cut a deal with the Elders of the Children. I told them I would collect and destroy the files, which I achieved.

"Around this time, I also became interested in refining my mortality – I had learned from the Children of some of their sacred rituals, their use of a chemical known as adrenochrome, and set off on my own research. For most of my life, I had a weakened immune system, and it wasn't until later that I learned that this was because of my father's lack of an immune system. I learned from the Chosen's archives that there was a researcher in one of their rival organizations that had been working on nanotechnology to create a super-immune system, and when I saw that this woman shared the same face as Tristan, I put that together with the information I had collected from Salmar that the boy was adopted. I needed a sample of Tristan's blood to create my own nanomachines, but with Charlemagne's private army protecting the pair of you, it was impossible to get anywhere close. My first opportunity came in England when I heard that Charlemagne was helping with a firestorm there and I saw that Tristan had been the subject of a terrorist attack. However, I failed to find you in that forest, so I retreated. The second opportunity came when one of my test subjects escaped into Allabrese, forcing me to place the entire town in containment as I searched for him, later learning that he of course went to Charlemagne for protection. I sent my own personal army and the other supersoldiers in to retrieve him and Tristan, but it appeared that it wasn't enough. As a result of my efforts, all of them were slain. Finally, my third opportunity came the following month when I received a phone call from Salmar that stated he had been visited by you two, because Tristan was interested in his parents. I sent in the Huntsman to do a simple job, and ended up intervening myself because seemingly, it wasn't a simple job when the pair of you continually evaded capture and then later escaped into the United States. Luckily, as an American citizen, that allowed me to fly in from my home in New York to Montana and pick up the trail. Tristan, you fool, in your advent, you led yourself not only into the open, but right to the home of the Order where I was able to find your mother. With Tristan's blood in my hands, I was able to finish my own superhuman serum, taking from my own superhumans under the care of Iustina and I, perfecting it outright. With this, all I needed was the scepter. And… you should know the rest of course. The Children captured me and tortured me for my failure."

Tristan uncrossed his arms and began to explain that, "We're stuck here because Charlemagne had the brilliant idea to meddle with both the time orb and space orb, creating a device he thought to be a time machine, but was instead a portal that travelled straight to this world. We got separated from him after we went in after him, because he had gone in looking for someone that he had lost – his son, Finn, and Finn's mother. We then had a fight and in Diana's rage against Charlemagne, she took hold of these crystals…" Tristan said, taking out the crystals from his pouch and showing them, "which took us to Georgia across the other side of the world."

Damian looked at the crystals with intrigue and then asked, "You managed to travel to the other side of the world with only those crystals?" Damian questioned with doubt.

"Yes," Tristan answered, "but for some reason, the crystals don't work anymore, except for last night when I went to rescue you. When I faced that supersoldier in the prison, they worked then when I needed them. I was sent to look for you because I was told that you were here and had the powers to take us back to Allabrese to reunite with Charlemagne."

Damian frowned at him and explained, "When these rocks become overwhelmed, they begin to break. They're not indestructible. A trip across the world with only these crystals – you're lucky they didn't shatter in the size they've been cut down to."

"Can they be fixed?"

"I don't know," Damian replied, "but their power should be the same. These are the crystals that I had given my supersoldiers, aren't they? Each of those crystals gave my soldiers the ability to travel up to ten kilometers at peak form. The power of each crystal exponentially grows. With two, you can travel one-hundred kilometers, and with three, one-thousand kilometers."

"And four... ten-thousand," Tristan said. "Shouldn't that be enough to get us across the Atlantic?"

"Yes," Damian responded. "There is some hope... When I came to this world, I had left behind a ring in the tomb, which contained a piece of the original orb approximately the same size as those pieces you have. Since a temple like that is difficult to come across, and most normal souls would die the instant they confronted the horror that meets them within, I believe it is safe to assume that it continues to be there."

"Then we have to travel to China," Tristan replied. "We need to find the Tomb of the Dragon Emperor and collect that ring."

"From where we are, the tomb is almost seven-thousand kilometers away. What are your plans to get there? Fossil fuels are a luxury to come across in this world and the only reasonable way to travel is via horseback."

"I have horses..." Tristan said.

"Hmph," Damian grunted, "it took the merchants almost a year to travel from China to Rome via the silk road, and you think we'll get there within a day?"

"I don't have naïve expectations," Tristan remarked back, getting slightly annoyed with Damian. "We have the crystals too. Can't you use them to get us their faster?"

Damian went quiet.

"It would still at least take us seven or eight days," Damian finally replied. "We would need supplies. I need clothes. I need a horse."

"Yes, yes," Tristan responded. "We have all that. Can you do it though?"

Damian looked back at them.

"What's in it for me?" Damian questioned.

"What do you want?" Tristan asked with a sigh.

Damian paused for a moment. "I don't want to be in this world, that's for sure. If I help you return to Charlemagne, then I want to return to the other world."

Diana and Tristan looked back at each other. Tristan sighed.

"Fine," Tristan reckoned, "but get us to Charlemagne before there's any promise. We'll do what we can to have you return with us, but I can't offer a guarantee."

"Good enough," Damian responded with contempt.

Act 8, Scene 2

The next morning from the day that Finn brought the car to a stop at a rest area on the Trans-Canada Highway, Charlemagne woke up to look up to the light grey skies above him. He brought a hand to his head and then slowly picked himself up, looking over to see the tents pitched at the side of the parking lot and a makeshift canopy brought over the rear of the truck. Charlemagne crawled out from the back of the truck and dropped down. He then went over to the fire between the camps and began to light it back up so that he could see to some breakfast.

Once Manon and Finn had awoken and eaten, they packed up their belongings and brought them back to the truck so that they could continue on the road. Charlemagne and Manon entered into the front cabin while Finn returned to the back. He picked up a jerry can and then went around to fill the truck with fuel before going back to sit down against the rear window and be near the machine gun pointed out back. Charlemagne started the engine and drove them out from the parking lot and back towards the highway so that they could continue their way towards Harlech.

The truck drove through the remainder of the distance which composed mostly of forest at the sides for the next hundred kilometers or so. The path that came towards Harlech was marked by a glimpse of the Harlech River from above as the highway passed by a bridge high above the water. Some more signs could be seen at the right-side of the road, stating that the next exit led out to Clements Mountain and Evergreen Plateau. Charlemagne continued to drive through until they reached the exit. On either side, there were still trees around them with no view of the city. Charlemagne carried on as he came by some abandoned cars on the side of the road, without tires, hoods raised, and gas covers left open. The next exit that came up was for Iris Heights and Iris Mountain as well as Middlefield. The truck drove through the rest of the forest as they approached this exit.

Finn looked out the side of the truck and down towards Upper and Lower Middlefield, as well as the rest of New Harlech, and by extension, the islands ahead. New Harlech had been totally wiped out from the sides of the mainland it existed on. No structure could be seen intact, and instead, there was nothing more than charred remains of buildings all around up to the water. Around Middlefield Avenue, where there were some skyscrapers, there were some more composed ruins, but they were nothing more than low-level ruins and rubble of what used to be up to thirty-story apartment buildings or commercial buildings. From Eastford all the way towards Oakley, this was the sight to see with burnt structures towards the Westford area and districts that surrounded. Finn also looked ahead towards the islands to see that they were in a similar state to how they had been previously if not more doomsday-in-appearance and ruined.

The view of the city disappeared as they were surrounded by trees on approach towards Caledonian Highlands and Northgate. Charlemagne carried on and they passed his exit to make their way towards the Ford Bridge and Westford itself. Charlemagne saw the bridge below at Waterfront Drive had collapsed and that the Rutherford Dam had been blown out. He came into Legion Hill and carried on as he made his way towards Penultimate Bridge. Charlemagne quickly made his pass by the Mount Harlech and North Harlech exit, which was when Finn noticed a pair of trucks like theirs behind them.

"Oh, damn…" Finn cursed, crawling over and picking up a set of binoculars.

Finn saw that both of the pickup trucks were armed with machine guns pointed straight towards them.

"Charles!" Finn shouted. "We've got company!"

Charlemagne looked into the rear-view mirror and then into the side-view mirror to see the pickup trucks on approach.

"Oh dear…" Charlemagne remarked. "Manon, you will have to help our son to fend these poachers off."

"What?" Manon questioned.

"Or you can drive if that's what you prefer," Charlemagne offered, "but we don't have time to switch seats. Finn, get on that machine gun, but do not open fire until we're certain they're hostile!"

Finn grabbed ahold of the MG42, readied the gun by laying down the latch over the feed of bullets and then held the handles as he stood in the back of the truck. The trucks ahead began to open fire towards them.

"They're hostile!" Finn shouted.

"Open fire!"

Finn placed his hand on the trigger and began to return fire on the machine gun, aiming towards the hostiles, which proved difficult as Charlemagne began to swerve out of the way to evade their own gunfire. Smoke blew off from the rapid-fire gun while bullets automatically fed in by demand and by the ammunition belt from the cartridge canister on the floor.

Charlemagne slowed down to make the sharp turn at the part of the highway that began to head south towards Penultimate Bridge. Both Charlemagne and Manon looked ahead towards the bridge down the hill as they began to rush along, picking speeds of an excess of one-hundred miles per hour. The side-view mirror cracked as a bullet hit it and then tore it off. Charlemagne looked into the rear-view mirror and saw the bandits would not let out.

The truck drove towards Penultimate Bridge, but as Charlemagne got closer, he began to notice some more pickup trucks with machine guns mounted on the back pointed towards them. There was a blockade established at the bridge with sandbags mounted atop of each other and a chain-link fence in front. There were also watch towers on the side of the bridge that went to King Island. The truck pulled out from the highway just as they were about to pass over the bridge, coming off an exit and then making a sharp turn eastward as they came onto Waterfront Drive.

"No way we'll be able to take them all on there," Charlemagne remarked. "We'll have to lose them through the ruins."

Charlemagne began to drive through Westford as they were joined by four pickup trucks on their tail. Finn continued to fire back, slowing down his firing as he came to the end of the belt. Charlemagne noticed that Finn was low on ammunition, so he took a detour off Waterfront Drive and into the ruined suburbs where the charred remains of homes provided ample protection as he began to drive left and right aimlessly in an effort to stop the firing back at them. Finn took the moment to lift the latch and place another belt of cartridges in from another canister. He then laid down the latch and pulled the lever to cock the machinegun. Charlemagne saw that Finn was ready and began to drive down the road back towards Waterfront Drive.

Finn proceeded to open fire again towards the hostiles, hitting the front of one of the pickup trucks up to the windshield. Charlemagne turned onto Waterfront Drive before he could see anything else. Only three cars could be seen coming out from around the corner as they sped down Waterfront Drive. Finn looked over to the remains of the Diamond Center and then forward as he slowed down his firing to limit how much smoke blocked his face.

"Don't forget the bridge has been blown out!" Finn shouted.

Charlemagne listened and quietly turned onto Legionnaire Way to drive uphill back towards the highway. Finn continued to lay down fire as he came to the last bullets in his band and then he was spent. Charlemagne drove onto the entrance ramp and came into the highway again, going eastbound and across the Ford Bridge.

Finn quickly reloaded the machine gun as the rear of the truck began to become pelted with bullets. He cocked the gun and then began to open fire on the hostiles from behind, hitting the tires of a car ahead and causing it to spin out. Charlemagne drove out at Caledonian Highlands and then began to head down the remains of Caledonia Road to come into Eastford. Finn missed his shots with the MG42 while Charlemagne swerved across on the wide road ahead of them.

Charlemagne turned onto Waterfront Drive and continued eastwards as he made his way into Eastford. Finn continued to miss his shots at the trucks, but in return, they were unable to hit them. Charlemagne kept left as he came to the five-point intersection with two roads going east. He continued down and went into Lower Middlefield via Waterfront Drive.

Finn continued to line his shots, slowing down as he came to the last of his bullets. Charlemagne drove through the waterfront where they could see an unobstructed view of the calm water of Walham River. They passed the former industrial portion past the metropolitan core and began to come towards Rosalynn Park and Oakley. At the end of Waterfront Drive, Finn ran out of bullets.

Charlemagne made a sharp turn and saw that Finn had stopped firing. He made his way into the ruins of Oakley Village and then held on as they blew a tire. The truck began to spin out. Finn held onto the side of the pickup while he shifted his weight down so that he didn't fall out. Charlemagne attempted to regain control of the car, but the pickup truck flew into some trees where it was stopped.

"Dammit!" Charlemagne remarked, hitting the steering wheel.

Finn stood up and picked up their last drum of rounds. He then began to ready the machine gun again while Charlemagne took his rifle. The trucks closed in on them. Charlemagne raised his rifle before quickly backing out into cover as they shot towards them. Finn ducked down.

"Finn! Forget it! Get down from there!" Charlemagne shouted.

"Let me finish! I can take them out!" Finn argued.

Charlemagne aimed his rifle out and attempted to open fire, but his gun was jammed. He quickly came back into cover while Finn continued to fiddle with reloading the machine gun. A truck drove past them and pointed its machine gun towards Charlemagne and Manon as they were in cover. Charlemagne raised his hands, which followed with Manon doing the same.

Finn span the tripod around so that he could aim towards the trucks. Charlemagne jerked his neck over and noticed.

"Finn, stand down!" Charlemagne yelled at him. "We're beaten!"

Finn didn't move his hands from the machine gun.

"We can beat them," Finn encouraged.

"Finn, stand down or you'll get us all killed," Charlemagne barked. "Let them have whatever they want!"

Finn growled and let go of the machine gun, raising his hands up slightly. Some of the bandits in the truck hopped out and began to approach them.

"You're under arrest!" one of the bandits remarked to them.

"Arrest?!" Charlemagne questioned. "In what world? There's no civil government anymore! How could you arrest us?! On what grounds?"

"You are in territory that constitutes the Commonwealth of Harlech," an officer said. "A civil state that follows the rule of law, and your fate will be determined by Lord Protector Salmar Cabernet, the overseer of the Court of Law."

"Lord Protector? Salmar" Charlemagne questioned before giving a sigh of disbelief. "How very typical of him to have himself appointed king in that manner. How can you be ruled by the rule of law while also have him as your 'Lord Protector?'"

"Silence!" another office yelled out. "Bandits are forbidden from this land, as are these items you are in possession of. You are also under arrest for the possession of these weapons, evading arrest, reckless driving, and the serious bodily harm and death that you've done to our peacekeepers. If you are citizens of the Commonwealth, you have certain rights and privileges, including the right to seek legal counsel, if not, well…"

"What? I can only imagine the sort of kangaroo court that awaits us," Charlemagne snarked. "We're not citizens – and we're not bandits. Let me speak with Salmar!"

"You will have a chance to explain yourselves in court. Lord Protector Salmar Cabernet will preside over your preliminary hearing, but I assure you given the egregious charges, your fate is sealed."

"Oh, that very much depends on what state of mind Salmar is in…" Charlemagne muttered.

"Enough! You do have a right to remain silent, so take advantage of it or anything you do say will be presented to the Lord Protector as evidence of your wrongdoing, including badmouthing!"

The officers went ahead and handcuffed the three of them. Charlemagne shook his head and said, "How in the world did Salmar manage to declare himself king of these lands?"

Act 8, Scene 3

Tristan rode Tempest out from Jerusalem, dressed in his armor with Diana's arms wrapped around his waist as they came into the desert. Behind them, Damian rode atop of the black horse that they had taken from the prison. He wore a set of long-sleeved black robes that wrapped over at the front, hiding the tunic underneath. Around his waist he wore a black leather belt. At his hands he wore black leather gauntlet gloves, similar to Tristan's. At his legs he wore baggy black trousers and tall black leather boots. Over his head, he wore a scarf that wrapped around his head to cover and conceal himself. Tristan wore his own cloak that wrapped around his back and held a hood that covered his head, while Diana wore her white dress and veil.

The three of them made their way into the desert a fair distance until they reached the top of a hill that looked across the land ahead. Diana and Tristan turned to face Damian.

"Alright, is this good enough?" Tristan questioned.

"The crystals," Damian requested, extending his hand outwards.

Tristan rode closer to Damian so that their horses were side-by-side, facing the opposite direction. He took the crystals from his pouch and into his gloved hand. Tristan looked at Damian with skepticism.

"How do I know you won't abandon us?" Tristan questioned.

"You? Maybe. Diana? Not a chance," Damian responded. "Where would I go? I can't travel to Harlech without my ring and I can enter into the dragon tomb without one of you to go through the poisonous gas."

Tristan frowned at Damian and gave him the crystals.

"If you don't want to get left behind, then grab on to my horse," Damian said. "I've never done this with horses, so this might spook them a little. Hold on."

Diana extended a hand outwards towards the reins of Damian's horse while Tristan grabbed onto the saddle. Damian closed a fist around the crystals and waited until they were ready. He then closed his eyes and they vanished.

The three of them appeared in a desert one-thousand miles from Palestine, in the middle of nowhere where the heat was equally impactful and air as arid. Tempest panicked as they touched down at the slope of a hill. Tristan immediately tried to calm the horse down as she thrashed around. They then regrouped at the top of the hill where Damian looked out from atop.

Tristan looked ahead and saw that they had a stretch of desert to cross ahead of them. The sand in this region was finer and less coarse than in Palestine, but there were some small patches of grass here and there.

"So?" Tristan questioned.

"So?" Damian repeated. "It'll take at least a day before we can make another jump like that, so... we may as well keep at it as much as we can before sunfall."

Damian led the way. Tristan watched him off before he began to lead Tempest behind. Tristan sighed.

"You know," Tristan quietly said, "I had my doubts, and I know you had yours, but he's the kid that I saw in those visions. It's weird – I don't see him as Zimmerman anymore. I see him as Damian."

"I'm not sure what you saw in those visions to say the same," Diana quietly responded, but I have noticed him to be acting a little... friendlier towards us, even if he can be sarcastic towards you. It's as if... since we know the truth about him, he doesn't have to pretend to be that person we knew him as. It's as if… he's himself around us."

"I can see the pain within him though," Tristan remarked. "His attitude – it's like the attitude of a teenager towards his parents. He has a bit of resentment towards us – me at least, because of who we are and what we represent. I wonder… what he really thinks of us, I mean. He spent the last ten years keeping an eye on each of us – who does that without a shred of care?"

"Tristan, don't forget that he tried to kill you," Diana reminded him. "He killed your mother, your aunt and uncle, my dad, and countless others."

"Except he didn't kill me," Tristan said. "In that church, after he stole my blood, he could have finished me, but he didn't. He only left us with that bomb. He said it himself – he has never wished harm against you in the least, and yet he left us with that bomb, you included. He expected both of us to make it out safely, but that begs the question of why even leave behind a bomb?"

Diana didn't respond.

"I want to help him, Diana," Tristan said. "He can be saved if he knows there's someone that cares for him. If I can see the good that I know to exist in him, then it might just be worth bringing him back with us and everything will go according to plan without a hitch. He can help make a difference in that world, which was lost here."

"Have you told him about Iustina? Helene? The other kids?"

"No," Tristan replied. "Not yet."

"He'll be devastated to learn that they're all dead, so please don't build these expectations. As far as I'm concerned, he's still Zimmerman."

Tristan didn't respond. He instead gave a look of pity towards Damian.

• • • •

The next few days went by in this manner: from where Diana, Tristan, and Damian appeared approximately one-thousand kilometers from Palestine, they travelled via horseback for thirty or so kilometers into the desert until sunset came and they stopped to build a fire and lay down their blankets to sleep. In the morning, they travelled a few more kilometers until it was noon again and they could teleport another approximate one-thousand kilometers eastward where they came out into an even flatter desert region. From this area, they continued east via horseback for another thirty kilometers, stopping at sunset to camp, and then continued in the morning.

On the fifth day, they arrived in a mountainous region that was far from the Middle Eastern deserts and entered into a wasteland where the ground composed of large rocks scattered around with tall mountains in the background – taller than the Caucasus and with peaks covered in snow. The weather was drier, but cooler with the skies covered by clouds. The day was shorter in this region as it darkened sooner.

The three of them stopped in the midst of the plateau where they lit a fire and camped for the night. Diana went to sleep while Tristan and Damian sat by the fire. Tristan looked over to Damian.

"I understand why you hate me," Tristan said to Damian. "To you, I'm the person that abandoned your mother, but I'm not. I should hate you for what you've done to me: you killed my parents, and my aunt and uncle, but I don't hate you. And that's not because of you bringing Diana into my life the way that you did, because that wasn't you – that was mere chance on Charlemagne's part to adopt me. Instead, I'm sorry for the way your life turned out. I'm sorry that the me of this universe refused to recognize you. You needed a father. Every boy needs a father. I can understand that, because I wished I had my father, even though I was fourteen when I lost my uncle. Luckily, I had Charlemagne…"

Damian growled and looked aside. Tristan's view of Damian was slightly obscured as the flames divided them.

"I never needed anything," Damian quietly responded. "I've *never* needed anything in my life. The sooner I was able to drop my expectations in people, the sooner I stopped being continually disappointed in other people. You should learn the same."

"I *was* the same," Tristan retaliated, "and it was miserable. You can't hide yourself from others. We need the other people in our life, even if they disappoint us sometimes; that's life. You don't try to hide from that. You own up to it and carry on."

"We don't need anything," Damian fiercely replied. "We only need ourselves."

"So, is that why you sheltered yourself with good people who you trusted? Iustina? Helene? You can't seriously convince me to believe you're as independent as you claim to be."

"They never knew," Damian responded, pausing for a moment, "about the life I led behind them. They never knew about the Wells Project, or my intentions with them. I lived my life with them like a masquerade, hiding my true self from them."

"Did you expect that a person like Iustina, who I heard to be extremely humble and kind, would accept what you intended for the other people?"

"Shut up about Iustina," Damian sneered.

"What exactly was your plan?" Tristan questioned. "What was your plan when you thought you travelled back in time?

You said you didn't intend to help the Children, so what then? What was the point of all this scheming?"

"You already know it," Damian replied. "All I've ever wanted was to create a New World, and it would have been beautiful. A world free from the scum of the Earth... and I would be at the top of the hierarchy, as the most powerful being that has ever walked the Earth. Iustina would have been my queen – she'd never know that it was I who created this new world, and my children... a new humanity. At first, I thought the world would be a better place without humans, but when I met Iustina, I wanted a world with people like her. Humans are filthy creatures – remnants of the animals they once were. Superhumans, however, are what we should have been. A perfect world would be beautiful and natural, and populated by these people; the evolution of humanity."

Tristan didn't respond.

"And who would stand against that except the enslaved masses whose malice wishes the rest of us – those that have raised themselves into higher beings, to join them in the hell they live in. What a senseless waste of human life... I hated everything about the old world – the senseless materialism, the senseless obsession of everyday topics, politics and religion, war and peace. What a waste... especially when there are better and more reasonable matters to concern oneself with, such as the beauty of the human form, the creation of art, acceleration of knowledge and technology, and the exceptionalism of mankind. And this isn't some sort of naïve dream of mine, because the dream was so close, you know that. I was this close to realizing my dream before I was forced back here."

"You would have killed millions of innocent people," Tristan remarked. "Innocent lives... What did they do to deserve that?"

"What should I even care about these people? Innocent? Don't make me laugh. Nobody is innocent. Humans are nothing more than the degenerate animals that pre-date them; minds focused on sex and other pleasures. To exterminate the lot of them would be no different than exterminating a wasp nest – useless drones."

"You're wrong," Tristan denied. "There's good in other people. You can't blame them for the way they are, and you can't pretend like you're any better. We're all sinners. We all deserve forgiveness and a second chance to uplift ourselves... The world isn't as evil as you believe it to be."

"What is evil but that which opposes us? Whether it's God, the Catholic Church, people, the Chosen, or the Children of Moloch. I have as much contempt for one as I have for the other. I hate all of the above, because they've all gotten in my way, even when I've attempted to go to them with open arms. All of them have slapped me in the face. You can't go anywhere expecting to be able to call someplace home, or someone family. We don't live in that kind of world. And I would love nothing more than to see all of these obstacles torn apart."

Tristan didn't respond.

"Ever since I was a kid, I've been told that I was destined for greatness, or that I would do great things for all of humanity, but they never told me why I should do great things for others when nobody was there to help me when I needed help most. All my life, I tried to live up to these expectations, wanting to do good for the world, but life was always unfair to me in return, punishing me even though I thought I was being fair and compassionate," Damian said, shaking his head. "I've never believed myself to be chosen by God the same way the Chosen see themselves. I'm simply a man of great talent and skill, and I'll use those talents and skills to achieve my dream and leave others in a state of perplexity as death faces them, of why this has happened to them, but I'm not a man of malice, because I would never expect them to beg for forgiveness for the wrong they had done to me. I am a man of mercy, and my mercy is to uplift them from the burden of their miserable lives. All of these people, they're better off dead than alive."

"What about Diana and me?" Tristan asked. "What was our place in this 'New World' of yours? Would you have seen us die just like the others? Would you have killed your mother because she did not live up to your standards in human beings? Would you have killed only me, led her to suffer because of your contempt for you father and because he did not meet up with your bizarre standards for human beings? Or are you so arrogant, that you believe you could decide for her what makes her happiest."

Damian didn't respond.

"You're not detached. You're conflicted. When you were with Iustina, Helene, and the other children, you were not wearing a mask, but you were your true self. Every time you stepped out though, you put on a mask then. I know, because I was there too, putting on an invisible mask. As long as you continue to love Diana because she's the essence of your mother, you'll have to let both of us live, and because of that, you could never have the world that you want or be the person you think you are – that you think you want to be, but who you aren't. Think about that."

Tristan stood up and left Damian on his own. He then went to join Diana down so that he could lay down. Damian simply looked back to the fire with a frown.

Act 8, Scene 4

Charlemagne, Manon, and Finn were arrested by the sheriffs that had pursued them through New Harlech, cuffed with hands behind their back, weapons and cache seized, and thrown into the back of a van where they were driven across Penultimate Bridge and into King Island. Charlemagne looked out around them as the back of the van opened and they were led out and taken into an underground parking lot.

A sign near the elevators they were at stated that they were at the Provincial Court of British Columbia. Charlemagne also observed that lights were on in the sublevel, which allowed him to see. The three were led out from a rundown provincial sheriff car and taken to a set of doors the sheriff in front of them unlocked and then they were guided through. Each of them had their fingerprints imprinted, pictures taken, and then they were thrown into a holding cell in the sublevel of the courts where a sheriff watched them through closed-circuit cameras in the corridor outside of their cell. The walls of the holding cell were a dull concrete grey and the lights were a dull halogenic white.

"Well, isn't this nice," Charlemagne sarcastically remarked, sitting down. "We've traveled a thousand miles only to be imprisoned so that we can appear before my deranged brother."

"Deranged?" Finn questioned.

"My brother hates me," Charlemagne said. "Four years ago, in the present that is, he attempted to kill me so that he could inherit Cabernet Industries."

Charlemagne sighed.

"But what if this isn't the same world that we're from," Finn noted. "You said that the Medici fellow told you about an arrangement of things that you said never happened."

"He could have lost his mind for all I know," Charlemagne remarked, sighing again. "However, if it is the year 2052 and Salmar is alive, acting as the king of the city, he must be… just around eighty-years old. Perhaps he'll have forgiven me, or…"

"If Salmar's mind is one, he will surely recognize us and we can explain the situation to him," Manon instead said. "If Diana and Tristan are here, then he can help us."

"We did evade his security forces," Charlemagne pointed out, "and kill a few of them. He tried to kill me once. What makes you think he won't do so again…?"

"We'll see…" Finn said.

"Blood for blood – after all that's happened in the last couple weeks, we definitely all deserve to be in prison," Charlemagne grunted.

"Sorry?" Finn questioned.

"You tried to kill me," Charlemagne responded.

"Oh, right…" Finn replied. "And I suppose I killed those guys that were coming after us, and…"

"Please, just stop…" Charlemagne begged.

"What?" Finn questioned. "You think you're so innocent? You practically genocided those Italians into inexistence looking for me, and all those times before you've had to take up arms."

"It's different when it's a matter of life or death," Charlemagne argued. "I didn't take up arms to slay them like a mad barbarian! It was justified action taken out of defense!"

"Yeah, that's me then…" Finn noted. "A 'mad barbarian' just looking for my next murder for the lolz."

Charlemagne didn't respond. Finn maintained his frown with his arms crossed. After a moment passed, he sighed and looked over to Charlemagne.

"Do you think that I just woke up one day and decided, 'You know what I want to do? I think I'll shoot up a place for no goddamn reason,' or, 'I think I'll bomb an oil refinery for the fun of it.' That's not what happened with me. When you've stared at the state of the world in which innocent people suffer from the greed of others, you grow depressed and frustrated because there's nothing that you can do to help them. You become helpless. I wasn't that sort of person. I'm not some wanker that sits in his basement and cries for the world. I act. I got tired of waking up in the morning and seeing the way the world was – the people that were suffering and the people that were dying – my people, our people – our blood and race, and I had to do something. I did what I had to do because I had to. It's because sometimes good men need to do what is necessary and what others should not so that others may live in peace. It's a fact of life – our ancestors didn't raise us to the position we're in as pacifists and with peace. What we live today is a comfortable circumstance of their sacrifice. They killed so that they, and by extension, us, could survive. It's a privilege of Western Civilization that today, the common man does not have to take a life in order to survive, but it's not a weakness of that same man to have restraint to killing – in taking a life, because it is abhorrent to kill. It is a sign of our civility and decency that murder gnaws at us, because it is an animality to kill mercilessly. I had restraint… but I also saw what was at stake and so I had to do what was necessary, and that necessity allowed me to overpower my restraint. At that moment, I knew I wasn't a kid anymore. It takes a man to make those sorts of difficult moral decisions and to live with the consequences…"

Charlemagne looked back at Finn with pity. He uncrossed his own arms.

"Do you at least regret what you've done? The lives that you have taken?" Charlemagne quietly asked. "The people you have killed?"

"No," Finn denied, looking to his father with sadness, "I don't."

Charlemagne looked to the ground with disappointment in him. Finn looked to the part of the ground that he looked at and then back at him.

"But that doesn't mean that my conscience doesn't ache," Finn added.

The three of them remained in the holding cell for several hours until a sheriff came to fetch them for their trial before the Lord Protector of the commonwealth. They were escorted out from the basement and upstairs to the court rooms. The three then entered through one of the larger court rooms in the courthouse, where ahead where the judge would sit, was a throne from where an elderly man looked down upon them.

Charlemagne looked at the eighty-year old Salmar. He wore the standard court dress of a court judge: black robes with a white collar. He appeared to be old and frail with the top of head completely bald and his face wrinkled. His eyes were sunken and tired. His arms were placed atop of the rests of the chair and he looked down towards the sheriffs and the trio with a bored glance, but his eyes soon widened as he saw the prisoners. Around his face was a trimmed white beard. Charlemagne looked straight at him.

"I don't believe it!" Salmar remarked. "Charlemagne? Is that you?"

"Yes, it is," Charlemagne responded. "This is me, Manon, and my son, Finn."

"How is this possible? I thought… I thought you were dead, the boy was dead…?"

Charlemagne looked at his brother with anxious eyes.

"Am I hallucinating?" Salmar pondered aloud.

"No, you're not," Charlemagne said, "but if you'll dismiss your guards, then I'll explain to you what is going on."

"Yes," Salmar agreed. "Guards, leave us at once."

The sheriffs looked towards Salmar and then to each other. They quietly left. Charlemagne stepped forward towards his brother.

"Salmar, what do you remember of me? Was it a bitter memory between us, of your time in prison because of me?" Charlemagne questioned.

"Prison?" Salmar responded. "I've never been to prison, Charles, and I don't have any bitter memories between us. If anything, our last moments together were happy... up until that tragic accident... How is that you're here now? Are you ghosts?"

"No," Charlemagne denied. "Tell me more about me, Sal. I need to know more so that I can understand what kind of a world that I'm in."

"What on Earth are you talking about?" Salmar questioned.

"Tell me more about me!" Charlemagne requested. "How did I die in this world for instance? Was it Finn that killed me?"

"Finn? How could your son have killed you when he died long ago? Don't you remember? You spent the last years of your life in pain over it... After you learned that you had a son from Manon, you sought him out, but it was too late. The son that you two had was the perpetrator of a deadly massacre that killed Aidan Cunningham of Cunningham Industries. You were never the same after that..."

"What else can you tell me? What kind of person was I before this supposed incident with the boy?" Charlemagne asked.

"Well, you were you," Salmar answered. "I had never seen you happier. Do you remember Diana?"

"Yes," Charlemagne replied. "Diana and Tristan – I remember them."

"Yes, you adopted Diana when she was ten-years old. I helped you gain custody of her. It was over forty years ago in this very courthouse. You took her into your home, and by God, she was such a wonderful girl, Diana. You loved her very much and so did I – it's a shame what came of her."

"What did come of her?" Charlemagne inquired.

"She died," Salmar remarked. "Liver cancer in her mid-thirties. How could you remember the name of that Tristan boy, but not how Diana died? Well, I suppose you had died at that time. You are a ghost, aren't you, Charles?"

"How did I die?" Charlemagne finally questioned. "Please, tell me."

Salmar sighed and then explained, "After Diana's funeral, I had discovered your body in your lab and phoned the police. They reviewed the security footage to see that Diana's son, Damian, had been through and made a hasty escape. They searched for him, but couldn't find him. He disappeared. The police believed that he had killed you, but it was never really solved because the boy was never found."

Charlemagne looked over to Manon and back to Finn. He then looked to Salmar.

"How did I overcome my cancer?" Charlemagne questioned.

"Easily," Salmar answered, "because of your friend, Judith Lambert – Do you remember her? She warned you that she had been diagnosed for cancer, and because of that, you were able to locate a tumor in your arm that had metastasized. Unfortunately, she didn't make it, but you were able to amputate your arm to prevent the spread, and because of that, you lived almost twenty years more."

"That's it then," Charlemagne quietly said. "This isn't our future," he said a bit louder and looking to the others. "Everything I've heard from the locals in this world has been similar, but not quite the same as what's happened in the present we came from. Finn didn't die when he attacked Aidan Cunningham, and I never amputated my arm when the cancer was in an early stage."

Charlemagne looked back towards Salmar and towards the ground.

"But that means Arturo really did die too, as did those children, and Diana... I adopted her when she was ten-years old?" Charlemagne questioned. "And Tristan..."

Charlemagne looked over to Salmar.

"What do you know about Tristan Merrick?" Charlemagne asked Salmar.

"Tristan Merrick?" Salmar repeated. "Isn't he the father of Damian?"

"Possibly," Charlemagne responded, "but did you not adopt him?"

"No," Salmar replied. "I have never adopted a child in my life. Charles, what is going on? What are you doing here?"

"I believe I have a suspicion of what is going on here," Charlemagne said. "I thought that I had come to the future, but this is not the future of a world that I had come from. I am in an alternate reality, and it still perplexes me how that is possible, but at least I am beginning to gain a grasp of the issue. Salmar, I believe that I have travelled from a different reality from almost thirty-years ago. In this reality, certain events have been similar, but others drastically different. In my reality, Diana and I did not meet until she was fourteen-years old, and Finn here... He lives!

My cancer though… I never got a chance to amputate my arm because by the time I had learned about it, it was too late. And you… you were different too! You were crazed and vengeful towards me, seeking to take control of Cabernet Industries at any cost!"

"That certainly sounds crazy," Salmar responded, stroking his beard. "I would never in my life take an arm against you, Charles. Like I said, the last years of your life were some of my most cherished memories between us, taking care of you in the depraved state that you had come into over the loss of your son and the deterioration of your health. We lived together in the manor where I made sure you didn't spend a moment alone while Diana had gone to university. In your grief, you stepped down as chairman of the board of directors and had me step in your place, but I never stayed in that position for long because of course, the war happened and then after that, everything went to hell… Cabernet Industries continues to a certain extent, but not as it once was, but we can discuss that later. If you are here from another 'reality' as you said, then what brings you here?"

"Well, that would be a very long story, but originally we were in Allabrese and I was with Diana and Tristan. You see, in my present, I adopted not only Diana, but also Tristan. It appears that in this alternate reality, I only adopted Diana, but the pair seemed to have made acquaintances anyways. I had travelled with both of them, but we became separated. I thought that Diana may have returned home, which as you know, would have meant here, so I am asking you if you've had any other travelers come through from the outside in the last four weeks or so."

"Hm…" Salmar thought aloud, "not that I can think of. This region can be very quiet… there are not many survivors in these northern parts, but they may be around in the south. I'm not sure if you know this, but Harlech has been divided between myself and an anarchic band to the south that controls Jarsdel and Cliffe Island, as well as Walham Valley to a certain degree. These crazed savages are a sporadic bunch of former criminals and psychopaths – the worst sort of people you could imagine, and they've made their own in the region below. If the people you search for are in Harlech, they are not in my kingdom."

"Could you help us search for them?"

"Well, that would depend on whether they are still alive," Salmar noted. "Our neighbors are not the type to take prisoners. For years we've attempted to take control of the entire region, but we lack the appropriate equipment to launch an amphibious invasion across the Henley River. Marke Bridge is destroyed so there is no connection between our two islands."

"I need to establish a search and rescue party then," Charlemagne said. "Can you spare me the men and resources to form a search party to search for Diana and Tristan?"

Salmar looked to Charlemagne with confidence.

"An expedition of that degree would be expensive," Salmar remarked, "but I will assist you in exchange for your own help. We have wanted to attack the band for a long time, and this may be our opportunity. I will have you meet with my general – an old family friend of ours, you may know him. His name is Kodiak Alexandrov."

"The name is familiar, but in my present, he is not a friend," Charlemagne said. "Where can I meet him?"

"Do not worry," Salmar said. "Guards!" he shouted. "I will have you released from those shackles and you can travel from here to Cabernet Tower to meet with him. If you explain your situation to him, we may be able to put together a plan of attack."

"Very well," Charlemagne responded as the doors opened.

"Guards, release these three here at once! They are not prisoners, but honored guests in this city. Escort them to Cabernet Tower and summon Commander Alexandrov."

"Yes, sir," a sheriff responded.

"And Charles," Salmar said, standing up. "After the police investigation underwent to search for this boy – Damian, the one they suspected to have murdered you, there was another group that came around the manor in search of artefacts that belonged to you. They identified themselves as federal authorities and presented a warrant to search for items they said belonged to them. Luckily, I had moved a lot of your inventions and other possessions to Harlech, and placed them in storage, so if you travel to the basement of the tower, you should find some of your inventions and see if there is anything that could prove useful in your quest. You're welcomed to them. All of it should be as it was, as I placed great respect towards your things… seeing them as all that was left of my older brother. When the war broke in the states, which bled into Canada, I took more with me when I was evacuated from Allabrese, and I made my home here ever since. You are welcomed to stay here as long as you need, and we will find Diana and this Tristan boy too."

"Thank you," Charlemagne said. "I appreciate your help, Salmar, I'm also glad our relationship turned the way it had in this world if not in ours."

Salmar nodded and then fluttered his hand.

"I will meet you at the tower later this evening," Salmar said. "Until then, farewell, my dear brother!"

Charlemagne, Manon, and Finn were escorted out from Salmar's court. He took a deep breath as he looked to the others.

"Well, at least we know that this isn't the future, right?" Charlemagne whispered to them.

"No, but it's opened up a whole lot more questions," Manon replied to him.

Act 9, Scene 1

From the courthouse, Charlemagne was taken out onto Earle Street and escorted in a former Harlech Police Department cruisers to Cabernet Tower. Charlemagne took an opportunity to look out at the remains of downtown, which was not as decrepit as Allabrese. The lower levels of buildings were boarded and the streets were clear of traffic. The traffic signs were functioning regardless and the streets were surprisingly cleaner than in the present. Closer to Dominion Square and Campbell Street, there was a lot more pedestrians at the side of the road as the square had been converted into a marketplace. There was also some more vehicular traffic in this area. Charlemagne was astonished.

"How common is gasoline in these parts?" Charlemagne questioned their driver.

"We don't use gas anymore," the man replied. "Everything in Harlech is dependent on electricity, which we have plenty of thanks to the fusion reactor at the power plant."

"Really?" Charlemagne responded. "And what's the population of Harlech nowadays?"

The man hesitated to respond and then said, "When the war came, there was a large influx of people in and out – a lot of foreigners fled to their own countries, and then there was a blast in the New Harlech Harbor when some munitions blew, and that wiped out almost the entire north side, a part of Keswick and the Industrial District, and caused a fire that couldn't be put out in Westford. Thankfully, that was all the action we ever saw – What about you? Where are you three from?"

"We're from the interior," Charlemagne responded.

"Ah," the peacekeeper replied, "the war was really fought there I suppose. After the war ended, a lot of people left to go south and into the countryside. I wasn't old enough to remember much about pre-war Harlech, but from what I've heard at least ninety-percent of the population left because of food shortages. We get our food from local farming towns, such as Douglas, and they sell in the market year-round, and in return, we sell them some of the goods we produce in the factories here, but business is limited since they don't have electricity. Lord Protector Salmar Cabernet wants to absorb Douglas into the commonwealth in return for access to power, but the townspeople there are skeptical. They're ruled by a small council – a sort of democracy, and it's so inefficient that they're divided on the subject of joining the commonwealth, but from what I've heard from the vendors in the market is that they would very much like to join."

"It seems like Salmar has done well for all of you," Charlemagne responded as they came into the downhill ramp that went into Cabernet Tower.

"Yes, compared to the other cities in the world, we've been able to have steady lives."

Once the car came to a stop, Charlemagne, Manon, and Finn exited and walked towards the elevators. The peacekeepers followed them.

"Manon, why don't you go with our peace-loving friends and up to the penthouse so that you can wind down. This Commander Alexandrov will meet us there along with Salmar later in the evening. I'm going to take Finn downstairs to the storage so that I can have a look at what I've left behind."

Manon did not object. She walked into the elevator with the peacekeepers and then they left Charlemagne and Finn behind. Charlemagne called the elevator back so they could go down.

"I died," Finn said as the two were alone. "In this world, I die."

"Yes, so do I."

"But you live more than me," Finn responded. "You... you fall into 'grief' because of me, even though you never met me, or..."

"I didn't have to meet you to love you," Charlemagne replied. "You're my son, and although Manon may be more skeptical around you, she loves you too – probably more than I do. The women that are silent of their love usually love more, but she's skeptical of you because she does not want to be let down. It hurts her. It hurt her to let you go once."

"I'm a terrible son," Finn pointed out. "I held her hostage and I almost killed you because... I don't even know what came over me, I was just..."

"Do not worry about it, Finn," Charlemagne said as the elevator arrived. "We forgave you. You forgave us. Let's not dwell on the past anymore and focus on the future ahead of us."

The elevator doors closed and they were taken down to the sublevel. The doors opened and Charlemagne stepped out into a familiar room atop of a familiar platform that looked down to an open space around.

"Before I had this room cleaned out to make space for my own laboratory here in Harlech, this was a storage room," Charlemagne said, looking around. "Let's see what I've invented that could be of use."

Charlemagne and Finn went down the platform and then down the steps as they looked around all the rubbage that was stacked upon each other in the sublevel storage room. Where the desks were placed in the laboratory in the present, there were filing cabinets two-story tall with a ladder at the side. Charlemagne saw lots of furniture, most taken from Cabernet Manor and covered with bed sheets. He also saw some portraits and frames stacked in a corner. Finn walked over to the corner of the room where there was a set of doors that led into the tunnel going towards the parkade. Charlemagne linked up with him and began to see a lot more of his personal items, including a plasma cannon and some containers.

"Well then," Charlemagne said, picking up the cannon. "This would be handy… if we ever encounter a ghost."

"Ghost?"

Charlemagne looked back at him.

"Has Tristan never told you about the great many adventures he's had under my care?" Charlemagne questioned.

"Tristan doesn't speak much about himself," Finn responded. "Even if he wanted to tell me, I'd think he'd be mad to say that ghosts were real, and that's coming from me."

Charlemagne laughed with a smile, "You have no idea then, of the peculiarities in this world, my dear boy. I suppose though, this is your first adventure with me and it is quite a strange one. Here we are, in the future of a world that isn't our own, surrounded by people and places that are familiar to us, but at the same time, unfamiliar to us. I've explained to you psionics already, so let me explain now more."

Charlemagne went on to explain his theories on psionics, as elaborated by him on what Maximillian Bauer once shared, and the abilities of some human beings to be receivers, transmitters, and transceivers of psionic waves of energy. He then went into his theories on how this was possible, which came down to the topic of a soul. He explained to Finn what happened in their timeline in Allabrese four years ago where his prototype fusion reactor unleashed a particle that caused spirits of all kind to freak out. He also explained how he used this cannon, based on similar technology of the fusion reactor to entrap the spirits so that he could study them. Charlemagne finished off with remarks of that tale.

"During that moment in my life, I learned of the importance of my comrades around me," Charlemagne reminisced. "Diana and Tristan had taught me of the importance to share my passion, and in that time I also learned of the curse of negligence, but my dear friends Judith and Barry – Sabrina… they all taught me to appreciate those around me and not shut them out. You have no idea how happy it was for me that, although we had thought you had died and we never met in England, that in the least, Tristan was able to earn your friendship and enjoy what we had thought to be your last moments, with him. Friends are not easily won, but they are easily lost. Do not take your friendship with Tristan for granted."

"I don't," Finn replied. "I love him like a brother."

"He may as well be your brother," Charlemagne replied, looking over to the other items. "Diana too – your sister that is."

"I thought she was my cousin," Finn said as Charlemagne went to look at the other items, "which is something I'd very much like to have explained to me."

"Diana is a distant cousin of ours," Charlemagne explained, "through our common ancestor on my grandmother's side of the family, Ophelia Cabernet, who married my grandfather, Derby Cabernet. She is the daughter of Louis Mountbatten, who was the Earl of Burma once upon a team and Admiral of the Southeast Asia Command of the British Navy. His mother was Princess Victoria, granddaughter of Queen Victoria, and his father was Prince Louis Battenberg, a German prince and relative of the wife of Tsar Nicholas II. Our relation with Diana comes through Queen Victoria, because Diana's father, William Cambridge, was the grandson of King Edward VIII, born from a lost child conceived between him and his wife, Wallis Simpson, taken from them by the Allies during the Second World War II to gain their compliance in the war effort, and placed in foster care here in Canada. King Edward was of course the son of George V, who was the son of Edward VII, who was the son of Queen Victoria."

"That's insane," Finn replied.

"I thought so too, so I took Diana's DNA, tested it with my own, and we share enough DNA that one could call us cousins, although distant. We are fifth cousins, while for you she would be your fifth cousin, one time removed because of the generational gap between you."

"That's insane," Finn repeated.

"Yes," Charlemagne responded.

"How did you ever figure this out?"

"I didn't," Charlemagne answered. "I developed this work from a report that was handed to me by a man named Damian Sutherland, who was the second-in-command of the Harlech Syndicate. This work was developed by them, based on intel they had inherited from the remains of the British Union of Fascists and infiltrators that had worked for the Office of Strategic Services – Good Lord!"

Charlemagne rushed over and removed the sheets on an object in the corner. The pair looked at the item and saw that it was an object similar to the time machine that was in the basement of Cabernet Manor in the present, but incomplete.

"So, I went ahead and built one in this world too," Charlemagne said. "If that's the case, then there must be… of course! If this is not the future of our present, but of an alternate universe, then there must be an alternate pair of the orbs somewhere around here – somewhere close-by too. If we can find those, we could put together this machine and it will surely take us home. We'll have a portal between our two worlds."

Finn proceeded to search this space of the room with Charlemagne until they found a reinforced case. Finn raised it up and placed it on a table nearby. He then opened it and saw that there was space in the case for two spherical objects, both of which were missing. Charlemagne saw and frowned. Finn then saw him go towards the time machine to search the compartment where the orbs were to be inserted.

"They're not here," Charlemagne concluded. "They've been taken."

"Who would take them?" Finn asked. "Who would take them, knowing what they do?"

"I'll have to ask Salmar that exact question."

Act 9, Scene 2

Diana, Tristan, and Damian rode along their horses as they followed an abandoned, overgrown road in a valley of mountains with a river at the side. They passed by some signs with letters in Chinese as well as some destroyed tanks left behind, reaching the end of the road where a bridge had been blown out at the cliffside. Damian stopped and then turned around.

"Well, this is as far as we'll come," Damian said. "We have one more jump before we're in the forest, and then a little more from there. We should be at the tomb before sunset."

Tristan rode Tempest so that they could position themselves for transport. Damian took out the crystals from a pouch on his belt and then held them in his hand. Diana and Tristan grabbed on, and they vanished. Tristan calmed Tempest as they touched down, arriving on another road in the midst of a tall and dense monsoon forest.

"Is this it?" Diana questioned. "Are we close?"

"We should be within a couple of kilometers from it, yes," Damian responded.

"Why couldn't you just take us straight there?" Tristan asked.

"For the same reason I never bothered to simply teleport into the shrine in the first place, all these years ago after I got ahold of the amulet. There's a protective aura around the tomb and this was the closest I could place us."

"Wait, I remember this road," Tristan said, looking around. "This is where the PLA ambushed us."

"Then you should know just how close we are," Damian replied. "Come, we can travel down this road, but then we'll have to venture through the forest. There are probably bandits nearby, so keep your head up. All of China may have collapsed and most of its people may have died of starvation, but this is roach country. Keep your eye out for roaches."

"Roaches?" Diana quietly questioned to Tristan as Damian went ahead.

"He's being racist," Tristan responded in a dull tone with a sigh. "It's an epithet. He's talking about the Chinese."

"Oh..." Diana replied.

The three of them continued down the road as they went through the monsoon forest around them. Tristan looked occasionally into the shaded and dense woods, looking into the distance as if he were looking for someone in the darkness until looking back towards Damian and his horse. The road made a gradual curve as the land raised them to the left to form a gentle slope with pockets that had slid down onto the road. They continued until they reached a fork in the road where it continued in the same curved direction while also turning to the right to go in the perpendicular direction that way. The three stopped and Damian shifted his horse to face left.

"Alright, this is the marker," Damian said, hopping off and leading the horse into the woods by the reins. "We'll have to travel on foot."

Diana got off the horse so that Tristan could drop down and lead the horse. She then pulled herself back on so that she wouldn't have to walk. Damian and Tristan then led the horses into the dense woods where they began to travel through with caution and a slower pace. Tristan looked at his compass and saw that they were going northwards. Diana held on to Tempest as the path became rougher.

The three of them walked for several minutes, a couple of kilometers, until they reached the cliffside that went down to a river below that was a murky color. At the edge of the cliff, where they had come out of, trees had been cut down by approximately ten feet and replaced with a rusted railroad. However, the margin had become overgrown as nature retook its course.

"I don't remember this railroad," Tristan said, "but I remember the river."

"Probably an addition in the thirty-or-so years," Damian responded. "We'll continue east and follow the tracks."

Damian hopped back onto his horse. Diana moved away from the reins so that Tristan could come back onto Tempest. They then began to follow the rails that ran atop of the cliff. The railroad in turn followed the river. The margin narrowed as they came up against some cliffs to their right as well before curving as the road curved to go away from the cliff. They soon found themselves in the middle of the forest again with a cliff that stretched on their right before settling down as the road continued due eastward through the forest. Damian stopped as he looked ahead.

Tristan caught up with him and looked forward. Ahead of the rail tracks there was a fence gate with watchtowers at the side of some sort of abandoned encampment. To the right of the camp were some stone cliffs that rose up. Tristan took out his binoculars and got a better look. He looked forward to see that there were some concrete structures past the fence inside. He could also see some movement around. Tristan passed the binoculars to Damian.

"I see people inside," Tristan stated. "At least four."

"Probably scavengers," Damian noted, looking forward and through the binoculars.

"Should we try to bypass, or…?"

Damian quickly lowered his binoculars and brought his horse to rear as a bullet hit down below them. Tempest panicked and kicked off to the side. They each went into the forest on opposite-sides, into cover. Diana hopped off Tempest so that Tristan could get off. She then climbed back on while Damian came off his horse at the other side. Some more gunfire shot towards them.

"We can't retreat," Damian said. "We need to pass through here and follow the river to get to the tomb. Help me take them out."

"Yeah, I'm with you," Tristan responded, turning to Diana. "Stay here and out of sight. We'll be right back."

Diana nodded. Damian began to go into the woods, which prompted Tristan to quickly cross to the other side so that he could join him. They ventured through the dense woods and came around to the side of the encampment, which was right by the river. Tristan took out his bow and shot towards the bandit at the watch tower.

"Go on ahead," Tristan said to Damian. "I've got you covered from here."

Damian went on as Tristan shot another arrow towards the bandit at the other watch tower, aiming for the torso as opposed to the arms and shooting rapid, lethal shots. Once the bandits at the tower were taken care of, Tristan went forwards atop of the downed portion of the fence he saw Damian run off into.

Tristan jumped back as a bandit appeared from around the corner suddenly, waving his rifle as he attempted to hit him. Damian dropped down from atop of the concrete structure behind and brought his arm around his neck, strangling him. The man dropped his rifle. Damian took a dagger and then slit his throat. The man fell forward and onto the ground. Damian picked up his rifle.

"Four more from what I could see above," Damian said. "Keep up."

Tristan frowned at him.

"I'll split on. Take point at the end of the alleyway," Damian instructed.

Tristan went ahead while Damian went the other way. He stopped at the end of the alleyway and shot towards some Chinese bandits near some decayed tanks. Damian soon got into position to lay down some of his own fire from further ahead. Suddenly, the tank that the Chinese were hiding behind detonated and exploded, killing the two that were behind it. Tristan moved ahead and took cover from the other side to face towards the two other bandits that were within the ruins of a structure on the second floor. Tristan was unable to get a shot on them, so he hid back into the alleyway so that he could move up.

Tristan could hear the gunfire settle down as he moved around the back of another structure. He then stopped as the gunfire returned towards him. He looked into the structure where there were decayed and decrepit trains inside, their sides rusted. A bandit shot towards him from a platform above on the second floor. Tristan stayed in cover and prepared an arrow. He then came around the corner to quickly snipe his target, hitting him in the abdomen. The bandit fell over. Tristan moved on ahead and came out to the other side of the supply camp.

Damian had miscalculated how many bandits there were as the one that Tristan had shot was an extra to the other two at the ruined factory ahead that Damian was up against. Tristan saw several donkeys with wagons at the end of the camp with various scrap metal thrown in. He moved across and came to an entrance into the structure. The bandits were inside, hiding behind old barrels placed on the second-floor platform. Damian could be seen behind a pillar towards the west-side.

Tristan readied and arrow, but held back as it was impossible to make a shot at the hostiles in cover. Damian's bullets hit against the hallowed barrels, causing an echo to pitch in from inside. Tristan then saw one of the bandits come out from cover to retreat back. He took his arrow and sniped him in the side, causing him to fall over. Damian's bullets finished him off. He then moved up. Tristan stayed where he was.

"I'm running low!" Damian shouted to Tristan. "I have one magazine left. Don't just stand there – do something!"

"You're the gifted one," Tristan barked back. "Why don't you make him panic or something?"

"I just travelled one-thousand kilometers across Asia," Damian replied. "Do you really think I have the mental strength to cause this chink to panic?"

Tristan rolled his eyes, fell back and came out of the structure. He could hear the bandit shoot towards Damian. Tristan came around and found an entrance underneath the platform the bandit was on. Blood dripped down from above. Tristan looked around and saw a ladder ahead at the opposite corner of the room where Damian had come from. He then looked back out into the alleyway and saw a platform extend from the structure next to him. He went in and climbed up the set of stairs that went to the second floor. He then crossed through, got to the other doorway and prepared an arrow, shooting and hitting the top of the barrel. Damian looked over and extended a hand over, closing his eyes. Tristan then watched as the platform beneath the Chinese bandit's feet began to shake and break off from its hinges before collapsing onto the ground.

"Now!" Damian shouted.

Tristan went in and aimed an arrow at the collapsed bandit. He withdrew his arrow and saw that the hostile was disarmed and down. He dropped down and picked up his rifle, tossing it aside and then going over to grab the bandit by the neck, punching him out. Tristan then took a deep breath and moved away.

Damian went to grab the assault rifle and take out the magazine. He then fetched some magazines from the unconscious bandit and the dead one. Tristan looked away as he brought a hand his face to take a deep breath and calm down from the action they just faced. He then jumped as he heard a gunshot fire. Tristan looked behind him and saw that Damian had shot the Chinese bandit that he had knocked out. Damian held a deep frown and looked away from Tristan as he took a strap on the rifle and brought it around his back. Damian left the warehouse without looking to Tristan, while Tristan glared at him with bitterness.

The pair left the encampment and went back to their horses.

"We have to cross the river ahead and have at least ten more kilometers afterwards," Damian said, climbing onto his horse. "We should get there before sunset."

Damian went ahead towards the cleared camp. Tristan looked to Diana.

"Everything okay?" Diana questioned.

"Yeah, it's fine," Tristan responded. "Just a little bloody, but we did what we had to."

Tristan climbed up onto Tempest and then began to follow Damian ahead. They walked through the encampment and then began to follow the river until it narrowed so the horses could cross the water. Afterwards, they hopped off and continued on foot as they returned through the forest and made their way towards the mountains ahead where the Tomb of the Dragon Emperor would be.

Act 9, Scene 3

Charlemagne and Finn traveled up the elevator to the penthouse of Cabernet Tower. There, they exited out and were confronted by royal foot guards at either side of the front entrance, dressed in a scarlet tunic, black trousers, and white belts like British redcoats or British royal guards. The doors of the penthouse were much the same, large and wide. The guards saluted, and then opened the door for them as they then entered in. Charlemagne immediately noticed that the penthouse had never been renovated, but was instead maintained in this timeline in its original form. The walls of the penthouse consisted of squared panels at the bottom half and chestnut reddish-brown painted walls at the upper half. The immediate corridor from the main entrance was closed-off from the loft with three double doorways at all four directions. Incidentally, there was no loft as this was a renovation completed by Allodia that was not completed in this timeline. Instead, the corridor from the main entrance led into an expanded sitting room that looked out to the south of the city, towards the rest of the two islands and beyond. The room was only one-story tall with concrete support beams between the thick reinforced windows. The patio was much the same, but instead of large black tiles and a reinforced glass half-wall railing, there was the original thick half wall and a flagstone floor that accompanied the small garden with a fountain in the corner. The furniture in the sitting room was traditional, like that which can be found in Cabernet Manor, and included a dark red sofa with chestnut wood frames. Atop was a brass chandelier. To the left there was a set of double doors that were open and went into a dining room, which had a long dining table and more windows at the side that looked out to the garden and city. Behind this dining room was a smaller door that went into the kitchen. Charlemagne and Finn walked into the sitting room, but could not see anyone.

Finn looked around and saw that there was a portrait behind the couches in the living room that contained various family members of the Cabernet stock. The portrait appeared to be recent, at least compared to the timeline that Charlemagne and Finn were from. The picture was taken at the steps that went up to the patio from the gardens at Cabernet Manor. At the front row were four individuals, Charlemagne in a three-piece black suit, next to Allodia, a man with short blonde hair, and another man with longer light blonde hair. Before Charlemagne was a young girl with dark hair in a white dress. At Charlemagne's side was an older couple, one of a man with a bald head and another of a woman with short light-blonde hair. At the other side, next to the man with medium-length blonde hair, was another older couple of a man with neat dark hair and another of a woman with blonde hair. Charlemagne saw Finn looking at the picture and looked back at it. Finn continued to stare at the picture.

"Hm, this picture is unique to this reality," Charlemagne said, "but nonetheless, I recognize every one of these faces. Here you have my parents, your grandparents, Everest and Vienna Cabernet, and there is of course me, there's Diana in front of me – she looks similar to when I had just adopted her in our reality. Next to me is my sister, Allodia and that man… I don't believe it. That man's name is Sergei Bykov, Allodia's fiancé in our reality who she never married because he was arrested. He placed all of us, especially Diana and Tristan, in danger for selfish gain," he explained, sighing. "They must have wed in this reality. What a shame. At any rate, next to that man is my brother, Salmar, who was also incarcerated in our reality, and next to him is my aunt and her husband, Britannia and Warren Vickery."

"Quite the family," Finn remarked.

"Yes, your family" Charlemagne noted and agreed. "I believe this is the most recent and complete picture of the family that has been taken, but it is incomplete, especially to our reality."

The main entrance doors opened. Charlemagne and Finn stepped in to see Salmar arrive, out of his barrister gown, and dressed in a brown gold-striped three-piece suit with a dark red tie and crème-colored dress shirt. Salmar stepped over to them and extended a hand out.

"My God, it is you, Charles," Salmar said, taking his hand and hugging him. "You have no idea of the joy in my heart to be able to see you again after all these years…"

Charlemagne awkwardly hugged his brother. He then stepped back and looked to Finn.

"It's a pleasure to meet you too," Salmar said, taking his hand and hugging him. "Yes… where's Manon?"

"I'm not sure," Charlemagne replied. "We had just arrived. I told her to take a moment to rest, so that must be what she is doing."

"Good," Salmar responded. "Commander Alexandrov is waiting for us downstairs in the war room. Come and meet him."

Charlemagne and Finn left with Salmar out from the penthouse and back to the elevator. They then entered and Salmar took a card from his suit jacket and swiped it on the panel. He then pressed one of the sublevel buttons and they began to go back down into the deep sublevel of the tower to the bottommost floor. Charlemagne and Finn stepped out with Salmar as they arrived, and they then walked down a dim corridor where there were guards like the ones above at the side with assault rifles in their hands.

The royal guards saluted Salmar as he approached. They came to the end of the corridor where Salmar took his keycard and scanned it. He then approached a biometric panel and had it scan his eyes. The doors opened and he was able to step in. Charlemagne and Finn followed, and they came to a large, dim room where there was a circular black table in the center alongside tall monitors before them. At the side of the room there were individual desks that were mostly empty. At the circular table in the center there was a fair-skinned man dressed in service dress, which included a black coat and black trousers, red beret, white-shirt and black tie. At the front of his coat were colored bars and across his chest was white sash. He was an older man, younger than Charlemagne currently was, with short white hair. The man looked at Charlemagne suspiciously.

"Charlemagne?" the man questioned in a Russian accent.

"Kodiak, this is indeed my brother," Salmar said. "From the past… not a ghost."

"Perhaps I should explain," Charlemagne interrupted.

Charlemagne explained to the both of them in detail of what had occurred in which Charlemagne gone looking for Manon and Finn, which prompted Diana and Tristan (who he explained to them to be one of his adopted-children as well as the partner of Diana), to come in looking for them. However, they were separated and now Charlemagne was looking for them with his biological son, Finn. Salmar then briefed Kodiak on how they believe that if Diana and Tristan had come to Harlech, they may be in the anarchic state to the south, which is why he has been summoned to brief all of them of the war situation.

"You would think that to conquer anarchists would be simple, but to the south, every single resident is a partisan of the cause, and every one of these residents are unpredictable, former criminals that have made the islands their home," Kodiak explained, showing them the map of Harlech on the monitor screen. "An invasion from King Island would be costly and pointless at this point of time. We abandoned the islands because they were a haven for these criminals and it was too costly to control them. The precinct certainly did not have enough space to hold that many fugitives, so we gave them the island and severed connections with the south. We also thought they would fade away, but the opposite has happened. They've organized themselves and even expanded southwards into the valley to gain control of their fields in order to feed themselves."

"However, the anarchic regime is an unstable one," Salmar explained. "Our operatives within the autonomous zone have said that infighting within their government has been plagued by political assassinations, but at the moment they've settled on a leader who holds the monopoly of force. Until one can topple him, they appear to be in a period of minor stability."

"Even then, there is no reason to invade the lower islands because we do not need the space and to rule these degenerates... would be costly and near impossible," Kodiak said.

"But Diana and Tristan could possibly be within this zone," Salmar replied, "and I would rather have this zone under control under my rule before I die to unite the islands, liberate Walham Valley, and crush the presence of anarchism so close to our settlement."

"How many anarchists are believed to be living in the southern islands?" Charlemagne queried.

"Far less than the population of the island," Kodiak answered, "but far more than our entire armed forces. The Commonwealth has two companies of armor and a battalion of motorized infantry, all totaling less than a thousand men. Our weapons and armor are produced by factories within the island

and encompass electrical engines so that we don't have to rely on our diesel reserves, which are kept for the warships we inherited from the old regime at the naval base at King George VI Park. Our air force is non-existent. If we invade the south islands, we could have every one of these criminals against us in large numbers – it would be a massacre on their end."

"But I will have it," Salmar assured him. "We have the firepower and should organize ourselves to crush these bastards once and for all. What do you think, Charles?"

Charlemagne looked at the map of Harlech that noted the influence of the anarchic state in relation to the Commonwealth.

"Perhaps we should not focus on modern doctrine simply because we have modern toys at our disposal," Charlemagne said, stroking his beard. "If we lay siege to the islands, that could be enough to force their submission. The islands appear to be easily defendable, but they're isolated without an inch of farmland to themselves. If you mobilize your navy to destroy the Grafton Bridge and bombard from the sea, you could strangle them easily and lay siege. They would be disconnected from their territory in Lennox. What kind of firepower would they carry?"

"Our intel suggests close to none. Although the Hemlock Garrison is under their jurisdiction," Kodiak said, "and a lot of the equipment was moved out during the civil war and what was left behind for civil defense would require diesel to operate. However, they do control sufficient arms to arm every citizen."

"But we must capture these islands and eradicate these communists once and for all," Salmar justified, "especially if something has happened to my niece and her husband!"

Kodiak looked at Salmar with disbelief, "It would be a massacre – think of that reputation on your name in the future."

"No," Salmar denied, "what future generations will see and learn is the cause of the Great Calamity because of decades of greed under the ideas of globalization and liberalism. What they will see and learn is that the Third World War was fought between anarchic-totalitarians and the defenders of the old regime. They will look on us poorly if we allow these people to survive anymore. My decision is final – organize your army and prepare to enact Case White."

"Yes, my lord," Kodiak responded in submission, bowing to him.

"With your permission, Sal," Charlemagne said, "may I join the frontline so that I can search for Diana and Tristan. I wish to partake."

"If that is what you wish, Charles, then who am I to stop you?" Salmar responded before turning to Kodiak. "How soon can the army be mobilized?"

"I will disseminate your orders to the high command at once – We will be ready for combat before sunrise," Kodiak replied.

"Good."

• • • •

Charlemagne and Finn returned to the penthouse late at night. Salmar had returned earlier than them. Charlemagne led Finn into the corridor to the right from the main entrance, which in Allodia's penthouse in their universe was a simple corridor that connected with the library, but in the original architecture, was a stairwell corridor that connected to the library as well as the second-floor. The stairs were constructed of a carved chestnut wood and was in its same U-shape. Charlemagne took Finn upstairs and into the corridor on the other end. On the second floor atop from the living room, dining room, and kitchen in the original design, there were more bedrooms than there were presently in Allodia's penthouse. Charlemagne and Finn stopped in the middle of the corridor.

"We have an early rise tomorrow," Charlemagne said to Finn. "I'll see you in the morning."

"Goodnight," Finn responded.

Finn entered into his bedroom. Charlemagne then went into his across the hall. He closed the door behind him and then began to remove his vest and poncho. He then went to the bathroom to wash himself, taking a moment to shave as well. Charlemagne exited from the washroom in a white robe, drying his face with a towel. He then heard a knock on the door.

Charlemagne went to answer the door and saw Manon on the other side. She was dressed in her own bathrobe and slippers.

"Manon," Charlemagne greeted.

"Where have you been?" Manon quietly questioned, stepping inside and closing the door behind her. "You disappeared, *Charles*. What is going on?"

"Tomorrow morning, an invasion will be launched to eliminate the anarchist state to the south from King Island. I'm going to take Finn with me to search for Diana and Tristan in this land, and I do not expect you to come with us. You'll be safer here in the tower."

"An invasion?" Manon questioned.

"It's all that can be done to search for the couple," Charlemagne assured her. "Believe me, and from what I've heard from Salmar – the anarchists are criminals. It's a win-win. He unites the islands and we can learn of the fate of Diana and Tristan, and retrieve the crystals we need to return home."

"What if something has happened to them?" Manon asked in a worried tone, turning her back to Charlemagne.

"Diana and Tristan can handle themselves," Charlemagne replied in an annoyed tone. "I've told you. They're not ordinary children. The island is a big place, and they've more than likely they've taken refuge someplace. Tristan is an intuitive boy."

"And what if something happens to you?" Manon asks, looking to Charlemagne, "or *Louis*? *Charles*, you cannot leave me in this world, alone..." she said, bringing a hand to his cheek and then embracing him. "All I want is to return home."

"You will in due time," Charlemagne responded. "Listen, I've found a machine in the basement. I believe it may be possible for us to return home through it without the need of psionic power. All we need though is a space orb to match the time orb that I have. Diana and Tristan have the crystals, so I need to find them before we can return. I will not fail them, Finn, or you. I will return alive... If I'm going to die, it will be at my own home because of the cancer than at the hands of a bunch of degenerates."

"Oh, *Charles*," Manon cried, parting from him and then embracing him again. "I'm sorry for all of this. All of this could have been avoided if I simply kept *Louis* with me. He would never have become the boy that he is under my care as a single mother. I could have taken him to Jacques in the least. He could have had my father to look up to. Anything but the way he is... and then, this would have all been avoided."

"Manon, you cannot blame yourself for the way that Finn has become. It was a one-in-a-million chance that he would become a far-right radical. You are not the sole person responsible for himself. He's twenty-years old. His being is his own..." he said, holding her before sighing. "They say that mothers who undergo stress before child birth are destined to have children that are more authoritative and militaristic, because stress causes the release of hormones that affect the child, preparing them, so that they will be more capable in the environment they will be born into. I manifested stress onto you when I betrayed you and left you alone. Finn is our creation, to the very way that he was made, and that is okay. He is a good boy. I assure you."

Finn parted his ear from the door. He wiped a tear from his eye and then resigned to his bedroom while his parents consoled each other.

"But I will not leave you alone a second time," Charlemagne said. "If there is one thing that I wish from you, Manon, something which I have no right to ask from you now that you know that I'm dying, please… will you marry me?" he asked. "Not for any reason except for the fact that I love you."

"*Charles*…" Manon responded, parting from him. "*Charles*, how could you?"

Charlemagne looked at her with disappointment, lowering his head down.

"I've wished to be known as *Madame Manon Madeleine Cabernet* since I was a little girl… and when you broke my heart, you broke the dream of the little girl that you had known since you were a little boy. Now, to ask me to have that again…" Manon said, turning to the side as tears streamed down her face. "*Charles*, there has never been any other man for me than you. Yes, I will marry you, but on one condition… two conditions!"

Manon looked to Charlemagne with happiness in her face.

"Firstly, you will return to me alive so that you can propose to me properly, and secondly, you will not leave anything to me even if I am to become your spouse. I want all that would be mine to go to *Louis*, so that the family name Cabernet may live in him. All I want from you, is that *gift* that should have been mine."

"Done," Charlemagne simply responded.

The couple embraced and kissed. Manon pushed Charlemagne back as their lips continued to meet, sitting Charlemagne down as they spent the night together in unity.

Act 9, Scene 4

Diana, Tristan, and Damian ventured through Guangzhou in the southern region of China, travelling through the forest and coming into a hilled land that finally reached the cliffside where the sculpture of the maw of the Chinese dragon stood out from the side with steam pouring out from the nostrils. The three of them looked down and then carried on so they could take the horses across the very shallow stream of water that ran down the base of the mountainside. They then walked uphill towards the entrance into the cave, but stopped halfway as the horses grew hysterical.

"Tempest!" Tristan complained as the horse shook her head.

Damian's horse simply refused to come an inch closer.

"Well, it looks like this is where one of us parts," Damian said, hopping off and looking to the others. "It's up to one of you to go in and retrieve the ring, because I can't and won't do it."

"I've been exposed to the gas before," Diana said. "I should be resistant to the effects of the toxin."

"You, maybe," Tristan replied, "but our son isn't. If you go in there and that toxin seeps into your placenta, it could kill our child. Stay here with Damian and let me go in."

"Tristan, you have no idea what awaits you in that cave," Diana warned. "It's more than your simplest fear that this toxin makes you hallucinate, but an expression of yourself – your inner demon. For me, as you know, that was a dragon with eyes just like mine and a coat as dark as my hair. For you... who knows what that could be, or how dangerous it could be. Are you ready to face that?"

Tristan looked at her and then over to the entrance into the tomb.

"I've been through a lot in the past several weeks," Tristan said, "and I've put a lot of thought into it, but I believe I'm ready to face what I should have faced last year instead of you. If I don't return, then do not go in after me."

Diana's hands trembled. She looked sad.

"God protect you, Tristan," Diana simply said in return. "Please be careful."

Damian rolled his eyes and uncrossed his arms.

"Yes, this is very sad – you might not get to see Tristan ever again. Can we get a move on? Some of us want to get out of this godforsaken land."

Tristan glared back at Damian and then looked to Diana. He gave a warm smile to her and then turned back to face the slope that went up into the mouth of the dragon. He then went inside and took out his flashlight so that he could see forward and down the corridor that led to the atrium where Bogdan had shot Diana in their world. He looked around and then stopped before the corridor that led to the shrine. Tristan took a deep breath and removed his sword from the scabbard and took his shield into his arm. He then went onwards into the dark tunnel with cautious steps.

"Alright, Mika," Tristan quietly said to himself. "Here we go…"

Tristan continued on with even more cautious steps, eyeing the light at the end of the tunnel and slowly making his way over there. He came out of the tunnel and entered into the Tomb of the Dragon Emperor as it had been described by Diana to him with curved stairs at either side that reached up to a landing. At the sides of the stairs were torches that lit the way and came up to the shrine where the emperor laid. The walls of the tomb were cavernous and from the ceiling there were sharp stalactites. The only difference from this tomb to what Diana had described to him was the floor. The floor was slightly flooded with water, less than an inch of water like quicksilver, which created a reflection of Tristan at his feet. Tristan looked down and then around.

"Where's the dragon?" Tristan questioned, looking about.

Tristan proceeded to walk towards the stairs and climb up to the shrine. The basin in the center where the Tears of the Dragon fell overflowed and caused a puddle to form around, spilling over the edge where a crease in the floor caused it to pour down. Tristan began to look at his feet for Damian's ring, but he couldn't find it. He looked over to the shrine of the Dragon Emperor and into the mirrors behind. The rack where the scepter used to be was empty, but that was not why Tristan looked at the mirror curiously. He had no reflection. Tristan looked down at his feet and saw that he didn't have a reflection in the water either as he had when he entered the room.

Tristan pivoted around as he looked to his feet and the looked up as he stared before him, a mark of himself, an opaque and solid being that had Tristan's form, his face and hair, but a shadowy complexion as his skin, hair, tunic, trousers, and boots were all in a darkened greyscale with sinister eyes that glowed a bright red. Tristan's shadow simply looked at him in exact mirror of his pose with a sword in hand and shield in the other. Tristan took a side-step, and his shadow took a step in the opposite direction. He took a step back and his shadow took a step away from him too Tristan to stare this figment of his imagination down, anticipating a strike from him until finally, Tristan raised his sword and brought it down towards the being.

Tristan's shadow mimicked Tristan's exact move, which caused their swords to clash. He attempted a horizontal slice, and his shadow returned the move. He then took a side-step and raised his shield, bringing the sword down and causing them to hit each other's shields. Tristan looked back at the sinister representation of himself and frowned.

"How is this supposed to work if I can't strike you?" Tristan questioned himself aloud.

"Like this," Tristan's shadow replied in an echoey voice like his own, jabbing his sword towards him.

Tristan quickly pointed his shield at the sword and took in the hit. He then stepped back as he looked at his foe with more alert as he became more active. Tristan's shadow brought his sword down for a vertical slice. Tristan deflected and attempted to perry, but the shadow anticipated the perry and deflected back with his own sword. The two separated from each other, but continued to stare the other down with hot feet. Tristan rushed in to swipe down at his shadow, but his shadow simply jumped out of the way and returned the attack. Tristan quickly raised his shield up to take in the hit, following by a bash from his foe's shield.

Tristan's shadow then sliced Tristan down the arm, grazing the chainmail at his shoulder, but hitting the tender wound sustained from his fight with Arkady and causing him to cringe. Tristan moved back up as the basin in the center of the landing had disappeared as had the shrine and burial coffin. The stairs around them had also shortened so they were closer to the ground below than they had previously been. Tristan stayed where he was at the top of the stairs while he looked over to his shadow. Tristan's shadow began to move in and then threw a horizontal slice.

Tristan raised his shield and the sword bounced back. He then brought the sword down and Tristan clashed his own sword, but they began to pit their strength against each other until each of them backed off and took a step back, causing Tristan to come down a step. He tried to climb back up, but his shadow jabbed his sword towards, prompting Tristan to raise his shield, but the force caused him back down a step, almost falling over. Tristan quickly jumped back onto a step to reconfigure his balance. His shadow came down the steps and loomed over him. He came down another and jabbed towards Tristan. Tristan took the jab into the shield.

Tristan's shadow then hit next with a slice that Tristan took into his shield. Tristan went in with a jab afterwards, but his shadow took it in. He moved back and came off the stairs, moving further back so that his shadow would have to follow him off the stairs as they came to the center of the room where the water was. Tristan then moved in and went in with a vertical slice. His shadow's sword clashed with his, so Tristan parried and attempted to get a swipe at the next, but his shadow countered the blow. They then retrieved their swords, but not before Tristan went in again with a jab. His shadow blocked the jab with his sword and then attempted a parry of his own, but Tristan very barely jumped out of the way as the tip of the sword came for his left eye. Tristan went in for a diagonal slice, but his shadow's shield. Tristan's shadow then went in with another jab, which hit into Tristan's armored side and caused him to grunt and quickly move back.

Tristan began to pant, gritting his teeth as he absorbed the pain and turned it into anger. He quickly rushed towards his foe and began to swipe sporadically at him, left and right. His shadow deflected each one and then parried to swipe at Tristan on the cheek. Tristan jumped back and felt the blood begin to drip down his face. He took a step forward and back, and then lurched forward to bring his sword down before pivoting around to hit at his shadow in the side. His shadow staggered to the side as the hit came, but no cut or blood came out. Instead there was only an echoed grunt, followed by a step back. Tristan took a step back and stared down his foe with hot feet.

The pair began to pace around each other until Tristan's shadow hopped forward and jabbed towards Tristan. Tristan deflected with his sword this time and attempted to parry to swipe at his shadow's face, but he deflected the parry and the two instead pivoted around each other so they stood where the other had stood. Tristan's shadow then brought his sword down for a vertical slice. Tristan raised his shield and attempted to jab, but predictably hit his foe's shield. Tristan's shadow then brought his sword down onto Tristan's sword before raising his up to swipe towards Tristan's neck. He backed away as the blade nearly slit through. In a panic, Tristan hit his foe's sword with the side of his shield.

Tristan backed up and breathed slowly, wiping the blood on his face and causing his entire cheek to stain. He then went in with a backhanded diagonal slice, nicking his foe's shield and then bringing his sword down atop of the shield before going in for a jab. He hit his shadow's shoulder and pushed him back before he could counter. Tristan took a step back and then quickly rushed in with careful steps, inching around the side for a horizontal slice, hitting the side of the shield and then blocking an attempted jab.

The pair proceeded to circle each other as they attempted to hit around the side. Tristan took a step back and jumped forward, bashing his shield into his shadow and then jabbing his sword into his side. His shadow hit at Tristan on the upper arm again, slicing just below where his chainmail came to an end. Both of them grunted. The pair stepped away from each other.

Tristan looked to his shadow as he dropped his defensive stance and then fell backwards with arms spread out from his body, sword and shield still in hand. The collapse into the water caused a splash as if he had fallen into a pool and not a shallow puddle. He disappeared from Tristan's sight, but Tristan quickly jerked his head up to the top of the stairs where he re-emerged from the water and looked at him from above. Tristan quickly put his sword and shield away, taking out his bow and drawing an arrow. He raised his bow and aimed for the shield as his shadow anticipated the hit, but then quickly dropped down to hit the knee. The shadow shouted out in pain. Tristan raised his bow to aim another, more lethal shot, but as the arrow flew, the shadow jumped back and fell through the water.

A shadow emerged in the water ahead. Tristan quickly put his bow away and took out his sword and shield, raising it in anticipation as his shadow emerged out from the water. Tristan instantly went in and bashed him with his shield, hitting him against the wall beneath the top of the stairs and then slicing at the arm that held his sword with a backhanded cut. Tristan's shadow hit back, but Tristan's bashed him back again, causing him to fall through the water and disappear again.

Tristan backed up and came to the center of the room, anticipating a strike from his shadow from any angle. He then quickly pivoted to two-hundred degrees as he heard a splash out from the water and his shadow came at him with a jump, sword raised up. Tristan swiped at him in the torso before he could get the drop on him and Tristan's shadow fell onto his side. Tristan went in to finish him, but he rolled out of the way and then jumped back onto his feet. Tristan went in for a slice at the foot before he could turn around, hitting him.

Tristan's shadow was nudged over, but quickly span back around, side-stepping so that he was away from the wall that Tristan had pinned him in last time and then dropping back so that he could disappear into the water again. Tristan readied himself for another strike from any angle. He stayed where he was and looked around for a quick minute until finally he heard a splash from behind him at close to two-hundred and seventy degrees. Tristan quickly span around with his sword extending a horizontal slice. Tristan's shadow fell over and into the water as though it were a puddle.

Tristan quickly went over as he saw his foe on the ground. He lunged and brought his own sword down, hitting him in the shoulder and keeping him down. He then jumped atop of him, placing one foot on his back to keep him pinned. Tristan's shadow then sliced at Tristan's feet with his sword, causing him to fall to his knee. His shadow then raised his sword up with both hands to deliver a strike down onto Tristan. Tristan deflected with his shield. His shadow then hit him with a violent strike against the shield until finally he grabbed it off him and tossed it aside. Tristan then deflected the incoming strike with both hands on his sword as he continued to stand on a knee.

The pair pitted their strength against each other. His shadow then hit him in the eye and then brought a hand around his wrist to elbow him in the face and remove his sword. Tristan felt the blow in his sword. He also heard his sword crash in the water. His shadow brought a hand around his waist and another at his thighs, preparing to lift him. Tristan retaliated by dragging his feet up and dropping his weight to the ground, placing his arms around his shadow so that he picked him up as Tristan's body fell onto the ground. He then brought his shadow's head into the ground and caused him to fall over.

Tristan quickly recovered and went over to subdue his foe, but his shadow disappeared into the water as he grabbed his own sword. He instead went to pick up his sword and then reach over for his shield, but as Tristan went for the shield, he heard a splash rise up from behind him. Instead of spinning around to counterattack, Tristan summersaulted towards his shield and picked it up, sloppily raising it over his body to absorb the blow. Tristan's shield then fell over as he couldn't control it, blocking the next blow with his sword at a horizontal angle as his foe's sword came down vertically. Tristan then transferred the energy from the strike back at his shadow, slicing across his face and causing his hands to separate from the sword.

Tristan's shadow tilted his face down as he grunted. Tristan quickly went in and threw a backhanded slice at his wrist, causing the sword to collapse to the floor, and then going for the side. Tristan's shadow caught the sword and pulled it off Tristan, throwing aside as he took a defensive stance and raised his arms upwards.

Tristan raised his own hands and the two stood apart from each other with hot feet again. His shadow went in with some kicks at the side to test the water, but Tristan kept his distance. Tristan didn't dare move in until another kick came and he pulled at his leg, bringing himself over and proceeding to attempt to subdue him. Tristan's shadow came around and atop. He punched at Tristan while Tristan attempted to kick his legs back at him while his shadow attempted to hold on. Tristan eventually managed to push him back and around so that he was atop of him. He placed his body atop of his shadow so that his shadow's legs were wide apart, making a counterattack as he had done impossible. Tristan also placed the weight of his torso atop of his shadow, bringing an arm around his neck to choke him out.

Tristan's shadow struggled with his legs. Tristan was pushed back, but he maintained his grip around the neck and took his legs and pelvis aside so that his foe's legs could not make contact with his body. Tristan began to punch at the head of his foe until he settled down. He then looked to the side and saw that his foe had grabbed ahold of his own shadow sword. He raised an arm to block the strike towards his head, grabbing it and struggling with his shadow to gain control of it. Tristan's shadow refused to let go of the sword, but Tristan overpowered him.

However, Tristan caused the sword to fly off to the other side of the room. He looked to his right-side and saw his own sword nearby. Tristan punched his shadow and then rushed over to grab the sword. Tristan's shadow slowly recovered in the meantime, looking over to Tristan as he picked up his own sword. He then went over towards his shadow and hit him in the side, causing him to fall over again. Tristan kicked him back and then with both hands, brought the sword down and through the chest, causing his shadow to screech out a terrible yell that echoed out.

Tristan's shadow's body began to become overcome with a darkness while the eyes beamed out until finally, the entire body collapsed into nothingness, much as had happened to Heyl. He looked down at where the body of his shadow had been, and then he looked around him before looking forward. He was no longer in the arena he had been hallucinating, but instead within a dark tunnel with light ahead of him. Tristan stood up from where he was bent over and put his sword away. He saw his shield on the floor nearby and went to pick it up, bringing it around and behind him. He then walked forward and came into the actual tomb that was lit by a shred of light that poured in from cracks above.

Tristan took out his flashlight and looked closer at the room, which was exactly as Diana had told him. There was no water on the floor though. He looked across the floor at the base of the room, but did not see the ring. He then climbed up the stairs to the very top where the basin and shrine was. At the base of the fountain he saw something glitter at his light. Tristan leaned in and picked it up and it was Damian's ring as he had told him. He wrapped his hand around the ring and closed his eyes.

"Thank you," Tristan whispered, placing the ring into a pouch.

Tristan walked up to the fountain and placed his arms around the side of the basin. He then looked over to the mirror and saw his reflection. The cut on Tristan's face remained as did the pain in his shoulder. Tristan brought a hand into the water and then cleaned his face. The dragon's tears did their work and healed his wound. He took a moment to drink from the fountain what little was left before he stepped back and began to leave.

Without hesitation, Tristan traveled back through the tunnel, through the atrium entrance of the tomb, and back outside where a mild downpour had begun as twilight set in. Diana looked over to the entrance as Tristan appeared. Damian turned around and looked over to Tristan with surprise. Tristan took the ring from his pouch and showed them.

"You... you did it..." Damian said in shock.

Tristan walked over and gave the ring to Damian. He then went over and hugged Diana. Damian looked back over to Tristan still in shock. He then took the crystals out from his own pouch and placed them together with the ring. Tristan and Diana continued to hug as tears fell from her eyes in relief.

"Very well," Damian simply said, looking to them with a frown. "Tomorrow at noon, we shall travel to Harlech."

Tristan didn't turn around to respond. Neither did Diana. The two simply continued to embrace each other as Tristan had survived the fatal trial within the Tomb of the Dragon Emperor.

Act 10, Scene 1

Charlemagne looked out from the ruins of the structure he was in through a pair of binoculars. Around him in the distance, he could hear the echoes of gunfire and the shouts of enemy combatants and friendly combatants. Charlemagne was not dressed in his Protection Squad uniform, but a modern urban combat uniform given to him by the Harlech Militia, which included a reinforced helmet. Behind him, within the rubble and ruins of the second-floor bedroom he took refuge in, Finn slept on a mat nearby, dressed in the same uniform as him. Their rucksacks were lined against the wall and Finn's assault rifle nearby. Charlemagne looked down the street and towards the ruins of some electric motor tanks down N Slade Drive.

The signs around them placed them on the outskirts of Saffron as many of them were in Mandarin, while a billboard ahead contained English, Persian, and simple Chinese characters, advertising a realtor. Charlemagne scanned the space ahead of them and began to see some movement. He could see some enemy combatants dressed in thick grey-brown coats, vests atop, and trousers armed with Colt C8 assault rifles, patrolling towards them.

Charlemagne moved away from the opening in the wall and put his binoculars away. He picked up his own rifle and went to Finn, waking him as he knelt down to shake him.

"Wake up," Charlemagne said to his son. "We've got hostiles down the street."

Finn woke up and pushed himself off from the ground. He quickly rolled up his mat and then brought it over to his rucksack while Charlemagne took his. Finn also picked up his rifle as they made their exit from the building they were in.

A week had passed since Charlemagne, Manon, and Finn had arrived in Harlech, and with that, the Battle of Harlech continued between the anarchists and commonwealth. The platoon that Charlemagne travelled with into Lincoln had been ambushed and they were separated from the frontline as the battle took a bloody turn. In the distance, the volley of shells from the destroyers in the sea could be heard bombarding Cliffe Island and Harthdam. The air around the city was smoky from the fires that raged on to develop a haze that covered the skies in a yellowish fog.

Charlemagne and Finn made their escape out from the building they had slept in and fell into the alleyway behind where they remained hidden as they saw the patrol pass. Charlemagne then looked to Finn.

"We have to regroup with the others," Charlemagne quietly said to Finn. "Hopefully the others have had better success than us. We'll need to retreat and keep up with these folk until they run into the infantry. After that, we can ambush them – get back at them for doing the same to our own."

Finn nodded. The two of them went down the alleyway and came out to the other side where they saw the patrol continue to pass. They stopped at the end of the alleyway where Finn pulled on Charlemagne's sleeve to point out another patrol advancing from Hudson Street. Charlemagne looked over and waited for them to pass. He then looked to Finn. Finn looked back at him.

"We'll need to proceed cautiously and from behind. Follow me," Charlemagne whispered.

Charlemagne went down the street and towards the street corner. He looked down and could not see more than a block ahead through the smoke. Finn joined him.

"Wait here and take point," Charlemagne said. "I'll continue from the other end."

Charlemagne rushed across the street and took cover at the opposite street corner. He then signaled Finn to stay put until he began to lose sight of the anarchists ahead. They went onwards down the street and took cover behind some ruined and charred cars. The patrol stopped ahead at the street intersection. Charlemagne could hear vehicles approach from the north. The patrol began to retreat. Charlemagne got into position to fire at them and then he opened fire. Finn joined in. The hostiles quickly spread out at the intersection as they got the jump on them, but the approaching vehicles came closer and began to open fire. Charlemagne and Finn cleaned up the hostiles before they remained hidden as the armored personnel carriers could be seen.

The pair raised their hands up in surrender to the vehicles so they could be seen. The APC stopped and the hatch opened from the top to reveal an officer looking towards them, waving his arms for them to come over. Charlemagne and Finn picked up their rifles and ran over.

"We're survivors from the Second Armor Company, Second Platoon that was ambushed last night," Charlemagne said, looking over to the officer. "Major Cabernet," he said, pointing to himself, "and Sergeant Cabernet," he said, pointing to Finn. What are the casualties from the counter-attack last night?"

"Second Lieutenant Larson, sir, and this is my platoon. According to the morning briefing, we received heavy losses from both the Second and Third platoons at Slade and Shai, but the First Armor Company was able to push through at Burnes and have taken defenses at the Boundary-Burnes intersection, while fighting continues in South Port Burnes. We can't push on until we get the rest of Boundary-Bering under control."

"We were ambushed on our way to Lincoln Drive. They then overran us. I have no idea what sort of defenses await there, but it seems to be all the same – blockades at every intersection and enough smoke that it is impossible to see more than couple meters ahead of you."

"The anarchists are a crafty bunch, aren't they? Intel says hostiles across the river set the forest on fire to create all this smoke. To make matters worse, we had to set fire to the forest on University Hill because our guys were getting ambushed at Shai Street by hostiles hiding in the woods. Command had no other option but to set it on fire and drive them out – made the drive to Riverside that much easier and now a Delta Company are taking the university as we speak. Speaking of which, we can't fall behind. CO wants City Hall taken today. Intel says the anarchists are on a shortage of food, so they should be on their last breaths. We're due to link up with the First Armor Company at Lincoln Drive. You can come with us or return to HQ up north."

"We'd rather carry on," Charlemagne responded. "We can re-organize later. Onwards."

Charlemagne and Finn climbed up and joined the platoon, which consisted of three armored personnel carriers, each with a section, or patrol of two fireteams. Each fireteam consisting of four soldiers, and car included with a driver and gunner.

"The other half of the hostile patrol you caught were travelling down Hudson Street," Charlemagne explained. "They'll have returned to their command by now if the platoon driving down Hudson Street hasn't caught them. Is there another platoon coming down Rupert Street?"

"Yes," the Platoon Commander replied. "They're to travel down Radisson Street to the end at Rupert Street and move further down at Fraser Street, while the platoon that came down Rupert Street makes a lap around to double-check Nelson Street. They are all then to join us at Lincoln Drive for the push to City

Hall. CO believes we'll have the island within a week before the anarchists starve to death. Enemy casualties so far are estimated to be approximately five-thousand so far. The navy spotted row boats attempting to make a run over the river from the south mainland – blew them to shreds, but somehow food is still getting through, probably under the cover of night."

The APC made a sudden halt.

"We must be here," the lieutenant said, standing up and climbing up the ladder.

Charlemagne followed him as he made his exit. He then observed from above as the platoon that had travelled down the street to the right of Slade Drive (Radisson Street) and passed them as they went down Rupert Street. The Lincoln-Slade intersection was dead ahead due south. Charlemagne waited several minutes, tapping his fingers at the rim of the hatch. He then looked down to Finn.

"Finn, come on," Charlemagne said, impatiently. "We're going on ahead."

Charlemagne climbed out of the hatch and stepped down. Finn joined him.

"We're going to go ahead and do some reconnaissance before the push to Lincoln Drive. Be careful," Charlemagne said, turning to Finn so they could move on. "We've wasted enough time in the last week pushing through Saffron and Port Burnes. We need to move quickly."

The pair went across the street from where the ruins of La Galerie Shopping Center were at the northeast corner of the highway ahead. They went down Radisson Street and then into an alleyway where they went down and made their way to Fraser Street. They were still too far to be able to see the intersection from where they were. Finn observed one of their platoons eastward at the Rupert-Fraser intersection. The pair crossed the street again and then made their way down towards the three-way street corner so they could look towards the highway intersection they were supposed to move to yesterday night – the highway of which was collapsed.

Slade-Lincoln was barricaded with all sorts of furniture collected throughout the city, which blocked the path ahead. Charlemagne could not see any anarchist soldiers around the barricade. He took a step back and looked to Finn.

"It appears as though they've abandoned the intersection, but this damn smoke is so dense that I cannot see further ahead. They've resorted to deep defense and ambushes in order to counter our heavy armor. They could be hiding amongst the commercial office buildings like rats. We should report back and have the company proceed with caution."

Charlemagne and Finn returned to the platoon where he met up with Lieutenant Larson to explain what they had seen. Afterwards, they boarded the top of the APC as the other platoons arrived for them to proceed. The front-most APC went ahead and began to approach Slade-Lincoln. Charlemagne and Finn looked around suspiciously with their weapons ready. Many of the structures within the district were in such decay and ruin that they offered nil cover inside for the anarchists to operate from, but the skyscrapers were a different story and there many of them along Lincoln Drive. Charlemagne suddenly saw a flash of fire ahead followed by the crash of a debris that hit nearby.

"Bloody hell!" Charlemagne remarked. "We're under fire!"

Charlemagne and Finn hopped off from the APC and separated. The anarchists had launched a burning mound of garbage towards them. The infantry soldiers in the APC exited out through the rear and spread out. Once the section was out, the APC drove forward and began to open fire towards the anarchists as they emerged from the smoke. Each of the APCs in the platoon spread out to offer heavy fire support from their machine gun turrets. Charlemagne looked over to the other six APCs.

"Get a platoon on the east flank at once!" Charlemagne shouted. "The remaining platoon shall join this one and brush them back!"

"Yes, major!" a voice shouted out.

The APCs repositioned themselves in the formation that Charlemagne instructed. A platoon covered the east flank, while two covered the south front. The highway to the west was collapsed and there were no signs of hostiles on that end, although three APCs parked nearby so they could open fire.

Charlemagne and Finn opened fire against the anarchists as they shot back through the smoke towards them. Another volley of debris came towards them and missed the armor.

"Second platoon push to Urhan Street!" Charlemagne shouted. "Everybody else, push forward down Slade Drive!"

Charlemagne and Finn went ahead. The hostiles could be seen from the second and third floor of the commercial buildings above the shops ahead. The armored personnel carriers ahead began to drive forward, through the debris as they paved a path for the infantry. Charlemagne and Finn followed as they went towards Urhan Street, using the APCs as cover.

The APCs ripped through the remains of the structure and took easy care of the hostiles who were forced to retreat.

"Third platoon goes west down Urhan Street and down Damitz Street towards Schull Street!" Charlemagne shouted. "Someone get in radio contact with command to let them know of our advance so that Second Platoon can continue through!"

"Aye, sir!"

"Four more blocks to City Hall!"

Charlemagne and Finn continued onward down N Slade Drive as they made a slow push towards Schull Street, Durrus Street, and finally Taghman Street. The number of hostiles that hid on upper levels soon became so numerous that fireteams infiltrated into the buildings at the side and began to fight door-to-door while the armored personnel carriers took care of the street fighting. Charlemagne and Finn stayed near the APCs where there was sufficient cover for them to hide from the hostiles above.

At Taghman Street, there was a stronger blockade where they were stalled for close to half an hour. Charlemagne reloaded his rifle and looked to Finn.

"At least they've stopped sending wave assaults that have forced us back," Charlemagne said. "They must have a lesser manpower than at the start of the invasion – an attack like that must be too costly. This may be the final push for their command center. City Hall is just past Colin Street next."

Charlemagne ducked his head at the sudden explosion that hit a structure at the southwest corner of the intersection. He then looked west down Taghman Street to see a platoon of tanks arrive from South Port Burnes. Another shell hit another side of the structure on the southwest, causing it to collapse. The infantry cheered the arrival of the armor. Charlemagne lowered his arms and looked over with relief.

"There we are…" Charlemagne muttered. "Come on, Finn. We're almost there."

Finn stood up from his knee and followed Charlemagne as they went over to the tank.

"About time you lot showed!" Charlemagne yelled.

The frontmost tank opened and a lieutenant appeared.

"Major Cabernet, there you are. Command was worried of your survival, but we heard you were with the Third Company here," the lieutenant explained. "Commander Alexandrov will let the Commander-in-Chief know."

"Nevermind that for now," Charlemagne responded, climbing the tank. "Onwards, City Hall awaits our final capture – hopefully then we can end this war."

The tank column proceeded down Slade Drive where City Hall could be seen in the distance through the smoke as they approached Colin Street. At the side of City Hall was a park where two sections proceeded through, while another continued into the building on the left. The tanks aimed their cannons towards the city hall, which was a chateauesque structure similar to the Windsor Hotel, built at the start of the last century with a clock tower that faced either side. The tanks shot towards the structure while the armored personnel carriers went forward and opened fire at the hostiles in cover before the steps of the civil center.

Charlemagne and Finn hopped off the tanks and took cover behind them, watching the armor rip to shred the hostiles that started to retreat inwards into the building. The tanks moved forward right up to Boundary Drive where they stopped as they laid siege to municipal building. The infantry soldiers that fought through the park made their approach up the steps of City Hall and began to position themselves on the exterior, as the buildings across the street were cleared by the section that went through. Charlemagne and Finn rushed across the street to link up with these soldiers so they could participate on the assault through City Hall and eliminate the Harlech Defense Council.

Act 10, Scene 2

Shots flew back and forth through the entrances into the lobby of City Hall. All sections with the Second Platoon took cover against the many doorways on the west face of the civic center that entered into the main floor. The main lobby of City Hall consisted of a polished greenish-grey stone floor with beige stone brick walls. There were other doorways on the north and south faces, which was where the other platoons had lined up and returned fire inside. At the east face there were a set of wide curved stone stairs that wrapped around to the second floor that circled around with balustrades as railings. In addition, there was a third story that wrapped around, accessible by either the elevators at the top of the staircase or via a stairwell at the side. In the middle of the room, hanging from the ceiling, was a large and wide chandelier. Anarchists inside had barricaded much of the balustrades so that they could hide behind and hold their ground as the defended the heart of the anarchic state. Within the ground floor there were also crates of ammunition spread out as it seemed that a great deal of supplies had been transferred to City Hall to assist in the defense. In the middle of the room from the ground floor, underneath the chandelier, furniture was stacked up and a bonfire lit which burned a cloud of black smoke that made it difficult to see.

The structure shook as a shell from the tanks hit the side of the building. Charlemagne observed as the militia put pressure on the anarchists, but more and more appeared from the doors as they knocked on the door of the wasp hive. Hostiles could be seen on every floor.

"Watch that AT on the second-floor!" a soldier shouted.

Charlemagne observed as some rockets were fired down from anti-tank weapons above. The rockets missed and hit above, but still caused rubble to collapse towards them and cause a cloud of dust to spring upwards. Another shell hit from the tanks parked outside. Charlemagne looked out as supplies arrived from Saffron. He reloaded his rifle and then looked over to Finn.

"Let's return some heavy ordinance and flush them out!" Charlemagne shouted.

Some soldiers retreated down the steps while men at the supply trucks unloaded crates of ammunition. Rocketeers came up the steps and began to return rocket fire inside, causing cover to be blown, exposing the hostiles as well as doing heavy damage. A rocket hit the top of the chandelier, causing it to come crashing down atop of the bonfire. A large cloud of dust flew out at either entrances, which caused a brief cease of fire as it spread out. The anarchists took the opportunity to retreat. Very little of them remained as they started to retreat into the depths of the municipal building.

"Advance! Push them back!" an officer yelled.

Charlemagne reloaded his rifle and then moved up towards one of the crates spread out. There were still hostiles above them on the third floor, which prevented a full advance into the main lobby. Soldiers moved in to put pressure on hostiles above. The gunners sporting light machine guns were able to do heavy damage, while grenadiers blew the hostiles out of cover. The anarchists were linear in their arrangement, unclassed as one could expect a society that boasts to be classless. Charlemagne moved in as the third floor began to clear. A section on either side of the north and south entrances moved in at doorways on the ground floor, east side, just at the side of the stairs where gun fire continued through. Another section moved up to the doorway beneath the landing that the staircase wrapped around, while another two sections moved up the stairs and to the second floor to continue fighting into the second floor. Charlemagne and Finn joined the sections that went upstairs. Another two sections moved up with them, but spread out around the second floor where cover remained, and another two sections began to make their way towards the stairwell so they could climb up to the third floor. Charlemagne positioned himself back as the two sections against the south wall pushed into the press room.

Soldiers moved up the steps with flamethrowers equipped, while rifleman and grenadiers held their positions at the doors into the press room. The flamethrowers then stepped into the line and began to ignite the room with the hostiles within. They then stepped aside to allow soldiers to storm the room. Charlemagne moved in and looked into the city council press briefing room. There was a small theater of seats on the closest side followed by a long countertop table that extended across the other half of the room, fit for eleven seats and facing towards a podium in front of the small theater. Across the back of the room, the logo of the City of Harlech was tagged with the word 'Autonomous City-State of Harlech' in graffiti paint.

Hostiles retreated backwards into the room behind. Soldiers moved in and opened fire into the council chamber. The flamethrowers moved in and exhausted out a fireball into the room, which caught the remaining hostiles on fire. Some hostiles retreated out into corridors at the side. The council chamber was a dark room with no windows and instead dark grey walls with a round table in the middle fit for eleven seats. On flag poles at the back of the room were anarcho-communist flags set with the self-made flag of the autonomous city-state. The table and the flag in the room were set alight. Hostiles were flushed out and into the corridor where soldiers gunned them down.

"Any sight of the leadership?" Charlemagne questioned the troops as they regrouped in the press room.

"Negative," a soldier responded.

"They must be in the building someplace," Charlemagne said. "We'll have to fight our way to the top. The mayor and councilmember offices are on the ninth floor."

Charlemagne and the section left the room as they cleared out the hostiles on the second floor. They went to the stairwell and proceeded to make their way up to the fourth floor where a section had positioned themselves at the entrance where hostiles fought back from the corridor on the other side. The floors from the fourth floor to the ninth floor were designed in an I-shape with elevators on the east face, and a T-intersection on the left and right with a short corridor around the corner next to the elevators on each side with a window at the end. A longer corridor was towards the west side with offices on the side and the end of the west side at the very end. On the west side there were also office-spaces with cubicles between the two long corridors which took up most of the space on each floor, and these offices had windows at the west end that looked out west towards the city. The building shook as another shell from the tanks hit the side of the building. Charlemagne stopped at the top of the stairs.

"I need a runner to tell the armor to stop firing!" Charlemagne yelled. "They'll trap us all in this building if they keep shelling the outside of the building."

"Aye, major," a soldier responded.

"Get the flamethrowers up front and clear a way in!" Charlemagne then ordered. "I want every one of these anarchists eliminated, except for the high-command. They're to be taken alive!"

The flamethrowers moved in and began to send a fireball into the corridor while others moved into the corridor.

"Grenade out!" a soldier called, throwing a frag grenade.

A section stayed behind to control the stairwell as they went through the fourth floor to clear out the hostiles. From the corridor, they pushed them back into the office cubical space at the center-west side of the building where light poured in from a hole in the side of the building caused by the tanks. The bombardments against the side of the building had stopped. Charlemagne and the section regrouped at the stairwell where they fought their way upwards to the fifth floor and repeated the same process.

Charlemagne stayed behind at the stairwell as the section moved into the corridor. The runner returned and took cover behind Charlemagne.

"Message from Lieutenant Larson, sir. He says that his men have secured the ground floor, second floor, and third floor. No sight of the anarchist's leadership or of any prisoners."

"Tell him that we've secured the fourth floor and we're on our way up to the ninth. We'll take position here at Boundary for the night if we have to and then continue through the rest of the island tomorrow if we cannot capture their leadership now."

"Copy that."

Charlemagne moved into the fifth floor to join Finn as they were about to move into the office space within. He placed a hand on his shoulder.

"No sight of the leadership," Charlemagne told him. "No sight of Diana and Tristan either. I'm growing to worry that they may not be here, or even alive."

"Tristan isn't a pussy," Finn replied. "He'll be alive, with Diana, somewhere. We just have to secure the islands."

The sections moved into the fifth-floor office space and culled out the anarchists from within. They searched the bodies of men and women, but saw none of them to match the photos of the anarchist high-command or the warlord. With the fifth floor under control, they moved onwards to the sixth floor and then the seventh floor. At the eighth floor, the number of anarchists began to dwindle. The sections moved up the stairs to the ninth floor where they received heavy resistance.

Soldiers from the stairwell on the other side cleared the way for hostiles to move out of the open and take point within the office-space in the center as well as from the private offices on the side. Despite being the top of the public office, the stairs continued upwards to the roof, which forced a section to stay behind and keep watch of the stairs going to the tenth floor. Charlemagne moved in to join the others as the flamethrower sent a fireball into one of the former city council member's offices. At the end of the south corridor was the mayor's office. An assault group moved up to the doors into the mayor's office while another returned fire from within the civil servant office. The flamethrower moved in and ignited the hostiles within the room who hid behind desks for cover. Charlemagne joined Finn with the team that was about to breach the mayor's office.

"Remember, we take the scumbag alive," Charlemagne noted.

The team leader of the section tossed a flash grenade in. The doors were then pushed open so that they could open fire within the office. Hostiles returned inaccurate fire and were shot down. The team then moved in to finish off any survivors while also checking the identities to see if they matched any of the wanted. The team leader then walked over to Charlemagne.

"Not here sir," the sergeant said.

"Dammit," Charlemagne cursed. "We'll have to continue upwards to the clocktower. Secure the floor before we advance."

"Yes, sir."

Charlemagne and Finn exited out from the office and went towards the office-space as the other assault group cleared out the room. There was no sight of the warlord from anywhere on the ninth floor.

"Shall I send word to Lieutenant Larson and command, major?" the runner questioned.

"Negative," Charlemagne replied. "We have one more floor to secure."

Charlemagne looked over to the sergeant of the other section that was travelling up the north stairwell.

"One more floor, sergeant. To the very top!"

"Aye, major," the sergeant replied.

Charlemagne and Finn moved with the section they travelled with and joined the other in the stairwell. They went up the stairs and to the attic of the building where hostiles opened fire against them. The hostiles stalled for almost ten minutes until the section was able to push in and spread out. The attic had a similar I-shape, but with no offices on the side and instead brick walls with an open ceiling that reached up to the eleventh floor where the mechanics of the clocks could be seen alongside platforms and other maintenance items. Where the office-spaces were, there were rooms with more maintenance equipment. Where the elevators were, there was a closet for elevator maintenance. Charlemagne saw that the tank shells had caused a massive hole in the roof where light poured down from.

The soldiers moved in on both sides with caution as hostiles were able to shoot at them from the platforms above. Most of the hostiles retreated into the open room above the office-spaces where there was plenty of cover. The flamethrowers moved and shot a fireball into the confined spaces on both sides. The fighting dragged on for close to twenty-minutes as the last of the anarchists were taken care of. The militia sustained close to no casualties, especially within the section Charlemagne travelled with. The soldiers checked the corpses of the soldiers to identity the warlord and other high command, but there were none.

"Cowards!" Charlemagne cursed. "They've fled their capital and left the drones to guard it. Outrageous! Inform the OC so that command knows that we've captured the city hall."

"Yes, sir," the runner replied.

Charlemagne looked to Finn.

"Come, let's meet with the field command below and see what we can do next," Charlemagne said with disappointment. "We could be here for another week or two."

Act 10, Scene 3

The day after Tristan had secured Damian's ring from the Tomb of the Dragon Emperor, they took the morning to rest from their travels before coming together atop of the horses so they could teleport across the ocean.

"Ready?" Damian questioned.

"We're going to Allabrese, right?" Tristan asked. "No tricks."

"We're going to Harlech," Damian responded. "Why on Earth would we travel to Allabrese?"

"Because that's where we left Charlemagne – and that's where he'll be looking for Finn, if he hasn't found them, and probably us too."

"You told me that Diana's last words to them was that she desired to go home, which was why you were sent to Georgia. Charlemagne isn't a moron. He'll have paid close attention to these words and assumed that Diana was teleported to a place she considers to be home, which would be Harlech. They'll be there."

Tristan didn't respond.

"Grab on," Damian said.

Diana and Tristan grabbed onto Damian's horse from theirs. Damian closed a fist around crystal and ring, and in an instant, they vanished and reappeared less than ten-thousand kilometers across the Pacific Ocean, in the remains of the City of Harlech. Diana and Tristan opened their eyes as they reemerged and touched down.

Tristan set off to control Tempest as she panicked. He also looked about to see the ruins they were around. The skies above them were cloudy with a thick smoky haze that was lit by the fires that raged beyond. It was also mildly dark as it was nighttime in this region of the world. Damian had teleported them to a small clearing of grass near the Lincoln-Slade intersection and by the collapsed highway. Tristan looked around and saw the destruction that had swept through the city.

"Now this is an apocalyptic mess," Tristan remarked as he settled Tempest. "Why here?"

"It's the center of the city," Damian said, closing his eyes. "Hm..."

"What is it?" Tristan asked.

"I feel... someone's presence nearby. A psionic energy from someone other than myself... Charlemagne."

"Charlemagne has been dabbling with psionic powers," Diana explained. "You can sense him?"

"Yes, he's nearby," Damian stated. "Follow me."

Damian went ahead on his horse and began to go down Slade Drive. Tristan followed and sped up to catch up with Damian as he went off. They began to approach the column of tanks and armored personnel carriers in front of City Hall.

• • • •

Charlemagne heard the neigh of a horse echo through the main lobby of the civic center. He exited out from the council chamber where field command had set up operations. Charlemagne was alone as the rest of operations had retired for the night. He entered into the press room where he woke up Finn who was sleeping on the floor with the rest of the platoon. Finn heard the neigh from outside and stood up, taking his rifle with him as he went to investigate with Charlemagne. The pair exited out and came to the second floor where they looked down to see Tempest and Damian's horse with the pair hopping off and then looking up towards them.

"I don't believe it," Charlemagne remarked, coming down the stairs with Finn. "Oh, Heaven's alive! What a relief!"

The pair met up with the couple, while Damian looked on from the side with a frown.

"Where's Manon?" Diana asked.

"She's at Cabernet Tower," Charlemagne responded. "Safe and sound. Where have you been?"

"You'll never believe us," Tristan responded, "but I guess we have lots to explain to you."

"Likewise," Charlemagne replied with a smile before looking over to Damian with a frown. "Zimmerman…"

"Zimmerman?" Finn questioned.

"He's a part of the explanation," Tristan said, "and also the reason why we were able to find you from where we vanished to."

Tristan began to explain his and Diana's story in brief from where they arrived when they had their argument, to where they travelled to and how they found out they were in the remains of Georgia by the Caucasus Mountains. He told them how he had to sell Diana's engagement ring in order to pay for their house, sword, and horse, as well as use his knowledge of Russian to communicate with some locals. He then explained that he had met with Mika, but in his spiritual form and perfect form, and that he told him that they were not in the future, but in an alternate reality. He told him to seek out the son born between himself and Diana in this timeline, a man named Damian, who was held captive by the Children of Moloch in Jerusalem. So, Diana and Tristan set off from Georgia and made the two-week journey south to Jerusalem where Tristan rescued this man named Damian who in fact was the man they knew as Zimmerman. Tristan then briefly explained that Zimmerman had been transported back to this world, which he is from, when he laid his hands on the time orb in their universe, with his dark crystal ring equipped, and he was sent back. He was subsequently captured by the Chosen when they sensed his presence, and they took him to the prison where they tortured him. Charlemagne questioned why they did this and how it was possible that Damian/Zimmerman had come to their universe in the first place, or why a second universe even exists.

"Because I created the world that all of you come from," Damian begrudgingly explained. "After the Children lost the war, they thought they had fought so eloquently; they unleashed the catastrophe that has come to be known in this world as the Great Calamity. In the aftermath, there was no more world to conquer and barely any Chosen left to rule. I became a member of the Chosen of Moloch when I was kidnapped by them at the age of eighteen. They tortured me, brainwashed me, and led me to believe that I was one of them, a man named Audric Zimmerman, of Ashkenazi descent. At the time of my capture, I was proficient with the powers of the orbs taken from the Scepter of Alexander the Great and the Amulet of Ra, so they used me as a human test subject to create their own psionic program – this all occurred under the organization known as the Global Defense Project at the end of the 2030s, which was later dissolved and the remainders incorporated into the Israeli Defense Force, since by then, the GDP was nothing more than a puppet to the Children, financed by the other countries of the world. The program stayed with the IDF, while I was transferred to work with Mossad to do the dirty for the Israeli war machine. By the time that the Great Calamity happened, I was an experienced operative with Mossad, but unknown to them my brainwashing had begun to fade. When the dust settled from the Great Calamity, I presented to the remainders of the leadership of the Children a proposition where I would test a power I believe I possessed, the ability to travel back in time. I told them that I would travel back in time to a point not too far back, where I could set the conditions right so that the events of this timeline could be evaded and a Greater Israel established to bring in a messianic age. I had no intent in doing so. I needed permission so they could authorize this project and I could collect the resources I would need to travel back in time comfortably with the knowledge I would need to be able to succeed. On May 14, 2042, six years from the one-hundred year anniversary of the start of the Israeli occupation, I unleashed my power and created your world, but I didn't realize this until I had come back to this world in which I was remembered as a man that had failed the Children since their world still existed. And then I met with Diana and Tristan, and Tristan explained to me that this world was an alternate reality to the world that he and Diana had come from, as spoken to them by an 'angel,' or whatever."

"I knew it," Charlemagne remarked. "I knew that this world seemed strange to the world that we had come from and that this couldn't be our future."

Charlemagne explained his experiences over the past several weeks, from the attack by Medici, his encounter with Dino Medici who explained to him what happened in Allabrese, to his travel with Manon and Finn to Harlech after he recovered from some injuries. He then explained his meeting with his brother who is the ruler of King Island, of a kingdom known as the Commonwealth of Harlech. Charlemagne explained that he thought he would find Diana and Tristan somewhere here, so he convinced Salmar to attack the southern island that are home to anarchists, and they've been at war for almost a week now.

"This is interesting," Charlemagne noted. "A second universe next to our own – I can only imagine how dangerously unstable that is to the fabric of reality itself. I'll be honest, when

I invented the time machine, I had hoped I had invented a manner by which one could travel back in time so that I could change the past," he said, looking over to Finn, "but if this is the way that it is done, then I can imagine the process to be terrible and set an imbalance that could destroy all of the realities."

"Anyways," Tristan interrupted, "after we met with Damian, we gave him the crystals so that we could travel here, but before that, we had to collect a fourth crystal that was in his ring, which he left behind in the Tomb of the Dragon Emperor in China, so that's why it's taken us this long to get here."

"No matter," Charlemagne replied with a sigh. "We're all together, so that we can return home. Where are the crystals now?"

"Damian has them," Tristan said. "He- he wants to return to our world with us."

"What?" Charlemagne questioned with minor insult. "Is he mad?"

Damian frowned back at him.

"He's helped us reach you," Tristan argued. "He's probably the only one that's powerful enough to use the crystals and help all of us return to where we belong. Besides, all of his machines are destroyed and his company ruined. He has no power to threaten us with – No, instead he can help us. He can help us defeat the Great Satan that is the Chosen, or worse… When I was alone in Georgia, I had visions of a Beast that was far worse than the Chosen in my opinion. Mika told me that his name was Heyl and that he was the rebel angel that had led the separatist war thousands and thousands of years ago between their kind."

Tristan briefly explained to Charlemagne what Mika told him in relation to the aliens, how the corporeal form was not the true form of angels like Mika or Madonna, but that this was an avatar that fallen angels could assume and subvert, such as the rebels they fought against in 2018. Secondly, he explained that beings that did not elevate to a pure spiritual form had mutated to become the Nephilim, or Shapeshifters, who were the ancestors of the Chosen who escaped from Antarctic to South America then to North America, Siberia, and finally to the Middle East almost two-thousand years ago. Lastly, he explained the fate of Heyl, to being that had elevated, but in his wickedness, was constrained to his corrupted avatar and cursed to walk the Earth.

"This Heyl," Tristan said, "he's Lucifer – he's Satan. He's a powerful entity who can influence and tempt people, but needs to be destroyed if we're to hope for any peace in our world. The angels aren't prone to these realities; they can travel between them. The Mika I met was the Mika we knew. Likewise, the same is most likely capable by Heyl. Damian can help us fight him."

Charlemagne looked back to Damian who had said nothing.

"Do you honestly believe this man would do such a selfless act? He's attempted to have me assassinated in France two years ago! He almost had you killed Tristan, and Diana."

"I've never tried to have Diana's life put in jeopardy," Damian clarified. "Look, what happened in France was nothing personal. I had a job to do for the Children, sue me, but they hate me more than they hate you, probably."

Charlemagne looked at him suspiciously.

"You're the assassin," Charlemagne noted. "Of course, how could that slip my mind? You have the talent and the skills, and your eyes are the same. You were the one that I had fought in that ferry – and then in the United States, you went after the children yourself!"

Damian didn't respond. Charlemagne looked to Diana and Tristan.

"And you two knew? You knew that he was that very same assassin, the one that you feared so much, Diana, and you still wanted to bring him with us."

"Diana doesn't want to bring him with us," Tristan corrected. "I do, because he deserves a second-chance. He's not evil."

"He has nothing for him in our world," Charlemagne argued. "All that was his has been lost. He has no wife, no children, no nothing."

"What do you mean? What happened to my wife?" Damian asked, lowering his arms. "Iustina? The children?"

"What are you on about?" Charlemagne questioned. "What's he on about?" he then asked the couple.

Tristan dropped a look of anxiety.

"He doesn't know about Iustina, is that it?" Damian questioned Diana and Tristan. "They're alive, right?"

"No," Diana answered. "I'm afraid... I'm afraid she's dead. Helene too and all the children. They were killed in an assault on your castle by the Children of Moloch, led by a Cardinal Calavera. I'm sorry we didn't tell you..."

Damian's face was expressionless. Tristan could see the death within him.

"All this time, you knew something that could have been important to me, but you kept silent, all so... so you could return to your own timeline?" Damian questioned with frustration. "I don't believe this. You really are the scum of the Earth, aren't you? The pair of you, because clearly, your time with him has made you out from the saint that you were in my world. You're nothing..."

"Back off!" Tristan shouted. "You're one to talk when you've come out to be a literal psychopath! We'll get you your ticket back to the present, so hold your horse."

Damian began to give off a manic laugh that showed the anxiety in his own voice. He shook his head.

"No," Damian rejected. "I have no intent in returning to that world. You- you can do whatever you want, but you're wrong to believe that either the Chosen or that Fallen Angel, Lucifer, are your concern, because they're not. They are nothing. They are not Satan. Satan is not a person, but a title. A title conferred to that which opposes 'God' or goodness, or whatever the hell it is that created all life; whatever that is that is so puny, so pathetic, and so dated. Lucifer is either dead or a myth, and while the Chosen may have the arrogance to believe they together can become their own messiah and be the new Satan, they're wrong. Look at this world and see their incompetence to even be able to wage war. No," he said, pointing a thumb to his chest. "I am the Satan that you should fear; I am the Son of Ra, the only Son of the Devil who lies in Hell, because I am the most powerful creation on this planet since him," he said with a laugh. "I literally created an entire universe out of scratch, and you tell me that you're worried about a few old men in robes? Hah!"

Diana and Tristan were silent. Damian took off his pouch from his belt and took the crystals into his hand.

"Enjoy your time in this world, because it is where the three of you deserve to spend the rest of your lives in," Damian said. "Finn, now is the time. Give me the time orb."

"Finn?" Charlemagne questioned, turning to him. "What is he talking about?"

"You didn't think that I wouldn't have had a contingent in place, did you?" Damian remarked. "I thought it was too good to be true that I would find Charlemagne's long lost son in that forest, but nonetheless, there he was abandoned just as I had been once upon a time. I was the only one that approached him and made him feel secure. I gave him a home. I gave him a life. And now, it's time to repay your debt to me, so give me the orb."

Tristan looked to Finn as he produced the piece of the time orb from his belt. He held it in his hand.

"Finn… don't do this," Tristan said. "You don't owe him anything."

Finn didn't respond and instead walked to Damian. He looked over to Tristan and then to Damian. He handed him the piece of the time orb, but then quickly swiped the pouch off of Damian. Damian struggled with him as he attempted to pull off the time orb, hitting him across the face and onto the ground. He then walked over to him so that he could get the pouch back. Finn instantly disappeared.

"No!" Damian growled. "Son of a bitch!" he cursed, looking around. "Is that how he wants to play it? I'll show him…"

Damian took the time orb and brought his hands at either side of it.

"I'm through with everything and anything in existence," Damian said. "I would have created another world so that I could have a third-chance at success – one where I eliminate the three of you before any of you have the chance to meet, but instead… I'll do this."

The time orb glowed in Damian's hand. Damian concentrated hard as he held the orb. Tristan drew his sword and pointed it towards Damian. Charlemagne took a sidearm and pointed it at him too.

"Give us the orb," Tristan threatened.

"No," Damian rejected, extending a hand over to them.

Tristan grunted and lowered his head, closing his eyes as he resisted. Charlemagne dropped his pistol and grabbed the side of his head.

"You see, life is easier when you stop giving a damn about anything," Damian explained as they shouted in pain. "After a lifetime of attempting to do good, eventually you come to a point when you ask what is the point? I'm not for anything anymore. I am against everything. I've sped up the decay of the universe. I don't know how long it will take until a catastrophic event takes place that everything is destroyed, but it will surely happen eventually, and then, there will be peace."

Damian moved his hand away, causing Tristan to fall down onto a knee as he panted. Charlemagne fell over unconscious. Diana went over to Tristan to help him up. Damian extended a hand to her as he climbed up onto his horse. She fell over unconscious instantly.

"Diana!" Tristan shouted, standing up.

Damian extended his hand back to Tristan and continued to torture him. With the other, he lifted Diana up and brought her onto the back of his horse.

"You worthless fool," Damian cursed at Tristan. "Do you really think that you could confront me? I am the most powerful being in the entire world, and you… you're no less pathetic than the man that was my father."

Damian lowered his hand from Tristan and then raised him up, choking him. Tristan brought a hand to his throat. He then dropped him as gunshots began to fire towards him. Damian looked over and saw Finn shooting towards him. The horse panicked as a bullet grazed it near the butt. Damian quickly escaped from the main lobby of City Hall, but not before turning around outside and attempting to extend a hand to Finn again. Finn disappeared. Tristan went over to the pistol on the ground that Charlemagne had dropped and grabbed it. He then shot back towards Damian, but Damian escaped with Diana, leaving him behind with Charlemagne who collapsed to the floor.

Act 10, Scene 4

Tristan immediately went towards Tempest, but then stopped as he looked over to an unconscious Charlemagne. He growled and then went over to tend to the man who took him into his home. Tristan got down on a knee and turned him onto his back.

"Charles, are you alright?" Tristan questioned.

Charlemagne began to wake up. He sat up and looked around.

"What's happened?" Charlemagne questioned, bringing a hand to his head.

"Zimmerman," Tristan replied. "Damian – whatever. He's kidnapped Diana and gone off with the time orb. He said he's accelerated time itself, but I don't feel anything happening that's out of the ordinary."

"The early myths of the time orb from Ancient Egypt said there existed such power within the pharaoh to manipulate time in that manner," Charlemagne remarked, standing up and looking to Tristan. "Where's Finn?"

"I don't know, but I'm sure he's fine. He has the space crystals on him and he can't be too far," Tristan replied, going over to his horse.

"Finn!" Charlemagne shouted. "Finn, where have you gone?!"

Tristan hopped onto his horse. He then began to hear gunshots from outside. Charlemagne walked over to Tristan as he readjusted Tempest so he could go off.

"Wait," Charlemagne said, going over to him. "Take me outside – I'm not steady on my feet and I need to make sure Finn is safe."

"I have to go after Damian," Tristan argued. "He has Diana."

"You'll have your chance in a minute," Charlemagne scolded. "Firstly, we must make sure the space crystals are safe before you go off to confront Zimmerman."

Tristan sighed and extended a hand over to Charlemagne to help him onto the back of the horse. He then ran off and came outside, going towards the gunfire where he saw Finn running down the street.

"Finn!" Charlemagne shouted.

Finn continued down the street and then turned the corner.

"Where's he off to?" Charlemagne questioned. "After him."

Tristan whipped the reins for Tempest to chase after Finn. He turned around the corner at Rhea Street and went north. Tristan followed, but then stopped as the horse reared. He looked ahead and saw a dark cloud of smoke around a familiar unholy figure. Tristan saw Heyl stand ahead, looking in the direction that Finn ran towards.

"Oh no…" Tristan muttered. "Not again."

Tristan drew his sword and then had Tempest charge forward. He sliced his sword towards the demon, but he disappeared before his sword could make contact, leaving behind a plumage of a dark smoke.

"What on Earth was that?" Charlemagne questioned.

"Lucifer," Tristan replied. "Come on, Finn could be in trouble."

Tristan rode down and turned right on Colin Street, seeing Finn ahead while Heyl floated from behind.

"Finn!" Tristan shouted. "Slow down!"

Tempest neighed and reared before she charged down the street after the demon and Finn.

"Do you notice a fluctuation in the temperature?" Charlemagne asked. "It appears as though it is nighttime, but I feel a draft every so often. When I heard of these tales of time manipulation, I imagined the skies rolling between night and day, but realistically I suppose that would be impossible without the Earth moving faster and the entire world trembling by that sudden acceleration."

"Uhuh," Tristan responded. "Kind of a little busy to be thinking about that right now."

Tempest continued to charge down Colin Street before turning left onto Walham Street. Tristan put his sword away and took out his bow. He pulled an arrow and aimed for Heyl. The arrow went through where Heyl was travelling and caused the figment to disappear. Tempest continued down the street, almost missing the turn that Finn had taken right onto Lincoln Drive towards the roundabout.

"If what Zimmerman has done is manipulate time – that could mean interstellar time, as in, the age of the universe. My mind comes to think of the sun, waking from its slumber to cause havoc and rapidly age. I think of the acceleration of the decomposition of material, the decay of matter. Who knows how fast that madman could have had time accelerate by."

Tristan ignored him and continued down the street as Finn went into the small forest that exited around where Jarsdel Park used to be in the middle of the roundabout. The forest was dense with a tall grass and close-together trees. Tristan stopped Tempest right at the entrance and hopped off.

"Stay here in case he comes out," Tristan said, "and be careful with that thing lurking around. I'm going after Finn before anything happens to him."

Tristan took out his sword and shield, and then went into the forest. Charlemagne stayed behind as asked. Tristan slashed at the overgrowth in the forest as he made his way into the depths of the roundabout park. He then stopped at the center as he saw some light pour in from above, near the remains of a path and a park bench. He saw Finn looking around. Tristan rushed out and met with Finn.

"Finn," Tristan greeted. "What are you doing?"

"He's here," Finn responded. "That thing – did you see it too?"

"Yes," Tristan replied. "That thing came after me too in Georgia – it's the Lucifer I was talking about."

"When I came to Allabrese, that… that thing came to me by the bridge over the river. He approached me and he showed me these bizarre hallucinations – I thought I was going mad. They were about my father, Charles, and his early life. How he met my mother when he was a year-old, growing up together in France, their early work together as explorers, and then their later years when they started to date. He then showed me the night that my father abandoned her at the Eiffel Tower. He showed me his fraternization with that other woman. He then showed me my mother's grief and decision to have me adopted – she said it was to give me a better life, but in that vision, I heard her say that it was because of him. I was adopted because she couldn't stand to look at me as a reminder of him. And Charles… he abandoned her for a woman! My life could have been so much different if only he had stayed with her. I saw the way that he raised Diana in this world, the love and affection that he gave her – that could have been me! I could have traveled with him. I could have helped him invent stuff – but I was forsaken? Why? Because they were selfish. My mother argues that I would have suffered as the child of a single-mother, but at least then I would have known who my father was and there could have been some hope that I would have met him sooner rather than never."

"Finn… people make mistakes. We're human," Tristan explained. "None of us are perfect, but it takes a decency to forgive. You're not the only one that was adopted and abandoned by his parents. Look at me. My mother didn't tell my father that she had a child either – the man never found out until he died. My mother placed me in the care of my aunt and uncle. Look, I know what you're talking about, especially about those visions. I didn't say anything when we reunited, but that thing, Lucifer, came to me too when I was vulnerable. He showed me Diana's early life in this world, the loss of her mother, and her upbringing under Charles where without me, she becomes a hopeless romantic. And do you know what happens later in her life? She meets me – and I thought for a split moment that it was because we were fated to be together, but that's not the cause. Diana and I hooked up in this world and then I abandoned her with child. The only reason why Diana and I ever met in our world was because Damian made it so."

"I want to make it so that I can be happy," Finn remarked. "I want it to be so that I can have the life that was taken from me. I die in this world, and in our world… nothing better happens."

"Damian wanted the same," Tristan argued, "but you're wrong. Something better did happen in our world, ironically because of Damian. We met. I stopped you from attempting to kill yourself in your hellbent revenge against a man who was never even your father, and because of that, you met Damian and came here. I don't know or care what conditions were behind your arrival, but you're not the same as him. Even if you were to try and tear reality so you could create your own timeline, you wouldn't live that life. It's impossible. Look at the life you have now – you've met your parents, but you've pushed them back when you got mad at their reasons as to why you didn't get the life you wanted."

"This is all easy for you to say," Finn remarked. "You didn't live the life that I did. You lived the life that I wanted to live."

"My life was never easy!" Tristan shouted. "In this world, I become a weak, pussy who abuses a woman for my own pleasure and abandons a child! That was the life I got living with my aunt and uncle, and them alone. I have no idea how that was possible, but in this world, the only blessings I got was that I didn't come out like that and that I got to meet Diana under different circumstances. My time with Charlemagne – it's scarred me! I've seen people beheaded, people shot at, massacres, and the abuse of innocents! I didn't want anything of this – How could you want what I got? I wouldn't even wish it on my worst enemy to receive the life that I received. Only by some grace have I been able to come out of that as a better person, but that's not the same for everyone. Look at you – with your life, you've risen out from that too. What Lucifer was trying to do to you by showing you that blatant pornography of a different life was that he was trying to manipulate you, the same way he was trying to manipulate me, in order to consume you into his reach. You taught me to slay dragons, Finn. He's a dragon that needs to be slayed – your resentment of the past is a dragon that needs to be slayed."

"It's… it's too late," Finn responded. "When that thing came to me on the third night, he… he became one with me and we struck a deal. He offered me a better life in return for allegiance, and I took it. It's why he's returned for me. He needs me."

"What are you talking about?" Tristan questioned. "He doesn't own you, Finn. Come with me and I'll take you back to your dad – I have to go after Damian and rescue Diana. You're safe. We'll be able to return to our world if you come with me with those crystals."

Finn shook his head and stepped back from Tristan.

"I already tried to kill them once because of him – my parents. He'll make me do it again. I – I have to hide. I… I can't return. I thought I could hide, but he's found me again! I don't want to kill them, Tristan!" Finn expressed with distress.

Tristan stepped towards Finn, putting his sword and shield away as he extended a hand towards him.

"It's okay," Tristan quietly said to his best friend. "I'm here, Finn. I'm not going to let anything happen to you. I risked my life to save you once, and you've saved mine by being my friend. I'm not going to abandon you."

Tristan's eyes looked behind Finn at the giant that appeared from the shadows. Heyl approached Finn. Finn noticed the shift in Tristan's eyes and turned around. Tristan quickly took out his sword and shield. Heyl opened his robe and engulfed Finn in a mist of darkness that passed through him. Finn fell to his knees and began to convulse. Heyl had disappeared. Tristan quickly put his sword and shield away and ran to his friend, dropping down to support his neck. Finn's eyes rolled back to show the white of the eyes as the spirit of Heyl ran through him, causing the veins of his face to show.

"No!" Tristan remarked, holding him down. "Finn! Fight it! Finn!"

Tristan brought his body over Finn's torso as he attempted to embrace him and hold him steady.

"Finn, please!" Tristan cried out. "Mika, help!"

• • • •

Charlemagne continued to wait out by the roundabout street until he turned his attention to the craw of a loud bird nearby. He looked over and saw a large black raven atop of a lamppost followed by a wind that picked up. Charlemagne stood up from the fallen log he sat at and looked behind him, seeing a goldenrod glow shine from within. He left where Tristan had told him to stay and stepped into the forest where he began to hear the cries of Tristan from within. Charlemagne quickly put his sidearm away and hurried through, following the glow of light, similar to the wisp of Curtia Kingston from years ago, which led him to where Tristan was on the ground at his knees, struggling with Finn.

The wisp of light instantly flew forward and came over Finn. Tristan moved his body back as he saw the light hit his friend. The convulsions of Finn's body became worse. Charlemagne quickly moved over to hold Finn down at the legs.

"What's going on?!" Charlemagne questioned.

"Lucifer," Tristan responded. "He's trying to possess him again…"

"Again?" Charlemagne asked. "You'll have to explain to me later."

The two were instantly blown back as the light that came from Charlemagne flew back into him. The convulsions on Finn stopped. Tristan quickly sat up and looked over to see Finn doing the same. His face appeared sickly and pale, and worse of all, the iris of his eyes were red. The possessed Finn took the bag of crystals from the ground and instantly disappeared. The two were left alone.

"No…" Tristan quietly remarked, standing up and going over to Charlemagne to help him. "He's gone."

Act 11, Scene 1

Tristan explained to Charlemagne what had occurred when he found Finn, his attempt to escape Heyl, the visions that Finn had when he arrived in Allabrese as when he was alone in Georgia, the deal Finn made with the Devil, and how Heyl had consumed him.

"If only I understood of all this back then," Charlemagne said with despair. "Of this punishment against me, my son, and my love for my own sins! I would have never have left Manon for her! What more can I do when I've done all that I can, apologizing and even attempting to make things right with him?! If only I had more time in my life so that I could spend it with him...!"

"Focus!" Tristan responded. "We need to find him if we want those crystals. He could be anywhere – He said that the last time the Devil had overcome him, he tried to kill you and Manon."

"Yes," Charlemagne replied. "Two weeks after you and Diana had left, he took Manon hostage and used her to drag me out of hiding so that I could confront him. He overpowered me though and very nearly killed me had I not explained to him that you and Diana were in danger, and that he needed to take my place in searching for you. I'm not sure what, but that was enough to break the possession that must have overcome him."

"He'll go after Manon then," Tristan concluded. "Where is she?"

"At Cabernet Tower," Charlemagne said. "She'll be protected by the royal guards, but..."

Charlemagne and Tristan were interrupted by a terrible and violent quake of the earth. They held their feet firm on the ground while the leaves and branches of the trees rustled as if there was a wind passing through. The crack of some trunks and the split of the concrete on the decayed path could be heard. The tremor lasted just under a minute. Charlemagne and Tristan looked around as it settled in silence.

"We should leave and go into the open before an aftershock happens," Charlemagne remarked. "Come."

The pair left the woods and came back to Tempest who was panicking in the midst of the street. Tristan went to calm her down. He then looked over to Tristan.

"You were saying?" Tristan asked him.

"A tremor that powerful must have been between a seven and an eight on the Richter scale," Charlemagne instead said. "What could of...?"

"Careful, behind you," Tristan interrupted, seeing some anarchists ahead, unarmed.

Charlemagne turned and drew his sidearm. He looked over and saw the group of people, walking around in a disoriented manner. He noticed they were unarmed and raised his sidearm to point it upwards. Charlemagne looked at them suspiciously, especially as one began to vomit.

"As I was saying..." Charlemagne quietly said to Tristan with slow words. "If I can speak from experience, Finn may be possessed in the same manner by which Nero was able to possess and influence Arturo several years ago."

"What was the solution to that?" Tristan asked, eyeing the anarchists ahead as he drew his sword and shield. "I don't remember."

"If I recall, I spoke to Arturo with words of encouragement, but I hardly believe that would be as effective as it were," Charlemagne answered. "You see these three ahead? What..."

Charlemagne silenced himself as the three anarchists began to fight each other like savage beasts. He looked on nervously.

"Perhaps we should leave before they notice us," Charlemagne remarked, stepping back. "I have a bad feeling about…"

Tristan looked away and then behind him as he noticed more of them, walking around like zombies.

"You don't suppose he's raised the dead, do you?" Tristan asked Charlemagne. "Either one of them that is – Damian or Lucifer?"

"Take me to Cabernet Tower regardless of that fact," Charlemagne remarked. "If what you've told me is true about Finn, then he'll be going after her this moment as we speak. She's more vulnerable – he won't take mercy on either of us, and he doesn't need to use her to get to me because he'll know I'm on my way. He'll slaughter her the very same way that Arturo slaughtered his own mother, Bianca, and then do the same to me, but I won't let that happen this time."

Tristan hopped onto Tempest and then helped Charlemagne come up behind him. He then directed Tempest to gallop off and away from the roundabout where many anarchists began to appear, behaving in a bizarre manner. He rode down Lincoln Drive.

"Do you think you can handle him on your own?" Tristan asked with uncertainty. "He'll overpower you the same way as last time."

"Would it be too much to ask for your help?" Charlemagne questioned. "I know that Diana is in danger at this very moment, but we need those crystals to return home and Manon's life could be in more danger than Diana's at Zimmerman's hands. It's not my place to ask this of you though… this is my fault and if anything happens, it is my punishment."

"I won't abandon Finn," Tristan said with certainty. "Damian won't kill Diana. I don't know what he's planning, if anything, but he'll want to keep her alive. He's not evil enough to kill the woman that represents all that is good to him. Right now, Diana is all he has."

"Thank you," Charlemagne replied.

Tristan reached Lincoln-Slade where a small mob of the undead, at least a dozen of them, roamed around. Tempest reared as they were about to crash into one. The anarchists crazily flailed its arms as Tempest punched the deceased in the head and knocked them over.

"Whoa, girl," Tristan quietly remarked.

"There's been so much death in this land that I can see why they'd be risen up to form an undead army," Charlemagne said. "These are the remains of anarchists that we've fought against for the past week. I never thought such an unholy feat were possible like this, even after what we lived through with the spiritual uprising."

Tristan attempted to navigate Tempest around the zombies, but she reared again as they were about to come onto Slade in the midst of the intersection. He quickly drew his sword and swiped it to cut-off the head of one of the zombies as it attempted to grab ahold of Tempest.

"I've had enough of these guys," Tristan said. "They're slowing us down."

Tristan managed to come onto Slade Drive where he continued down, navigating through the many undead that had awakened by the dark powers at work. He swiped his sword at them as they made their approach towards Tempest, who would occasionally frighten as one of the undead would charge towards them, attempt to grab onto the side of the horse, or attack them. Tristan made his way through a crowd of them on his way to Frontier Street, where the density of them worsened.

In return, Tristan sped up his pace, knocking past them and trampling over them as he hurried down towards Saffron Street. In the distance, coming from the opposite island, Tristan could hear sirens and screams. Tempest turned left as Tristan steered her towards the entrance ramp that went onto the highway northbound. Tristan slowed down to come onto the highway and then sped up again as he made his way towards the remains of Marke Bridge where an armored-vehicle launch bridge covered the gap over the river where the bridge had been destroyed. Tristan led Tempest onto the metal ramp and over the platform that connected Jarsdel Island with King Island. He then continued down the highway only to stop as he saw fires rage across the remains of downtown Harlech. The flash and wail of sirens could also be seen and heard. Directly ahead, Tristan could see the flight of spirits similar to the sight that Charlemagne was familiar with from the Halloween uprisings.

"Good Lord," Charlemagne remarked. "Here too?"

Unlike Jarsdel Island, there were no undead anarchists, but the presence of spirits that flew around, wreaking havoc while the city burned.

"Get me to Cabernet Tower at once," Charlemagne requested. "We'll need to retrieve something from storage if we're to hope that we can make it to Finn in one-piece."

"I don't think my sword will do much against a ghost," Tristan acknowledged, putting his sword away. "What street should I take?"

"The lower level tunnels are cordoned off," Charlemagne directed. "Come off here and go into Bromley. Take the roads there to reach Cabernet Tower."

"Got it," Tristan affirmed, directing Tempest towards the off-ramp and around where she jumped over the concrete barriers at the end.

Tempest reared as a police cruiser passed them from the Industrial District and went into Bromley. Tristan carefully made his way onto the sidewalk so that he could continue into Bromley where he stopped at Bailey Drive. The city was in mass chaos as spirits attacked police cruisers, police officers, and civilian bystanders near the remains of Pentateuch Cathedral and the fortified Harlech Police Precinct. Tempest stopped and reared at the intersection as a spirit approached them.

Tristan directed her away and then drew his sword as he saw more spirits ahead down Bailey Drive. He made his way down and sliced at one as it flew over them. The slice caused ectoplasm to come down on them, but directed the spirit away and into the side of a building. Tristan swiped the gunk off his face and then continued to direct Tempest down towards Campbell Street, turning left.

"Why go to this length? What is either Zimmerman or this 'Heyl' attempting to achieve?" Charlemagne questioned. "Zimmerman has set his course. He wants the total destruction of the entire universe. Heyl though?"

"Heyl is Lucifer," Tristan remarked as they went down the street. "Lucifer wants nothing more than the humiliation of mankind, God's creations, at least that's what Mika told me."

"No, of course, that is exactly what is known about Lucifer. His pride sent him to Earth where he took the shape of a serpent and led Adam and Eve to sin on false promises. His entire motive is to direct people away from God, but why Finn?"

"Finn is a remarkable person," Tristan suggested. "Lucifer is interested in remarkable people. He knows the power within people and wants to use their power. Finn could do great, but terrible things, especially under his control."

"Or perhaps, simply," Charlemagne pondered. "All of this is simply the action of chaos. Lucifer is the angel of chaos after all, and it is by chaos that he thrives – like these anarchists."

"Hm," Tristan responded. "Maybe."

Tristan saw the corner of Cabernet Tower in the distance. He diverted Tempest to the sidewalk and continued his approach as he made his way to the tower where Finn surely was.

Act 11, Scene 2

Tristan rode Tempest up to the front of Cabernet Tower where like in their own timeline, shutters were pulled down at the side of the building, preventing anyone from getting in or out. Tempest reared as Tristan stopped her halfway across the building and then took her around so that they could go down Earle Street and then around the tunnel that went into the sublevel parking lot. The garage shutter into the parking lot was left open with a police van crushed underneath. Tristan rode Tempest through, and they found themselves in the underground parking lot of the tower.

Tempest rode around Sublevel One and went down a ramp to Sublevel Two where the express elevator to the penthouse was before the VIP parking stalls. She reared just before though as Tristan and Charlemagne saw some spirits ahead, vandalizing some parked cars. Tristan drew his sword while Charlemagne hopped off the horse. He then followed and took out his shield.

"Call the elevator," Tristan said to Charlemagne. "I'll hold them off."

Tristan made a slow encroachment towards the spirits while Charlemagne went around to call the elevator. The spirits soon noticed his presence and began to approach him. Tristan went over and attempted to jab at one, cutting through only to cause an ooze of ectoplasm to drop down. He withdrew his sword and sliced at the head of the spirit, which was enough to cause it to stop approaching Tristan as the head fell to the ground and rolled away. Tristan stepped back as a ghost attempted to claw at him. He then went in to slice its arms off before raising his shield as it threw up on him.

Charlemagne looked behind him as he watched, and a ding marked the arrival of their elevator. Tristan finished off the spirit before he went over to join Charlemagne. The two of them watched over to the spirits as the chopped off body parts simply disintegrated into puddles of ectoplasm, while new parts grew at the stubs. Charlemagne closed the doors and typed in the pin-code to get the elevator to drop down to the sublevel.

Tristan put his sword away and threw off the ectoplasm from the face of his shield before he brought it around him.

"What disgusting little things," Tristan cursed. "How did you put up with them for almost a month?"

"I wasn't hacking at them," Charlemagne replied. "Luckily, in this timeline like in ours, there was a spiritual invasion where I invented my plasma cannon to contain these creatures, and that same plasma cannon is downstairs in storage."

The elevator slowed down and then the doors opened. Tristan looked out as the motion sensors turned on the lights and he saw that they were in the same room that Charlemagne's laboratory was housed in their timeline. He stepped out and looked down at all the stored goods, while Charlemagne went around and down the stairs to go to his personal belongings.

Charlemagne came to the corner of the room with the garage shutters and picked up the plasma cannon on the table. He examined it carefully so he could familiarize himself with the device. Tristan joined him and looked around. He saw the time machine in the corner of the room and went over to it. Charlemagne saw.

"So, even in this timeline, you went and produced this," Tristan said.

"But I never finished," Charlemagne replied. "It's unfinished, and from what I was able to deduce, the parts that went unfinished were mostly components that Barry had worked on. I can only imagine that our fates were different in this world than in ours."

"Yeah, it seems like that's the case with a lot of people and their relationships," Tristan responded. "Some of us did better in this world, while others did worse."

"The people in this world have lived their lives," Charlemagne noted. "What you need to understand though, particularly in your case as you have expressed, is that the people in this universe are not literally the same. I mean, the souls of these people are different even if genetically they are the same. Do you suppose that a monozygotic twin shares the same soul as their other half?"

"No," Tristan responded.

"No," Charlemagne affirmed. "Even though the genotype of monozygotic twins are the same, and one is essentially the clone of the other, their essence is separate. Likewise, our souls are separate from the people of this world, and their being by extension is separate. I am not burdened by the manner that Charlemagne in this world wasted his life, knowing that I was able to do more than him, even though we both lived in shock over Finn's death. I lived my life, and he has lived his. And for you... your counterpart lived his life, and whether his negligence over his child has damned him, it is inconsequential to you. You have risen to be a far better person, and I'm certain that you will not abandon that child of yours."

Tristan nodded.

"Come now," Charlemagne encouraged, "while the me of this universe created the same device, it appears to function a little differently, but I will adjust. First off though, I need to charge the device with a bit of plasma taken from a fusion reactor. It was my intent to have a miniature reactor power the tower, so I wonder if the me of this universe ever completed that. We'll have to find out before we go upstairs."

Charlemagne took some plasma containers and attached them to his belt. He then picked up the plasma cannon and looked over to Tristan.

"There is a war room below where the Commander of the Commonwealth Militia should be," Charlemagne said to him. "Coincidentally, you'll never believe that this man is the son of Bogdan Alexandrov, Kodiak. He'll know where the fusion reactor may be."

Tristan nodded. The two went through the storage room and back towards the elevator. Tristan pressed the button as Charlemagne walked over to him. The elevator doors instantly opened. He stepped in with Charlemagne, and then Charlemagne pressed a button to go down to sublevel six, pressing in the pin-code to override the security function. The doors closed.

The elevator then went down before beginning to malfunction within a few seconds. The car jiggered, the brakes screeched, and the lights flashed. Above them, Tristan and Charlemagne heard the patter and maniacal laughter of a spirit above them. There was a metallic creak noise that came next before the car then collapsed. Tristan and Charlemagne held on as the car hurled down before making a sharp impact below.

Tristan looked around from where he held on and looked over to Charlemagne who had fallen over. He went to him and checked on him. He then helped him onto his feet. A red glow emitted in the elevator from the emergency light. Once Charlemagne was on his feet, Tristan saw that the elevator doors had fallen apart, exposing the other side where it was dark and decrepit. Tristan pulled out his flashlight and shined out. They were in the deepest depths of Cabernet Tower.

"Charles, how many floors down does Cabernet Tower have?" Tristan asked.

"Well, when the tower was constructed, there was almost ten-stories beneath the earth, but half of them were abandoned in the eighties, and that is where I built the new laboratories in our universe. In this universe, they built the underground bunker at least to the sixth floor. I'm not sure how many more they could be."

"Well, prepare for some spelunking, because we're down under," Tristan said, crawling out. "We should be able to find a ladder, or stairs, or something right?"

"Oh, yes," Charlemagne encouragingly said. "There should be something of the sort, somewhere."

Tristan shined his light around where they had landed. The walls around them were composed of brick. There was a discontinued logo for Cabernet Industries against the wall before them. The floor was dirty and dusty, and the walls appeared to have been torn apart. Charlemagne joined him and turned on his own flashlight, looking around.

"Back in the day, this used to be a Research and Development Division, which was the prelude to Cabernet Technologies. My father had this division shut down, and when I took over, I reorganized the efforts into Cabernet Tech, building the structure in Allabrese so that I could be close-by and for the benefit of skilled-workers to live in a small, cheap community."

"Fascinating," Tristan sarcastically remarked. "Which way to the exit?"

"Hm... if the design of these sublevels were any similar to the design of the offices above, then the exits should be at the side someplace," Charlemagne surmised. "Follow me."

Tristan followed Charlemagne down a corridor and towards a set of double doors. They walked through and found themselves in another corridor. The pair stopped as they felt a small earthquake rock itself through. Tristan held on to a wall as they froze for a moment. The quake lasted less than a minute. They stayed put for another minute before they continued onwards.

"How fast do you think Damian sped up the flow of time?" Tristan asked as they continued through. "How much time do we have before something cataclysmic happens as he hopes?"

"I have no idea," Charlemagne responded. "Zimmerman has demonstrated though that he has no real devastating power if this is all that he can conjure. Of course, were he to get his hands on the crystals that Finn has, then I would be worried, because by his power, he could create a third replica of the universe, and that would be such a destabilizing event that it could result in the destruction of all universes. The old Egyptian tales said that Pharaohs could skip seasons with a snap of the finger. For all I know, every second could be the equivalent of an earth year, and with that I'd hold on to my initial theory that the Sun is still our worse fear – not a comet or asteroid. The Sun is set to become hotter in years to come as temperatures rise, bringing us to the end of the Ice Age. You know this. You also know though that the sun is sporadic in its behavior. It will be a many millennia before the effects of the Sun's awakening are felt to a devastating level. The end of the world, regardless of the existence of humanity, is guaranteed to be a billion years away with the expansion of the Sun, and then its death billion years later. Zimmerman believes he can accelerate time to the end of the time itself, but that won't be so easy. He'll be waiting for a very long time."

"A thousand seconds is what? A couple minutes?" Tristan questioned.

"And a billion seconds would take many years," Charlemagne replied, "and this assumes we are going at the pace of time that I have estimated. We could be going either faster or slower. As a Christian though, none of this upsets or scares me because I hold on to the end of times as being whenever Christ has decided to come again – the Second Coming. I know that this may not be what others, such as yourself believe in though…"

"No, I believe," Tristan corrected. "Ever since Diana made us attend Mass, my opinion on spiritual matters has been skeptical. When my father and mother died, I became an atheist, and worse off, a nihilist and a misotheist around the time that we returned from Asia. When Mika came to me as an angel though, I began to understand… I'm not a non-believer anymore. Wait… How did you know I didn't believe? I always pretended to be a believer to satisfy Diana, so how did you figure it out?"

"Finn told me," Charlemagne responded. "He told me of your nihilism, which was only a short improvement, in my opinion, from Finn's Deism. Deism is nothing more than the uncertainty of agnosticism mixed with the moral pride of Protestantism. Nonetheless, as a believer in Christ, hold fast, because these are not the end of times for humanity."

"I know."

"Nobody knows when Christ will return."

"No."

The pair stopped as they reached a door that led into a square stairwell that travelled upwards. They then began to move up the stairs until they reached the top that exited out to a door. Tristan pushed against the door, but it was stuck. He bashed his body into it a couple of times until the door released and they found themselves in the dim corridor of the underground bunker. Another earthquake began to shake at their feet – stronger than the previous one. The pair held on to the door frame as dust fell down from the ceiling above them.

Once the earthquake stopped, they proceeded forward to exit out into the main corridor that led to the war room. There were no guards to be seen around. Charlemagne led Tristan into the war room where he could see more people, including Kodiak at the table, on the telephone, while others rushed around. Kodiak looked over to Charlemagne and Tristan as they arrived. He lowered the telephone and looked to them.

"Mr. Cabernet," Kodiak greeted with a tired face. "Where have you been? Pandemonium has taken hold of the city... I've lost contact with Salmar while the city is being overrun. I sent guards in to search for him, but I've lost contact with them too. Who is that with you?"

"My son, Tristan," Charlemagne responded. "Where was Salmar last seen?"

"He retired for the night an hour before the chaos," Kodiak responded. "I'm having reports of these bizarre creatures on the street on King Island, and at Jarsdel Island, the army has met with an army of the undead."

"They're all undead," Charlemagne replied. "I don't have much time to explain, but have the police attempt to electrically stun the spirits on the street – that's all I can suggest to help them. A similar situation occurred here in Allabrese in 2017 and that's why I've taken this out. I need to know where there is a fusion reactor so that I can charge these canisters with plasma."

"There should be one on the third sublevel," Kodiak replied. "What are you going to do?"

"If Salmar is at the penthouse, both he and Manon could be in danger. Tristan and I are going to face the demon that awaits us at the top of the tower. Stay here in the meantime. I'm sorry the situation may seem bizarre, but you're safest here where you can direct the militia and peacekeepers."

"Alright then," Kodiak replied, looking to the both of them before focusing on Charlemagne, "and while the situation is bizarre, Mr. Cabernet, it is no more bizarre than the moments that I have spent with the Huntsman serving the Cabernet family."

"No matter," Charlemagne responded. "Thank you for your service."

Charlemagne and Tristan left and exited out back into the corridor.

Act 11, Scene 3

Charlemagne and Tristan went down the corridor that led to the elevator, stopping before it as Tristan opened the doors wide. He then took out a flashlight and shined it towards a ladder on the side.

"Watch your step," Charlemagne said as he went in.

Charlemagne went in behind him.

"If you wait for me to charge the plasma cannon, it may be too late to save Salmar or Manon – we've wasted enough time as it is. I'm going to go into the third sublevel, while I want you to go up to the top. You'll have to come up to the main floor, go up to the second floor and take an elevator upwards to the eighty-eighth floor. From there, you can re-enter this shaft and climb up to the penthouse."

"Got it," Tristan replied as they climbed.

Charlemagne stopped at the third sublevel and hit a switch to release the doors on the opposite-side from the storage. He then climbed out and looked over to Tristan who stopped to look down to him.

"Be careful," Charlemagne said to him. "I'll be less than ten minutes behind you."

"Understood," Tristan replied. "You be careful too."

Tristan continued to climb upwards as he left Charlemagne behind to charge his weapon. He went up through the parking lot where he felt a humid warmth as he went to the top floor. He then found himself at the end of the ladder as he arrived at the main floor. Tristan hit the switch to open the doors and then found himself in the main lobby where there were some spirits around. Some of the spirits that lingered around appeared to be non-hostile as they simply cowered in corners of the room in distress of their existence in this realm, while others fought each other. Tristan attempted to avoid provoking any of them as he went to the escalator and climbed up to the second floor, going over to the elevator shaft, but stopping as he saw two more spirits at each other.

The spirits kept bashing into each other like wild animals. Tristan drew his sword and approached them, which caused them to shift their attention to him. He sliced at them as they attempted to attack him, which gave him some time so he could call an elevator. Tristan then turned around and faced them again, anticipating their reconstruction as the fallen body parts turned into ectoplasm and the parts that were missing regrew. The creatures then turned back to face Tristan and attack him. He cut at them again, which disarmed them momentarily once more.

Tristan quickly entered into the elevator as it arrived and hit a button to go up to the top-most floor that these elevators went to. The doors then shut and the lift climbed upwards. Tristan cleaned off the ectoplasm on his sword and then put it away with his shield. He then waited for the elevator to go all the way up to the top only for it to begin to malfunction as it staggered and came to a halt. Tristan backed up into a corner as he felt the elevator and lights above him failed.

"Oh no…" he muttered.

Tristan held on for a minute until he realized that the elevator had simply failed around the seventieth floor. He looked around and took a step forward. He was safe. He approached the lift door and pulled it forcibly open, seeing that he was stuck up against a wall. He took out his sword and poked out the hatch above before putting his sword away and jumping up to pull himself to the roof. Tristan looked around the wide elevator shaft at the north-face of Cabernet Tower with a mild fright. He then went over to the shaft doors nearby and pulled them open so he could climb out onto the seventy-first floor. Tristan then made his way down the corridor and around so he could find the fire escape doors at the corner of the floor.

The floor he had come to was dim, but there were emergency flood lights that lit up around. Tristan took out his sword and shield and began to navigate through the office-space of the seventy-first floor, following the 'Exit' signs until he reached a stairwell. He then pushed through and began to climb up the flight of stairs in the concrete stairwell, stopping for a moment as the tower began to shake as another earthquake passed. He then continued upwards when he stopped once more as another earthquake came – this one was much more violent than any of the previous ones.

Tristan hugged a corner near a doorway out of the stairwell at the seventy-ninth floor. The light fixtures that were turned off due to the blackout collapsed and the glass panes at the side of the building shattered, bringing in a humid heat that had arisen outside. The earthquake continued and the concrete steps began to collapse ahead and the landing he stood on began to crumble at the edges. Tristan saw and immediately moved himself out of the way and into the floor he was at where he fell over, came onto his rear, and stayed sat there until the rumble passed within a few more seconds.

Once the earthquake stopped, Tristan stood up and looked around at where he had come to. He was in an open-floor office with various desks around. He picked up his sword and went over to the stairwell in which the landing inside had collapsed as with the steps immediately ahead. He stepped away and proceed out from the open-office and into the corridor on the other side. He then navigated through the corridor to come outside of the elevator shafts where he saw a spirit on the floor, bashing its fists into another spirit. Tristan raised his shield and made his approach over.

Tristan raised his sword and decapitated the spirit, knocking the body over and then stabbing through the other to decapitate it. He then continued forward and around the corner so that he could reach the other stairwell at the end of the hall. The windows in the stairwell had been blown out, but most of the concrete steps were intact on this side. Tristan entered and began to continue his ascent up the tower until he reached the eightieth floor where the steps were ruined, and the gap was too far to jump.

At the eightieth floor, Tristan came out into a corridor where he went down and back around to the main corridor before the elevator shafts. There, he saw an overweight spirit at the end, sat on its rear with its back to Tristan. The spirit had a yellowish glow around it and appeared to be in distress as it made a rabid noise. Tristan quietly made his way over and attempted to skirt around it so he could continue on his route without confrontation. However, as he went down the corridor, the spirit looked over to him and gave off a terrible shout. Tristan instantly drew his sword and raised his shield as it began to charge at him. He side-stepped out of the way and sliced his sword through the brittle body of the being, causing it to collapse into two on the floor. Tristan stepped over the remains and then hurried on to the other stairwell he had formerly been going through.

Tristan cut through another open office, this time with architect desks and more open space. He went to the stairwell and looked inside. The stairwell was in a poorer condition, but the steps up to the next floor were intact. He was able to travel up to the eighty-third floor before the steps were out of order and he was forced to divert through another open office and back out into a corridor. Thankfully, there were no spirits on this floor, which allowed Tristan to cut through and come to the other stairwell without a hitch other than the fact that the steps in this stairwell were collapsed too. Tristan took a step back and then put his sword and shield away with a sigh.

From the corridor, Tristan returned to the elevators where he went to the closest elevator shaft door and began to pry it open forcibly, which happened with ease since the power was out. He then looked down and saw the elevator he had travelled in below with a ladder at the side. Tristan carefully made his way over and grabbed hold of the ladder so that he could continue his ascent to the eighty-eighth floor.

Suddenly, another earthquake passed through. Tristan held on to the rails of the ladder as the tower shook. An elevator car broke off from its wires and began to tumble down below Tristan where it crashed into the first sublevel floor. The earthquake was relatively mild to the others that had passed. Tristan held on and stayed where he was for a split moment before he began to climb upwards again, reaching the eighty-sixth floor. There was then a sudden activation of mechanical engines and the flood of red lights in the shaft. Tristan looked around and then below as he saw the elevator he was in begin to rise up towards him at an alarming pace.

Without hesitation, Tristan climbed up the remainder he had left, seeing that the eighty-eighth floor was the very top of the shaft. By the time he reached the eighty-seventh floor, the elevator was almost halfway towards him. He quickly went up to the eighty-eighth and then looked around for the emergency release switch. The elevator car was right beneath him. He hit the switch and then jumped through the doors as they opened, crashing onto the floor and looking behind him as the elevator car opened its doors at its arrival. Tristan stood up from the ground and then looked around to notice a burning smell from nearby as well as a horrible sight around him.

The bodies of various men in red coats, royal guards, could be seen around with the splash of blood against the walls from the massacre that ran through this room. Tristan looked nauseatingly around him at all the bodies, also noticing the mark of bullet holes against the walls where a gunfight must have taken place. He stepped to the side corridor and then moved away so he could carry on lest more life be lost.

Tristan faced the elevator shaft door that went up to the penthouse from the eighty-eighth floor and approached it to pull the shaft doors open. He then looked inside to see the ladder and then looked upwards to see the final stretch. Coincidentally, a plume of smoke came own from above and there was a warm glow and crackle of fire. Tristan quickly grabbed ahold of the ladder and began to continue upwards to the top of the penthouse where he intended to confront Finn and put an end to this conflict once and for all.

Act 11, Scene 4

Tristan climbed out from the elevator shaft and found himself in the ruined entrance corridor that went to the front door of the penthouse. A disaster had swept across the penthouse rooftop since Tristan and Charlemagne had arrived at the tower as there was a hole in the ceiling that looked outside and blood stains on the wall. The smoke came from segments of the wall and floor that continued to burn. The floor at Tristan's feet was wet from the pipes above that had sprayed water down, but were now torn apart. The door ahead was left ajar, so Tristan pushed through it and came into the foyer corridor where he immediately saw the doors ahead to be wide open and the corpse of a man to his left with his back against the wall.

The penthouse was more exposed than Tristan imagined as almost the entirety of the roof and second floor had been destroyed as well as walls exposed to other rooms. Tristan looked around and could not see anybody else in his immediate vicinity. He went over to the older man that had his back up against the wall. He was dressed in a brown suit and Tristan did not recognize him as Salmar although he was. He went to him and touched his wrist to feel no pulse. He then dropped his hand down and closed his eyes before continuing forward into the sitting room. The windows were completely shattered and a humid wind blew in and a light rain poured down from above.

Tristan turned around to leave the sitting room and saw a ruined portrait on the ground behind the sofa. The portrait had been slashed through where there was a figure next to what appeared to be Allodia with Sergei, Salmar, and a couple Tristan recognized to be Charlemagne's aunt and uncle. Tristan recognized the couple to the right of the removed figure to be Charlemagne's parents. On closer inspection, there were two figures that had been displaced in the torn portrait – they were Diana and Charlemagne. Tristan left the room and came into the stairwell. The stairs went to nowhere since the ceiling was exposed and second floor destroyed. Tristan walked into the library and looked ahead to see Finn looking out to rest of the city.

"Finn…" Tristan said, looking to his best friend. "What have you done?"

Tristan looked around the library as he walked over to his best friend who continued to face the city where to the horizon in the east, despite the fact that not even midnight had passed, the sun could be seen rising from over the western horizon, through the smoke as it shined a red-orange glow and appeared to be larger than usual. Tristan also noticed that through the smoke, the moon could be seen much larger by at least four times its typical size, giving off an appearance as if it were about to drop on the Earth – its face was scarred too.

"Where's Manon, Finn?" Tristan asked. "Where's Manon? Please don't tell me you've killed her."

Finn didn't answer. Tristan saw on closer look that Finn held a rifle in his hand.

"Finn, answer me," Tristan demanded. "Talk to me. Finn, dammit. I've never had someone in my life the way I had you – you're the older brother I never thought I wanted. Please, talk to me."

Finn turned around to face Tristan. Tristan looked at him unrecognized eyes. His face was pale, eyes serious, and irises red.

"There's nothing you can say that can change me," Finn said, taking out the bag of crystals from his belt and showing them. "With these, I will confront Damian and usurp him, and then I'll abandon this world so that I can start my own as he did."

"You idiot!" Tristan remarked, shaking his head as he instantly calmed down. "You can't create your own world! You'll kill us all – don't you feel it? Time is accelerating ahead and sooner or later, the Sun will become too hot for the Earth and life on this planet to handle. Finn, I know this isn't you. You can't deceive me – Do you hear me, Heyl? I will not be deceived, because this is not my friend! I know you're in there, Finn – you're not dead yet!"

A flash of lightning showed the spirit of Heyl floating behind Finn with his arms outstretched and bony hands apart as each finger flexed and extended separately as if he was a puppet-master to Finn.

"That's where you're wrong," Finn replied, forming a fist around the bag of crystals.

Tristan observed that his hand shook. Finn put the bag back onto his belt.

"I- I cannot be – redeemed," Finn said in slow words as if he was struggling to speak. "Tristan, you bastard..." he then said, bringing a hand to his face as if he was having a headache, "I'll... I'll... I'll kill you. I'll kill you because of what you've done to me."

"What I've done to you?" Tristan questioned under his breath.

"For what you have that I do not. I'll kill you for what you share with Diana, which should have been mine! I'll kill you...!" he shouted at the top of his lungs, raising the rifle upwards with both hands.

Tristan lurched forward and immediately took the muzzle of Finn's rifle with his hand, slapping down on the stock of the gun and then quickly launching the muzzle of the gun into the back of Finn's face, knocking him back. Tristan threw the rifle overboard and then quickly grabbed Finn by the arm to prevent him from falling over, grabbing hold of him around the shoulders to pull him out. Tristan pulled him in as he struggled and held him closely.

"Finn, snap out of it," Tristan pled. "Please, Finn. It shouldn't be like this – you were the one that always inspired me. I don't have any words of wisdom to give you except that the past is over. Whatever trauma you have, I know that I don't share them; I'm here with you to share in the emotion of that trauma, because I've suffered too, but all of that is over. You have parents that love you. Diana loves you. I love you. Please come back home with us, Finn."

Finn squirmed. Tristan observed and with a look of optimism, but also sadness and pity for his friend, as he continued to restrain him.

"Finn, fight back. Fight this demon. You were made to be better than this, Finn. You were made to be great, not horrible. Fight this," Tristan quietly said to him. "Fight him."

In a sudden motion, Finn elbowed Tristan back with a brute force, straight across the face. Tristan quickly grabbed the bag of crystals from Finn's belt while Finn took a sidearm from his belt and pointed it towards Tristan. Tristan instantly vanished as he saw the barrel of the gun pointed at him.

When Tristan appeared at the other side of the penthouse, he heard the echo of the gunshot that very nearly killed him. Tristan poured the crystals into his hand and then stashed them into a pouch in his belt. He then picked up some rubble on the floor and poured it into the bag. Tristan then placed the bag on his belt as a decoy.

The rain intensified. Tristan looked at where he had come and saw that it was the kitchen. He took out his bow and readied it, crouching behind a counter as he prepared an arrow. A tear fell down the side of Tristan's face, but he did not look sad, but serious. Tristan quickly wiped the tear and raised his chin up with determination. He then stood up.

"Where are you?!" Finn shouted from the library. "Give me back those crystals! Give me back what is mine!"

"Not a chance," Tristan whispered, moving out.

Tristan went onto the patio balcony and began to make his way around the dining room and towards the living room. There, he stopped behind a pillar and then looked around as he saw Finn making a careful approach, looking at every direction around him with paranoia as he anticipated Tristan's sudden appearance. Tristan held his bow with hesitation to fire.

"Not like this…" Tristan muttered to himself. "I don't want to kill him…"

Tristan cowered behind the pillar as a gunshot went straight past him.

"There you are!" Finn shouted, opening fire.

Tristan quickly moved around the other side and came into the dining room, firing his arrow towards Finn and missing him. Finn pointed the gun to him and Tristan vanished. He appeared in the ballroom to the north of the penthouse, which was much the same in this timeline except that there was no bar to the right. Tristan made his way into the crossed corridor that connected the foyer corridor to the dining room and another room, which in their timeline was a trophy room. From what Tristan could see through the rubble, this room was a study. Tristan took cover around the corner towards the foyer as he looked over to see if he could see Finn.

Finn made his approach out from the living room and into the foyer corridor where he continued to search around him as he waited for Tristan to appear. Tristan prepared another arrow and took a deep breath. He then pivoted around from the corner and attempted to shoot towards Finn. Finn quickly saw Tristan's sudden appearance and ducked down. Tristan side-stepped towards the other corner and prepared another arrow, shooting it towards Finn and hitting him in the thigh. Finn shouted out in pain.

Tristan hid around the corner and prepared another arrow. He peaked around the corner, but Finn shot towards him keeping him back. Tristan peaked around the corner again after two shots were fired and saw Finn pull the arrow out from his thigh. He then shot another bullet at Tristan before he quickly reloaded. Tristan came out as he reloaded and shot a third arrow at him, hitting him on the chest, which barely had an effect on him as the arrow to the thigh. Finn finished to reload and shot towards Tristan. Tristan instantly vanished as he saw the danger and re-appeared in the library.

The library in the penthouse appeared to be smaller, at least from the second floor as the bookshelves were closer to the wooden railings. The stairs were also more regal, and after the damage that swept through the penthouse, were more intact to go upstairs. Tristan went ahead and began to go up the stairs and exit out into the corridor on the other side, which had collapsed. He stopped just at the door and looked down and over to where Finn was. He had left. Tristan stayed in the library as he breathed steady breaths.

There was no sight of Finn. Tristan hopped down and made his way over to take cover by the door frame that looked into the foyer corridor and across into the cross-corridor where he couldn't see Finn. Tristan looked towards the living room and the door frame into the dining room and saw that it was clear. He then took careful steps forward. His ears twitched as he heard footsteps from nearby. He moved into the cross-section and looked over to the ballroom where he saw Finn wrapping a bandage around his thigh before standing up as he continued to look around. Tristan hid behind the corner and prepared an arrow. He looked at his bow with hesitation and took a deep breath.

"I'm sorry, Finn," Tristan muttered to himself, pulling the arrow back.

Finn looked over as Tristan stepped out and shot an arrow towards him. The arrow lodged into the barrel of the pistol right as Finn fired, causing the barrel to explode in his hand. Finn quickly dropped the firearm as he raised his hand up with a shout of pain. Tristan instantly put his bow away and proceeded to charge towards him. Finn saw and stood his ground, grabbing Tristan as he attempted to tackle him onto the ground. However, Finn underestimated Tristan's abilities.

Tristan didn't grab Finn by the torso, but by the thighs as he picked him up and then threw him onto the ground. He restrained him, which caused Finn to shout out in anguish as he squirmed in Tristan's grip hold. Tristan looked about and saw the remnants of the fire that continued to burn to spread around rapidly. If it wasn't for the rain, they would have been surrounded by fire. Tristan then heard the collapse of some of the structure from around. He lowered his head, but maintained his grip over Finn, holding him down.

"Finn, stop," Tristan quietly said. "What do I have to do to expel this demon within you? What do I have to say? Please, Mika – God, anyone! Finn, stop!"

"Tristan!" Charlemagne shouted from above.

Tristan looked over and saw that Charlemagne was on the remnants of the second floor with his plasma cannon.

"Charles!" Tristan shouted back. "Thank God – help me! Heyl is nearby – stop him!"

Charlemagne looked down as Tristan moved his back in position so that he could continue to hold down Finn. Finn continued to squirm demonically. Charlemagne then looked ahead of the boys as a flash of lightning struck. An aura lit up around Charlemagne in the same goldenrod color as at Jarsdel Park, but Charlemagne didn't pay attention to that, but instead over to the presence of Heyl over the boys. Charlemagne pointed his plasma cannon over to Heyl and fired at him.

The hit from the plasma cannon caused a blinding, bright white light to reflect out from the fallen angel and for a terrible screech to echo out. The fallen angel lurched back with its arms spread out and Charlemagne struggled to maintain control as the cannon shook violently, more violently than it ever had with all of the spirits that Charlemagne had ever confronted. Finn had calmed down as Heyl was preoccupied. Tristan felt the difference as he simply held Finn down, keeping his body atop of him as he avoided the blinding light. Heyl's eyes began to glow out with a burst of fire that shot outwards.

Charlemagne was barely about to see, but through the corner of his eye he saw the sudden appearance of balls of fire at the hands of Heyl that were shot towards him. Charlemagne disengaged the plasma cannon and ducked into cover as the balls of fire exploded nearby, rupturing the remaining structural integrity of the penthouse and causing the second floor where Charlemagne was to collapse. Charlemagne slid down and was separated from the others.

Finn resumed to struggle against Tristan. Tristan kept him down with his weight until he felt Finn grab the small sack at his belt filled with rubble. He then felt himself teleport with Finn as the crystals in Tristan's belt-pouch activated with their physical connection. Finn had the pair of them appear in the stairwell foyer where they impacted against the floor and Finn was able to break-free.

Tristan quickly stood up as Finn ran from him, holding the bag of crystals in his hand. He looked towards him with a smirk and then towards the bag as he realized he had been duped.

"Nice try," Tristan remarked, going over to him.

Tristan grabbed hold of Finn again by the thighs and pinned him into the corner of the structure where he squirmed in resistance. Tristan repositioned his grip and then attempted to pull him down onto the ground. Finn punched Tristan across the face and broke free again, falling to the floor where he crawled away. Tristan felt blood pour out from his nose from the punch at Finn had given him. He went towards Finn and grabbed his leg as he attempted to kick him. Tristan then pulled him out from the corner and slammed him down onto the ground, ripping off the pouch with the crystals from his own belt and tossing it aside.

"Now, Charles!" Tristan shouted.

Charlemagne appeared from along the second floor again as the ceiling had caved in the foyer corridor. He pointed the plasma cannon forward but could not see Heyl until a flash of lightning showed him near the ruined stairs. He opened fire and hit at the torso of the fallen angel, causing the same reaction as before as a bright white light reflected off and shined brightly around them. Charlemagne attempted to pull the fallen angel over so that he could entrap it, but the resistance was too much. He peaked down below where he noticed that Finn was calm with Heyl distracted and in peril.

"Get him away, Tristan!" Charlemagne encouraged Tristan. "Pull him away – break the bond!"

Tristan heard this and squinted over to Charlemagne. He then stood up and picked Finn up, seeing that the exit to the foyer corridor was blocked, so he went into the library. Heyl drifted towards Finn, but the beam cannon pulled him back. The fallen angel screamed out in agonizing pain. The plasma beam began to expel a large amount of heat around, which began to burn Charlemagne's hands. Tristan fell onto a knee with Finn in his arms, placing him on the ground as he had fallen unconscious.

Charlemagne lost control of Heyl again, which caused the fallen angel to fade out of sight again, but not without retaliation. Charlemagne ducked down as he saw balls of fire form out from the air and come towards him, hitting the structure again and causing it to collapse. Tristan looked down to Finn with pity as he heard the explosion behind them, jerking his neck to look behind him. He then looked back down to Finn as he suddenly opened his eyes. Finn launched his hands around Tristan's neck, pouncing at him and pushing him back. Charlemagne climbed back up to the second floor and began to make his way carefully around the rubble so that he could come into the library.

Meanwhile, Finn continued to force himself down to Tristan, choking him out. Tristan brought his legs up and kicked back at Finn, hitting the dense ballistic vest and launching him backwards. He then went over and quickly grabbed his thighs to tackle him back down as he knelt up. Tristan sat down atop of Finn's abdomen and punched him across the face. He then grabbed his arms and pushed them down onto Finn's chest as he restrained him. Finn thrashed his head around as he attempted to lurch forward and bite at Tristan.

"Charles!" Tristan shouted. "Now!"

Charlemagne heard Tristan from the second floor and quickened his pace as he navigated along the ledges of the ruined ceiling before he came out to the balcony and took his plasma cannon over. Charlemagne pointed the cannon towards where he anticipated Heyl would be.

A sudden flash of lightning showed him out from the darkness and he fired. The impact hit Heyl in the chest and caused another reflection of white light to bounce out and shine around. Tristan loosened his grip on Finn's arms as he settled down and passed out again. He then got off from him and picked him up so that he could leave up the stairs and go over to where Charlemagne was. However, they were trapped.

Tristan lowered Finn down and sat him against a wall, kneeling before him to check that he was breathing. Charlemagne struggled with Heyl who began to form fireballs in his hand again and throw them towards Charlemagne. A wind began to pick up though and the balls were hurled away. Charlemagne noticed and then saw the aura around him reappear. Tristan witnessed this and then realized there was a spirit similar in shape to how Mika appeared to him, but in a goldenrod yellow, behind Charlemagne.

The angel rose up and branched out its wings, extending an arm outward towards Heyl, which caused a sharper wind to blow. Tristan then saw a breath of fire breathe out from Heyl like a dragon, but the angel blew the fire away before shooting outwards towards Heyl, causing the body of the fallen angel to shatter like glass. Charlemagne released his grip from the trigger as he heard the sharp yell of the fallen angel and the sudden disappearance of him from before them.

Tristan moved his eyes out of the way and then back over to Charlemagne whose face was wet with rain and sweat. He panted heavily. A wisp of the same goldenrod light hovered over him, splitting in two with half going into Finn. Tristan jerked his head over to Finn and saw him begin to wake.

"Finn!" Tristan cheered, smiling with intense emotion. "Finn, wake up!"

Finn opened his eyes and looked over to Tristan with confusion.

"Oh, thank God," Tristan remarked, hugging his best friend. "Finn…"

Finn looked onwards around him with shock and confusion as he felt the embrace of Tristan.

"What happened?" Finn questioned. "Where am I?"

Charlemagne walked around and looked down to Finn with the plasma cannon in one hand. He gave a look of relief to his son.

"What happened?" Finn asked again, looking towards Charlemagne.

"What do you remember?" Charlemagne questioned.

Finn looked ahead of him while Tristan pulled away and looked to him with an emotional smile.

"Was I possessed?" Finn surmised.

"Yeah," Tristan replied, looking to him with relief.

"Worse than at the manor," Charlemagne noted, "seeing that you cannot even remember. You said to Tristan that you had made a deal with the Devil, and that he would be looking for you. Well, he found you, but we were… by some miracle, just able to expel him – hopefully for good. Tristan, help Finn down from there… We need to get off from the top of this tower before it collapses."

"Sure," Tristan replied, standing up and helping Finn onto his feet.

Finn walked with a sudden limp coming from the same leg that Tristan had shot. Charlemagne walked downstairs, turning around to look over to the boys as Tristan helped Finn walk with Finn's arm across the back of Tristan's neck, resting on his shoulders.

"Where's Manon?" Charlemagne questioned. "I… I saw what had happened to Salmar, but…"

"I'm not sure," Tristan interrupted. "I haven't seen her… wherever she could be. I'm sorry about Salmar though…"

"What about Salmar?" Finn questioned with alarm. "What did I do? Where's my mum?"

Charlemagne turned behind him as he heard a sudden creak. Tristan and Finn looked over to a bookcase shelf that suddenly began to open, and out from the small room behind, Manon appeared, dressed in the same clothes she came to this world in, slightly tattered.

"My love," Charlemagne expressed, going over to her as he dropped the plasma cannon down. "What happened?"

Manon looked over to Finn with minor fear. She then placed a hand on the bookshelf as she was barely able to stand on her own.

"Salmar... he is dead?" Manon questioned.

"I'm afraid so," Charlemagne replied. "What happened to you?"

"Salmar said that there was an attack and that something was coming up to the apartment. He told me to hide here, and all I could hear was the fight that happened. You tell me though, what has happened here?"

"In a moment... First, we need to leave," Charlemagne replied, helping her stand. "Can you walk?"

"Yes," Manon replied, pushing off from the bookcase to stand on two feet.

"Follow me then," Charlemagne said, going over to the rubble.

Tristan placed Finn down on the ground and went over to help Charlemagne move the rubble so that they could enter into the corridor. He then went over and picked up the pouch on the floor, which he opened to drop the crystals and ring into his hand. Tristan then faced Charlemagne who extended his hand to him.

"Hand them to me," Charlemagne requested. "I'll teleport us somewhere safe…"

"Take us either to the parkade or the bunker," Tristan requested. "I… I have to go and save Diana. Did you see the moon? The sun? However fast Damian made time go by, it's doing a number on the solar system."

"I know," Charlemagne responded. "I believe the Moon was struck by a meteorite, which caused one of the larger earthquakes, if not all of the earthquakes. Give me the crystals."

Charlemagne took the crystals and the ring into hand. The two of them then went back into the library. Tristan picked up Finn and then walked over to Manon and Charlemagne. Tristan extended a hand towards Charlemagne, who took ahold of Manon. Charlemagne then closed his eyes and the four of them teleported downstairs.

The group reappeared in the underground parking lot where it was hot and humid. Tristan lowered Finn down against a column while Charlemagne walked over to him, removing something from around his neck, which presented to be a medium-thickness gold chain necklace with a golden medallion dangling from it. Tristan watched as Charlemagne knelt down and presented it to Finn.

"This necklace was your great-grandfather's," Charlemagne said to Finn. "May God protect you, Finn, by the image on this medal, from the demons that lurk and seek to take hold of you. May St. Gabriel watch over you more than he watches over me…" he explained, bringing a hand to Finn's forehead so that he could bless him with the Sign of the Cross traced by his thumb. "May the Lord turn His face to you and grant you peace."

Finn didn't respond and simply took the necklace into his hands while Charlemagne moved his hand away. Tristan watched and then looked back at Charlemagne as he looked to him. Finn held on to the necklace and looked at both of them.

"I'm going after Damian and Diana," Tristan stated. "He has her and the time orb, and without the orb, we can't stop what's happening out there, no less, return home without the two of them."

"Perhaps..." Charlemagne said. "I believe if I place these crystals into my time machine downstairs, finish some of the minor works, we could teleport back to our universe through it. If my time machine were capable of bringing us all the way here, then that means electrical power is far more powerful than the power that comes from individual humans. We don't need the time orb for that..."

"If that's the case, then if I don't return and it seems like it's too late to wait for me, then leave with Manon and Finn," Tristan said, looking to Charlemagne before looking away.

"Even then, I suppose, he must be stopped," Charlemagne noted. "The destruction of this universe could spell hazard for ours."

"I have to try then, not just for Diana's sake..."

"Do not blame yourself for the way that monster came out," Charlemagne remarked. "He was not your son, and that child in Diana's womb does not share the same fate as him. Every child that is born is the result of an ovum and the seed of a man that comes together. Every sperm is distinct from the other, and likewise for an ovum. The chance that the same two gametes came together to produce the same child that Damian is, is astronomical. Even then, your child has two-loving parents, where, as I'm aware, and Damian was born out of lust from two naïve children. You cannot save him."

"I'm not going to try and save him," Tristan said, looking back to Charlemagne. "I'm going to save Diana and retrieve the half of the time orb that can stop this apocalypse, and if necessary, take us back to our timeline."

"Please be careful, Tristan," Charlemagne warned, looking at the space crystals before presenting them to Tristan. "Take at least one – it could prove to help you."

Tristan looked at the crystals with temptation.

"Damian expects me to bring him just what he needs to escape," Tristan remarked. "I have to do this without – just, make sure you're ready to leave when I return and that you're here in the parkade where you're accessible for a quick escape."

Tristan began to leave so he could go over to Tempest who waited for him.

"Tristan," Charlemagne called out, "may God bless you on your quest, and…"

Tristan stopped.

"… thank you for all you've done for me and my family."

Tristan didn't turn around and instead continued to walk over. Finn sat up and looked over to Tristan, stepping forward as he saw him off. Tristan climbed onto Tempest and then quickly dashed forward to exit the parkade, leaving behind Charlemagne, Manon, and Finn, expecting to never see them again.

Act 12, Scene 1

Tristan rode out from underneath Cabernet Tower from atop of Tempest and returned back outdoors via the ramp out from the parkade. The skies above were a mixture of bright red and grey, smoke and cloud, and sirens could still be heard throughout the city, but it was much quieter than it had been almost an hour ago. The screams of civilians, gunfire, and sound of general destruction of vehicles, property, and other items had come to an end. The rainfall continued to come down, but the thunder and lightning stopped with Heyl's disappearance. There was also a temperature shift as it was no longer humid and warm, but cold and dry, much as it had been when Tristan arrived in Harlech, but more severely so. Tristan rode out from the parkade ramp and came onto Earl Street.

From Earle Street, Tristan had Tempest hurry down onto Campbell Street where he took a moment to analyze his surroundings. There was less commotion and motion on the streets. Tristan saw that the spirits had disappeared and returned to their realm as the chaos had left with Heyl's vanishment. Tristan turned Tempest so that he could face east, down Campbell Street, and then began to motion her to gallop forward. He raised her to gallop as fast as she could be pushed to run as he hurried on his way to rescue Diana. Within a short moment, Tristan was back at Bailey Drive where he turned around and then continued down, past Pentateuch Cathedral, and then around onto the double-road that passed underneath the highway. Tristan had Tempest jump over the concrete barrier onto the on-ramp. They then came up onto the highway where they made their way towards the edge. Tristan slowed down to lead Tempest across the makeshift platform bridge extended out from the armored vehicle-launched bridge, covering the gap over the Henley River at the remains of the Marke Bridge. Once at the other side, Tristan came off the highway as it was collapsed further ahead and impassable. He came off onto Saffron where he went down to the intersection with Slade Drive. Tristan then turned right and continued down Slade Drive where he had Tempest speed up again.

Tempest galloped forward with a mighty speed. Tristan observed that the undead anarchists had collapsed as well and that the bodies were strewn across the street. He rushed past them and carried on forward down the war-torn street, coming across Frontier Street, carrying on to Lincoln Drive, and then onwards to the frontline at Boundary Drive. The tanks and armored personnel carriers were still parked before City Hall, which appeared to have suffered structural damage from the many earthquakes that had passed. Tempest stopped at the Slade-Boundary intersection where she reared as she came to a sudden halt.

Tristan looked around for a brief moment before he decided to carry on down Slade Drive. He looked up to the sky behind him and saw that the bright moon continued to shine down on them in its immense size. The sun had darkened as time continued to flow in outer space at a rapid pace. Tristan came into enemy territory with Tempest, rushing forward as he went into South Lincoln, which was less metropolitan and more rugged than the urban center.

Tempest continued to gallop forward as they were soon into the heart of Northton at the intersection with Slade-Caledonia. The streets in these parts were abandoned with no sight of any hostiles. The area suffered a lot of damage from the earthquakes as just about every structure was in rubbles. Tristan continued down to the very end of Slade Drive, reaching the familiar area just before the movie studios. He turned right onto Riverside

Drive and passed the small road that crossed over the rail line. He then made his back towards the highway intersection where he took Tempest up a ramp, hopping over the midline so that he could go down and make his way towards Durham Bridge. Tempest reared as they made their way towards the start of the bridge to see that it was destroyed with at least a hundred-meter gap between each of the separate sides over Durham River. Nonetheless, from atop of the highway, Tristan could see ahead where he needed to go to: Aegis Castle, by the dark storm cloud that surrounded the south of Cliffe Island.

Tristan pulled Tempest back and then made their way back around, coming off the highway and back into Jarsdel Island where they continued down Riverside Drive going towards Harthdam. Tempest galloped down the drive, passing the ruins of the many retail chains on the left as well as the rail tracks at the side. He passed the Boundary-Riverside intersection and then steered left as they quickly made their approach to the Thames-Harthdam-Riverside intersection. Tristan turned left so that he could cross the short alternative bridge that connected Jarsdel Island with Cliffe Island.

Thames Bridge was in a poor state as well because of either the earthquakes or the anarchists. Half of the bridge was submerged under water on Tristan's end. Tristan stopped at the start of the bridge and looked forward. He then led Tempest down the ramp of the bridge, keeping on the right-side as he was able to have Tempest jump over a short gap and come to a flat section on the other side. This section then connected with a collapse portion of the left-side, which allowed him to cross over and then continue down into a gulp just before Thames Street. Tristan had Tempest jump over to the other side again so they could come up a ramp formed out of the street and then bring them into Cliffe Island properly.

At the top of the gulp, Tristan looked out around him. He took a deep breath and looked towards the southeast from him. He then continued down Thames Street to come into Attlewood. The atmosphere on Cliffe Island was more devastating and apocalyptic than anywhere else. Almost every structure was in ruins and collapsed. The area was also totally abandoned like Northton and much of north Jarsdel. From where Tristan was atop of a hill, he could therefore see out across the island towards Aegis Castle, which was intact aside from one of the towers. The forest around the castle was decayed too without any leaves and only the branches of the trees that were curled up and burnt. Tristan looked over to the castle with focused eyes before he continued down south, via Thames Street, and made his pass through the abandoned and ruined district.

Tristan passed Reading Street, Beech Street, and then found himself at the center of Attlewood where he could see the remains of the clocktower, Chelsea Tower, and the burnt-out police precinct. Near the intersection there were various wrecks of burnt out cars on the side of the street as well as the disturbing sight of decomposed bodies hung from a rope along the frame of a collapse structure. He carried on down the street, passed Denton Street and then York Street until he slowed down because of the presence of many corpses on the street from anarchists. Tristan was perplexed by the presence of bodies far from the frontline, so he slowed down to look.

The corpses of the anarchists appeared to be fresh as there were no signs of decay, but the most disturbing aspect of the bodies was they were posed as if something terrible had swept them that caused their eyes to melt, but bodies remain as they were in a split second that their deaths overcame them. Tristan took Tempest down the street slowly, eyeing these corpses with the perplexity that all of these bodies were pointed towards him, almost as if they were arranged to look at him or greet him. The corpses of the anarchists had their weapons pointed to him, some of them had bottles of Molotov cocktails in their hands and were about to throw them, but all of them were dead.

Tristan continued down from York Street, through Wimbledon Street, and then halfway towards Elberton Street where this horrible sight passed and was replaced with the sight of people fleeing from what came to them. Tristan held a look of deep disturbance as he passed through, reaching Elberton Street and then continuing forward with speed as he came out of the ruins of Attlewood and into the ruins of Southton.

On approach towards the beachfront, Tristan saw the grassland before the beach to be completely replaced with a burnt, black dirt surface with the trees that once were at the side to be barren and charred. Tristan came down Plymouth Drive at the side of the beach where the forest on the left was in a similar state, completely barren with every tree smoldered and without a single leaf up to the top of the hill where the ruins of houses could be seen.

Ahead, to the south, Tristan could see Grafton Bridge destroyed from the bombardment from the navy. Like on Jarsdel Island, much of the highway had collapsed, but Tristan continued down Plymouth Drive to the point that was the end of the island where the bridge extended over the river because there was an underpass that ran underneath. Tristan saw that the underpass was intact, allowing him to travel through to the other side and come to the south of Leicester.

Tempest was led left onto Norwich Street and Tristan took her down the road as he came closer to Aegis Castle. The size of the castle was readily visible as he came out from underneath the bridge. Aegis Castle sat atop of a hill where in Tristan's universe, the home of Damian and Iustina, was surrounded by a dense forest of oak trees, but in this world could be seen for the immense size that this fortress was. Norwich Street came around to the north base of the hill where Aegis Castle rested on. Tempest was led forward at another intersection for a street that came around the rear of the castle, continuing forward with the tall iron gate fence to his left. On his right was the slope of a hill that went up to Fisherman Road where on the other side was the rest of Leicester. The slope of the hill was in a similar state to everything in this area – singed mud that was impassible in the heavy rain.

Tristan pulled Tempest back, causing her to rear as he arrived at the front gate of the castle, which was left slightly open. He came off Tempest and went forward to push against the iron bars, opening the gate and looking ahead to the stone brick road that came up and around the side of the hill to the very top where the castle was. The slope of the hill was steep and impassable due to the rain. Tristan went back to Tempest and hopped on.

Tempest reared and then went through as Tristan began to make his ascent to the castle with a hasty determination, eyes focused forward as he went up the steep slope at the side of the castle, coming around the curve and then continuing straight. Tempest moved forward quickly with haste to the end of this stretch before coming around the next curve and then going straight forward again. Tristan rode Tempest around to the end of the final stretch, which then curved at a ninety-degree angle as opposed to one-hundred-eighty, ending at the front wooden gate of the outer walls of the castle. Tempest reared at the wooden gate as he saw two anarchists at either side of the gate with spears at their sides.

Tristan hopped off and drew his sword, looking to them as he also brought his shield into his arm. He looked towards the anarchists through the darkness and saw that there was something strange to them. Their eyes were unfocused, and they moved like dolls as they approached Tristan, eyes not even looking to him. Tristan prepared his shield as they jabbed towards him. He then stepped out of the side and with his sword, he went to them and sliced at them. The cuts on their bodies had no effect on their morale. They simply took it. The bewitched anarchists attempted to bring their spear down on Tristan, but he raised his shield and then jabbed his sword forward into their unarmored bodies where blood naturally poured out. Tristan then shifted his focus onto the other.

The bewitched anarchist brought his spear down and into the ground as Tristan jumped back. He then moved in and slashed downwards before spinning around to pick up momentum and hit the torso of his foe with steady force. He then brought his sword down onto the neck of his foe, which caused blood to spatter out. Tristan finally jabbed his foe in the abdomen, and the pair of them simply fell over like ragdolls as the spell left them and they bled out.

Tristan looked at these fools with pity, but instead of wasting his limited time to mourn them, Tristan put his sword and shield away and approached the gates, pushing the doors open so that he could pass through with Tempest. Tristan then returned to Tempest and rode through into the front courtyard of Aegis Castle. Just as Diana had described this courtyard, the sides consisted of arcades that looked out to either side where there were gardens between the outer walls and the façade of the castle. However, in this universe, there was nothing to admire as the gardens were nothing more than pens of mud. Tristan came to the front doors of the castle where another pair of bewitched anarchists waited for him. He looked at this display unimpressed and hopped of Tempest to draw his sword and shield. Tristan then faced these foes.

The anarchists lunged forward with their spears, and Tristan skirted out of the way to get around them, going in for a slice until he had them weak enough for a fatal blow. Tristan jabbed his sword through the neck to cause enough trauma for the body of the anarchist to collapse on its own. He then turned his attention to the other and stabbed him in the thigh. He then dealt a devastating impact on the neck, which was enough to cause the anarchist to collapse. Once these pair of fools were down, Tristan put his sword and shield away again so he could come up to the front doors and push through, entering into the castle where Diana had led the Chosen once and fought the shapeshifter.

Act 12, Scene 2

Tristan stepped into the foyer of Aegis Castle, which even in this universe, given the tremors in the last two hours, was still much the same as how Diana had described it to him. Directly across from the main entrance into the castle foyer was the circular stain glass window, which had been shattered, leaving a circular hole through the wall. In front of the window, the statue of the Virgin Mary had been shattered by vandals, literally defaced and arms in pieces. There were no banners or any furniture. The floors were dirty, but somehow, there was light as every torch in ever sconce was aflame. In the ambience, there was only the rain and the faint echo of a melancholic tune being played on an organ from somewhere in the castle. Tristan stepped forward into the center of the foyer, looking to his right at the large set of doors that led into a great hall similar to the one at the convent in Montana, but much larger with tall arched windows to the right that looked out the northwest side of the castle and the remains of the gardens. He came up the steps to the top of the landing, just before the statue of the Holy Mother, going around behind to look through the circular window, which looked out to the south courtyard.

From where Tristan stood, he was just able to peek out and over the window, but he could also see the towers that Diana had told him about, with the east tower being directly ahead, another, slimmer tower at the top of a domed structure to the right (the south tower), and then just in the corner of his vision to the very right was the west tower where the Fountain of Youth was alongside a belfry. From what Tristan could see, the south tower also contained a belfry at the top, but much smaller than the one in the west. Tristan moved away from the window and drew his sword and shield, going towards the west-side of the tower as he entered into one of the larger corridors on the second floor.

Tristan walked down the corridor and then turned around the corner to come into contact with some more bewitched anarchists who held halberd spears. He walked cautiously towards them, keeping his distance as they attempted to jab at him. He moved around the side where he was able to enclose on one of them and go in for a stab in the chest. He then moved back to deal with the other, keeping his distance and shuffling around his foe while he evaded the attempted jabs. Tristan stabbed the second anarchist in the chest and then pulled his sword back as his foe fell over and the mind control left them.

Tristan carried on down the corridor to reach another junction which had a set of large wooden doors directly ahead. He pushed the doors open and came into a small sanctum, which was where the Fountain of Youth was. The room was also just as Diana had described to him with the tympanum and sculpted face of the fountain ahead, the columns around – Tristan closed his eyes and took a deep breath as he stepped forward. The only difference in this room was that the pool was empty. Tristan frowned, but listened to the music as he noted that it was closer than it had been previously. He came around to the arched corridor that led into the stairwell, but the music did not come closer, so he did not climb up to the belfry and instead made his way out back into the wide corridor. Tristan looked both directions and then started to make his way to the left where he came around to another set of large wooden doors.

Through the large wooden doors, Tristan looked out and saw that a large library extended outwards along the west face of the building with overhang windows at the very top. The music was fainter here, so Tristan backed out. He looked to another door at the end of the corridor he was in, walking towards it and pushing through, but saw that it came out onto the outer wall, which encircled the castle and another courtyard, the west courtyard, next to the library. In the midst of the courtyard was a ruined fountain with a destroyed statue of a man in a robe atop. Tristan exited back into the corridor and went the other direction, which led down a corridor that took him around to a set of windows that looked down to the south courtyard as noticeable by the large circular gap where the stained glass window in the main foyer had been.

Tristan turned right and came towards a large stairwell with a set of stairs that took him down to the ground floor. He then walked down a corridor parallel to the arcade of the courtyard, which then led him out into this courtyard where the music was noticeably close, but not as close as it had been in the west tower. The south courtyard was plain in appearance as the decade of neglect since the fall of the city had left what must have formerly been a grass field into a track of mud with a barren tree in the corner. In the midst of the courtyard there were more bewitched anarchists with halberds pointed towards him. Tristan approached them with caution, especially given the slippery track of the muddy floor at his feet.

The bewitched anarchist made an approach towards Tristan and extended the halberd out to jab him. Tristan blocked with his shield and came around, hitting the pole of the spear with his sword. He then went in for a jab towards the anarchist, backing up as the other attempted to jab him while he was attacking. Tristan deflected the jabs against him with difficulty as his legs continually slid in place on the mud. Finally, he backed up and took out his bow, shooting arrows at the anarchists through the necks so that he could continue with haste.

Tristan looked across the courtyard and noticed a tower that he had just realized to exist, to the north. The tower was short, but sure enough, there was a fourth tower. His eyes scanned across the roofs as they found their gaze upon the east tower where in his universe, Damian's workshop was at the top. Tristan looked at the east tower with certainty and began to cross the courtyard to make his way over.

From where Tristan was, he went down to the south-side of the courtyard where there were a pair of wooden doors. He attempted to push through, but they were locked from the other side. Tristan brought his ear to the door and could hear that the music was strong from the other side. He stepped down the arcade he was in and looked into a window into the room, seeing that it was empty and that it was simply a fairly-sized foyer with steps that went up to the base of what must have been the domed structure where the south tower was. Tristan came around the arcade and found another door that went into the east side of the castle.

Tristan walked down the corridor and entered into a stairwell which took him up to the second floor. The music was faint as he moved away from the source of the music, but he continued onwards and exited out into a wide corridor similar to the one on approach to the west tower. He went down to the end of the corridor and reached a set of double doors, which led into a circular room with an arched doorway that led into a stairwell around the side. The height of this circular room was only two-stories. This circular tower was part of the north tower. Tristan exited out as the music was even more faint here.

From the north tower, Tristan came out and stepped out onto a walkway that looked into courtyard near the east tower. Tristan walked down to the center of the wall that wrapped around the courtyard and noticed that he was in the same east courtyard where Diana had confronted Iustina in. To his left was the north tower, which was next to an extension of the outer wall with an arched tunnel that went out to the gardens. Across from Tristan was the alcove with the door that led into the parliamentary-like room, which connected to the east tower. Tristan continued around the wall and came around to the other side where he exited out a set of double doors.

Tristan entered into a small foyer where he heard the music to be in the same volume as it had been in the west tower. The room was slightly diagonal in shape, or polygonal, with a set of double doors to the left against the left wall, and a small arched alcove with a wooden door to the wall perpendicular. This wall was arched slightly and was a part of the east tower. Tristan went to it and saw that it led into the stairwell that went up to the top. The music was fainter in this tower, so Tristan avoided it. He instead went towards the set of large doors, which led into a stretched room that connected with the top of the parliamentary room, facing perfectly eastward. Tristan saw that this was a chapel.

The chapel nave extended straight outwards from the foyer corridor towards a curved chancel at the end, which was in complete disarray. The altar was ruined. The tabernacle without its doors and bare open. The stained-glass windows that overhang above were somewhat intact as some of them were shattered somewhat, but other than the structure of the chapel, they were all that was intact. The pews of the chapel were missing as was the presider's chair, podium, tabernacle, and any decorations. Tristan only looked briefly at the sad sight of this sacred space before he left as the music was as faint in this room as it was in the east tower stairwell.

Tristan came out and continued straight into another set of double doors, which led into a corridor with steps that went back down to the ground floor, up to another set of double doors. He walked through and came into a medium-length corridor with a third set of double doors at the very end, but an obstacle before him. The ambience of the tune played on an organ was strongest in this corridor. The obstacle before him was a large, tall and stocky brute dressed in similar clothes as the anarchists Tristan had faced up until now, but with a different weapon. He carried with him a spiked ball and chain flail and looked to Tristan with blind hatred through his mind-controlled eyes. The tall figure, who was at least six feet and six inches tall, stood before the door with the handle of the ball and chain flail on the ground like a staff, his feet apart. Tristan bent his knees as he raised his sword and shield, making his cautious approach.

The brute flailed his mace in an intimidating manner, smashing the ball into the stone floor as he made his own, less cautious approach towards Tristan. Tristan cowered back as he raised his shield, seeing the sporadic movement of the ball and chain as it literally flailed around as the brute waved it forward. Once the brute had Tristan pinned with his back to the wall, he raised it and brought it down. Tristan raised his shield up to cover himself. The brute smashed the iron ball into Tristan's shield with a brutal impact.

Tristan then quickly jabbed his sword forward, hearing the scratch of the top of his shield as the ball was pulled off. Tristan quickly retracted his sword before he could make contact as he saw the ball come around to hit him in the side. He then quickly fell onto his side and rolled over to come around his foe, slashing his sword at his thigh before jumping back to avoid being bludgeoned by the spiked-ball as the brute began to twirl it around again. Tristan kept back as the large man came over to him.

The brute launched the ball and chain towards him, and this time, Tristan ducked out of the way as he had previously done, coming behind the brute and hitting his sword against the back of the brute, which cut into the dense ballistic vest that he wore under his jacket. Tristan jumped back out of the way as the ball came twirling to him again. The brute laughed at him and began to move faster.

Tristan jumped back and felt the ball and chain scratch his shield as it passed directly over it. He ducked out of the way and then jumped up, grabbing the brute by the neck and raising his sword up so that he could pull it down on him. The ball and chain then hit Tristan in the side, right in the chainmail before he could stab, knocking him over and against the wall. Tristan quickly recovered so that he could avoiding being hit with the ball again as it came directly down on him, barely missing his head as he raised his shield, being hit with a brutal impact again. Tristan quickly stood up then and motioned back.

The brute twirled the ball and chain again as he made his way over to him. Tristan breathed quickly, moving back as the brute came towards him. Once he had his back against the wall again, Tristan attempted to jump down and make the same feint against the brute as before, but instead the ball hit him again against the torso, causing him to roll to the side. Tristan lost control of his sword and his body was atop of his arm, which was awkwardly against the top of his shield. He pushed himself off from the ground and raised his shield up as he huddled to take in the impact of the ball against him. He then went over and took his sword, picking it up as the ball came towards him again.

Tristan quickly threw his sword like a javelin, piercing through the head of the brute and causing the ball to hit him in the side and throw him against the wall. He looked over as he leaned against the wall, recovering from the impact, and saw the brute fall forward onto his knees and then collapse to the floor. Tristan walked over and kicked the brute onto his back so he could pull his sword out.

Tristan's sword was stuck deep and it took a bit of effort to pull it out. He looked down at his foe with pity and then carried on through the door so he could enter into the large foyer corridor at the south-end of the south courtyard. The door to the courtyard was blocked by a wooden plank that locked the door. Tristan held his sword and shield in hand as he took a moment to recover from the fight he just had.

Once Tristan was ready, within a short minute, he stepped forward to where he heard the music come from, through a set of large double doors to his left, in the midst of a curved wall to the very south of the room. Tristan stopped before the door and put his sword and shield away, and then with both hands, pushed against the door, and entered through into the throne room.

Act 12, Scene 3

Tristan stepped forward and entered a large room with a domed ceiling similar to the sanctum at the base of the west tower. The room followed a crimson carpet with gold rims that came down from the entrance and went little more than halfway through the room where it abruptly stopped. The polished marble floor continued onwards to reach a set of steps at the end and before the large stone throne that was built into the side of this greater sanctum. Around the sides of the walls were arched windows with columns before them to form an ambulatory in the space between. Atop of these columns there was a small viewing gallery from the third floor just before the point where the walls began to arch out to form the domed ceiling. At this level, there were smaller arched windows where light poured in from. The level only curved around three-quarters of the room as the space above the throne was exempt and there were no columns and only arched windows. Likewise, there was no arched window behind the throne and instead a large circular stained-glass window similar to the one in the foyer, smashed and exposing the outdoor chill inside. Tristan looked ahead and saw Damian sat on the throne, at his side, on the floor, was Diana collapsed and unconscious, enveloped by a byzantine purple aura, and to the side of the room there was a possessed anarchist on the organ.

Damian looked towards Tristan with a smirk on his face. He rested his right elbow on the arm rest of his throne and his right fist tightened underneath his chin, resting it atop. The other arm was stretched out and relaxed. Over Damian's torso he had placed a gold-rimmed chest-piece which gave him a defined appearance. Once Tristan reached the end of the carpet, he stopped and took out his sword and shield, which caused Damian to smile brighter and laugh.

"I'm impressed," Damian remarked to Tristan. "I didn't expect you to come, no less work your way through all of the adversaries that have been placed before you – from that supersoldier in Jerusalem, to your own inner demon – did you enjoy the pawns from the underworld that I placed as your warm-up?"

"Hardly," Tristan responded, frowning at him.

Damian raised his relaxed hand and pointed it towards the bewitched anarchist on the organ. There was a sudden bang on the piano and then the man began to scream out in pain, clutching his head before a fire burned out from his eyes and he fell over dead. Damian then relaxed his hand again and placed it on the rest.

Tristan was alarmed by this and breathed sharply. He looked at the dead man and then back to Damian.

"Do you see that? This is the level of power that you have decided to confront," Damian said. "Do you know why I take the crown of Satan? It's because there has been no being since Beliyal, the Devil himself, Moloch-Baal that has existed with this much power. Look at all that I've been able to do despite my own adversity – the hoops that I had to jump to get to where I am."

"And now it's all over for you," Tristan said. "You have no way of escape – you've set the world to end, and with it, even you will die. I hope you enjoy an eternity in Hell with your master."

"Hmph," Damian remarked, "but I won't die when the universe dies out. My powers are so great that I will survive and be all that remains – myself and Diana that is… her in stasis, a deep freeze, but with me where we will be alone, together forever."

"You're mad," Tristan grunted back. "Stop all of this, please."

Damian laughed and replied, "Of course you would plead rather than seek to fight me."

"Actually, I'd rather fight, but had to give you a fair warning," Tristan responded.

Damian stood up and stepped forward. He brought his hands forward where a sword began to materialize out of thin air. Tristan was astonished. The sword was made of a dark metal and was neatly crafted. It was slightly larger than a broadsword, but smaller than a claymore. In his other arm he formed a black metallic shield. Damian took each into his hands and then waved the longsword around, cutting through the air with it.

Tristan trembled at the sight before him of what he had to face.

"I thought that if you would come that you would at least be cowardly (and stupid) enough to bring me my ring and those crystals, but…" Damian said, taking a deep breath. "I don't sense them with you," he remarked. "The most likely explanation to that is that you couldn't bring them. Finn – that treacherous ingrate!"

"Actually, I could have brought them, but didn't," Tristan replied. "I don't need them to defeat you. All I need is my sword and shield – and even if these break, I'll outmatch you. Just you see."

"Humorous and cute," Damian responded, "while I didn't think you'd come, I hoped it. I was never satisfied with the way that my father died in this universe. He was a miserable man that lived a pitiful life – I wasn't the only child that he abandoned, and my mother was not the only woman that he betrayed. He was weak and easy to kill, but not you… You have confidence, but perhaps that is just your youth. Even then, you are far stronger than he was, but no more stronger than me. I want this fight to last well and true, so I'll make you a deal."

Damian took out the time orb from his pocket and raised it up through telekinesis, placing it on a windowsill above his throne. He then stepped forward again so that he was down the steps of his throne and closer to Tristan. He tightened a fist and Tristan saw around him a sort of transparent field separate them from the outer edge of the room where Diana was.

"This will not be a test of our psionic abilities, but purely of a man's physical strength," Damian announced. "All I ever had in a man was myself to teach me these ways, but you had your uncle, even if it was for a short time, and then you had Charlemagne. Let us see whose upbringing was superior from the other. The only manner by which you can 'save' Diana is if you strike me down, causing this force field around her to disappear, so I challenge you to that. Strike me down. A fight to the death while the world ends around us would make me more than happy, if not emotional – it is dramatic, and I like that. Save the woman you claim to love, and your unborn child, or else I will save both of them, and that child in particular from the pitiful fate that awaits him."

Tristan's frown worsened and he began to groan. He took sword in hand and charged towards Damian, bringing his sword down. Damian raised his longsword up and blocked the incoming blow. Tristan bounced back and continued to scowl at Damian. With one hand Damian brought his longsword back and then down towards Tristan, hitting his shield. Tristan was barely able to absorb the blow as his arm was pushed back towards him, nearly crushing into him.

Tristan took a step back, which caused Damian to lower his arm and shield down so he could calmly step closer to Tristan. He then moved back and Damian raised his guard. Tristan stepped closer forward, came around the side and then attempted to jab towards Damian's arm. Damian blocked out of the way and kept his longsword back, charged, and ready to come down. Tristan side-stepped in the other direction, dropped down to side roll, and then brought his sword down to hit the back of Damian's thigh. The sword impacted and Damian lurched forward in surprise. Tristan then brought his sword down again, hitting the armor on Damian's chest before raising it to cut him on the shoulder.

The third impact hit his shield. Damian recovered and raised his sword up and brought it down towards Tristan. Tristan quickly backed up and kept his distance from him as the sword fell down and into the stone floor. The two foes came to the center of the sanctum where they began to circle each other. Tristan kept hot on his feet, going towards Damian before jumping back, in again, and then back as the sword came down towards him. Tristan moved out of the way, rolled to the side and then brought his sword back down on the thigh with a heavy blow.

Damian lurched forward, but pivoted around the side. Tristan instantly attempted a jab at the top of the thigh, but missed as Damian swung his sword to block the incoming jab. He then moved aside as Damian attempted to bash his shield towards him before bringing his longsword down. Tristan pointed his sword forward and managed to hit Damian in the torso armor, but that did nothing. Damian raised his shield up and charged his sword again as he faced Tristan.

Tristan took a step back and stayed hot on his feet. Damian then lunged forward to crash his shield into Tristan's, hitting shield with shield, which caused Tristan to lurch back. Damian brought his sword down, but Tristan rolled out of the way and attempted to hit him in the back of the thigh a third time, but the impact missed and hit his shield as Damian quickly pivoted to block the incoming feint attack. Tristan then brought his sword down and hit his shield, side-stepping out of the way before Damian could parry or hit him back.

Damian turned to face him from where he was. He raised his sword and attempted to hit him, but Tristan ducked out of the way to the left, attempting to hit him again with a feint attack before going the other way as he hit the shield to do the same. Tristan hit Damian's shield again as he kept up with him, but then Tristan tried something new and brought the sword down on Damian's arm. Damian took a step back as he maintained his grip on the longsword despite the cut that had hit him on the gauntlets.

Tristan backed up too. He raised his sword upwards as he kept his shield pointed to his foe. Damian held on to his stance, gritting his teeth as he faced Tristan. He then suddenly straightened up and let go of his sword, causing it to hover before him. Damian then launched the sword with a fierce might towards Tristan as he cowered back, causing Tristan to quickly roll out of the way. Tristan looked towards the sword and then saw it come back to Damian.

Damian grabbed hold of his sword and began to charge towards Tristan, bringing it down at him. Tristan rolled out of the way again, panting as he was forced to move and move. Damian brought the sword back down on him once more, but missed as Tristan stayed out of the way. He backed up and looked over to Damian. Damian suddenly began to multiply.

Tristan looked around the room at the doubles that emerged, each with a sword and shield. The appearance of so many foes caused Tristan to panic and his eyes to widen. They all began to charge towards him, so Tristan held his ground and raised his shield in the direction that he had seen Damian foremost. The sword came down and hit against the shield. All of the projections simply went through him while the real Damian hit the shield.

Enraged, Damian bashed his shield into Tristan's, which gave Tristan an opportunity to strike upwards and into the arm that held Damian's shield, stabbing upwards into the shoulder. Damian lurched backwards and threw his arm up as the sword cut through. He screamed out in pain and then growled loudly. He swung his sword horizontally and finally hit Tristan in the side, causing him to fly off and slide down the floor. Damian's right arm dangled. Damian quickly relocated his shoulder joint and then picked up his sword from the floor to charge towards Tristan.

Tristan stood up and slid out of the way, standing up again and looking to his foe. Damian launched the sword again telekinetically, missing Tristan as it hit a pillar instead. He recalled the sword back into his grip and began to levitate like Heyl. Tristan raised his shield and deflected the sudden blow that came towards him as Damian jumped from where he was and zoomed across the room to hit Tristan.

Damian raised his sword up to come down on Tristan as he was exposed, but Tristan took the opportunity to cut at Damian's thigh once more, causing Damian to come down on one knee. Tristan pointed his sword towards Damian's neck, but he raised his own shield and blocked it. Damian then raised his sword and brought it down towards Tristan, but he moved out of the way and came around to the other side of the room. Damian recovered and looked back to Tristan, panting just as he was.

Tristan then saw that Damian projected a dozen more images of himself. Damian raised his sword up and then jumped forward altogether. Tristan raised his shield and blocked the incoming blow and then blew his sword up to strike Damian across face, cutting upwards. Damian grunted, dropped his sword and brought his hand to his face. Tristan didn't stop as he went in with another blow to the arm while Damian raised his shield to cover his face. He sliced the bicep and then came down on Damian's shoulder, but missed. Tristan's sword fell through the air and came down.

Damian jumped backwards to the other side of the arena as he touched his face once more. He then raised his sword up as it was underneath Tristan's feet. Tristan rolled out of the way as it came up and then went back into Damian's hand. Damian then launched it towards Tristan, which caused him to duck out of the way as it horizontally sliced through and then fell. Tristan clashed his sword against the sword and knocked it off balance. Damian extended a hand towards it to bring it back to him, but then looked over to Tristan as he charged at him.

Tristan jumped and raised his sword, pointing it forward so he could jab at Damian's neck. Damian extended his hand towards him. Tristan bashed his sword against Damian's. Tristan closed his eyes for a moment as he anticipated the head-aching pain to come to him, but opened them instantly to see the blue spirit of Mika come out and between them. Mika pointed a hand towards Damian, which redirected the psychic energy back at Damian, causing him to scream out in pain as he grabbed his head. Tristan then pierced through Damian's neck at the jugular notch, which caused him to tilt his head up and take slow breaths.

Damian looked up with shock. His shield fell off his arm, and both it, his chest-piece, and his sword disappeared into nothing. His body shook. A blue aura encapsulated Tristan. Tristan pulled his sword out from Damian's neck. Damian fell onto his knees and then collapsed to the floor.

Tristan whipped his sword and then took a step back, looking at Damian with pity as his eyes began to water. The aura around Tristan then faded and a bolt of lightning struck nearby as Damian was dead. The force field disappeared, but purple aura remained around Diana. Tristan wiped the tear from his eye and then took more steps back.

"Why did it have to be this way?" Tristan questioned aloud. "Why did I have to kill him? He lived such a sad life... only for this to come over him? Tell me, Mika, why?"

Tristan jerked his neck up and above the throne as he was suddenly met with an angel, or rather, a fallen one. Heyl appeared and hovered over the throne, looking down towards Tristan and the corpse of Damian. Tristan frowned at him and took a defensive stance.

"You again..." Tristan muttered. "Don't you die?"

Heyl looked down to Damian's body and ignored Tristan. He stepped down and walked towards it. Tristan saw that Heyl walked barefoot with his pale feet. His hood was pulled back and showed his bald, pale head as white and grey as marble stone. Heyl looked down at Damian with contempt.

"Such a pity," Heyl spoke in an effeminate, yet masculine voice. "My finest work, brought to an end... yet, he was contingent – how naïve of him to think he could usurp me."

Heyl squatted down and placed a hand on Damian's back. Tristan stepped forward and then watched with wide eyes as Heyl's body began to flow into Damian's, causing Damian's corpse to spring back to life as a gasp was let out.

"Oh no you don't," Tristan remarked, rushing forward and bringing his sword up.

Tristan stabbed down into the back of Damian where Heyl had entered in. The corpse fell down again. Tristan pressed his sword down, using a foot to keep the body down. The body did not resist until a minute passed and it began to shake like Finn's body had shaken. Tristan pulled his sword out and brought it back down into the back of the neck, causing a terrible screech to come out, as if it was the screech of a thousand damned souls speaking out.

The aura that was around Tristan restored even brighter than before. Damian's body began to mutate and morph. Tristan withdrew his sword and took many steps back as he witnessed the transformation of what was now Damian-Heyl, taking the form that Diana had described to him, horrifyingly, as the true shape of the shapeshifter. However, this was no mere shapeshifter as it was larger and more grotesque, for this was the King of Shapeshifters.

Damian-Heyl was slightly different than the true bestial form of Cardinal Mario Calavera in that his appearance was as follows: the beast had not great horns, but instead great tusks and a snout like a pig. Instead of yellow eyes, it had dark purple eyes. Its composition was a mixture of different animals, the arms were bull-like with hooves at the end, while its head was a mixture of boar at the face and a lion around the skull where a dark reddish-brown-haired mane protruded out. The torso was buff and wide like a bear, hairy too, but abdomen smooth and muscular with a lizard-like tail. The hind legs were like that of a rhino. Damian-Heyl let out a terrible roar towards Tristan – the beast towered over him, almost double his height and incredibly long.

Tristan looked forward at the beast with great fear. He took an uncertain step back, which was when the beast reared onto its hind legs. Tristan put his sword and shield away as he took out his bow and opened his arrow pouch so he could prepare an arrow. The beast made its charge towards him. Tristan shot an arrow out and hit the beast in the eye. He then ducked out of the way and saw it crash into a pillar and collapse onto its feet. Tristan took out his sword and instantly went over to the hind leg of the beast, slashing away at it.

The beast was startled by the assault on its body and stood up. It then mule-kicked its legs out before coming around with its tusks coming straight for Tristan. Tristan jumped back and began to run to the other side of the room. The beast went after him. Tristan allowed it to chase him for less than a minute until he took out his shield and began to hit on it like a drum with his sword, causing a loud noise to echo. Unlike the bells of the west tower, the banging on his shield was not enough to paralyze the creature, but enough to cause it some mild pain. The beast howled out, giving Tristan a chance to escape to the other side of the room.

Tristan put his shield away and his sword, taking out his bow as he stared down at the beast. The beast settled down and its purple eyes began to glow a magenta color. Tristan then observed as the rubble from the pillars rose up and began to fly towards him. He ducked out of the way as the rubble came over, hitting the floor nearby. Once the dust had settled, Tristan stood up on one knee and saw the beast come towards. He quickly prepared an arrow and shot it towards the beast, blinding it momentarily and giving him a chance to jump out of the way. Tristan switched out his bow for his sword as the beast rested on its legs again from crashing into a pillar.

The beast howled as Tristan slashed at its back. He then jabbed his sword into the spine of the creature right as it began to stand back up. Tristan held on and mounted the top of the beast, causing it to jump sporadically like a bull in an attempt to lose him. He held on by pressing the sword down until finally, it was too much for him and he pulled out. The recklessness of the beast as it thrashed around caused two more pillars to be kicked out. Tristan landed on the ground and on his side. He saw the beast turn to him and quickly stood up. The beast howled and then charged towards him.

Tristan didn't have enough time to blind it, so he simply jumped out of the way. The beast stopped right before a pillar and looked side to side before looking back to Tristan. Tristan took out his shield and began to bang it with his sword, causing a nuisance for the shapeshifter as he escaped to the other side of the room. He then put his shield away and looked over to the creature as it calmed down. Tristan kept his shield in hand as he looked over to the beast with focused eyes.

The beast stamped its feet in the ground. Tristan breathed quickly. His face was bloodied with cuts and gashes, and his legs trembled. The beast's eyes began to glow and some of the rubble from nearby began to lift up and fly towards Tristan. Tristan raised his shield and blocked the rubble as he covered his head and upper torso. He then jumped out of the way as a larger piece came. The beast then stamped its feet forward and began to charge towards where Tristan lay.

Tristan attempted to stand up, but he fell over again. Instead, he took his sword and threw it towards the head of the beast, piercing between the eyes. The beast stopped in its tracks and raised its hooves up, stamping them down as it attempted to get the sword out from its forehead. The impact of its hooves against the ground caused some of the ceiling to collapse downwards. Tristan took the moment of distraction to take out his bow and shoot some arrows at the side of the beast, but he soon stopped as he saw they had no impact.

The beast panicked and thrashed around, hitting its head into a pillar where it was finally able to get the sword off. The sword slid towards another pillar. Tristan quickly went over and picked it up, and then he went to the beast to slash at the side of its torso before taking it through and cutting in. The beast instantly stood and thrusted its body towards Tristan, knocking him back. The beast then attempted to stomp on him, but he moved out of the way.

Tristan was barely able to stand up to make his escape. He held sword in hand and took out his shield, banging on it as he ran to the other side of the room and then knelt down for a moment while the beast howled. He saw the beast calm down and took to banging on his shield again, which alarmed it. Finally, Tristan stood up and continued to bang on the shield while he stepped forward and then side-stepped so that he stood behind one of the pillars that were blown out already.

The beast calmed down as Tristan stopped banging. Tristan kept his shield in his hand and looked down towards the beast. Its eyes glowed again and rubble floated upwards and began to make its way towards Tristan like cannon fire. The rubble missed as Tristan held his ground and protected himself with his shield. He then looked forward to see the beast come towards him. The beast charged and Tristan took his sword and swapped it out for his bow, shooting a quick arrow at the beast's eye and then hopping out at the last second.

Tristan looked over and saw the beast crash into the side of the wall, causing the wall to shake and for pieces of the ceiling to collapse down. However, the structure held. Tristan took out his sword for his bow, and then went over to the exposed underbelly of the beast. He rushed forward, both hands at the grip of his sword, and stabbed into the underside of the beast, pushing through to make an incision and expose the belly. Tristan then withdrew his sword out.

The beast cried out and flailed its legs until it was able to stand and then thrash around. Tristan was knocked back and into a pillar. The beast knocked its head into the side of the wall and then went towards the pillar that Tristan was in front of, bashing its head into the pillar. Tristan shielded his head with his arms, but he was unaffected. The beast then tore its head through the pillar, destroying it while Tristan took the chance to escape.

Tristan turned around as he heard the beast cry out and stamp its hooves, facing towards him. He then looked up to the platform above as it began to split in half, and one-half collapse down atop of the beast, and the other follow suit. The beast began to stagger from side-to-side as though dazed, hitting its head into the other pillar to cause more of the structure to collapse, and then the entire wall that was behind it to come forward. Tristan instantly rushed out of the way as the wall came down, crushing the whole beast underneath and causing a cloud of dust to blow through.

Act 12, Scene 4

Once the dust had settled, Tristan looked over to where the beast had been, seeing it collapsed underneath all of the rubble, motionless. He took a moment to catch his breath before he put his sword away and then went towards the throne where Diana still was. Tristan walked carefully towards her and then knelt down, placing a hand on her shoulder. He shook her. Diana didn't wake.

"Diana?" Tristan questioned. "Diana, wake up."

Tristan continued to shake Diana. He then went over and placed a hand on her wrist, checking her slow pulse. He placed a hand underneath her nostrils and felt warm breath come out. He then continued to shake her, looking across to the ground where the time orb had fallen due to all the seismic activity. Tristan stood up and went over to it, picking it up and seeing that it was in one-piece.

Diana's aura faded as Tristan looked at the gem. He put the rock into a pouch and then went over to her, shaking her even more. Diana slowly opened her eyes and looked to Tristan as the aura faded.

"Tristan?" Diana questioned. "Is that you?"

"It is, believe it or not," Tristan responded with a smile. "You have no idea what I've been through so that I could see your beautiful eyes again."

Diana smiled in return. Tristan helped her onto her feet. She looked around and saw the ruined room. She then saw the beast ahead and looked at it curiously.

"Where's Damian? Where are we?"

"You're at Aegis Castle," Tristan responded, "and Damian is no more. Come on, I can explain later. Charlemagne is waiting for us – I've got the time orb. We can return home now."

The couple stopped as they were about to leave as there was a sudden movement from beneath the rubble. Tristan looked over with disbelief as he saw the eyes of the shapeshifter, Damian-Heyl, open.

"Oh no…" Tristan muttered. "Hurry, we need to leave."

The beast attempted to stand up with all of the rubble that lay atop of it. Tristan took Diana's hand and the couple proceeded across the room towards the exit.

"What's going on?!" Diana questioned. "What is that? Is that a shapeshifter? That can't be Damian – he was my son… Who is that?"

"It's Heyl!" Tristan responded as they ran. "Damian and Heyl – Damian-Heyl – Whatever, it's a shapeshifter for sure!"

Diana and Tristan came out to the south courtyard foyer. Tristan took her to the other side of the room where he let go and quickly picked up the heavy plank and then plopped it down. He then pushed against the doors so they could travel through the south courtyard. The rain continued to fall outside. Tristan took Diana's hand, and the pair began to exit out into the courtyard as the beast broke out from its restraint and roared out. Diana and Tristan crossed into the other side of the courtyard, entering into the east wing of the castle where Tristan took Diana up to the second floor.

The beast crashed through the foyer and came into the south corridor just as they went in. They then went up the stairs, turning left as they came into a wide corridor, but then pausing as the castle shook as if something had bashed its head against the castle walls. Tristan and Diana staggered for a moment before they then continued into the foyer and then down the stairs. They went straight to the exit of the castle, which was when the beast tore through the remains of the circular stained-glass window, the statue of the Virgin Mary, and then stomped towards them as they went into the front courtyard where Tempest waited. The beast charged to them.

Tristan helped Diana onto the back of the horse. He then looked over as the beast bashed through the front of the castle, causing rubble to fly out. Tempest reared. Diana attempted to calm her. Tristan pulled himself up and over, and then nudged Tempest to get them out of the castle.

Tempest stomped forward and went through the front gates of the castle, and then around the curve so they could go downhill. The beast chased after them. Diana held on to Tristan as they galloped downhill, and then went through the gates onto Norwich Street. The beast was right behind them. Tempest galloped forward, around Norwich Street to the very end, and then around into the tunnel that went underneath Grafton Bridge.

The beast tore through the tunnel and then continued after them as they went alongside the remains of the beach. Diana looked behind her as she saw the beast that was Damian-Heyl rampaging behind them while up in the sky, she saw a bald eagle in flight. Tristan turned onto Thames Street and then made his way uphill into Attlewood. The beast continued uphill, tossing left behind cars on the sides of the street with its tusks.

Tristan steered forward into the horrifying depths of Attlewood, past the remains of the anarchists. The beast simply trudged through them, destroying what was left of them, and then continuing down. Tristan looked up to see the eagle ahead of them, with them. They made their way to the Thames-Queen intersection and then continued forward towards Thames Bridge. Once at the bridge, Tristan steered Tempest through the obstacles with Damian-Heyl right behind them.

Tempest hopped over the gap between the bridges and then over the cross-section. With the beast's stomps, the remains of the bridge behind Tristan began to collapse into the water indefinitely. Tristan made his way across the final gap and then up the ramp formed by the collapsed road, reaching the top. Tempest reared and the couple looked over to the sight of Damian-Heyl struggling to cross the water before ultimately drowning.

Tristan looked forward with a deep sigh as Tempest came down onto her front legs and settled down.

"Thank God for that," Tristan remarked, holding the reins. "Stupid thing couldn't even…"

Suddenly, Damian-Heyl appeared from the depths of the water, climbing onto the side of Thames Bridge that they had just come up from.

"You've got to be kidding me!" Tristan complained, kicking Tempest off.

Damian-Heyl continued after them as they went down Riverside Drive. The beast stomped forward with heavy steps. They went underneath the highway and then continued down through Northton until they reached the Riverside-Slade intersection where they turned left. Tristan followed the bald eagle through Jarsdel Island as it guided them on their path.

Tempest galloped along uphill and then they went straight forward. The beast began to gain on them as they travelled in a straight line. Tristan noticed and steered them right on Caledonia Street, causing the beast to come to a sudden halt at the sudden turn so it could reposition. Tristan then turned left onto Bering Street, which took them around a bent road. Tempest galloped along where they stayed straight, or curved, and then went around again on approach to the roundabout.

Tristan turned left on the roundabout and came around, exiting onto Lincoln Drive, and then going around this curved road until they reached Slade Drive again. The beast struggled to keep up as they went around these non-linear roads. Tristan turned right onto Slade Drive, following the eagle, and then they moved onwards straight towards Frontier Street.

The beast followed and began to gain on them again. Tristan turned at right Frontier Street and then turned right again at the next intersection. He then turned right once more onto Slade Drive to slow down the beast. Tristan went to the end of Slade Drive, and then turned onto Saffron Street, which took them towards the highway. The beast kept up and was about to get them as they arrived at the on-ramp.

Tempest turned and went up the ramp, onto the highway. She then hurried forward as they approached the armored vehicle launched bridge, coming onto the metal platform. The beast caught up to the start of the makeshift bridge before they could come to the other side. Tempest quickly jumped the remainder distance as the beast tore its tusks into the end of the bridge and caused the entire thing to tumble over and into the water. Tristan stopped and turned Tempest to her side so he could look over to the beast as it roared towards them. Tempest reared and Tristan looked back at the creature without remorse.

The beast began to run off from them. Tristan watched and then saw that it turned around at the end. Without hesitation, he kicked Tempest off, and they went down the highway. The beast jumped across the gap and landed at the other side, causing the highway to shake and crumble. Tempest quickly made her exit at Tristan's steer, coming onto Bailey Drive. The beast was right behind them.

Tristan led Tempest down Bailey Drive, looking with focused eyes at the intersection with Campbell Street. He growled and looked up to the eagle.

"I can't bring this thing right to Charlemagne, no less the rest of the townspeople," Tristan acknowledged. "I'm going to have to finish it off here…"

"How?" Diana questioned.

"I'll think of something," Tristan replied, going straight and coming into the remains of Keswick.

There was little left behind in what was Keswick, as most of it had been caught in the blast that struck the harbor and destroyed New Harlech alongside with bits of the northern side of the industrial district. Diana's family apartment had been taken in that disaster. All that remained of Keswick was an open field of rubble alongside the walls of some structures. The eagle began to fly in circles nearby before it perched itself on some rubble. Tristan came into the district and then rode Tempest into a medium-sized clearing where rubble mounds surrounded them. He then rode Tempest up along the side while the beast came down and into the field, slipping and falling over. Tristan stopped at the top and kept Tempest here, hopping off and pulling his sword out.

"Stay here," Tristan said, stepping forward to go finish off the beast.

"Wait, let me help!" Diana petitioned. "Give me your bow in the least."

Tristan didn't take the time to argue, so he removed his bow and bag of arrows, giving them to Diana. He then slid down the rubble and went to confront the beast as it stood up and looked towards Tristan. Tristan looked back at it, sword and shield in hand.

Damian-Heyl cried out towards Tristan and began to make its charge towards him. Diana took the bow and opened fire from atop of Tempest, hitting the beast in the eye. The beast stamped upwards and reared. Tristan took the opportunity to go forward, coming around to the side of the beast where he slashed near the wound in its underbelly. The beast stamped heavily into the ground before knocking Tristan back.

Diana continued to aim the bow and shoot arrows at the beast while Tristan recovered and looked towards the beast. She noticed the cut on the underbelly, but was unable to hit it. The beast turned towards Tristan and began to charge at him. Diana aimed the bow and hit the beast in the eyes again, causing it to panic and rear blindly.

Tristan took his sword and began to come around the other side of the beast where he went ahead and slashed at it. He then began to jab at the side of the creature, which caused it to suddenly pivot and bash Tristan away and back onto the ground. Diana shot another arrow at it so that it couldn't see. Tristan pushed himself off from the ground and then looked at the creature. He hurried down to get away and then banged at his shield to get its attention towards him. Tristan could barely stand on his feet and his movements had become slowed and labored.

Damian-Heyl turned to Tristan. Diana held the bow as she waited for the beast to charge towards Tristan. She then opened fire and blinded it once more. Tristan ran forward and came around the side of the beast, sliding underneath and slashing at the innards of the creature, causing it to stamp even more violently, but ultimately do nothing more than that. Tristan rushed forward from the other side and then turned around as he saw the beast continue to the thrash about.

"No matter what I do," Tristan said as he breathed quickly, "it won't die…"

Tristan then noticed that his body continued to hold the same blue aura that had never left him. He looked at his hands and then tightened a fist, whipping his sword in the air.

A bolt of lightning struck down nearby. Tristan looked towards where the bolt fell and then to his metallic sword. He began to bang on his metallic shield to get the beast's attention. The beast hollered and then looked towards him as he stopped.

Tristan threw his shield aside and then only held his sword, taunting the beast to come towards him.

Damian-Heyl began to charge towards Tristan. Tristan stepped forward as it came. Diana shot arrows at its eyes and blinded it once more. The beast reared on its feet, stamping up and down on its front legs. Tristan held his sword like a javelin and aimed it towards the beast. He waited for it to rise up before he threw it as it was about to come down. The sword split through the forehead and caused the beast to panic even more, shouting even louder.

"Now, Mika!" Tristan yelled.

A bolt of lightning struck down and connected with Tristan's sword, conducting the intense electricity through the whole body of the shapeshifter in a blinding display. Tristan shielded his eyes and felt the earth rumble. He then looked down at the feet of the shapeshifter as the ground beneath the shapeshifter's feet began to collapse.

Diana observed the earth swallow the demonic beast as it collapsed downwards into the abyss. Tristan looked ahead and fell onto a knee, resting his arm on his thigh while he tilted his head down. The aura around him left. His head was wet with both rain and sweat. Diana saw and looked down with worry.

Tristan stood up and went to go pick up his shield, placing it around his back. He then went over and began to make his ascent atop of the mound Diana was at. He helped her down and then embraced her. Tristan held a plain face as he held her.

"It's over," Tristan proclaimed. "It's finally over."

"Let's go and rejoin the others," Diana suggested. "I want to go home…"

"Me too."

Act 12, Scene 5

Tristan rode Tempest out from Keswick and back into downtown Harlech where they came into the parkade. The rain had stopped, but the moon continued to stare down at them. Tristan came around to the lower level of the parkade where he found the shutter that went into the tunnel, which went to the storage, open. There, he saw Charlemagne and Finn by the modified device constructed out from the time machine, and Manon nearby, sitting on the ground. The device looked as though Charlemagne had torn the time machine apart as opposed to fix it. From a segment of the machine, there were some thick rubber wires that connected to an outlet in the wall. This piece was the roof of the machine, which was connected to a pole that protruded outwards.

Charlemagne looked to them with astonishment, but also confidence. He gave a warm smile and Tristan rode Tempest gently over to the device they had innovated. Tristan took out from his pocket and silently handed the time orb to him. Charlemagne took it into his both hands and then held it.

"It's time to restore time and get us the hell out of here," Tristan said. "Can you do it?"

"I'll give it a try," Charlemagne remarked, holding the hemispherical orb before him.

Charlemagne closed his eyes and concentrated. He stood in silence for close to a minute before opening his eyes and exhaling out.

"I- I can't do it," Charlemagne admitted. "I thought that if I concentrated, I could revert the actions that Zimmerman had done, but…"

"Hand it back then," Tristan said. "I know that God won't condemn this world – there must be a way to stop this carnage."

Tristan took the orb in hand and concentrated hard. Charlemagne saw the orb brighten for a split moment before Tristan opened his eyes.

"Never mind," Charlemagne said to him. "We need to leave before the temperatures become too hot for us to even be here – before the sun rises."

Tristan gave the orb back to Charlemagne, who gave it to Finn. He then looked over to the device before them.

"Did you fix the machine you found?" Tristan asked, moving over with Tempest.

"Not quite," Charlemagne answered. "I've decided to take a different approach, using what I now know about the crystals, where we are, etcetera. I've connected the device into the power grid of the tower, placed the crystals in the receptacle for them, and when I press this button, the electrical power should give enough electrical power to the crystals so that when I place my hand on this handle, made of mjolnium, I should be able to teleport to a great enough distance so that we simply return to our dimension."

Tristan observed that Charlemagne wore rubber gloves with Zimmerman's ring on one of them. The other three crystals were placed in the receptacle.

"What about the flow of time in this universe?" Tristan questioned Charlemagne as he went to the machine.

Charlemagne turned around.

"We'll have to see about it when we return to our timeline," Charlemagne simply said. "For now, there's no sense for all of us to be here. It's time to return home."

"And if we can't stop it from our universe?" Tristan questioned.

"Tristan, right now I'm preoccupied in returning the rest of us home," Charlemagne noted. "Please, one problem at a time. I realize that all souls in this universe may be doomed, and I also realize that if this universe comes to a rapid end, that may spell trouble for our universe too, but please… let Manon and Diana return home before we focus on that issue."

Tristan didn't respond. He looked over to Finn who was looking at him

"Come on now," Charlemagne said, everybody come over so they can grab hold of me.

Tristan rode Tempest closer.

Charlemagne looked at him.

"I'm bringing the horse with me," Tristan said. "Is that okay?"

Charlemagne shook his shoulders and replied, "It shouldn't be a problem. My love, come form a bridge between Tristan, Diana, and the horse. Finn, stay where you are on my right-side."

Manon stood up and walked over. Diana held onto Tristan. The two of them sat atop of Tempest. Manon took Tristan's hand and Charlemagne's hand. Charlemagne put a hand on the metallic pole that was a lever, and Finn placed a hand on his father's forearm.

"Everybody ready?" Charlemagne asked.

"Ready," Tristan confirmed.

"We're ready, *Charles*," Manon quietly said.

"Do it," Finn said.

Charlemagne pulled the lever, causing the machine to come to life. An arc of electricity formed atop of the machine. Tristan looked over at the blinding sight and then to Finn who reached into his jacket pocket and at the other hand, let go. His eyes widened, but he couldn't do anything. Charlemagne teleported them out from this alternate reality using the machine, which caused the three crystals to shatter and leave nothing behind.

The group came to the front of Cabernet Manor with a loud crack of noise and an expel of excess energy that blew back like a minor blast wave. Tempest reared at their arrival and Tristan immediately tried to calm her before looking around and seeing that they were back in their dimension as Cabernet Manor was intact and the skies above them were clear with the sun shining down. He took a deep sigh of relief and then looked over to Charlemagne, Manon, and Finn. His smile faded.

"Finn?" Tristan questioned, looking down to the causeway as he saw Finn on the ground.

Charlemagne was on his knees at Finn's side. Diana and Tristan came off Tempest. Tristan went over to the other side.

"No response," Charlemagne remarked, pressing into his thumb and then bringing his cheek to his mouth. "No breathing."

Charlemagne brought his mouth to Finn's and gave two breaths. He then attempted to resuscitate him as he pressed into his chest. Tristan looked down at Finn's hand and saw the time orb in it – he had taken the time orb into his hand. He looked at this with confusion and picked up the half-orb, which was cracked like the space crystals had been.

"Someone call an ambulance!" Charlemagne remarked.

"I'll go," Diana said, walking up the stairs and to the door. "The door is locked!"

"Manon, my cellphone is in a pocket in my belt. It should be off, but charged."

Manon knelt down and took the phone. She then began to turn it on. Charlemagne continued to beat down on Finn's chest in an attempt to resuscitate him.

"Tristan, you take over..." Charlemagne said, falling backwards as he exhausted himself.

Tristan took his mouth to Finn's and blew two more breaths. He then proceeded to push his hands into chest for thirty more beats before bringing his mouth back to his. Finn lurched his abdomen up, taking a large gasp of air, but he did not open his eyes. He was still barely conscious Tristan moved back.

"He's breathing, Charles!" Tristan said.

"Oh, thank the Lord!" Charlemagne remarked, looking over to Manon. "Let them know he's awake, but that we still need that ambulance."

Finn groaned. Charlemagne stood up and took out his house keys. He then went over to open the front door.

"What the hell did you do?" Tristan questioned Finn.

"I..." Finn replied, stopping for a moment. "I... had to save those people."

Charlemagne stopped before he came up the steps and looked down to Finn.

"What do you mean?" Charlemagne questioned. "Save those people?"

"The... the time crystal," Finn clarified. "I thought... if I took it into my hand, conducted power through me, and focused on stopping what Damian had done, I could save those people before anything else happened."

"Why would you do that?" Charlemagne asked. "We would have solved the problem anyways."

"Because... time slows down in that universe," Finn explained, sitting up. "A day here is almost six days there, but that wasn't always as it was – only when we went in. You told me that Manon went in thirty-minutes after I had disappeared, but it was forty-five minutes before I saw her appear. I thought that could have been an easy oversight between us, but after that, you said it was two and a half days before you came to join her, but in reality it was six days for us. That's an exponential growth in the difference one-to-one-half – the only factor that changed was people going through the time machine – that's the purpose of the time crystal in the machine. It multiplies by one-point-five so that when I went through, one day was a day and a half, and then when Manon went through, a day here was two and a half there, and then when you came through, a day was almost four days there, and then Diana and Tristan came through, which should have made a day here equal to six days there.

"But I've been through multiple times…" Charlemagne stated. "How then?"

"Every time you came back, the difference reset," Finn stated, "you told me that when you return, you use both crystals, but you shouldn't have to unless both time and space were affected. You thought it was because you were travelling forward and backwards in time, but that was not the case. You were resetting your position between universes and the flow of time. Since we only teleported back to this dimension since you've exhausted your powers, this difference should still affect the other universe."

"If he's right, then there would have been a ratio of one-to-six between how many hours before we met Charles," Tristan said, looking to Charlemagne. "Diana and I went through the time machine almost eight hours after you had left."

"I was gone for almost a day and a half," Charlemagne remarked back. "He's right. How did this detail brush over me? All this time, I thought time was equal in both dimensions. That was very observant of you, Finn."

"Time was equal," Finn clarified. "The time machine distorted it with every pass through."

"Is it done though?" Tristan asked Finn. "Did you stop the rapid progression of time?"

"I- I think so," Finn replied. "We'd have to go and check, but I think I did it. I didn't want any more harm to come to those people, given all that happened to them because of me alone…"

The sirens of an ambulance could be heard in the distance. Charlemagne could see the flash of lights come over Nattau Bridge.

"Well, I suppose I should be relieved that you figured that out then," Charlemagne said. "An hour here would have been six hours there, times whatever speed Zimmerman had set outside the earth to run at. We would have been doomed."

"Come on, let's get you to a hospital," Tristan said, helping him stand as the ambulance arrived at the gates of the manor.

Charlemagne stepped over to Manon, watching Tristan take Finn down as the paramedics came out and prepared their stretcher.

"Is it all true?" Manon questioned. "He saved them?"

"I told you he wasn't evil," Charlemagne said. "He was only misguided and misled. I'll travel through with what remains of the crystals to check, but I believe him. If everything is fine, I'll return to destroy them – After all that's happened, I've realized that these crystals are too powerful to be left around."

Diana heard this and gave a soft nod. The sun began to set and cast a warm orange glow across the horizon. She watched from atop of the hill as Charlemagne and Manon went to join the ambulance as the paramedics took in Finn. Manon stayed with him, while Charlemagne and Tristan came back as the truck drove off.

"Well, it's true," Charlemagne said to Diana as they regrouped. "It's April – Easter Sunday as a matter of fact. Time had slowed down while we were gone, which I suppose is a relief for all of us. I'm shocked that I let this pass me, but I suppose it's not that much of a surprise given my age and stamina."

"You're not getting old, Charles," Diana replied. "You were just overwhelmed."

Charlemagne nodded.

"I'm going to change out of this tunic and armor, and then I'm going to go and meet up with Finn at the emergency room," Tristan said. "We should also have a check-up on the baby…"

"I have one more thing I have to do – check on the other universe to see that time has reset, and then destroy the crystals."

"Destroy them?" Tristan queried. "Why?"

"Because they're too dangerous. I'd rather store them safely, but even that may be too dangerous given what we had just lived through and barely survived through."

Diana nodded again.

"Do whatever you have to Charles," Diana replied, "and… I'm sorry for what I said to you and what I did to cause all of this. I'm sorry for lashing out against you – it was unfair."

"No matter," Charlemagne responded. "I believe I should apologize to both of you for keeping my illness from you. I thought I could cure myself without need to alarm you, but… all my efforts have failed. I have no choice but to simply accept that my time is short, and to enjoy that time with Finn while I can. Thank you, both of you, for all that you've done for me. I do not know how I can repay you for all of this…"

"You don't have to repay us," Diana responded. "The moments you gave us for the past four years was enough. In the other universe, you adopted me when I was ten-years old. That means a lot to me. However, it's this universe that I'm glad to be from, because in this… Tristan and I got to be together, and you got to meet Finn. You've taught us a great deal, Charles, to both of us, and these lessons will not be lost on us as we grow older. They'll be lessons we share with our son," she said, touching her belly, "and many more children to come. You've truly given us an experience we couldn't have had anywhere else. For me at least, I was able to find that fourth level of happiness you wanted us to find in God, and through this child of mine."

"I've found it too," Tristan chimed in, "because of all that's happened, I was able to find what was lost on the me of the other universe. I was able to rise up and find God, and I've never been happier than I've been now, with Diana, our son, and the dedication I owe them to be the best they can be."

"The pair of you me make me very proud," Charlemagne concluded. "You've taken not only my lessons to heart, but the lessons of my grandfather. This is not the end, however, because there is much more to learn. At the same time, for your age, the pair of you have learned more than any normal individual can experience and learn in a lifetime. With that, I believe you to be both wise and mature children, and whatever happens to you, I know you will triumph and succeed. It was in my opportunity to be your father that I was able to learn the lesson that was lost on me by my grandfather, and that was the duty to share in what I had learned, with younger generations. At the age of fifty-five I had only just learned that, so the fact that the pair of you were able to learn that so soon, leaves so much more time and room for the pair of you to become wiser than I could hope to be. The child that is in your womb, Diana, is blessed to have such parents as yourself, and I know that this child will grow up to be Great. May God bless the pair of you, your son, and the ends of the Earth so that others too may take part in the Greater Glory of God, in what God calls for all of His children, to be born and raised by a loving mother and father, whose sacrifices are redeemed in Heaven and Earth. Amen."

Epilogue I

"The good news is that Finn really did stop the rapid flow of time in the other universe – not only stopping it, but resetting it, although whatever damages that came are irreversible," Tristan explained. "After we looked around to see that everything was peachy, we returned and he took out the crystals from the time machine," he added as he drove through Allabrese. "He put the time orb together and then he placed Damian's ring in a reinforced box, which he put a pin-code on. Only me, Finn, and him know the combination to the box, but it's going to be put into storage where it can be hopefully forgotten."

"What's the bad news?" Diana questioned, looking over to Tristan who was dressed in regular clothes, but had retained his beard, which was thicker.

Tristan sighed for a moment and then replied "Charlemagne only has two more months to live, according to his doctor. He's going to spend that time with Finn, but he wants us to stay here for the baby's birth and his early moments."

"Of course," Diana agreed, looking down with a saddened face "I'd rather he be born here – it's more convenient, and then of course, Charlemagne can see him while he can. We won't leave once he's born either."

Tristan nodded and then said, "Hey, before we go for dinner, I want to make a stop someplace. It's a surprise."

"Sure," Diana permitted, "but what took you so long before you came out?" Diana asked. "You were with Charles in his study for almost two hours."

"Oh, he was…" Tristan said, hesitating before taking a deep breath. "He was giving me a detailed account about what happened when we separated in the other universe, during that whole adventure we had."

"Oh… what for? A testimony?"

"No, it was because I asked him to tell me," Tristan replied.

"Why?"

Tristan sighed and then explained, "Ever since we met, I've recorded the adventures we've had in a journal I have so that I can write them down at a later date as a novel," Tristan responded. "It's a little project of mine that I don't really pay much attention to."

"Wait, really?" Diana questioned. "All this time? I had no idea."

"I was just able to fill in the fourth book, but when the time comes, I want to type them out so that our children can read them. I think they'd make a good story."

"They'll never believe us…" Diana remarked, "but maybe it'd be good if it came to them through a fictional angle."

"Yeah," Tristan replied, smiling. "It would be."

Tristan drove Diana to Lord Phoenix Secondary where pulled over at the curb at the rear of the school, behind the field where there were some houses and parked cars nearby. He turned off the engine and then looked over.

"This is your surprise?" Diana questioned. "Manon and Charlemagne getting married in secret is a surprise. This though… is just confusing."

"I think you know where this is going…." Tristan remarked, looking across the field. "Come on."

The couple exited out from the truck and Tristan took Diana's hand. They then walked around and entered through an opening in the chain-link fence where they began to walk peacefully towards the edge of the soccer field.

"You know, it's really put a sock to my plans to know that you're now going to give birth on our anniversary date," Tristan said. "I wanted to get married on that day."

"We'll have to choose another day to be our special day," Diana replied. "The twenty-ninth now belongs to our son – which by the way, you were right about."

"I wasn't right, Mika was right," Tristan responded. "Mika – St. Michael the Archangel."

"It's tempting to baptize him under that saint name," Diana said, "but my mind is set…"

"It is?"

"I don't want to jinx fate, Tristan, but after all that's happened, I do feel pity for the boy that was Damian. I know you do too. I want to name our firstborn son Damian given that it was both his name, and also Scot's, and we'll keep the saint name the same: St. Allan."

"Damian Allan Merrick," Tristan said. "The other Damian was Damian Allan Cambridge. You can't change the last name if we get married."

"It'll be the distinguishing feature," Diana said as they walked along the side of the field. "The fact that this boy was born in paradise through our love rather than in hell by apathy and lust. This boy will be raised by his father, who will love him very much and never abandon him."

The couple stopped behind the stands that looked out towards the field. They came to the concrete platform and stopped in the middle where they parted hands.

"Do you know what's special about this place?" Tristan asked with a cheesy smile.

"Yes," Diana replied, looking over to the pole where she sneaked a cigarette at. "It's hard to believe that almost four years ago we met, and now we're in this way."

Tristan came down onto a knee and took out a small velvet box from his jacket.

"If I can't have our anniversary date as our wedding date, then I'll have the place that we met as the place that I propose at," Tristan said, smiling. "Diana Anne Cambridge, will you make the careful decision, and not only be my wife, who together we will assist each other in our path to salvation through Christ, and together we will have numerous children who we will raise in the same path of our Lord?"

Diana returned a soft smile, which soon caused her eyebrows to frown as she began to cry. She nodded and embraced him. Tristan hugged her. She cried into his chest and then moved back so that Tristan could place the engagement ring, which was cast of mjolnium with a small fragment of both the time and space crystals placed together. Diana looked at the beautiful ring and then embraced Tristan, looking at the ring with glee.

"Here's to the many more adventures we will have," Tristan proclaimed.

"And the ultimate happiness that will never come to an end."

Epilogue II

A man rode forward atop of a horse with a dark brown coat. The horse then reared at the edge of a cliff. The man had long brown hair that glowed to a slight blonde through the sunlight and stretched just to the back of his neck. He was of fair skin, slightly tanned, and over his face was a thick red beard, which in reality was a mixture of light-brown hair and golden blonde hairs. He was a handsome young man, muscular by the outlines of his military uniform, and he had fine eyebrows that were the same shade of brown as his hairline. His eyes were a dark blue. The uniform that he wore was of a woodland digital camouflage with black combat boots, tactical trousers and jacket, and a ballistic vest atop of his torso. At his wrist, he wore a multifaceted handmade analog clock watch, and around his neck was a golden necklace with a charm of St. Allan.

Before the man was the stretches of an evergreen forest that went for miles, with more forest behind him as well as sharp-peaked mountains. Likewise, behind him, two men approached in a similar uniform, looking over to Damian who turned around to look back at them with a confident smile.

"Sir, the rebels are on the move and we await your orders," one of the officers remarked. "We have four divisions of infantry and armor at your disposal across the frontline

"The rebels are numerous, I suggest that we retreat," the other officer advised.

"Retreat?" Damian questioned. "If we retreat, then hundreds of civilians would be left behind so that evil forces can have their way with them. We make our stand here, in the Rocky Mountains, and defend our home, captain. My parents taught me that one should never abandon their family or give in when all seems lost. They never gave in on me... and I won't give in on our people. Mobilize the army and prepare a defense. We will make our stand here for the fate of our people… and we'll put our trust in Almighty God that he should deliver these heathens into our hand, for the glory of the Church. Hail Christ!"

"Hail Christ," the officers responded.

Damian looked back over the cliffs and ahead towards the east. He took a deep breath and closed his eyes, bringing a hand to his charm as he looked forward and up to the sky. He gave a warm smile and then turned back around so he could travel back to their encampment and prepare for the battle that came.

"From the beginning of creation, God made them male and female. For this reason, a man will leave his father and mother and be united with his wife, and the two will become one flesh; so they are no longer two, but one. What therefore God has joined together, let no man separate."

– Mark 10:6-9

www.ingramcontent.com/pod-product-compliance
Lightning Source LLC
Chambersburg PA
CBHW072016020726
47501CB00006B/1833